W9-BSD-163

"The spunkiest, funniest, and most engaging private investigator in Santa Teresa, California, not to mention the entire detective novel genre."
—*Entertainment Weekly*

Back in 1969, a lot of young people were hitting the road and disappearing. More than one of them wound up dead—including the girl in daisy-patterned pants who was found in a quarry off Highway 1 in Lompoc, the victim of multiple stab wounds. Eighteen years later, she's still a Jane Doe—and the cops who found her are still haunted by the case. Anxious to solve it, but no longer in their prime, they turn to Kinsey Millhone for help. If nothing else, they'd just like to identify the body. But this ice-cold case heats up more quickly than they expect. And for Kinsey, it will lead to a lot of dangerous discoveries—including some about her own past . . .

"Grafton is so good that when you're immersed in one of her books—and even afterward—you believe that there is a Kinsey Millhone in Santa Teresa, California, who is a private investigator and lives in a converted garage and dines fairly often on Big Macs."
—Cleveland *Plain Dealer*

"Kinsey Millhone is Grafton's best mystery, one that has been unfolding deliciously since the letter 'A.'"
—*San Francisco Chronicle*

"[A] first-class series."
—*The New York Times Book Review*

continued . . .

"D is for Dependable. Sue Grafton returns with *Q is for Quarry*, the seventeenth spoonful—and one of the tastiest—of her mystery alphabet soup . . . Based on an actual, unsolved murder . . . [the book's] foundation in fact is apparent throughout and provides a grounding in procedural detail . . . that is convincing . . . cunning . . . one of the most satisfying stories to come from the ever-dependable Grafton in years."

—*The Washington Post Book World*

"Q is for quite a good read. Sue Grafton's alphabet thrillers just keep getting better . . . *Q* is quintessential Grafton. It is so well written that many readers might consider it her best . . . Fans will love *Q* because there's a strong focus on Kinsey's past . . . tasty tidbits for those of us who know that Kinsey is still trying to come to terms with her parents' deaths . . . One of Grafton's most admirable traits as a writer is her respect for the victims of a crime as well as the people who solve them. Solid methodology and a straightforward writing style are the groundwork for Grafton's two decades of success. *Q* is so neatly and superbly unraveled, it's sure to inspire many a fan to return to *A is for Alibi* and begin the series again." —*USA Today*

"Well written . . . wonderfully realized . . . Kinsey plumbs the closeness and isolation of these tiny desert towns . . . This faint poignancy is intensified once the reader learns that Grafton has built her book on an actual unsolved case, extrapolating a fictional solution from available evidence. Her final bare account of this young girl who remains unidentified provides its own haunting epilogue."

—*The Houston Chronicle*

"Involving . . . It's narrated by Kinsey with her usual wry humor and eye for telling detail." —*The Orlando Sentinel*

"Sue Grafton still spins a wicked mystery." —*Marie Claire*

"Another class act from Grafton . . . Should a contest be held to name the credible private eye in mystery fiction, Kinsey Millhone would certainly rank at or near the top. The central figure in Sue Grafton's long-running series conveys a verisimilitude, in both her professional and private lives, that makes most of her competitors seem like cartoons. Believability is once again the cornerstone of Grafton's latest and most ambitious novel, fiction founded on fact . . . an intriguing story, convincing in detail and satisfying in development. Still, what lifts this above the crowd is the character of her protagonist Kinsey Millhone, who rings true both as a detective and as a woman." —*The San Diego Union-Tribune*

"*Q is for Quarry* is a different approach for Grafton, who now has the name and the clout to try some real-life crime-solving . . . This book was inspired by real unsolved homicide in 1969 . . . and readers are encouraged to come forward with any information . . . one of Grafton's best." —*Hartford Courant*

A NOTE TO THE READER

<u>Q is for Quarry</u> was inspired by a real case in which the body of a young woman was found in Santa Barbara County, California, in 1969. The victim remains unidentified; however, with such advancements as forensic reconstruction, it is still possible that someone may recognize this Jane Doe, and that the case might even be solved. A reconstruction of the victim's face, created by Betty Gatliff, an internationally recognized forensic artist who is a fellow of the American Academy of Forensic Sciences, appears on the final page of *Q is for Quarry*. It is the hope of the Santa Barbara Sheriff's Department and Sue Grafton that, even after all this time, a reader or two may recognize Jane Doe and come forward with her identity.

TITLES BY SUE GRAFTON

Kinsey Millhone Mysteries

A is for Alibi
B is for Burglar
C is for Corpse
D is for Deadbeat
E is for Evidence
F is for Fugitive
G is for Gumshoe
H is for Homicide
I is for Innocent
J is for Judgment
K is for Killer
L is for Lawless
M is for Malice
N is for Noose
O is for Outlaw
P is for Peril
Q is for Quarry
R is for Ricochet
S is for Silence
T is for Trespass
U is for Undertow
V is for Vengeance
W is for Wasted
X

and

Kinsey and Me: Stories

IS FOR QUARRY

SUE GRAFTON

G. P. Putnam's Sons
New York

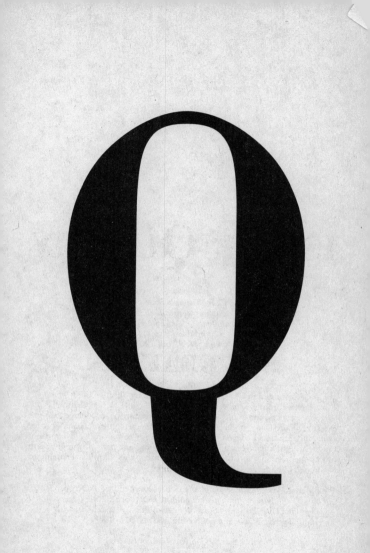

MIDLOTHIAN PUBLIC LIBRARY

PUTNAM

G. P. PUTNAM'S SONS
Publishers Since 1838
An imprint of Penguin Random House LLC
375 Hudson Street
New York, New York 10014

Copyright © 2002 by Sue Grafton
Cover design and art copyright © 2002 by Thomas Tafuri
Excerpt from *R is for Ricochet* copyright © 2004 by Sue Grafton
Penguin supports copyright. Copyright fuels creativity, encourages diverse
voices, promotes free speech, and creates a vibrant culture. Thank you for
buying an authorized edition of this book and for complying with copyright
laws by not reproducing, scanning, or distributing any part of it in any form
without permission. You are supporting writers and allowing Penguin to
continue to publish books for every reader.

First Marian Wood/G. P. Putnam's Sons hardcover edition / October 2002
Berkley mass-market edition / October 2003
First G. P. Putnam's Sons premium edition / March 2016
G. P. Putnam's Sons premium edition ISBN: 978-0-399-57518-1

Printed in the United States of America
10 9 8 7 6 5 4 3 2 1

This is a work of fiction. Names, characters, places, and incidents either are the
product of the author's imagination or are used fictitiously, and any resemblance
to actual persons, living or dead, businesses, companies, events, or locales is
entirely coincidental.

If you purchased this book without a cover, you should be aware that this book
is stolen property. It was reported "unsold and destroyed" to the publisher, and
neither the author nor the publisher has received any payment for this "stripped
book."

THIS BOOK IS DEDICATED TO

Bill Turner and Deborah Linden
Bob and Nancy Failing
and
Susan and Gary Gulbransen.
Thank you for making this one possible.

ACKNOWLEDGMENTS

The author wishes to acknowledge the invaluable assistance of the following people: Steven Humphrey; Dr. Robert Failing; Retired Sergeant Detective Bill Turner and Retired Chief Deputy Bruce Correll, Criminal Investigations Division; Sergeant Bob Spinner, Forensics Science Unit, and Diana Stetson, Jail Administration and Custody Operations, Santa Barbara County Sheriff's Department; retired Coroner's Investigator Larry Gillespie, Santa Barbara County Coroner's Office; Betty Pat Gatliff, Forensic Sculptor; John Mackall, Attorney-at-Law; Lucy Thomas and Nadine Greenup, Reeves Medical Library, and Anna Bissell, R.N., O.C.N., Santa Barbara Cottage Hospital; Martin Walker, M.D.; Robert Sorg, Bob's Canvas Shop; Chuck Nation, Nation's Auto Upholstery; Linda Perkins, DeBrovy's Custom Canvas; Richard Madison; Anita Donohue, Julian Ranch; Lamar and Cheri Gable; Jay Schmidt; Maggie Harding; and Joe B. Jones.

Special thanks, also, to Joe Mandel, Gregory Spears, and Chris Kovach for the use of their names.

IS FOR QUARRY

1

It was Wednesday, the second week in April, and Santa Teresa was making a wanton display of herself. The lush green of winter, with its surfeit of magenta and salmon bougainvillea, had erupted anew in a splashy show of crocuses, hyacinths, and flowering plum trees. The skies were a mild blue, the air balmy and fragrant. Violets dotted the grass. I was tired of spending my days closeted in the hall of records, searching out grant deeds and tax liens for clients who were, doubtless, happily pursuing tennis, golf, and other idle amusements.

I suppose I was suffering from a mutant, possibly incurable form of spring fever, which consisted of feeling bored, restless, and disconnected from humanity at large. My name is Kinsey Millhone. I'm a private detective in Santa Teresa, California, ninety-five miles north of Los Angeles. I'd be turning thirty-seven on May 5, which was coming up in four weeks, an event that was probably contributing to my general malaise. I lead a stripped-down existence untroubled by bairn, pets, or living household plants.

On February 15, two months before, I'd moved into new offices, having separated myself from my association with the law firm of Kingman and Ives. Lonnie Kingman had purchased a building on lower State Street, and though he'd offered to take me with him, I felt it was time to be out on my own.

That was my first mistake.

My second was an unfortunate encounter with two landlords in a deal that went sour and left me out in the cold.

My third office-related error was the one I now faced. In desperation, I'd rented space in a nondescript cottage on Caballeria Lane, where a row of identical stucco bungalows were lined up at the curb like the Three Little Pigs. The block—short, narrow, and lined with cars—ran between Santa Teresa Street and Arbor, a block north of Via Madrina, in the heart of downtown. While the price was right and the location was excellent—in easy walking distance of the courthouse, the police station, and the public library—the office itself fell woefully short of ideal.

The interior consisted of two rooms. The larger I designated as my office proper; the smaller I was using as a combination library-and-reception area. In addition, there was a galley-style kitchen, where I kept a small refrigerator, my coffeepot, and my Sparkletts water dispenser. There was also a small fusty half-bath with a sorrowful-looking toilet and sink. The whole of it smelled like mildew, and I suspected at night wee creatures scuttled around the baseboards after all the lights were turned off. By way of compensation, the building's owner had offered unlimited cans of an off-brand paint, and I'd spent the better part of a week rolling coats of white latex over the former pulsating pink, a shade rem-

iniscent of internal organs at work. He'd also agreed to
have the rugs cleaned, not that anyone could tell. The
beige high-low, wall-to-wall nylon carpeting was matted
from long wear and seemed to be infused with despair.
I'd arranged and rearranged my desk, my swivel chair,
my file cabinets, sofa, and assorted artificial plants.
Nothing dispelled the general air of weariness that in-
fected the place. I had plenty of money in savings
(twenty-five thousand bucks if it's anybody's business)
so, in theory, I could have held out for much classier
digs. On the other hand, at three fifty a month, the
space was affordable and satisfied one of my basic princi-
ples in life, which is: Never, never, never to live beyond
my means. I don't want to be compelled to take on work
to meet my overhead. The office is meant to serve me,
not the other way around.

Since the bungalows on either side of mine were vacant, I was feeling isolated, which may account for a
newfound ambivalence about my single status in a world
of married folk. Except for two brief failed marriages, I'd
been unattached for most of my natural life. This had
never bothered me. More often than not, I rejoiced in
my freedom, my mobility, and my solitude. Lately, circumstances had conspired to unsettle my habitual con-
tent.

Earlier that week, I'd encountered my friend Vera
with her husband, (Dr.) Neil Hess. I was sneaking in a
late-afternoon jog on the bike path at the beach when I'd
spotted them sauntering along ahead of me. Vera was a
former employee of California Fidelity Insurance, for
which I'd also worked. She'd met Neil, decided he was
too short for her, and tried passing him off on me. I
knew at a glance they were smitten with each other, and
despite protests to the contrary, I'd persuaded her that

he was her perfect match, which had turned out to be true. The two of them were accompanied that afternoon by their eighteen-month-old son in his stroller and a grinning golden retriever pup, frolicking and prancing, tugging at his leash. Vera—massive, lumbering, milky, and serene—was clearly expecting again, apparently in mere days, judging by her swollen state. We paused to chat and I realized that in the three and a half years since I'd last seen her, my life hadn't changed a whit. Same apartment, same car, same work, same boyfriend in absentia in a relationship that was going no place. The revelation generated a prolonged pang of regret.

Meanwhile, Henry, my beloved landlord, was off cruising the Caribbean in the company of his siblings and his sister-in-law, Rosie, who owns the tavern half a block from my apartment. I'd been bringing in his mail, watering his houseplants once a week and his yard every couple of days. Rosie's restaurant would be closed for another five days, so until the three of them returned home, I couldn't even have supper in familiar surroundings. I know all of this sounds ever so faintly like whining, but I feel morally obliged to tell the truth.

That Wednesday morning, I'd decided my attitude would greatly improve if I quit feeling sorry for myself and got my office squared away. To that end, I'd gone to a thrift store and purchased two additional (used) file cabinets, an upright wooden cupboard with assorted pigeon holes, and a funky painted armoire to house my accumulation of office supplies. I was perched on a low stool surrounded by cartons I hadn't unpacked since I'd moved into Lonnie's office three and a half years before. This felt a little bit like Christmas in that I was discovering items I'd long forgotten I had.

I'd just reached the bottom of box number three (of a

total of eight) when I heard a knock at the door. I yelled "I'm here!" When I turned, Lieutenant Dolan was standing on the threshold, his hands sunk in the pockets of his tan raincoat.

"Hey, what are you doing here? It's been months." I got up and dusted my hand on the seat of my jeans before extending it to him.

His grip was strong and warm, his smile almost sheepish, as pleased to see me as I was to see him. "I ran into Lonnie at the courthouse. He said you'd rented this place so I thought I'd pop in."

"That's great. I appreciate the visit."

"I see you're getting settled."

"About time. I moved in February fifteenth and haven't done a thing."

"I hear business is slow."

"It is—at least the kind of jobs I like."

I watched while Con Dolan made a circuit of the room. He seemed ill at ease and covered his discomfort by wading through a steady stream of small talk. He chatted idly about Lonnie, the weather, and miscellaneous matters while I made what I hoped were the appropriate responses. I couldn't imagine what he wanted, but I assumed he'd get down to his purpose in due course. He'd never been the type to drop in unannounced. I'd known him for ten years, the greater portion of which he'd headed up the homicide unit of the Santa Teresa Police Department. He was currently out on a medical disability, sidelined by a series of heart attacks. I'd heard he was eager to return to work full-time. According to the scuttlebutt, his chances ran somewhere between slim and none.

He paused to check out the inner office, glanced into the half-bath, and then circled back in my direction.

"Lonnie said you weren't crazy about the place and I can see your point. It's grim."

"Isn't it? I can't figure it out. I know it needs something, but I can't think what."

"You need art."

"You think so?" I let my gaze trace the bare white walls.

"Sure. Get yourself some big travel posters and some double-sided tape. It'd perk the place right up. Failing that, you might at least wipe the dust off the artificial plants."

He was in his early sixties and his cardiac problems had left his complexion looking sour. The usual bags under his eyes had turned a dark smokey shade, making his whole face seem sunken in circulatory gloom. He was apparently marking the time away from the department by shaving every other day, and this wasn't the one. His face had tended to be pouchy in the best of times, but now his mouth was pulled down in a permanent expression of malcontent. Just my kind of guy.

I could tell he was still smoking because his raincoat, when he moved, smelled of nicotine. The last time I remembered seeing him he was in a hospital bed. The visit had been awkward. Up to that point, I'd always been intimidated by the man, but then I'd never seen him in a cotton hospital nightie with his puckered butt on display through a slit down the back. I'd felt friendlier toward him since. I knew he liked me despite the fact his manner in the past had alternated between surly and abrupt.

I said, "So what's up? I can't believe you walked all the way over here to give me decorating tips."

"Actually, I'm on my way to lunch and thought you might join me—if you're free, that is."

I glanced at my watch. It was only 10:25. "Sure, I

could do that. Let me get my bag and my jacket and I'll meet you out in front."

We took off on foot, walking to the corner, where we turned right and headed north on Santa Teresa Street. I thought we'd be going to the Del Mar or the Arcade, two restaurants where guys from the PD gravitated for lunch. Instead, we soldiered on for another three blocks and finally turned into a hole-in-the-wall known as "Sneaky Pete's," though the name on the entrance sign said something else. The place was largely empty: one couple at a table and a smattering of day drinkers sitting at the far end of the bar. Dolan took a seat at the near end and I settled myself on the stool to his left. The bartender laid her cigarette in an ashtray, reached for a bottle of Old Forrester, and poured him a drink before he opened his mouth. He paused to light a cigarette and then he caught my look. "What?"

"Well, gee, Lieutenant Dolan, I was just wondering if this was part of your cardiac rehabilitation."

He turned to the bartender. "She thinks I don't take very good care of myself."

She placed the glass in front of him. "Wonder where she got that?"

I pegged her in her forties. She had dark hair that she wore pulled away from her face and secured by tortoiseshell combs. I could see a few strands of gray. Not a lot of makeup, but she looked like someone you could trust in a bartenderly sort of way. "What can I do for you?"

"I'll have a Coke."

Dolan cocked his thumb at me. "Kinsey Millhone. She's a PI in town. We're having lunch."

"Tannie Ottweiler," she said, introducing herself.

"Nice to meet you." We shook hands and then she reached down and came up with two sets of cutlery, encased in paper napkins, that she placed in front of us. "You sitting here?"

Dolan tilted his head. "We'll take that table by the window."

"I'll be there momentarily."

Dolan tucked his cigarette in his mouth, the smoke causing his right eye to squint as he picked up his whiskey and moved away from the bar. I followed, noting that he'd chosen a spot as far from the other drinkers as he could get. We sat down and I set my handbag on a nearby chair. "Is there a menu?"

He shed his raincoat and took a sip of whiskey. "The only thing worth ordering is the spicy salami on a kaiser roll with melted pepper jack. Damn thing'll knock your socks off. Tannie puts a fried egg on top."

"Sounds great."

Tannie appeared with my Coke. There was a brief time-out while Dolan ordered our sandwiches.

As we waited for lunch, I said, "So what's going on?"

He shifted in his seat, making a careful survey of the premises before his gaze returned to mine. "You remember Stacey Oliphant? He retired from the Sheriff's Department maybe eight years back. You must have met him."

"Don't think so. I know who he is—everybody talks about Stacey—but he'd left the department by the time I connected up with Shine and Byrd." Morley Shine had been a private investigator in partnership with another private eye named Benjamin Byrd. Both had been tight with the sheriff's office. They'd hired me in 1974 and trained me in the business while I acquired the hours I needed to apply for my license. "He must be in his eighties."

Dolan shook his head. "He's actually seventy-three.

As it turns out, being idle drove him out of his mind. He couldn't handle the stress so he went back to the SO part-time, working cold cases for the criminal investigations division."

"Nice."

"That part, yes. What's not nice is he's been diagnosed with cancer—non-Hodgkin's lymphoma. This is the second time around for him. He was in remission for years, but the symptoms showed up again about seven months ago. By the time he found out, it'd progressed to stage four—five being death, just so you get the drift. His long-term prognosis stinks; twenty percent survival rate if the treatment works, which it might not. He did six rounds of chemo and a passel of experimental drugs. Guy's been sick as a dog."

"It sounds awful."

"It is. He was pulling out of it some and then recently he started feeling punk. They put him back in the hospital a couple of days ago. Blood tests showed severe anemia so they decided to transfuse him. Then they decided while he was in, they might as well run more tests so they can see where he stands. He's a pessimist, of course, but to my way of thinking, there's always hope."

"I'm sorry."

"Not as sorry as I am. I've known him close to forty years, longer than I knew my wife." Dolan took a drag of his cigarette, reaching for a tin ashtray on the table next to us. He tapped off a fraction of an inch of ash.

"How'd the two of you hook up? I thought he worked north county. You were PD down here."

"He was already with the SO when our paths first crossed. This was 1948. I was from a blue-collar background, nothing educated or intellectual. I'd come out of the army with an attitude. Cocky and brash. Two years

I knocked around, not doing anything much. I finally got a job as a pump jockey at a gas station in Lompoc. Talk about a dead end.

"One night a guy came in and pulled a gun on the night manager. I was in the backroom cleaning up at the end of my shift when I figured out what was going on. I grabbed a wrench, ducked out the side door, and came around the front. Guy was so busy watching to make sure my boss didn't call the cops, he never saw me coming. I popped him a good one and knocked him on his ass. Stacey was the deputy who arrested him.

"He's only ten years older than me, but he's the closest thing to a mentor I ever had. He's the one talked me into law enforcement. I went to college on the G.I. Bill and then hired on with the PD as soon as a job opened up. He even introduced me to Grace, and I married her six months later."

"Sounds like he changed the course of your life."

"In more ways than one."

"Does he have family in the area?"

"No close relatives. The guy never married. A while back, he was dating someone—if that's what you want to call it at our advanced age. Nice gal, but somehow it didn't work out. Since Grace died, the two of us have spent a fair amount of time together. We go hunting and fishing any chance we get. Now that I'm out on medical, we've done a lot of that of late."

"How's he dealing with all of this?"

"Up and down. Too much time on his hands and not a lot to do except brood. I can't tell you how many times I heard that one: guy retires after thirty years and the next thing you know he gets sick and dies. Stacey doesn't say much about it, but I know how his mind works. He's depressed as hell."

"Is he religious?"

"Not him. He claims he's an atheist, but we'll see about that. Me, I always went to church, at least while Gracie was alive. I don't see how you face death without believing in *something*. Otherwise, it makes no sense."

Dolan glanced up just as Tannie appeared with two large plates loaded with freshly made sandwiches and fries, plus two orders for the other table. Dolan interrupted his story to have a chat with her. I occupied myself with banging on the ketchup bottle until a thick drool of red covered the southeast corner of my fries. I knew he was leading up to something, but he was taking his sweet time. I lifted the top of the kaiser roll and salted everything in sight. Biting in, I could feel the egg yolk oozing into the bun. The combination of spicy salami and snappy pepper-hot jack cheese turned out to be the food equivalent of someone hollering *Hot Damn!* on the surface of my tongue. I made one of my food moans. Embarrassed, I looked up at them, but neither seemed to notice.

When Tannie finally left, Dolan stubbed out his cigarette and paused for an extended bout of coughing so fierce it made his whole body shake. I pictured his lungs like a set of black cartoon bellows, wheezing away.

He shook his head. "Sorry about that. I had a bad cold a month ago and it's been hard to shake." He took a swallow of whiskey to soothe his irritated throat. He picked up his sandwich and continued his story between bites, taking up exactly where he'd left off. "While Stacey's been laid up, I've been doing what I can to get his apartment cleaned. Place is a mess. He should be out of the hospital tomorrow and I didn't want him coming home to the sight of all that crap."

He set his sandwich down to light another cigarette,

rolling it over to the corner of his mouth while he pulled
out a cylinder of papers he'd tucked into his breast coat
pocket. "Yesterday, I went through a pile of papers on
his kitchen table. I was hoping to come across the name
of a friend I could contact—somebody to cheer him up.
Stace could use a little something to look forward to.
Anyway, there was nothing of that nature, but I did find
this."

He placed the curling sheaf on the table in front of
me. I finished my sandwich in one last bite and wiped my
hands on a napkin before I reached for the papers. I
knew at a glance it was a copy of a Sheriff's Department
file. The cover page was marked 187 pc, indicating it was
a homicide, with a case number following. The pages
were held together with fasteners, sixty-five or seventy
sheets in all, with a set of handwritten notes inserted at
the back. I returned to the cover page.

Victim: Jane Doe
Found: Sunday, August 3, 1969
Location: Grayson Quarry, Highway 1, Lompoc

Under "Investigating Officers," there were four names
listed, one of them Stacey Oliphant's.

Dolan leaned forward. "You can see he was one of the
original investigating officers. Stace and me were the
ones who found the body. We'd taken a Jeep up there
and parked off the side of the road to go deer hunting
that day. I guess there's a gate across the road now, but
the property was open back then. The minute we got
out, we picked up the smell. We both knew what it was—
something dead for days. Didn't take us long to find out
exactly what it was. She'd been flung down a short embankment like a sack of trash. This is the case he was

working when he got sick. It's always bugged him they
never figured out who she was, let alone who killed her."

I felt a dim stirring of memory. "I remember this.
Wasn't she stabbed and then dumped?"

"Right."

"Seems odd they never managed to identify her."

"He thought so, too. It's one of those cases really
stuck in his craw. He kept thinking there was something
he'd overlooked. He'd go back to it when he could, but
he never made much progress."

"And you're thinking what, to have another go at it?"

"If I can talk him into it. I think it'd make a world of
difference in his attitude."

I leafed through the photocopies, watching the pro-
gression of dates and events. "Looks like just about
everything."

"Including black-and-white prints of the crime scene
photographs. He had another couple of files but this is the
one caught my eye." He paused to wipe his mouth and
then pushed his plate aside. "It'd give him a lift to get back
into this and see about developing some information. He
can act as lead detective while we do the legwork."

I found myself staring. "You and me."

"Sure, why not? We can pay for your time. For now,
all I'm suggesting is the three of us sit down and talk. If
he likes the idea, we'll go ahead. If not, I guess I'll come
up with something else."

I tapped the file. "Not to state the obvious, but this is
eighteen years old."

"I know, but aside from Stacey's interest, there hasn't
been a push on this since 1970 or so. What if we could
crack it? Think what that'd do for him. It could make all
the difference." It was the first time I'd seen any animation in his face.

I pretended to ponder but there wasn't much debate. I was sick of doing paperwork. Enough already with the file searches and the background checks. "Stacey still has access to the department?"

"Sure. A lot of folks out there think the world of him. We can probably get anything we need—within reason, of course."

"Let me take this home and read it."

Dolan sat back, trying not to look too pleased. "I'll be over at CC's from six until midnight. Show up by eight and we can swing over to St. Terry's and bring Stacey up to speed."

I found myself smiling in response.

2

I spent the early part of the afternoon in my new office digs, hammering away on my portable Smith-Corona. I typed up two overdue reports, did my filing, prepared invoices, and cleaned off my desk. I started in on the bills at 3:00 and by 3:35 I was writing out the final check, which I tore from my checkbook. I tucked it in the return envelope, then licked the flap so carelessly I nearly paper-cut my tongue. That done, I went into the outer office and moved all the unpacked boxes back into the closet. Nothing like a little motivation to get the lead out of your butt.

My supper that night consisted of a peanut-butter-and-pickle sandwich, accompanied by Diet Pepsi over ice. I ate in my minuscule living room, curled up on the sofa tucked into the window bay. In lieu of dinnerware, I used a fold of paper toweling that doubled as a dainty lip wipe when I'd finished my meal. With spring on the move, it was not quite dark out. The air was still chilly, especially once the sun went down. Through the partially opened window, I could hear a distant lawn mower and the occasional fragment of conversation as assorted people walked by. I live a block from the beach on a side street that provides overflow parking when Cabana Boulevard gets jammed.

I slid down comfortably on my spine, my sock feet on the coffee table, while I settled in to work. I went through the file quickly at first, just to get the lay of the land. A detective named Brad Crouse was lead investigator on the case. The other investigating officers, aside from Stacey Oliphant, were Detective Keith Baldwin, Sergeant Oscar Wallen, Sergeant Melvin Galloway, and Deputy Joe Mandel. A lot of manpower. Crouse had typed the bulk of the reports, using multiple carbons, which Stacey had apparently then photocopied from the old murder book. Judging from the number of strikeovers, I had to guess Detective Crouse had not been first in his class in secretarial school. I fancied if I put my ear to the page, I'd pick up the churlish echoes of his long-ago curses embedded in the lines of print.

It's odd going through an old file, like reading a mystery novel where you spoil the ending for yourself by peeking ahead to the very last page. The final document, a letter from a soils expert in San Pedro, California, was dated September 28, 1971, and indicated that the sample submitted by the Santa Teresa County Sheriff's Department would be impossible to distinguish from samples taken from similar deposits across the state. Sincerely. So sorry. End of the line for you, bub. I went back to the beginning and started reading again, this time taking notes.

According to the first officer at the scene, the girl's body had been rolled over the edge of an embankment, coming to rest about fifteen feet down, some fifty feet from the highway. Con Dolan and Stacey Oliphant had

spotted her at approximately 5:00 P.M. on that Sunday—
1700 hours if you're talking military time, as this report
did. She was lying on her left side on a crumpled canvas
tarp, her hands bound in front of her with a length of
white plastic-coated wire. She was wearing a dark blue
Dacron blouse, white cotton pants with a print of dark
blue daisies with a dot of red in each center. There was a
leather sandal on her right foot; the matching sandal was
found in the brush a short distance away. Marks in the
dirt suggested she'd been dragged across the grass near
the road. Even from the top of the slope, Dolan and Oliphant could see numerous stab wounds in her chest. It
was also apparent her throat had been slashed.

Oliphant had made immediate CB contact with the
Lompoc PD. Because the location was in the county, two
on-duty sheriff's deputies were dispatched to the scene.
Deputy Joe Mandel and Sergeant Melvin Galloway arrived twenty minutes after the initial call. Photographs
were taken of the decedent and of the surrounding area.
The body was then removed to a Lompoc mortuary,
pending arrival of the coroner. Meanwhile, the deputies
searched the vicinity, took soil samples, bagged the tarpaulin along with a nearby broken shrub and two pieces
of shrub stem that appeared to be stained with blood.

On Tuesday, August 5, 1969, Mandel and Galloway
returned to the crime scene to take measurements—the
distance from the highway to the spot where the body
had been found, the width of the blacktop, the location
of the stray sandal. Sergeant Galloway took additional
photos of the various areas, showing the embankment,
damaged shrubs, and drag marks. There were no crime
scene sketches, but perhaps they'd become separated
from the rest of the file in the intervening years.

I took a minute to sort through the photographs,

which were few in number and remarkably uninforma-
tive: eight black-and-white prints, including one of the
roadway, one of an officer pointing at a broken shrub,
one of the embankment where the body was found, and
four of the body from a distance of fifteen feet. There
were no close-ups of Jane Doe's face, no views of her
wounds or the knotted wire with which her hands had
been bound. The tarp was visible beneath her, but it was
difficult to judge how much of the body, if any, had been
covered. Times have changed. Current practice would
have dictated fifty such photographs along with a video
and a detailed crime-scene sketch. In the same envelope,
I found an additional five photographs in faded color
showing the girl's sandals, pants, shirt, bra, and panties
laid out on what looked like a sheet of white paper.

The autopsy had been performed on August 4, 1969,
at 10:30 A.M. I squinted, inferred, surmised, and otherwise faked my way through the report, deciphering
enough of the technical talk to figure out what was being
said. Because her body was in a state of advanced decomposition, the measurements were estimates. The girl's
height was calculated at 63 to 65 inches, her weight at
120 to 125 pounds. Her eyes were blue, her hair dyed a
reddish blond that showed dark roots. In the left earlobe
she wore a thin gold-wire circle with a horseshoe configuration. In her right earlobe she wore a similar gold-wire
loop with a bent clip in its lower end. Her facial characteristics were indistinguishable due to skin slippage, gas
crepitation, and decomposition. Examination of the
body showed eight deep stab wounds in the middle of
the back below the shoulder blade area; two stab wounds
at the base of the neck on either side; five stab wounds
between her breasts; and a large stab wound under the
left breast, which had penetrated the heart. There was

considerable maggot activity. Because of decomposition, the pathologist was unable to ascertain the presence of any scars or identifying marks. There were no skeletal fractures or deformities, no visible injuries to the external genitalia. Her fallopian tubes and ovaries were unremarkable and her uterine cavity was empty. Cause of death was listed as multiple stab wounds of the neck, chest, heart, and lungs.

At the conclusion of his exam, the pathologist removed Jane Doe's fingers, the nails of which she had painted with silver polish. These were tagged by an officer and turned over for shipping to the FBI Identification Division in Washington, D.C. Films taken of her upper and lower jaws showed multiple metallic restorations. She also suffered from what is commonly referred to as buckteeth, with one crooked eyetooth on the left side. A dentist, consulted later, suggested that extensive dental work had probably been done in the two years before her death—that being 1967 through 1968. He judged her to be in her late teens to early twenties. A forensic odontologist, examining the maxilla and mandible at a later date, narrowed the girl's age to fifteen years, plus or minus thirty-six months, noting that she probably died before she reached the legal age of eighteen.

On Wednesday, August 6, Sergeant Galloway submitted the following clothing and evidence to the deputy in charge of the property room:

1. One navy blue, full-length, puffed-sleeve blouse of Dacron-voile material—make unknown—blood-stained.
2. One pair home-sewn female white pants with blue flowers with red centers—size unknown.

3. One pair bikini panties, pink—size medium, Penney's label.
4. One black bra, size 38A, Lady Suzanne label.
5. One pair female brown leather sandals—buckle type, with four brass links on leather straps. Size 7½. With gold letters "MADE IN ITALY" on inner sole.
6. One soiled canvas tarpaulin with blood and miscellaneous stains.

The dead girl's earrings, a clipping of her hair, and the plastic-coated wire taken from her wrists were also booked into evidence.

The Sheriff's Department must have sent the essential information about the deceased to other law enforcement agencies, because a series of follow-up reports over the next several weeks covered all manner of missing persons believed to match the description of Jane Doe. Three stolen automobiles were recovered in the area, one containing assorted articles of women's clothing in the rear seat. This turned out to be unrelated, according to handwritten notes entered at a later date. The second vehicle, a 1966 red Mustang convertible with Arizona plates, reported stolen from an auto upholstery shop in Quorum, California, was subsequently returned to its rightful owner. The third stolen vehicle, a red 1967 Chevrolet, was tied to a homicide in Venice, California. The driver was subsequently arrested and later convicted of that crime.

A vagrant was picked up for questioning but released. There was also a report of a twenty-five-year-old employee who'd absconded with $46.35 in currency and change stolen from a service station owner outside the town of Seagate. The caretaker at a nearby state beach park was contacted and questioned about any persons he might have seen in the area. He reported nothing unusual. In three separate incidents, hitchhikers were picked up for questioning, but none of them were held. This was the summer of 1969 and there was a steady stream of hippies migrating north along this route. Hippies were generally regarded with suspicion, assumed to be high on drugs, which was probably the case.

At 10:30 A.M. on August 6, 1969, Detective Crouse interviewed a clerk named Roxanne Faught, who worked at a minimart on Highway 101. She'd contacted the Sheriff's Department after reading about the murder in the papers and reported that on Friday, August 1, she'd seen a young girl who matched the description of Jane Doe. Miss Faught stated that the girl had helped herself to coffee and a doughnut, which she was unable to pay for. Faught paid for them herself, which is why the incident stuck in her mind. Earlier she'd noticed this same girl hitchhiking north, however she was gone when Faught left work at 3:00 P.M. The girl in the minimart carried no luggage and had no wallet or purse. Several other people contacted the department with leads, but none of these panned out.

As the days went on, calls came in reporting vehicles of various makes, models, and descriptions that had been seen near the quarry both before and after the body was discovered. As with any investigation, delving into the one crime seemed to bring a number of peripheral crimes into focus: loitering, trespassing, public drunkenness, petty theft—all of which turned out to be immaterial to the case. It was clear that many local citizens were busy remembering odd and freakish incidents that had occurred in the weeks prior to the homicide. For all anyone knew, one of these reports might hold a vital clue about the girl who'd been murdered or the person, or persons, who'd killed her.

Every phone call, every out-of-state inquiry, and every rumor was dutifully tracked down. At the end of each report, there was a list appended, giving the names, addresses, and phone numbers of those who'd been interviewed. The managers of the JCPenney stores in Lompoc and Santa Teresa were contacted with regard to the article of clothing that bore the Penney's label, but it was learned that the item was available at any store in the chain. In the end, the girl remained unidentified, and as autumn rolled into winter, new leads diminished. The stained canvas tarp bore no identifying labels. The plastic-coated wire was submitted to the crime lab for analysis. The lab determined that wiring of that nature "would most probably be utilized in low-voltage-amperage conditions where little or no tension would be exerted on its length and where maximum protection from abrasion and moisture was required, perhaps an auto light system, or small low-voltage lighting equipment." By December of 1970, the intervals between reports had lengthened and new information had dwindled.

Stacey had worked the case at various times during the following years. He'd consolidated the list of witnesses, and it looked as though he'd arranged them in order of their importance, at least from his perspective. Many had been eliminated because the information they'd provided was too vague or their suggestions too far-fetched. In some cases, it was clear from later file entries that their questions and concerns were not relevant to the investigation. He'd followed up on every call in which a missing girl had been reported. In one instance, dental records were not a match for Jane Doe's. In another, the police advised the Sheriff's Department that

the girl in question was a chronic runaway and had returned home within days. In a third case, the mother of
the subject called and informed investigating officers her
daughter was alive and well. Stacey had even tried using
telephone numbers listed in the reports in hopes of con-
tacting persons whose information seemed pertinent,
but many numbers were out of service or had been reas-
signed to other parties. Having reached the last of the
reports, I went through again, consigning the pertinent
dates to a stack of blank index cards, converting the facts
from their narrative form to disconnected bits of information that I'd analyze later.

When I finally closed the file and looked at my watch,
it was only 7:15—still early enough to catch up with
Dolan at CC's. I pulled on my shoes, grabbed my jacket
and shoulder bag, and headed out to my car.

The Caliente Café—or CC's, as it's known—is a neighborhood bar that offers an extensive menu of American
dishes with Spanish surnames. The food was probably
the management's attempt to keep the patrons suffi-
ciently sober to drive home without incurring any DUIs.
The surrounding property had undergone a transformation since my last visit two years before. The restaurant is
housed in an abandoned service station. The gasoline
pumps and below-ground storage tanks had been removed at the time of the conversion, but the contaminated soil had simply been blacktopped over and the
resulting quarter acre of tarmac was used to provide pa-
tron parking. As time went on, the neighbors had begun
to complain about the virulent seepage coming up from
the ground—a chemical molasses fierce enough to
darken the soles of your shoes. In the thick of summer

heat, the asphalt became viscous and smelled like oolong tea—which is to say, smoldering tires. In winter, the surface seized up, buckling and cracking to reveal a mealy substance so caustic it generated nosebleeds. Stray cats were subject to wracking coughs on contact. Wandering dogs would suddenly stagger in circles as though in the grip of neurological dismay. Naturally, the owner of the property wasn't interested in paying the hundreds of thousands of dollars required to excavate this hellishly befouled soil, but the EPA had finally stepped in, and now the parking lot had been uprooted in an effort to remove all the contaminated dirt. In the process, numerous Chumash Indian artifacts had been uncovered, and the site was suddenly embroiled in a dispute among several parties: the tribe, the landowner, the city, and the archaeologists. So complex was this litigation that it was impossible to tell who was siding with whom.

It was a testimony to loyal patrons that for months they'd continued to tromp across this malodorous earth, endured delays and inconveniences, suffered picketers, public warnings, posted notices, fumes, muddy shoes, and the occasional pratfall just to get to their daily drinks. The parking lot was now fenced off and the path to the front door consisted of a narrow walkway of two-by-four planks laid out end to end. Approaching the establishment, I felt like a gymnast teetering on the balance beam before an ill-timed dismount.

The red neon sign that hung above the entrance still hissed and sizzled like a backyard bug light, and the air wafting out smelled of cigarette smoke and corn tortillas fried in last week's lard. A shrieking duet of blender motors was accompanied by castanets of clattering ice cubes being whirled together with tequila and margarita mix. The Caliente Café opens at 6:00 every morning and doesn't shut down until 2:00 A.M. Its further virtue is that it's located just outside the city limits and thus provides an ever-present refuge for off-duty police officers who need to unwind at the end of a hard day—or after lunch, or after breakfast.

As I crossed the threshold, I confess I was hoping to run into a Santa Teresa vice cop named Cheney Phillips. Our long acquaintance had never progressed as far as romance—he had a girlfriend, for one thing—but one could always hope. Rumor had it the two of them had split up, so I figured it wouldn't hurt to put in an appearance.

Part of what sparked my interest was the fact I hadn't heard from Robert Dietz in months. He's a semiretired private eye who worked as my bodyguard in 1983 when a cut-rate hit man was hired to rub me out. Our connection since then has been intense and sporadic, with long, inexplicable intervals between visits. Only two weeks before, I'd called him in Carson City, Nevada, and left a message on his machine. So far, he hadn't bothered to call me back, which meant he was either out of the country or had moved on to someone new. Though I was crazy about Dietz, I'd never thought of him as my beau, my steady, my significant other, or my main squeeze (whatever the hell that is). Oh sure, Dietz and I had fooled around some over the past four years, but there was no commitment between us and no promises on either part. Naturally, I was irked at his neglect, even though I was equally at fault.

I caught sight of Dolan at the bar. He was wearing a worn brown leather bomber jacket. I paused for a moment to scope out the crowd and saw his gaze slide in my direction. Dolan's been a cop for too many years not to keep an eye on his surroundings, perpetually scanning faces in hopes of a match for one of the mug shots that had once crossed his desk. Off duty or on, no cop can resist the notion of a wholly unexpected felony arrest.

He raised a hand in greeting and I steered a course toward him, threading my way among parties waiting for tables. The stools on either side of him were occupied, but he gave the guys a look and one of them stood up to make room for me. I placed my shoulder bag at my feet and perched on the stool next to his. The ashtray in front of him was thick with butts, and it didn't take any of my highly developed detecting skills to note the number of cigarettes he'd smoked, including the one he was in the process of lighting from the still lit. He was drinking Old Forrester and he smelled like a Christmas fruitcake, minus the dried maraschino cherries. He was also snacking on a plate of poppers: batter-fried jalapeño peppers filled with molten cheese. I thought I'd avoid pointing out the continuing error of his ways. There's nothing more obnoxious than someone calling attention to our obvious failings.

I said, "I thought I might run into Cheney Phillips. Have you seen him?"

"I think he's in Vegas on his honeymoon."

"His honeymoon? I thought the two of them broke up."

"This is someone new, a gal he met in here five or six weeks ago."

"You're kidding."

"Afraid not. Anyway, forget him. He's not your type anyway."

"I don't have a type. Of course, I don't have a boyfriend either, but that's beside the point."

"Have a popper."

"Thanks." I took one and bit into it, experiencing the

spurt of melted cheese before the heat of the jalapeño set my tongue aflame. The jukebox came to life, and I peered over my shoulder as the strains of a country-western melody line-danced its way across the room. The Wurlitzer was ancient, a chunky, round-bodied contraption with a revolving rainbow of hues, bubbles licking up along its seams.

I turned my attention back to Dolan, trying to figure out how much he'd had to drink. He wasn't slurring his words, but I suspected he was so conditioned by his own alcoholic intake that he'd show no signs of drunkenness even if he fell off his stool. I wasn't sure if he'd been drinking continuously since lunchtime or had gone home for a nap between cocktails. A glance at the clock showed it was only 7:35, but he might have been sitting there since 4:00 P.M. I didn't look forward to working with the man if he was going to be pie-eyed from day to day. His constant smoking didn't appeal to me, either, but there was nothing I could do about it so the less said the better. "How's Stacey doing? Have you talked to him yet?"

"I called him at six and said we'd stop by to see him. Guy's sick of being poked and prodded, really wants out of there. I guess they'll release him tomorrow once the test results are back."

"Did you tell him your idea?"

"Briefly. I said we'd fill him in when we got there. What'd you think about the case?"

"I really love all that stuff. I usually don't have the chance to see police reports up close."

"Procedure hasn't changed that much the past twenty years. We're better at it now—more thorough and systematic, plus we got new technology on our side."

The bartender ambled our way. "What can I get for you?"

"I'm fine," I said.

Dolan lifted his whiskey glass, signaling for a refill.

"Aren't we on our way to see Stacey?"

"Right now?"

"Well, there's no point in getting into this if he's not going to agree."

I could see Dolan debate his desire for the next drink versus his concern for his friend. He pushed his glass back, reached for his wallet, and pulled out a handful of bills, which he tossed on the bar. "Catch you later."

I grabbed my bag and followed him as he headed for the door.

"We'll take my car," he said.

"What if you want to stay longer than I do? Then I'm stuck. Let's take both cars and I'll follow. That way, I can peel off any time it suits."

We wrangled a bit more but he finally agreed. I was parked half a block down, but he dutifully waited, pulling out just ahead of me as I came up on his left. His driving was surprisingly sedate as we cruised out the 101 in our minimotorcade. I knew if he got stopped and breathalyzed, he'd easily blow over the legal limit. I kept an eye out for cops, half-forgetting that Dolan was a cop himself.

Once close to St. Terry's, we found street parking within two cars of each other on the same block of Castle. It was now fully dark and the hospital was lit up like a lavish resort. We went in through the rear entrance and took the elevator to 6 Central, the oncology floor. The lights had been dimmed, and the wide, carpeted corridor muffled our footsteps. Three spare IV poles and two blood pressure monitors were clustered against the wall, along with a linen cart and a multitiered meal cart filled with trays from the dinner served earlier. I caught sight of a few visitors, but there was none of the lively interplay between patients and family members. Getting well takes work and no one wants to waste energy on superficial conversation. Passing the nurses' station, Dolan gave a nod to the clerk at the desk.

Stacey was in a private room, looking out on a darkened residential street. He seemed to be sleeping, his hospital bed elevated at a forty-five-degree angle. Poking out from under his red-knit watch cap were wisps of ginger-colored hair. Two get-well cards were propped upright along the wide windowsill, but there was nothing else of a personal nature. The television screen was blank. On his rolling bed table, there were a pile of magazines and a paper cup filled with melting ice.

Dolan paused in the doorway. Stacey's eyes came open. He waved and then pushed himself up on the bed. "I see you made it," he said, and then to me, "You must be Kinsey. Nice to meet you." I leaned forward and shook his hand. His grip was strong and hot, almost as though he were metabolizing at twice the normal rate.

While Dolan went about the business of rounding up chairs from opposite corners of the room, I said, "I believe you knew the guys who trained me—Morley Shine and Ben Byrd."

"I knew them well. Both good men. I was sorry to hear about Morley's murder. That was a hell of a thing. Have a seat."

"Thanks."

Dolan offered me one chair and settled in the other. While the two of them chatted, I studied Stacey. He had small mild blue eyes, pale brows, and a long, deeply creased face. His color was good, though it looked as though he hadn't shaved for days. He seemed to be in good spirits and he spoke with all the vigor of an active man.

After some preliminary conversation, Dolan brought

the subject around to the Jane Doe investigation. "I gave Kinsey the file to read. We thought we should talk about where we go from here. The doc still talking about letting you out tomorrow?"

"Looks that way."

The two of them chatted about the case while I kept my mouth shut. I don't know why I'd expected Stacey to resist Dolan's proposition, but he didn't seem at all opposed to our resurrecting the case. He said to Dolan, "Speaking of which, Frankie Miracle got out. His parole officer, Dench Smallwood, called me and said Frankie found a place in town. By now, he probably has legitimate employment."

"That'd be a first."

I said, "How does Frankie Miracle fit in? I remember his name from the file."

Dolan said, "He got picked up in Lompoc August 1, two days before Jane Doe's body was found. We always figured he was good for it, though he denied it."

Stacey spoke up. "He killed his girlfriend in Venice, July 29, during a meth binge. He stabbed the woman umpteen times, then he helped himself to her car and all her credit cards and started driving north. She was found a couple days later when neighbors complained about the smell."

"Dumb-ass signed her name to the charge slips every time he stopped for gas," Dolan said. "You'd think someone would notice a 'Cathy Lee Pearse' with no boobs, a mustache, and a two-day growth of beard." He shifted in his chair and then rose to his feet. "You two go on and get acquainted. Time for me to step outside and grab a smoke."

Once Dolan left, I said, "You have a theory why Jane Doe was never identified?"

"No. We expected a quick match, someone who'd

recognize her from the description in the papers. All I can think is she wasn't reported missing. Or maybe the missing-persons report got buried in the paperwork on some cop's desk. There's probably an explanation, but who knows what it is? By now, it's unlikely we'll ever find out who killed her, but there's a possibility we can get her ID'd and returned to her folks."

"What are the chances?"

"Not as bad as you might think. Once enough time passes, people are more willing to speak up. We might tweak someone's conscience and get a lead that way." He hesitated, taking a moment to smooth the edges of his sheet. "You know, Con's wife, Gracie, died a while back."

"He mentioned that."

"It hit him hard at the time, but he seemed to be pulling out of it. But ever since he got sidelined with this heart condition, the guy's been in a funk. As long as Gracie was alive, she seemed to keep him in check, but now his smoking and booze consumption are out of control. I've been trying to find a way to get him back on track, so the minute this came up, I jumped on it."

"You're talking about Jane Doe?"

"Right. I was happy you agreed to help. It'll give him a lift. He needs to work."

I smiled with caution, listening for any hint of irony in his tone. Apparently, he didn't realize Dolan had voiced the very same concerns about him.

When Dolan returned, he stood looking expectantly from me to Stacey. "So what's the game plan? You two have it all worked out?"

"We were just talking about that. Kinsey wants to see the crime scene before we do anything else."

I said, "Right."

Dolan said, "Great. I'll set that up for tomorrow."

3

Dolan picked me up at my place at 10:00 in his 1979 Chevrolet, Stacey in the backseat. He did an expert parallel parking job and got out of the car. He wore a dark blue sweatshirt and a pair of worn blue jeans. The exterior of the Chevy was a mess. By day, I could see that the once-dark brown paint had oxidized, taking on the milky patina of an old Hershey's bar. The back bumper was askew, the left rear fender was crumpled, and a long indentation on the passenger side rendered the door close to inoperable. I managed to open it by means of a wrenching maneuver that made the metal shriek in protest. Once seated, I hauled, trying to get it shut again. Dolan circled the car, shoved the door shut, and secured the lock by bumping it with his hip.

I said, "Thanks." Already, I was worried about his prowess at the wheel.

He leaned in the open window and held his hand out to Stacey. "Give me your gun and I'll lock 'em in the trunk."

Stacey winced audibly as he torqued to one side, slipping his gun from his holster and passing it to Dolan. Dolan went around to the rear and tucked the guns in the trunk before he got in on his side.

The car's upholstery was a dingy beige fabric that made it difficult to slide across the seat. I remained where I was as though glued in place. I turned so I could look at Stacey, who was sitting in the backseat with a bed pillow wedged behind him. His red knit watch cap was pulled down almost to his brows. "Threw my back out," he said by way of explanation. "I was moving boxes last week. I guess I should have done like Mother taught me and lifted with my knees."

Dolan's hiking boots were muddy, and waffle-shaped droppings littered the floor mat on his side. He adjusted the rearview mirror to talk to Stacey's reflection. "You should have left those for me. I told you I'd take care of 'em."

"Quit acting like a mother hen. I'm not helpless. It's a muscle pull, that's all; my sciatica acting up. Even healthy people get hurt, you know. It's no big deal."

In the harsh light of day, I could see that, despite the transfusion, his skin had gray undertones, and the smudges beneath his pale brows made his eyes appear to recede. He was dressed for the outdoors, wearing brown cords, hiking boots, a red-plaid wool shirt, and a fisherman's vest.

"You want to sit up here?"

"I'm better off where I am. I'm never quite sure when I'm going to need to lie down."

"Well, just let me know if you want to switch places."

I tugged at my seat belt, which was hung up somewhere. I spent an inordinate amount of time trying to get the mechanism to release a sufficient length of belt so I could clip it into place. Meanwhile, Dolan put the car in gear. The engine coughed and died twice, but finally sputtered back to life, and we were under way. The interior smelled of nicotine and dog. I didn't picture Dolan as the doggy type, but I didn't want to ask. The floorboards were strewn with gas receipts, discarded cigarette packs, and assorted cellophane bags that had once contained potato chips, cheese-and-cracker sandwiches, and other heart-healthy snacks.

We gassed up at a service station adjacent to the freeway and then he eased the car out into the traffic, heading north on the 101. As soon as we were settled at a steady speed, Dolan punched in the car lighter and reached for the pack of Camels he had resting on the dash.

Stacey said, "Hey! Have mercy. You've got a cancer patient back here."

Dolan again angled the rearview mirror so he could see Stacey's face. "That doesn't seem to stop you from smoking that pipe of yours."

"The pipe's purely recreational. At the rate you smoke, you'll be dead before me."

Dolan said, "Nuts," but left the pack where it was.

Stacey tapped me on the shoulder. "See that? The guy looks after me. You'd never guess that about him."

Dolan's smile barely registered, but it softened his face.

After the town of Colgate, the railroad tracks and the highway ran parallel to the ocean. To the north, the Santa Ynez Mountains loomed dark and gray, dense with low-growing vegetation. There were scarcely any trees, and the contours of the foothills were a rolling green. Much of the topography was defined by massive landslides, sandstone and shale debris extending for miles. Dolan and Stacey conducted a conversation that consisted of fishing and hunting stories—endless accounts of all the creatures they'd shot, hooked, trapped, and snagged; gutted, skinned, and toted home. This, with men, passes for a load of fun.

We sped past the state beach park, where camping sites consisted of adjacent oblongs of asphalt that looked suspiciously like parking spaces. I'd seen campers and RVs lined up like piano keys while the occupants set out aluminum picnic tables and chairs, stoking up their portable barbecues in areas much smaller than the yards they had at home. The children would gorge on hot dogs and potato chips, frolic in the ocean, and then bed down in the car, hair sticky, their bodies infused with residual salt like little cod fillets. For Dolan and Stacey, the sight of the line of campers triggered a recollection of another unsolved homicide—two teens shot to death on an isolated stretch of beach. After that, they spent time pointing out the various locations where past homicide victims had been dumped. Santa Teresa County had provided a number of such spots.

A few miles beyond Gull Cove, Dolan took the turn-off and headed west on California 1. I found myself lulled by the passing countryside. Here the hills were undulating, dotted with shaggy masses of the dark green oaks that marched across the land. The skies were pale blue with only the faintest marbling of clouds. The air smelled of the hot, sun-dried pastures sprinkled with buttercups, where occasional cattle grazed.

The two-lane road wound west and north. From time to time, the route cut through irregular, high-arching rock beds. On one of these stretches, thirty-two years before, a mammoth boulder tumbled down the slope, shattering the windshield of my parents' car as we passed. I was sitting in the rear, playing with my paper doll, scowling because I'd just bent her left cardboard leg at the ankle. I felt a flash of uncontrollable five-year-old rage because her foot looked all crookedy and limp. I was just setting up a howl when one of my parents made a startled exclamation. Perhaps the falling rock was briefly visible on descent, bouncing in a jaunty shower of smaller rocks and dirt. There was no time to react. The force of the boulder smashed through the windshield, crushing my father's head and chest, killing him instantly. The vehicle veered right, careening out of control, and crashed against the rocky hill face.

The impact flung me forward, wedging me against the driver's seat. From this confining cage of crumpled metal, I kept my mother company in the last, long moments of her life. I understand now how it must have felt from her perspective. Her injuries were such that there was no way she could move without excruciating pain. She could hear me whimper, but she had no way to know how badly I was hurt. She could see her husband was dead and knew she was not far behind. She wept, keening with regret. After a while, she was quiet, and I remember thinking that was good, not knowing she'd left her body and floated off somewhere.

Dolan swerved to avoid a ground squirrel that had skittered across the pavement in front of us. Instinctively, I put a hand out to brace myself and then I focused on the road again, disconnecting my emotions with all the skill of a vivisectionist. It's a trick of mine that probably dates back to those early years. I tuned into the conversation, which I realized belatedly had been directed at me.

Dolan was saying, "You with us?"

"Sure. Sorry. I think I missed that."

"I said, this guy, Frankie Miracle, we talked about last night? He got picked up on a routine traffic stop outside

Lompoc. The schmuck had a busted taillight, and when the officers ran the plate, the vehicle came up stolen and wanted by the Los Angeles County Sheriff's Department. Galloway reads him his rights and throws him in the hoosegow. Meanwhile, the car's towed to the impound lot. When Galloway sits down to write his report, he reads the APB, indicating the registered owner's the victim of a homicide. He goes back over to the jail and tells Frankie he's under arrest for murder and reads him his rights again. Two days after that, Stacey and I go deer hunting and come across the girl."

"Yeah, if it wasn't for the taillight, Frankie could've been in Oregon and we might not've tied him to the situation here."

"What about the weapon? I don't remember any mention of it."

"We never found the knife, but judging from the wounds, the coroner said the blade had to be at least five inches long. Rumor has it, Frankie carried something similar, though he didn't have it on him when we picked him up."

Stacey said, "He probably tossed it or buried it. Country up there is rugged. Search and Rescue came through and did a grid search but never turned up anything." He leaned forward and tapped Con on the shoulder, pointing to a side road going off on our right a hundred yards ahead. "That's it. Just beyond this bridge coming up."

"You think? I remember it was farther down, along a stretch of white three-board fence."

"Oh. Maybe so. You could be right about that."

Dolan had slowed from forty miles an hour to a cautious fifteen. The two peered over at a two-lane gravel road that cut back at an angle and disappeared from view. It must not have looked familiar because Stacey said, "Nuh-uhn. Try around the next bend. We could have passed it already." He turned and stared out the rear window.

In the end, Dolan made a U-turn and we circled back, making a second slow pass until they settled on the place. Dolan pulled onto a secondary lane, gravel over cracked asphalt, that followed the contours of a low-lying hill. Directly ahead of us, I could see where the road split to form a Y. A locked gate barred access to the property with its No Trespassing signs. On the near side of the gate and to the right, a Jeep was parked.

"Where's Grayson Quarry?" I asked, referring to the crime scene as designated on the official police reports.

"Around the bend to the right about a quarter of a mile," Dolan said. As he edged over on the berm and set the handbrake, an elderly gentleman in jeans, cowboy boots, and a leather hat emerged from the Jeep. He was small and wide, with a full-sized Santa belly pushing at the buttons of his western-style shirt. He approached our car, walking with a decided limp. Dolan cut the engine and got out on his side.

Stacey murmured, "That's Arne Johanson, the ranch foreman. I called and he agreed to meet us to unlock the gate."

By the time Stacey eased out of the backseat, I'd emerged from the passenger side and shoved the car door with one hip. Now that Dolan was in the open air, he lit a cigarette.

Stacey moved toward the old man and shook his hand. I noticed he was making an effort to appear energetic. "Mr. Johanson. This is nice of you. I'm Stacey Oliphant with the County Sheriff's Department. You probably don't remember, but we met in August of '69 back when the body was found. This is Lieutenant Con

Dolan from Santa Teresa PD. He's the fellow who was with me. Two of us were up here to hunt when we came across the girl."

"I thought you looked familiar. Good seeing you."

"Thanks. We appreciate your help."

The old man's gaze drifted in my direction. He seemed puzzled at the sight of me. "Like to see some ID if it's all the same to you." This was directed at the guys though his eyes remained on me.

Stacey moved his jacket aside to expose the badge attached to his belt. His badge specified that he was retired, but Johanson didn't seem to notice and Stacey didn't feel compelled to call it to his attention. Dolan rolled his cigarette to one corner of his mouth and took out a leather bifold wallet with his badge, which he held up. While Johanson leaned forward and studied it, Dolan took out a business card and handed it to him. Johanson tucked the card in his shirt pocket and glanced at me slyly.

"She's with us," Dolan said.

I was perfectly willing to show him a copy of my license, but I liked Dolan's protectiveness and thought I'd leave well enough alone. This time, when the old man's eyes returned to mine, I looked away. I pegged him as a throwback, some old reprobate who believed women belonged in the kitchen, not out in the "real" world going toe to toe with men. He had to be in his eighties. His eyes were small, a watery blue. His face was sun-toughened, deeply creased, and bristling with whiskers that showed white against his leathery skin. He shifted his attention to Dolan's cigarette. "I'd watch that if I was you. It's fire country up here."

"I'll be careful."

Johanson took out a set of keys and the four of us

walked over to the metal rail gate with its ancient pad-lock. His stride had a rocking motion that suggested an old injury. Maybe in his youth he'd worked the rodeo circuit. He selected a key, turned it in the padlock, and popped it off the hasp. He pushed the sagging gate aside, forcing it back to a point where it was anchored in the grass. The four of us passed through, Dolan and Stacey leading while I tagged behind them and Johanson brought up the rear.

"It was two cops who found her, coming here to hunt," he said, having either missed or forgotten the reference Stacey'd made to their prior meeting.

Dolan grunted a response, which didn't seem to discourage the old man's garrulousness. "We got wild boar on the property. Owner lets hunters come in now and then to cull the herd. Boars is aggressive. I've had 'em turn and charge right at me, gash a hole in my leg. Mean sons a bitches, I can tell you that. Peckers like razor blades is what I heard. Mating season, the female sets up a squeal brings the hair right up on the back of your neck."

"Actually, Lieutenant Dolan and I were the ones who found the body. We'd come up to hunt."

"You two. Is that right? Well, I'll be. I could've swore I knowed you from someplace."

"We're all a bit older."

"I can testify to that. I'm eighty-seven year old myself, born January 1, nineteen double ought. Broke a hip here a while back when my horse fell on me. It hadn't healed too good. Nowadays, they can take out the old joint and put another in its place. This gimpyness don't straighten out, I might get me a brand-new one. Say, what's this all about now, anyway? I'm not entirely clear."

Stacey said, "Sheriff's Department is going over some

old files, taking another look. We're reworking this case in hopes of resolving it."

"And you come up here why?"

"We wanted to see the crime scene so the reports would make more sense. Those old crime scene photographs don't tell how the area's laid out, relative distances, things of that sort." This again from Stacey. So far I hadn't said a word.

Johanson's eyes strayed to my face with the same thinly veiled curiosity. "I can understand that. I brung my son down here when they was hauling her body out of the ravine. He was fourteen and thought it was just fine and dandy hitchin' rides every time he had to go someplace. I wanted him to see where he could end up."

"You have a son that young?" I said, trying not to sound too surprised.

The old man grinned, showing blackened and crooked teeth. "Got two," he said. "I been married five time, but I never had kids until this last go-round. Youngest boy's thirty-two yesterday. I got him workin' on the ranch. Other boy's a bum. I guess I have to think of it as fifty percent success instead of fifty percent failed."

Dolan dropped his cigarette to the ground and crushed the ember thoroughly with his heel. "You think that's what happened to her? Someone offered her a ride and ended up stabbing her to death?"

"That'd be my guess. You know they never did figure out who she was. Pitiful, you ask me. All these years, her mom and dad never knowed what happened to her. Prob'ly still think she's comin' home and there she was laid out with her throat cut ear to ear."

Stacey said, "Identifying the girl is part of what we hope to accomplish."

Dolan was already firing up his second cigarette. "We

appreciate your time, Mr. Johanson. I'm sure you're busy and we don't want to keep you. Thanks for meeting us."

"Happy to oblige. You needn't bother about me. I'll just tag along 'til you're done and lock the gate again."

"We won't be long. We'll be happy to lock the gate after us when we leave."

"I don't mind the wait."

Stacey and Dolan exchanged a glance, but neither said another word as they trudged the remaining distance to the edge of the ravine.

Johanson trailed along after us. "Wadn't any gate here back then. I figure the feller must have cruised all up and down, looking for a place to dump her, and chosen this. He must not have knowed about the quarry. Lot of traffic on this road any time of day; fellers heading to the mine. Bad weather's different. Operation closes down if things get too bad."

"I'm surprised she wasn't found by one of the Grayson employees," Stacey remarked.

"Because she smelt?"

"That's right."

"Might've been for all I know. Lot of them boys are Mexican. Called 'em 'wetbacks' in those days. Made a point not to bring attention to theirself, especially where the law's concerned. Probably thought it was a dog if they caught wind of her at all. I'm sure the last thing occurred to them was some young girl been kilt."

Dolan's response was noncommittal, perhaps in hopes of squelching further conversation. Ignoring Johanson, he scrambled a few steps down the embankment. The ground seemed soft, though the surface was powdery with dust. He anchored himself with his right foot on the downside of the slope and stood with his hands in his jeans pockets studying the undergrowth. "She was right about here. A lot more brush in the area back then."

"We cut that back on account of the fire department," Johanson said. "They come out usually twicet a year. Owner won't clear brush without a threat. Too cheap."

"With the fire danger up here, you can't ignore the brush," Stacey said, ever so polite.

"No, sir. That's what I say. You'll find a few more trees. Back when that girl was throwed down there, that 'un and this one wasn't here. Both black acacias. Grow like weeds. I'd cut 'em down myself, but owner won't hear of it. Now, oaks I don't touch. Couldn't pay me to fell one unless it's eat out by rot."

Dolan and I were both ignoring the man. I watched Dolan as he scrambled back out of the ravine and stood scanning the portion of Highway 1 that was visible from where we stood. "My guess is he backed in and opened the trunk of the car. He probably used the painter's tarp to drag the body the short distance from there to here. The tarp was heavily soiled on one side and you could see a path through the underbrush where it'd been flattened by the weight."

"Kids used to pull in here for petting parties," Johanson said. "Monday mornings, ground'd be littered with rubbers, limp as snake skins. That's why we put in the gate, to keep cars out."

I looked at Stacey. "Was she wrapped in the tarp?"

"Partially. We believe he killed her somewhere else. There were blood stains in the grass, but nothing to suggest the volume you'd've seen if she bled out. He probably used the tarp to keep the stains off the interior of the trunk."

Dolan said, "If we'd had some of this new high-tech equipment back then, I bet we'd have found plenty. Hair,

fiber, maybe even prints. Nothing neat about this killing.
He just happened to get lucky. Nobody saw the murder
and nobody spotted him when he toppled her down the
slope."

Johanson perked up. "Neighbor down the road—this
is C. K. Vogel—I don't know if you remember this, but
C. K. seen a light-colored VW van on the particular
morning of July 28 up along that road over there.
Painted all over with peace symbols and psychedelic hippie signs. Said it was still there eleven o'clock that night.
Curtains on the winders. Dim light inside. It was gone
the next morning, but he said it struck him as odd. I
believe he phoned it in to the Sheriff's Department after
the girl was found."

Dolan's skepticism was unmistakable, though he tried
to be civil—not an easy task for him. "Probably unrelated, but we'll look into it."

"Said he seen a convertible as well. Killer could've
drove that. Red, as I recollect, with an out-of-state license plate. If I was you, I'd make sure to have a talk with
him."

I said, "Thanks for the information. I'll make a note."

Johanson looked at me with interest. Suddenly, he
seemed to get it: I was a police secretary, accompanying
the good detectives to spare them the tedium of all the
clerical work.

The breeze shifted slightly, blowing Dolan's smoke in
my face. I moved upwind.

"Something I forgot to mention about Miracle," Stacey said. "When we went back to the impound lot and
searched Frankie's car, we found soil samples in the floor
mats that matched the soil from the embankment. Unfortunately, the experts said it was impossible to distinguish
this sample from samples in other quarries throughout the

state. West Coast has the most extensive marine deposits in the world."

"I saw that report. Too bad," I said. "What'd Frankie say when you questioned him?"

"He gave us some long garbled tale of where he'd been. Claimed he'd been hiking in the area, but it was nothing we could confirm."

Dolan said, "He was higher than a kite the day they picked him up. Grass or coke. Arrest sheet doesn't say. He's a meth freak is what I heard."

"Everyone under thirty was higher than a kite back then," I said.

Mr. Johanson cleared his throat, having been excluded from the conversation too long to suit him. "Being's as you're here, you might want to see the rest of the property. This is the last ranch of its size. Won't be long before they tear down the old house. Probably build subdivisions as far as the eye can see."

My impulse was to decline, but Dolan seemed to spark to the idea. "I'm in no hurry. Fine with me," he said. He gave Stacey a look. Stacey shrugged his assent and then checked for my response.

I said, "Sure. I don't mind. Are we finished here?"

"For now. We can always come back."

Johanson turned toward his Jeep. "Best take the Jeep. Road's all tore up from heavy rains we had a while back. No point throwing up dust and gravel on that fancy car of yours."

I thought he was being snide. I checked for Dolan's reaction, but he was apparently in agreement with the old man's assessment.

We piled in the Jeep, Stacey in the front seat, Dolan and me climbing into the rear. The seats were cracked leather, and all the glassine windows had been removed.

Johanson started the engine and released the emergency brake. The vehicle's shocks were gone. I reached up and grabbed the roll bar, clinging to it as we began to lurch and bang our way up the deeply rutted gravel road. Like me, Stacey was clinging to the Jeep frame for stability, wincing with pain from the jolts to his injured back.

The grass on either side of us was rough. A hillside rose on our left and then leveled out at the top, forming a mesa where numerous pieces of heavy equipment sat. Much of the remaining ground was stripped and terraced, broad fields of rubble unbroken by greenery. "That's the quarry," Johanson said, hollering over the rattle and whine of the moving vehicle.

I leaned forward, directing my comments toward the back of his head. "Really? That looks like a gravel pit. I pictured limestone cliffs."

"Different kind of quarry. These is open pit mines. Grayson Quarry goes after the DE. That's diatomaceous earth. Here, I've got a sample. Take a look at this." One eye on the road, he leaned down and removed a chunk of rock from the floor of the Jeep, then passed it across the seat to me. The rock was a rough chalky white, about the size of a crude round of bread with irregular gouges in the crust. I passed it on to Lieutenant Dolan, and he hefted it as I had, finding it surprisingly light.

I said, "What'd you say this was?"

"Diatomaceous earth. We call it DE."

I felt a tingle of uneasiness run down my spine as his explanation went on. "DE's a deposit made up mainly of siliceous shells of diatoms. This whole area was underwater oncet upon a time. The way they tolt me, marine life fed on diatoms, which is these colonies of algae. Now it's pulverized and used as an abrasive, sometimes as an absorbent."

Stacey raised his voice against the crunch of the tires over gravel. "I used to use it to filter beer when I was making it at home."

The road began to climb and the Jeep labored upward, finally rounding a bend. The old house came into view—massive, dilapidated, Victoriana under siege. Clearly, the structure had once been regal, but weeds and brush were creeping up on all sides, consuming the yard, obscuring the broken lines of wood fence. Years of neglect had undermined the outbuildings so that all that remained now were the rough stone foundations and occasional piles of collapsed and rotting lumber.

The house itself was a two-story white frame, flanked by a one-story wing on either side of the facade. There were four porches visible, providing shade and sheltered ventilation so that doors and windows could be left open to the elements. A porch wrapped around the house at the front, with a second porch stacked on top. A widow's walk encircled the roof. The numerous paired windows were narrow and dark, many of the panes sporting the sort of tattered holes that rock throwers make when they score a hit.

Johanson waved at the house, scarcely slowing his speed. "Been empty for years. I'm in the gardener's cottage on 'tother side of the barn," he yelled.

I found myself averting my gaze as we passed the house and headed for a compound of structures I spotted in a shady area ahead. Barn, toolshed, greenhouse. There were arbors of grapevines as gnarly as rope. Weathered wooden tables were arranged under the trellises. I had the sensation of cold blowing down on the back of my neck.

Johanson pulled up in front of a ramshackle frame cottage. Beyond, I could see a raw wood barn that listed to one side, and beyond that there were endless stretches of three-board wood fence.

I leaned forward again and laid a hand on Johanson's shoulder. "Excuse me, who'd you say owns this?"

He killed the engine before he turned. "Miz LeGrand. I guess I should say Miz Kinsey to be accurate. She's a widder woman, must be ninety-some by now. Married to Burton Kinsey, the fella who leased the quarry from her pappy. He made his fortune off the mine, though the whole of it was rightly hers oncet the old man died. . . ."

I'd ceased to listen and the silence in my head seemed as profound as temporary deafness. He was talking about my maternal grandmother, Cornelia Kinsey, born Cornelia Straith LeGrand.

4

Friday morning, I arose at 5:59, switching off the alarm a moment before the clock radio was set to burst into song. I stared up at the skylight above my bed. No rain. Shit. I didn't feel like exercising, but I made a deal with myself: I'd do the jog and skip the gym. I leaned over and scooped up the sweats I'd left folded on the floor. I wriggled into pants and top. I sat up and tugged on a pair of crew socks, shoved my feet into my Sauconys, and had my key tied to the laces before I'd left my bed. It occurred to me that if I just made it my habit to sleep in my sweats and crew socks, it would be a lot more efficient. All I'd need were my running shoes and I'd be ready to go. I went into the bathroom and availed myself of the facilities, after which I brushed my teeth, splashed water on my face, and then used my wet hands to comb the sleep-generated peaks and valleys from my hair. I trotted down the spiral stairs, checked the thumblock on the front door and pulled it shut, then rounded the studio to the gate.

The neighborhood was quiet and the air felt damp. I

walked half a block down and one block over, crossing
Cabana Boulevard to the bike path that parallels the
beach. I began to jog, feeling sluggish, aware of every
footfall and every jolt to my frame. With me, jogging is
seldom a subject for debate. I get up and do the run,
unless it rains, of course, and then I burrow in my bed.
Otherwise, five mornings a week, I shake off the sleep
and hit the road before I lose my nerve, knowing that
whatever I'm feeling at the outset of a run will be gone
by the time I reach the end. The gym I can do without,
though I'd been good about lifting weights for the past
several months.

The sunrise had already presented itself in a dazzling
light show that left the sky a broad and unblemished
blue. The surf looked forbidding, a silt-churning cold,
applauded only by the sea lions who waited offshore,
barking their approval. I ran a mile and a half down to
the Cabana Recreation Center, did a U-turn, and then
ran the mile and a half back, finally slowing to a brisk
walk as I headed for home.

I'd been resisting the urge to ponder events from the
day before, but I could feel my thoughts stray. Dolan and
Stacey had both caught the name "Kinsey" as soon as
Johanson mentioned it, but my expression must have
warned them to keep any observations to themselves. I
had said little or nothing while the ranch foreman
showed us through the barn, the old orchards, and the
greenhouse, which was largely abandoned. Most of its
panes were intact. The air was humid and smelled of
mulch, peat moss, compost, and loam. In that protected
environment, alien vines and opportunistic saplings had
flourished, creating a towering jungle that pushed against
the glass on all sides, threatening to break through. The
minute we walked into the space, I knew I'd been there

before. Cousins I'd discovered in the course of a previous investigation had sworn I'd been at Grand's house when I was four years old. I had only the scantiest recollection of the occasion, but I knew my parents must have been there, too. The three of them—my father, my mother, and her sister Virginia—had been banished from the family after my parents eloped. My father was a mailman, thirty-five years old. My mother, Rita Cynthia Kinsey, was an eighteen-year-old debutante whose mother was convinced she was destined for someone better than Randy Millhone. Instead, my mother ran off with him, thumbing her nose at the entire Kinsey clan. Virginia sided with the newlyweds. Thereafter, all three were cast into the Kinsey family equivalent of the Outer Darkness.

Despite being exiled, my parents apparently made secret visits to the ranch whenever my grandparents were away. Rumor had it there were numerous contacts with the three remaining sisters, but I only knew of two occasions. On the first, there was an incident in which I'd fallen off a porch and hurt my knee. I did remember the sight of the scrape with its alternating stripes of dirt and blood, which smelled like iron. I could also remember the searing pain when my mother dabbed at the abrasion with a cotton ball that seemed to hiss on my skin. She and I took turns blowing on the wound, huffing and puffing to dry the medication and thus ease its sting. On the only other drive to Lompoc I remembered, my parents were killed before we ever arrived. My grandmother had known of my existence since the day I was born. I was still smarting from the fact she'd never bothered to make contact.

Walking the property with Arne Johanson, I'd dreaded the idea of entering the house, and I'd been hoping to avoid it when I realized Stacey's breathing had become

labored and much of the color had drained from his face.
I laid a hand on his arm and called, "Con?"

Dolan turned and looked back. Stacey shook his head,
making one of those gestures meant to assure us we
needn't worry about him. Johanson had forged on ahead
and he was still chattering about the ranch when Dolan
caught up with him. "Mr. Johanson? Sorry to cut this
short, but I've got a meeting coming up in town and we
have to get back."

"This won't take long. You don't want to miss the
house."

"Maybe another day. We'll take a rain check."

"Well. I guess that's that then. Whatever you say."

Within minutes, he'd delivered us to Dolan's car and
we were back on the highway. The drive home had been
low-key, with Stacey slumped on the backseat, the red
knit cap pulled down to shield his eyes.

"Are you all right, Stace?" I asked.

"Walking wore me out. It's my damn back again. I'll
be better in a bit." In the absence of animation, his face
looked old.

Dolan readjusted the rearview mirror, keeping one
eye on Stacey and one on the road. "I told you not to
come."

"Did not. You said the fresh air'd be good. Said I
ought to take advantage while I was up to it."

I said, "You warm enough?"

"Quit worrying."

I turned my attention to Lieutenant Dolan. "What's
next?"

Stacey answered before he could. "We'll meet at my
place tomorrow morning. Ten o'clock suit?"

"Fine with me," I said.

Dolan said, "Sounds good."

We dropped Stacey first. He lived close to downtown Santa Teresa, five blocks from my office, in a small pink stucco rental house perched above a pink cinder-block wall. Dolan had me wait in the car while he retrieved Stacey's gun from the trunk and then followed him up the six stairs to the walkway that skirted the place. I could see how tightly Stacey had to grip the railing in order to pull himself up. The two disappeared, moving toward the rear. Dolan was gone for ten minutes, and when he returned to the car, he seemed withdrawn. Neither of us said a word during the drive to my apartment. I spent the remainder of Thursday afternoon taking care of personal errands.

Having finished my jog, I walked the block between the beach and my place. When I reached my front door, I picked up the morning paper as I let myself in. I tossed the *Dispatch* on the kitchen counter and started a pot of coffee. As soon as it began to trickle through the filter, I went up the spiral stairs to take my shower and get dressed.

I was halfway through my bowl of Cheerios, sitting at the counter, when the telephone rang. I dislike interruptions at breakfast, and I was tempted to wait and let the answering machine pick up. Instead, I leaned over and grabbed the handset from the wall-mounted phone. "Hello?"

"Hello, Kinsey. This is Tasha, up in Lompoc. How're you?"

I felt my eyes close. This was one of my cousins, Tasha Howard, the only member of the family I'd ever dealt with at any length. She's an estate attorney with offices in Lompoc and San Francisco.

I'd met her sister, Liza, a couple of years before, and during our one and only conversation discovered hitherto unplumbed depths of disaffection in my otherwise placid frame. My reaction was probably only a side effect of the fact that Liza was telling me things I didn't want to hear. For one thing, she told me, in the giddiest manner possible, that my mother was regarded as an idol among her living nieces and nephews. While this was meant as flattery, I felt it dehumanized the woman whom I'd never really known. I resented their prior claim, just as I resented the fact that my pet name for our aunt Virginia, that being "Aunt Gin," was a term already in wide use among these same family members. So, too, was the penchant for peanut-butter-and-pickle sandwiches, which I'd assumed was a secret link between my mother and me. Granted, my reaction was less than rational, but I was left feeling diminished by the idle tales Liza told.

Tasha was okay. She'd bailed me out of a jam once and on another occasion she'd hired me for a job. *That* hadn't turned out well, but the fault wasn't hers.

Belatedly, I said, "Fine. How are you?" We always have conversations that sound like they're punctuated by transatlantic delays.

"I'm good, thanks. Listen, it looks like Mother and I will be coming down your way to shop and we wondered if you were free. We can have lunch if you like, or maybe get together for drinks later in the afternoon."

"Today? Ah. Thanks for asking, but I just started work on a case and I'm completely tied up. Maybe another time." I hoped I didn't sound as insincere as I felt.

"Must be a busy time of year."

"Feast or famine," I said. "It's the nature of the beast." I was really trying my best not to be prickly with her. Even in the briefest of conversations, we often manage to butt heads on the subject of family relationships. She favors closer ties while I favor none.

"I suspect you'd refuse no matter what."

"Not at all." I let a silence fall.

We breathed in each other's ears until she said, "Well. Mother will be down again on Tuesday. I know she's anxious to talk to you. Are you still in the office on Capillo?"

"Actually, I'm not. I've rented a bungalow on Caballeria. I just moved in a couple of months ago."

"I'll tell her."

"Great. That's fine. Not a problem."

"I don't want you to take offense, but I hope you'll be polite."

"Gee, Tasha, I'll try to behave myself. It'll be a struggle, of course."

I could hear the smile in her voice. "You have to give me credit for persistence."

"Right. Duly noted. I have you down for that."

"You don't have to be sarcastic."

"That's my dry sense of humor."

"Why are you such a pain in the butt? Couldn't you try meeting me halfway?"

"I don't understand why you insist on pursuing me."

"For the same reason you insist on rebuffing me. Being pigheaded is a family trait."

"I'll give you that. It still pisses me off that Grand thinks she could treat my parents like shit and then waltz in years later and make it all evaporate."

"What's that got to do with us? Pam and Liza and I didn't do anything to your parents *or* Aunt Gin. Why should we be held accountable for Grand? Yes, she behaved badly. Yes, she's a bitch, but so what? Maybe your mother and Aunt Gin delivered tit-for-tat. At the time your parents died, we were only kids. We didn't know what was going on and neither did you. It seems ridiculous to nurse such bad feelings. To what end? We're family. You're stuck with us whether you like it or not."

"So far, I've done very well without 'family.' So why can't you drop the subject and get on with life?"

"Why can't you?" She paused, trying to gain control of herself. "I'm sorry. Let's try again. I don't understand why every time I call we get into these *wrangles*."

"We don't get into wrangles *every* time."

"Yes, we do."

"No, we don't!"

"Name one conversation when we didn't come to blows."

"I can name three. You hired me for a job. We had lunch together that day and we got along fine. Since then, we've chatted on the phone two or three times without bickering."

"That's true," she said, reluctantly, "but I'm always aware of the anger percolating just under the surface."

"So what? Look, Tasha, maybe in time we'll find a way to settle our differences. Until then, we're not going to get anywhere arguing about whether or not we're arguing. I don't claim to be rational. I'm nuts. Why don't you let it go at that?"

"Okay. Enough said. We just wanted you to know we're still interested. We hoped yesterday's visit to the ranch would provide an opening."

"Ah, that. How'd you find out?"

"Arne Johanson called Pam. He said he saw someone who looked so much like your mother, it gave him goose bumps. I was surprised you'd even step a foot on the family ranch."

"I wouldn't have if I'd known."

"Oh, I'll bet."

"That aside, I do recognize what it costs you to keep in touch. I don't mean to be quite so belligerent."

"No apologies necessary."

"Uh, Tasha? That wasn't an apology."

"Skip it. I got that. My mistake," she said. "The point is, I'm a lawyer. I deal with belligerence on a daily basis."

"I thought you did estate planning. How could anyone get belligerent about that? It sounds so dull."

"Shows what you know. Anytime you talk money, there's the potential for folks to get nasty. Nobody wants to talk about dying and nobody wants to give up control of the family purse. When it comes to the beneficiaries, there's usually an undercurrent of entitlement," she said, and then hesitated. "On a related topic, you probably heard there's talk of razing the Manse."

"The 'Manse'? Is that what it's called? I thought a manse had something to do with Presbyterians."

"It does. Our great-great-grandfather Straith was a Presbyterian minister. In those days, the Church didn't have the money to build a parsonage so he paid for it himself. I think he intended to deed it over to the Church when he died, but cooler heads prevailed. At any rate, the house is a mess. It'd be cheaper, at this point, to tear it down."

"I take it Grand doesn't want to spend the money to bring the old place back."

"Right. She's tried to enlist the support of a couple of historic-preservation groups, but no one's interested. The location's remote and the house itself is a hybrid. Turns out it's not even a good example of its kind."

"Why not leave it as it is? It's her land, isn't it?"

"It's hers for now, but she's ninety years old and she knows none of her heirs has the money or the passion for undertaking the job. Besides, she's got another house in town. She hardly needs two."

"That's right. I remember now. Liza told me most of the family live within blocks of her."

"We're a cozy bunch," she said, dryly. "Meanwhile, she's got all kinds of developers sniffing around. Mostly local vintners with an eye on the slopes. Turns out the soil's perfect. Plus, she gets a lot of coastal fog, which means a longer growing period."

"How much land does she have?"

"Twenty-three thousand acres."

There was a silence while I tried to compute what she'd just said. "You're kidding."

"I'm serious."

"I had no idea."

"Doesn't matter for now because she'll never sell. Great-Granddaddy made her promise she'd keep it just as it is. The issue won't get sticky until she goes."

"Hasn't she put the estate in some kind of trust?"

"Nope. Most of those old trusts were established in the thirties—people in the east who'd had wealth in the family for generation after generation. Out here, all we had were ranchers, down-to-earth types much more likely to form limited family partnerships. At any rate, nothing's going to happen as long as she's alive," she said. "Meanwhile, if you change your mind about that drink just give me a call. You still have my number?"

"I better take it down again."

Once I hung up, I had to sit down and pat my chest. I'd actually ended up entertaining a few warm feelings about her. If I didn't watch myself, I was going to end up *liking* the woman and then where would I be?

*   *   *

On my way over to Stacey's, I popped by the office to make sure all was in order. I opened a window briefly to let in a little fresh air and checked my machine for messages. I took care of a few routine matters and then locked up again. I left my car where it was and walked the five blocks to his house, arriving in advance of Con Dolan. Stacey'd left his front door open and his screen unlatched. I knocked on the frame. "Hey, Stacey? It's me. Mind if I come in?"

He responded with a muffled "Make yourself at home."

I stepped inside and closed the screen door behind me. The floors were bare of carpeting, and the windows had no curtains or drapes, so my very presence seemed to set up an echo. I could smell coffee being brewed, but otherwise the place felt unoccupied. The room was stripped down, as though someone were moving in or out with the job only partially completed. The interior of the house couldn't have been more than eight hundred square feet, most of which was visible from where I stood. The space was divided into living room, kitchen, a bedroom, and a bath, though the door to that was closed. The floor was linoleum, printed in a pattern of interconnected squares and rectangles, blue on gray with a line of mauve woven in at intervals. The woodwork was stained dark; the walls covered with yellowing paper. In places I could see tears that revealed the wall coverings from three lifetimes down; a small floral print covered by a layer of pinstripes that, in turn, covered blowsy bouquets of faded cabbage roses.

Under the windows to my right, there was a mattress, neatly made up with blankets. A TV set rested on the bare floor nearby. To my left, there was an oak desk and a swivel chair. There was not much else. Six identical cardboard boxes had been stacked against the far wall. All were sealed with tape and each bore a hand-printed label that listed contents. A closet door stood open, and I could see that it had been emptied of everything except two hangers.

I tiptoed to the kitchen door and peered in at a small wooden table and four mismatched chairs. A Pyrex percolator sat on the stove, a low blue flame under it. The clear glass showed a brew as dark as bittersweet chocolate. The doors to all the kitchen cabinets stood open, and many shelves were bare. Stacey was obviously in the process of wrapping and packing glassware and dishes into assorted cardboard boxes. A heavy ream of plain newsprint lay on the counter, wide sheets that must have measured three feet by four. He was clearly dismantling his house, preparing his possessions for shipping to an unknown location.

"See anything you like, it's yours. I got no use for this stuff," Stacey said, suddenly behind me.

I turned. "How's your back?"

Stacey made a face. "So-so. I've been sucking down Tylenol and that helps."

"You've been busy. Are you moving?"

"Not exactly. Let's say, I may be going away and wanted to be prepared." Today his watch cap was navy blue. With his bleached brows and his long, weathered face, he looked like a farmer standing in a fallow field. He wore soft, stone-washed jeans, a pale blue sweatshirt, and tan sheepskin boots.

"You own this place?"

"Rent. I've been here for years."

"You're organized."

"I'm getting there. I don't want to leave a mess for someone else to clean up. Con's the one who'll come in."

The unspoken phrase *after I'm dead* hung in the air between us.

"Con told me they were trying new drugs."

Stacey shrugged. "Clinical trials. An experimental cocktail designed for people with nothing left to lose. Percentages aren't good, but I figure, what the hell, it might help someone else. Some survive. That's what the bell curve's all about. I just think it's foolish to assume I'm one."

Con Dolan knocked at the front door and then let himself in, appearing half a second later in the kitchen doorway. He carried a brown paper grocery bag in one hand and a smaller white bag in the other. "What are you two up to?"

Stacey put his hands in his pockets and shrugged casually. "We're talking about running away together. She's arguing for San Francisco so we can cross the Golden Gate Bridge. I'm holding out for Vegas and topless dancing girls. We were just about to toss a coin when you came in." Stacey moved toward the stove, talking to me over his shoulder. "You want coffee? I'm out of milk."

"Black suits me fine."

"Con?"

Dolan held up a white sack spotted with grease. "Doughnuts."

"Good dang deal," Stacey said. "We'll retire to the parlor and figure out what's what."

Con took his two bags into the living room while Stacey produced a tower of nested Styrofoam cups and poured coffee in three. He returned to the counter and picked up the pile of newsprint and a marker pen. "Grab those paper towels, if you would. I'm out of napkins and the only kind I've seen are those economy packs. Four hundred at a crack. It's ridiculous. While you're at it, you can nab that sealing tape."

I picked up the roll of tape and my coffee cup, while Dolan returned to grab two of the kitchen chairs. Then he came back and picked up the two remaining cups of coffee, which he placed on the desktop in the living room. He reached into the larger of the two bags and hauled out three wide black three-hole binders. "I went over to the copy shop and made us each one. Murder books," he said, and passed them out. I flashed on my early days in elementary school. The only part of it I'd loved was buying school supplies: binder, lined paper, the pen-and-pencil sets.

Stacey taped two sheets of blank newsprint to the wall, then unfolded a map of California and taped it to the wall as well. There was something of the natural teacher in his manner. Both Dolan and I helped ourselves to doughnuts and then pulled up chairs. Stacey said, "I'll take the lead here unless someone objects."

Con said, "Quit being coy and get on with it."

"Okay then. Let's tally what we know. That'll show us where the gaps are. For now, you probably think we have a lot more gaps than we have facts in between, but let's see what we've got." He uncapped the black marker and wrote the name "Victim" at the top of one sheet and "Killer" at the top of the next. "We'll start with Jane Doe."

I pulled a fresh pack of index cards from my shoulder bag, tore off the cellophane, and started taking notes.

5

He printed rapidly and neatly, condensing the information in the file as we talked our way through. "What do we have first?" He lifted his marker and looked at us. Like any good instructor, he was going to make sure we supplied most of the answers.

Dolan said, "She's white. Age somewhere between twelve and eighteen."

"Right. So that means a date of birth somewhere between 1951 and 1957." Stacey made the requisite note near the top of the paper.

"What about the estimated date of death?" I asked.

I thought Dolan would consult the autopsy report, but he seemed to know it by heart. "Dr. Weisenburgh says the body'd been there anywhere from one to five days, so that'd be sometime between July 29 and August 2. He's retired now, but I had him go back over this and he remembered the girl."

"All right." Stacey wrote the DOD on the paper under Jane Doe's date of birth. He went on writing, this time dictating to himself. Rapidly, we went through the basics: height, weight, eyes, hair color.

Dolan said, "Report says blond, though it was probably a dye job. There was some suggestion of dark roots."

I said, "She had buckteeth and lots of fillings, but no orthodontic work."

Stacey's mouth pulled down. "Maybe we should stop and have a chat about that."

Dolan shook his head. "They didn't do braces much when I was growing up. My family was big—thirteen kids—and we all had crooked teeth. Look here. Bottoms buckled up, but these top guys are good." He turned to me. "You have braces as a kid?"

"Nope."

"Nor did I," Stacey said. "Well. I'm glad we got that out of the way. So what's that tell us, the buckteeth?"

"Well, I'd say most kids with a severe overbite have already seen an orthodontist by the time they're ten," Dolan said. "My niece has three kids, so I know they start early—sometimes do the work in two or three stages. If this gal was going to have braces, she should've been in 'em by the time she died."

"Maybe her family didn't have the money," I suggested.

"That could be. Anything else?"

"Cavities like that, you're talking poor diet, too. Candy. Soda pop. Junk food," Dolan said, with a quick look at me. And then to Stacey, "Not to sound like a snoot, but kids from your basic middle- to upper-class families usually don't have rotten teeth like that."

I said, "Think about the toothaches."

Stacey said, "She did get 'em fixed. Matter of fact, the forensic odontist thinks all the fillings went in about the same time, probably in the year or two before she died."

I said, "That must have cost a bundle."

"Think of all the novocaine shots," Dolan said. "You'd have to sit there for hours with that drill screaming in your head."

"Knock it off. You're making my palms sweat. I'm phobic about dentists in case you haven't heard. Look at this," I said, showing him my palms.

Stacey frowned. "They ever circulate a chart of her amalgam fillings?"

Dolan said, "Not that I know. I've got a copy in here. Might come in handy if we think we got a match. We do have the maxilla and mandible."

I looked over at him. "Her jaws? After eighteen years?"

"We have all ten fingers, too."

Stacey made a note on the paper. "Let's see if we can get the coroner's office to run another set of prints. Maybe we'll get a hit through NCIC."

"I can't believe she'll show up, given her age at the time of death," Dolan said.

"Unless she got arrested for shoplifting or prostitution," I said, ever the optimist.

"Problem is, if she got arrested as a juvenile, her records would be sealed and probably purged by now," he said.

I raised a hand. "You were talking about why she was never recognized; suppose she was from out of state, some place back East? I get the impression the news story didn't get nationwide attention."

"Story probably didn't rate a mention beyond the county line," Dolan said.

"Let's move on to her clothes. Any ideas there?" Stacey asked.

I said, "I thought it was interesting her pants were homemade. If you add that to the issue of poor dental hygiene, it sounds like low income."

Stacey said, "Not necessarily. If her mom made her the clothes, it'd suggest a certain level of caring and concern."

"Well, yeah. There is that. Those flowered pants were distinct. Dark blue daisies with a red dot on a white background. Someone might remember the fabric."

Dolan said, "I'd like to go back and look at that statement the minimart clerk made about the hippie girl who came in. What's the woman's name, Roxanne Faught? We ought to track her down again and see if she has anything to add."

Stacey said, "I talked to her twice, but you're welcome to try. Is that store still open?"

"As far as I know. It was closed for a while, so it might have changed hands. You want me to take a drive up there?" Dolan asked.

"Let me do that. I can go this afternoon," I said.

"Good. Meanwhile, what else? What about sizes?"

We spent several minutes working through those details. This time Dolan flipped back through the pages, looking for the list of clothing booked into property. "Here we go. Shoe size—7½. Panty size—medium. Bra size was 38A."

I said, "That means she's got a fairly large torso, but a small cup size. Barrel-chested. Girls like that tend to look top-heavy, even if they're thin."

Dolan turned a page. "Says here her ears were pierced. 'Through the left earlobe is a gold-colored wire of a "horseshoe" configuration. Through the right earlobe a gold-colored wire with a bent clip in its lower end.' People might remember that, too."

Stacey added that to the list and then said, "Is that it?"

I raised my hand. "She wore nail polish. Silver."

"Got it. Anything else?"

"Not that I remember."

Dolan got to his feet. "In that case, if you'll excuse me. I gotta have me a smoke."

At lunchtime, I volunteered to make a trip to the nearest market and pick up the makings for sandwiches, but they'd apparently gotten wind of my peanut-butter-and-pickle fetish and voted to go out for Chinese. We took Con's car and made the crosstown trip to the Great Wall, with its pagoda facade and a gilded statue of the Buddha sitting over the front door. In the parking lot, I waited while Stacey and Con tucked their guns in the trunk of Con's car. The three of us went in.

The interior walls were painted the requisite Chinese red with red Naugahyde banquettes and round white paper lanterns strung like moons around the perimeter. Stacey didn't have much appetite, but Con seemed more than willing to make up for it. I was starving as usual. We ordered pot stickers and spring rolls, which we dunked in that pale Chinese mustard that cleans out your sinuses. We moved on to Moo Shu Pork, Kung Pao Chicken, and Beef with Orange Peel along with a dome of white rice. Con and I drank beer. Stacey had iced tea.

While we ate, the guys speculated about the killer, a matter in which I deferred to them: I have no formal training in homicide investigation, though I've encountered a few bodies in the course of my career. Given the nature of the murder, they theorized that the perpetrator was most likely male, in part because women tend to be repelled by close-contact blood-and-gore killings. In addition, the multiple stab wounds suggested a brutality more commonly associated with men.

"Hey, these days, women can be brutes," Con said.

"Yeah, but I can't see a woman hefting that body into the car trunk and hauling it out again. A hundred twenty-five pounds is a lot of dead weight."

"As it were," Dolan said. "You think this was planned?"

"If it was, you'd think he'd've worked out a plan for disposing of the body. This guy was in a hurry, at least enough of one that he didn't stop to dig a grave." He was making notes on a napkin and the pen made occasional rips in the paper while the ink tended to spread.

Con opened his packet of chopsticks and pried the two wooden sections apart, rubbing one on the other to smooth away any tiny wooden hairs. He doused both his chicken and his beef with enough soy sauce to form a shallow brown lake in which his rice grains swam like minnows. "I'm surprised he didn't pick a dump site more remote."

"That stretch of road looks isolated if you don't know any better. No houses in sight. He probably didn't have a clue about the quarry traffic running up and back."

"I'm with you on that. Forensics says the wire he used to bind her wrists was torn off something else so he must have grabbed whatever came to hand. Guy was making shit up as he went along." I watched as Dolan formed a pincer with his chopsticks and tried picking up a chunk of chicken, which he couldn't get as far as his mouth.

"Question is, did he target that girl in particular, or was he trolling for a victim and it was just her bad luck?"

Con said, "I think it was a fishing expedition. He might've tried five or six gals and finally one said yes." He shifted to a scooping technique, using his chopsticks like a little shelf onto which he pushed the bite of chicken. He got the hunk as far as his lower lip. Nope. I saw him shake his head. "I don't think we're dealing serial. This feels like a one-off." He tried again, this time lunging, his lips extended like an anteater's as he lifted his chopsticks. He captured a snippet of orange peel before the rest fell back onto his plate.

I grabbed a fork from the next table and handed it to him.

Stacey made a doodle on the napkin, which by now was completely tattered. "Hang on. Let's back up a second. Agewise, it seems to me like she's bound to be closer to the high end—sixteen, seventeen, eighteen, and up, instead of the twelve, thirteen end of the spread. Young girl like that, somebody's going to report she's gone, regardless of whether she leaves voluntarily or stomps out in a huff. You're a parent, you might shrug and not think too much about it, but when she doesn't come home, you're going to worry. You call around and find out her friends haven't seen her either and you're going to call the cops. If she's twenty and disappears, it might not raise any flags at all."

"Right. She could've had a history of taking off. This might have been one more in a long string of disappearances."

Dolan pushed his plate aside. "As long as we're making wild-ass guesses, here's another one. I don't think she's local. Killer didn't get into any facial mutilation so he must not've been worried someone would know who she was. He didn't know how long she'd be lying there. Suppose she's found the same day and they run a description of her in the paper? She's local, somebody's going to add two plus two and figure it out fast."

I said, "What if she's from another country altogether? England or Spain. There are probably plenty of places where dental care didn't rank that high in those days. It might also explain why she wasn't reported missing."

Dolan said, "A missing-persons report might've gone through Interpol and never reached us. It's worth checking. Maybe they have something on file."

"There's a note in there somewhere—woman claims she saw a hitchhiker who fit the girl's description outside of Colgate. This was a couple of hours before the clerk in the Gull Cove minimart saw that hippie girl on August 1. Could be she was working her way up the coast," Stacey said.

Dolan reached for his black binder with its incident reports already marked with torn scraps of paper. He turned a few pages and checked the marginal notes he'd written in a surprisingly wee hand. "You're thinking about Cloris Bargo. She says July 29, four-thirty in the afternoon, she saw a young white female, five foot two to five foot three, age sixteen to seventeen, navy blouse, flowered slacks, long blondish hair, leaning against the base of the Fair Isle overpass. Bargo saw a vehicle stop and pick her up, heading north on the 101."

"That's worth another look. If Jane Doe was thumbing rides, we might backtrack and see if we can figure out her point of origin, maybe rough out a timeline." Stacey reached for his map of California and unfolded it, flapping and spreading the unwieldy sheet across the tabletop. "If she came from the south, she'd have traveled the 405 as far as the 101," he said. "The main arteries from Arizona into California are Highways 15 from Las Vegas, Nevada, the 40 from Kingman, Arizona, the 10 from Phoenix, and 8 coming up from Yuma. Starting from anywhere else, she'd have taken a different route."

Dolan pushed his plate away. "You're never going to pin that one down. She could have come from anywhere. On the other hand, you talk about July 29. That's the same day Frankie Miracle killed his girlfriend and hit the road. If Jane Doe was thumbing rides, he could've picked her up."

We left the subject at that point and moved on to other things.

After lunch, Con dropped me at the office, where I caught up with the notes on my index cards and then spent a few minutes doing digital research, which is to say, walking my fingers through the telephone book. My job was to verify reports about the young hippie girl, hitching rides in the period between July 29 and August 1. Con was going to hit the phones and track down the whereabouts of Frankie Miracle's former cellmates, while Stacey searched out his legal skirmishes in previous years. We agreed to meet that night at CC's to share what we'd learned.

I had a prior address for Roxanne Faught, but nothing for Cloris Bargo. As it turned out, luck was on my side and starting with the obvious paid off for once. A check of the white pages revealed one Bargo, not Cloris, but a sister who didn't even bother to quiz my purposes before she gave me the current phone number and the Colgate address. Shame on her. I could have been a stalker or a bill collector.

I checked my city map and drew a bead on my destination—a tract of middle-class homes just beyond the Fair Isle off-ramp, where Cloris Bargo had seen the girl. I locked the office, fired up the VW, and took Capillo Avenue as far as the 101.

The day was mild and hazy, the landscape muted, as though washed with skim milk. I rolled down my car windows and let the speed-generated wind blow my hair to a fare-thee-well. Traffic was light and the trip to Colgate took less than six minutes.

I took the off-ramp at Fair Isle and headed toward the mountains, counting the requisite number of streets before I turned left on York. The house I was looking for was halfway down on the left side of the street. This was a neighborhood of "starter" homes, but most had undergone major renovation since the sixties when the area had been developed. Garages had become family rooms; porches had been enclosed; second stories had been added; and the storage sheds in the rear had been enlarged and attached. The lawns were well established and the trees had matured to the point where the sidewalks buckled in places where the roots were breaking through. The children, mere toddlers when their parents had moved in, were grown and gone now, coming back to the neighborhood with children of their own.

I pulled up in front of a two-story white stucco house with a frame addition on the left and an elaborate new entrance affixed to the front that involved arches, a rustic wooden gate, climbing roses, and a profusion of hollyhocks, hydrangeas, and phlox. I let myself through the gate and climbed the porch steps. The front door stood open and the screen was on the latch. From the depths, I could smell something simmering; fruit and sugar. The radio in the kitchen was tuned to a call-in show, and I could hear the host berating someone in argumentative tones. I placed a hand on the screen, shading my eyes so I could see the interior. The front door was lined up exactly with the back door so my view extended all the way to the rear fence that separated two yards. I called, "Hullo?"

A woman hollered, "I'm out here! Come around back!"

I left the porch and trotted along the walkway that skirted the house on the right. As I passed the kitchen

window, I glanced up and saw her standing at the open
window. She must have been near the sink because she
leaned forward and turned off the tap as she peered
down at me. Through the screen, she looked thirty-five,
a guess I upgraded by ten years once I saw her up close.

I paused. "Hi. Are you Cloris Bargo?"

"Was before I got married. Can I help you with something?" She turned on the water again and her gaze
dropped to whatever dish or utensil she was scrubbing.

"I need some information. I shouldn't take more than
five or ten minutes of your time." It was weird having a
conversation with someone whose face was two feet
higher. I could nearly see up her nose.

"I hope you're not selling anything door-to-door."

"Not at all. My name's Kinsey Millhone. I'm a private
detective. Your name came up in connection with a case
I'm working for the Sheriff's Department."

She focused on me fully, her gaze sharpening. "That's
a first. I never heard of the Sheriff's Department hiring
outside help."

"This guy's a retired north county detective reactivat-
ing an old murder case—that young girl stabbed to death
back in 1969."

She put something in the dish rack, dried her hands
on a towel, and then reached for the radio and turned it
off. When she made no other comment, I said. "Mind if
I come in?"

She didn't extend an invitation, but she made a gesture that I interpreted as consent. I continued down the
walkway to the rear of the house, where the concrete
drive widened, forming a parking pad. On the right, a
clothesline had been strung between a wooden pole and
a bolt secured to the side of the garage. White sheets
flapped lazily in the breeze. The backyard was nicely

landscaped; the flower beds bordered with prefabricated foot-high sections of white picket fence. Someone had recently put in flats of pansies and petunias, now drooping from the transplant process. A sprinkler head attached to a hose sent a fan of water back and forth across the grass. The outdoor furniture had seen better days. The hollow aluminum frames were pitted in places, and the woven green-and-white nylon webbing was faded and frayed. In the far corner, I could see a large expanse of tilled ground with several young tomato plants, a row of newly planted peppers, and five empty bean poles, like teepees, waiting for the emerging tendrils to take hold. I saw no sign of kids or pets.

I climbed six steps to the porch. She was waiting at the back door, holding it open for me. She stepped back and I entered. Her attitude had shifted in the brief time it'd taken me to circle the house. The set of her jaw now seemed stubborn or tense. There was something in her manner that made me think I'd best provide concrete proof of my identity. I handed her a business card.

She took it and placed it on the counter without reading it. She was trim and petite, in tan Bermuda shorts, a white T-shirt, no makeup, bare feet. Her dark hair was chin length and anchored behind her ears with bobby pins.

"Nice flowers," I said.

"My husband takes care of those. The vegetables are mine."

The heat in the kitchen felt like South Florida in June—not yet oppressive, but a temperature that made you think seriously about leaving the state. Two big stainless steel pressure cookers fitted with racks sat on burners over matching low blue flames. The lids were lined up on the counter nearby, their little pressure cooker caps resting on the windowsill. Freshly sterilized lids, seals, ladles, and tongs were laid out on white sack-cloth towels like surgical instruments. A third kettle contained a dark red liquid, as viscous as glue. I picked up the rich, hot perfume of crushed strawberries. I counted twelve pint-capacity Mason jars lined up on the kitchen table in the middle of the room. "Sorry to interrupt."

"That's all right." She returned to the sink. Everything about her smacked of Midwestern farm values—the canning, the sheets on the line, the truck garden, the unadorned face.

"You remember the case?"

"Vaguely."

I noticed she didn't ask to have her memory refreshed, so I volunteered the help. "A sheriff's deputy took a report from you. According to his notes, you spotted a girl hitchhiking near the Fair Isle off-ramp July 29, 1969."

"You mentioned the date before."

I ignored the minor reprimand. "You indicated seeing a vehicle stop and pick her up. Turns out she fit the description of the murder victim found in Lompoc a couple of days later."

Cloris Bargo's expression was modified by the appearance of two swatches of pink, like blusher applied by a department store cosmetologist. "You want iced tea? I can fix you some. It's already made."

"That'd be great."

She opened one of the kitchen cabinets and took down a burnished blue aluminum tumbler, which she filled with ice cubes. She poured the tea from a fat glass pitcher she kept in the refrigerator. I knew she was stalling, but I wanted to give her room to declare herself. Something was going on, but I wasn't sure what. She handed me the glass.

I murmured, "Thanks," and took a big healthy swallow before I realized it was heavily presweetened. I could feel my lips purse. This was equivalent to that noxious syrup you have to drink before blood draws designed to diagnose conditions you hope you don't have.

She leaned against the counter. "I made it up."

I set the tumbler aside. "Which part?"

"All of it. I never saw the girl."

"No hitchhiker at all?"

She shook her head. "I'd met the deputy—the one who wrote up the report. I was new in California. My family hadn't been here six months. I hardly knew a soul. There'd been a prowler in our neighborhood, and this deputy was sent out to talk to us. He'd gone house to house, asking if anyone had seen anything strange or unusual. I was off work. I'd just had an emergency appendectomy and I was still recovering. Otherwise, I wouldn't have been home. We ended up having a long talk. I thought he was cute." She stopped.

"Take your time," I said.

"A week later, the paper mentioned his name in reference to the murder investigation. I'd never told a lie in my life, but I picked up the phone and called the Sheriff's Department and asked for him. Once he got on the line, I said the first thing that came to mind."

"Your claim that you'd seen a girl whose description matched the victim's was completely false," I said, hoping I'd misunderstood.

"I just said that. A lot of people must have called in with information that didn't pan out. All I wanted was a chance to talk to him again."

I was silent for a moment, thinking, *Shit, shit, shit.* "Did it work?"

She shrugged. "I married him."

"Well, that part's good, at any rate."

Her eyes strayed to the window. I saw a car pass along the driveway, cruising toward the rear. I looked back at her.

She lowered her voice. "Do me a favor."

"Sure."

"Don't mention this to my husband. I never told him the truth."

"He doesn't *know*?"

She shook her head.

"Would it really matter to him after eighteen years?"

I heard the car door slam shut and her husband's hard-soled shoes *tap-tapping* across the pavement between the garage and the back porch. There was a pause while he checked his pansies and petunias. In my opinion, they needed watering. He apparently agreed. I heard the shriek and squawk of the faucet handle when he turned off the water, moved the sprinkler, and turned the water on again. He continued toward the back door while she went on rapidly. "Every time someone asks how we met he tells them the story of how I took the time to call in the report. He admired I was such a conscientious citizen. Says it's one of my best traits. He claims he fell in love with me on the phone. Then he said it seemed like fate since he'd seen me in person just the week before. He thinks I'm different. A cut above, he says."

"Tricky."

"You bet."

The back door opened. Her husband came in, pausing to wipe his feet on the mat before he entered. Nice-looking guy. He was in his fifties with steel gray hair and blue eyes, his lineage probably Dutch or Scandinavian. He was tall and lean in a well-knit frame, without an ounce of fat. He wore street clothes—tan dress pants, a dark blue dress shirt, and a tie with a pattern of blue and tan. He had his badge on his belt. I wondered what his job was after twenty years with the SO. He'd already removed his gun and his holster, which he'd probably locked in the trunk of his car. "What's tricky?"

"Getting the pectin just right," she said without batting an eye. Having lied to him once, she was apparently an old hand at this.

"I'm Kinsey."

"Joe Mandel. Don't let her fool you. She makes the best strawberry preserves you ever ate."

"I'll bet."

His face was creased, hair thinning as age began to take its toll. He looked athletic, and I assumed he was fast on his feet, still capable of tangling with the bad guys when circumstances required it. "Looks like a science lab in here. You two cooking up trouble?"

"More or less," I said.

He exhibited no particular curiosity about who I was or what I was doing in the kitchen with his wife. He leaned over, bussed her on the cheek, and patted her arm. "I'm going to change and do some yard work. We'll go to Sizzler tonight, get you out of this heat. You need help?"

"I'm fine, sweetie. Thanks."

"Nice meeting you," he said, with a quick smile at me.

I smiled and raised a hand in response. Cloris watched him depart, her expression fading from warmth to something more subdued.

"He seems nice."

"He *is* nice. That's why I married him. He's decent. It would never occur to him to lie to me."

"Why don't you tell him, then?"

"Why don't you mind your own business? I can handle this myself."

6

The drive from Santa Teresa to Lompoc takes an hour by car, but I stopped at Gull Cove, which marks the halfway point. In my heart of hearts, I knew why I'd volunteered for this part of the job. Aside from the fact I needed time alone, I was flirting with the notion of going back to Grand's old house. Like a newly reformed drunk, I'd sworn off with conviction just the day before and now found myself thinking maybe one more quick visit wouldn't do any harm.

I reached the Gull Cove minimart at 2:00 P.M. The business had been housed in an enormous shambling structure covered with cedar shingles, an appealing mix of modern and traditional, with a few Cape Cod elements thrown in for good measure. The building had also housed a twenty-four-hour diner, a curio shop, and a tiny two-station beauty salon. Even at a distance, it was clear the entire place had been closed down. I could see windows boarded over, and the asphalt parking lot was cracked and faded to a chalky gray. The surrounding grass was a dull brown with assorted weeds and wild-

flowers growing to knee height. On the hillside behind
the building, a lone tree had died and stood now like a
scarecrow, its twisted branches raised toward the sky as
though to beckon birds. The population of Gull Cove
was pegged at one hundred, but I couldn't for the life of
me spot so much as one.

I parked my car near the front steps and got out. The
wide wooden deck creaked under my feet. A notice
posted on the main door announced that the complex
was closed for renovations. Someone had drawn a Happy
Face in pencil with the mouth turned down. Someone
else had written "WHO CARES?" in ballpoint pen. A
third party, perhaps human, had taken a big dump near
the padlocked door. I peered through the minimart's
front window, which was dusty and streaked where winter rains had hammered at the plate glass. The interior
was stripped; not one fixture, counter, or display case remained. It looked like the renovations would be going
on for some time.

I turned and stared at the road. The Gull Cove complex was the only commercial structure for miles, a hundred feet from the highway and a natural stopping-off
point for travelers who needed to take a break. It was
easy to see why someone thumbing a ride might get
dropped off in passing. Perhaps after doughnuts and coffee, our Jane Doe found a lift as far as Lompoc, which
had turned out to be the end of the line for her.

I went back to the car and checked my notes, looking
for Roxanne Faught's last known address: Q Street in
Lompoc, thirty minutes to the north. Seemed like a long
way for her to travel for a clerking job. I fired up the engine and hit the road again, heading north, the Pacific
Ocean on my left. Today the swells were low and without chop, the color a darker reflection of the blue sky

above. Idly, I thought about Grand's house. It was possible I'd catch a glimpse of the place if I happened to pass that way. Surely, it was visible from the highway if you knew where to look. I turned on the car radio to distract myself.

I reached the outskirts of Lompoc. The town is flat and compact, a one-story panorama of wide streets and small houses. A constant wind blows off the ocean, funneled by the rolling hills that cradle the town. Three miles to the north is Vandenberg Village and beyond that, Vandenberg Air Force Base. The entire valley is given over to horse farms and cattle ranches, much of the agricultural land planted to fields of commercial flowers, many of them grown for seeds. Though I had no idea what I was looking at, I could see stretches of bright yellow and vibrant pink. Beyond them were acres of what appeared to be baby's breath. Many farms were being sold to real estate developers; the sweet peas, poppies, and larkspurs being crowded out by crops of three-bedroom houses in neatly planted rows.

The town itself boasts the Lompoc Municipal Pool and a substantial civic center along with all the standard businesses: the Viva Thrift Shop, banks, attorneys' offices, automotive and plumbing supplies, retail stores and gas stations, coffee shops, pharmacies, and medical complexes. Lompoc is a base town with neighborhoods of temporary residents whose military careers will always move them from place to place like pieces on a game board. It was hard to see what people did for amusement. There wasn't a bowling alley, a concert hall, or a movie house in sight. Maybe local culture consisted of everyone renting videotapes of last year's money-losing movies.

Q Street wasn't hard to find, coming as it did between

P and R. The address was on the left side of the street, and I slowed as I approached. The house, resting on cinderblocks, was an oblong wooden box covered with sheets of asphalt siding imprinted to look like dark red brick. A porch, stretched across the front, sagged in the middle. Two white-washed tires served as makeshift planters from which pink geraniums spilled. An old white claw-foot tub had been upended and half-buried in the yard. A blue-robed plaster Madonna stood in the shelter of the porcelain rim. I pulled in at the curb and got out.

An old man in overalls was in the front yard bathing a dog. The man looked ninety, if a day, and was still staunchly constructed. He'd strung a garden hose through the half-opened kitchen window, and I assumed the other end was attached to the faucet. As I crossed the grass, he paused in his work, releasing the hose nozzle, shutting off the stream of water. He had a square, jowly face, a lumpy nose, and a straight, nearly lipless mouth. His hair was slicked back, plastered down with pomade, and even then, so thin I could see through to his scalp. His skin was mottled brown from sun damage, interspersed with patches of red. His blue eyes were vivid dots under pale, sparse brows. The air smelled like wet dog hair and a pungent flea soap. A medium-sized pooch of no determinate breed stood knee-deep in a galvanized tub. He looked skinny and frail with his coat plastered to his frame, thinned to transparency. Dead fleas, like pepper, seasoned the flesh underneath. The dog trembled, whining, and wouldn't quite meet my eyes. I kept my gaze averted so as not to embarrass him.

The old man said, "Help you?" His voice was surprisingly high-pitched for a man his size.

"I hope so. I'm looking for Roxanne Faught and this is the only address I have. Any idea where she is?"

"Ought to. I'm her dad," he said. "And who might you be?"

I showed him my card.

He squinted and then shook his head. "What's that say? Sorry, but I don't have my specs on me."

"I'm a private investigator from Santa Teresa."

"What do you want with Roxanne?"

"I need information on an old case. Apparently, a girl came into the Gull Cove minimart when Roxanne was working there in 1969. I'd like to ask her some questions about the incident."

He squeezed the hose nozzle and the spray of water showered like a light rain over the dog's back and haunches. "That the one got killed?"

"Yes, sir."

"Well. I guess that's all right then. I know a sheriff's deputy came by a couple times asking the very same thing."

"You're talking about Stacey Oliphant, the guy I'm working with. Is your daughter still in the area?"

"Close enough. How about this. I'll go give a call and see if she's willing to talk to you. Otherwise, there's no point."

"That'd be great."

He laid the hose aside, lifted the dog from the tub, and set him on the grass. The dog gave one of those profound total-body shakes, flinging water in all directions until his coat stood out in spikes. The old man picked up a heavy towel and gave the dog a vigorous rub, then swaddled him in the towel, and handed him to me. "This's Ralph."

Since I was hoping to curry favor, I took the dog without protest. I could feel warm doggie bathwater seeping from the towel through my shirt front. Ralph lay in my arms, a damp bundle of bones, as trusting as a baby, his eyes pinned on mine. His tongue flopped out the side of his mouth, and I could swear he smiled. I jiggled him a bit, which he seemed to enjoy. I really don't understand how animals persuade human beings to behave like this.

The old man reappeared, closing the door carefully. He made his way down the steps. He wasn't quick on his feet, but he seemed to get the job done. He had a scrap of paper in his hand. "She's home right now and said it's okay to give you this."

I handed the dog over and took the paper, glancing down at the phone number and address. "Thanks."

"It's a little house off the highway. You go down here about ten blocks until you hit North Street and then turn right. Once you get to Riverside you turn right again. She's about five blocks down."

Roxanne Faught had turned her front porch into an outdoor room, with pale sisal carpet, a dark green painted porch swing, two white wicker rockers, occasional tables, and a double-sided magazine rack, one half stuffed with issues of *People* and the other with copies of *Better Homes and Gardens*. Five terra-cotta pots of bright orange marigolds lined the edge of the porch. When I arrived, she was sitting on the swing with a bottle of beer and a freshly lit cigarette. The house itself was white frame and completely nondescript. There were windows and doors in all the proper places, but nothing that made the house distinct. Roxanne was in her sixties and attractive, though the creases in her face were exaggerated by all the makeup she wore. Her hair was, in the main, a coppery blond, showing gray at the roots where four inches of new growth formed a wide band. Her brows were plucked to thin arches and her dark eyes were lined in black. The smoking had darkened her teeth, but they were otherwise straight and uniform, suggesting caps. She wore a long-sleeve navy T-shirt with the sleeves pushed up, jeans, and tennis shoes without socks. She took a sip of beer and pointed at me with the bottle. "You have to be the one Pop just called about. Come on up and have a seat."

"Kinsey Millhone. I appreciate your seeing me on such short notice. I wasn't sure where you were living so I started with him."

"I've been in town all my life. I guess I don't have much sense of adventure. My great-aunt died and left me just enough money to get the house paid off. I can survive without working if I watch my step." She paused and picked up a strand of two-toned hair, which she studied critically. "You can see I quit going to the beauty shop. Cheaper to color it myself, when I get around to it. I can't give these up," she said, gesturing with her cigarette. "I smoked so long I'm probably doomed, anyway. Might as well enjoy." She coughed once, loosening something deep in her chest. "What can I help you with? Pop says you're here about that girl got killed, what was it, twenty years ago?"

"Just about. Eighteen in August."

"You know what's interesting about her? She's got a grip on folks. Here she is dead all that time and she still has people out there wondering who she is and how to get her back where she belongs."

"And who killed her," I added.

"Yeah, well good luck on that. You got your work cut out. Sit, sit, sit. Can I get you a beer?"

"I'm doing fine right now, thanks." I settled on one of the white wicker rockers, which creaked under my weight. "I can see where you'd want to spend the day out here, watching traffic go by. Nice."

"That's the thing about retirement. People keep asking me, don't you miss work? Well, no way, José. I could go the rest of my life and never leave this porch. I'm so busy as it is I can't figure out how I ever had time for a job. Between housework and errands, there's half the day gone right there."

"What else do you do?"

"Read. I work in the yard, play bridge with some gals I've known for years. How about you? You like the work you do?"

"I'm not that crazy about being stuck indoors, but the field work's fun."

"So now. What can I tell you that you don't already know?"

"One thing I was curious about. Gull Cove is thirty miles south. Seems like a long way to drive for work you could have found in town."

Roxanne coughed again, clearing her throat. As with other smokers I've known, her coughing was habitual and didn't seem to warrant a remark. "That's easy. I was diddling the owner. That's how I got hired." She laughed. "Seemed like a good idea at the time. He moved on to someone else and I got fired. Big surprise. My fault entirely. It's like Pop used to say, 'Don't shit in your own Post Toasties, Roxanne.'"

"Live and learn."

"You got that right. Anyway, I was working seven to three. This was summer and hotter than blue blazes, even with the breeze coming in off the ocean. You know the place at all?"

"Actually, I stopped off there on the drive up."

"Then you've seen for yourself. Not a shade tree in

sight; building stuck there on the side of the hill. By August the sun's hot enough to boil water. Anyway, this was
a Friday morning. I remember because I got paid once a
week and I had bills up to here. So I'm working away—
it's just me by my lonesome. Business was never heavy
and I could handle it myself. This gal comes in. She's
checking the aisles, walking up and down like she has
some shopping to do. Then I see her move to the rear
where we had a coffee machine and a self-serve case of
deli sandwiches and sweets. Customers would serve
themselves, then come to the register to pay once they
had everything they needed. We kept tables and chairs
outside on the deck and most of 'em would take their
purchases out there and watch the ocean while they ate.
You had to look over the four lanes of traffic whizzing by
on the road, but you could see it all the same. Different
every day. I never got tired of the sight myself. Any rate,
she helped herself to a cup of coffee and a doughnut and
had both of them scarfed down by the time she got to
the front. She'd tossed the cup somewhere in back,
maybe thinking I wouldn't notice she'd just had her fill.
Next thing I know, she's halfway out the door. I rang up
the charges and then I caught up with her. That's when
she told me she was broke. Well, hell, I thought. I've
been broke in my day and I don't begrudge anyone some
brew and a bite to eat, so I told her I'd take care of it.
She said, 'Thanks. I mean that.' Those were her exact
words. 'Thanks. I mean that.' And off she went. Couldn't
have taken more than four minutes all told, and I'm
talking from the time she came in."

"I'm surprised you remembered her at all."

"Somebody tries to run out without paying? You better believe I remembered. Especially when she turned up
dead." She paused to stub out one cigarette and light

another. "Pardon my manners. I hope this doesn't bother you. Do you smoke?"

"No, but we're outside and I'm upwind. What else do you recall? Anything in particular?" I wondered how anyone could remember so brief an encounter after so much time had passed.

"Like what? Ask me questions. It's easier that way."

"How old would you say?"

"Twenties."

"Not in her teens?"

"Could have been. She was a good-sized girl."

"You mean fat?"

"I wouldn't say *fat*, but she was big. Big wrist bones, big feet. Had what Pop would call good child-bearing hips."

"You remember her clothes?"

"Oh lord, I think I gave that sheriff's detective all this same information at the time. Why don't you ask him?"

"I thought I'd go back over and see if anything new comes to light," I said.

"Pants and a blousy shirt—you know, big sleeves."

"Belt?"

She feigned irritation, giving me a mock cross look. "You get right down to the nitty-gritty, don't you? Scars, moles, other identifying marks? What do you want? I only saw the girl up close once."

"Sorry. I take it she wasn't wearing a belt."

"Don't think so."

I could feel her withdraw and knew I needed to pull her back. "What about her shoes?"

"I'd say boots if I had to guess."

"It's not multiple choice. Just whatever comes to mind. Take the pants. Were they patterned or plain?"

She brightened. "Now, that I do know. It's what I told the cops back then. Daisies."

"You remember the color?"

She shrugged. "Daisy colored. You know, yellow and white. Probably some green in there someplace. Is that important?"

"I'm just groping around. What about the shirt?"

"Plain. I hope you don't intend to ask me every little thing."

I smiled. "Really, I don't. Was the shirt dark or light?"

"Dark blue voile."

"Which is what? Sorry, but I don't know the term."

"I'm not sure myself, but I know that's right because I went back and looked it up."

"You kept notes?"

"I kept the clipping from the paper. It's in the other room."

I could hear a dim alarm bell ring. What I was getting was rehearsed. "Did you get the impression she was local or on the road?"

"Traveling, definitely. I saw her hitchhiking earlier when I was coming in to work. I'm sure she hadn't eaten in a while. She wolfed her food right down."

"She could have been stoned," I said.

"Oh. I hadn't thought about that. She probably was, come to think of it. That might explain where her money went. She spent it all on dope."

"Just a possibility. I wonder how far she managed to travel without funds. Or do you think she had the money and just didn't choose to spend it on food?"

"Hard to say. If I hadn't volunteered to pay, she'd have tennis-shoed the place so I'd've been stuck either way. Bet she panhandled, too. Your age, you probably don't remember those days."

"Actually, I do. I was in my late teens."

"Point is, all those hippies hung out, cadging any

change you had. Smoking these big fat joints. I forget now what they called 'em. Thumbs, I think. Me, I wasn't into that. Well, maybe a little grass, but never any LSD."

I murmured a response and then said, "Was she wearing jewelry?"

"Nope. Don't think so."

"No watch or bracelet? Maybe earrings?"

"Oh. I remember now. No earrings. Her left earlobe was torn through. Like somebody'd grabbed a hoop and ripped it right off."

"Was the injury recent?"

"Nope. It was all healed up, but it was definitely split."

"What about her fingernails?"

"Bitten to the quick. Nearly made me sick. She wasn't all that clean, and she'd picked at her cuticles until they bled. You ever see that? Nails so short the fingertips look all puffy. It's enough to make you lose your lunch."

"And you're sure you'd never seen her around town before."

"Not before and not since."

"How'd you happen to get in touch with the Sheriff's Department?"

"I didn't 'happen' to do anything. I read about the body in the paper and remembered she'd been in. Like I said before, the incident stuck in my mind because she tried to pull a fast one."

"What made you so sure it was the same girl?"

"Who else could it've been?"

"Ah. Well, this has been a big help. I appreciate your time." I reached out to shake her hand.

She complied reluctantly. "Don't you believe me? I notice you didn't take notes."

"I got it all up here," I said, tapping my head.

* * *

Once back in my car, I checked my road map. Roxanne was still on the porch looking out at me, probably wondering at the delay. Maybe she thought I was finally taking notes, recording the bullshit recollections she'd constructed over the years. I didn't think she'd lied. She'd simply told her story too often. By now, she was either vamping like crazy or remembering someone else. I folded the map in half, trying to gauge how far I might be from the ranch. If I continued south on Riverside and made a dogleg right, I'd hit the road that angled south and east, connecting with Highway 101 just about at Gull Cove. According to the map, the road was called Calle LeGrand, presumably named after my great-grandfather LeGrand, whose twenty-three thousand acres filled a sizeable chunk of the area. Twisting hairlike blue lines indicated creeks running through the land.

I started the VW and waved at Roxanne once as I pulled away. The last I saw of her she was sitting on the porch swing, a fresh cigarette in hand, taking yet another sip of beer.

I picked up Calle LeGrand and followed the road south, through low rolling gold hills that would turn as green as Ireland when the rains returned. In the areas where there were no structures in sight, I fancied I was looking through the eyes of the early settlers, marveling at the acres of untouched land, bare and silent except for the cries of birds. I missed the turn to the ranch and had to circle back when I realized I'd gone too far. On the return, I saw the side road where Stacey and Dolan and I had met Arne Johanson. The gate now stood open and a haze of dust on the gravel road suggested that a vehicle had recently passed that way.

I turned in, driving slowly, my attention drawn to the gulley where Jane Doe's body had been found. I could see now that a section of the road angled off to the left, ending in a cul-de-sac, and I remembered the passing reference to the VW van that was seen parked in the turnaround. Also, a red convertible with out-of-state plates. Offhand, I couldn't remember the name of the fellow who'd called it in, but the report might bear revisiting, as Arne had suggested. Somebody Vogel. I'd have to look it up. I eased the car up the hill, following the route Arne had taken in his Jeep. I was really hoping the No Trespassing signs didn't apply to me.

The house came into view, looking like something in an old horror film. I parked in the driveway and approached with a curious mix of anxiety and excitement. Bare wooden trellises affixed to the porch rails at intervals suggested that roses or morning glories might have climbed there once. Now the beds were overgrown. I climbed the front porch stairs, which seemed remarkably sound. The house, though a shambles, had been built to last. I remembered talk at some point of moving the house into the city limits, restoring it as a possible tourist attraction. I could see where the city would be reluctant to make a claim. Even the idea of renovating the house in situ would be an expensive proposition. To what end?

I tried the front door and to my surprise I found it unlocked. I pushed it open and went in, assaulted by the dense smell of soot and mildew. I spent the next thirty minutes wandering from floor to floor, sometimes awed at the grandeur that remained. High ceilings, the sweeping staircase in the foyer, all the marble and mahogany still gracing the rooms. A large butler's pantry opened

into a vast kitchen with servants quarters built on behind. A second staircase led up to the second floor from
there. I could feel memory stir. Vague images, shapeless
and filled with shadows, moved at the edge of my vision.
I could hear sounds, talking and laughing in another
room, without being able to distinguish the words.

I was standing on the wide second-floor landing when
I heard someone walking in the hall below. From the
bottom of the stairs, someone called, "Kinsey?"

For one wonderful moment, the voice was my mother's and she'd returned from the dead.

7

I crossed to the banister and peered over the railing. Tasha stood in the stairwell, looking up. "I saw your car parked outside."

"I'll come down."

I descended the stairs, embarrassed that I'd been caught poking around the house uninvited. She'd taken a seat on the third step up, leaning against the wall. I settled on the same step, sitting close to the rail.

"How'd you know I was here?"

"Arne saw your car pull in and called me. My office isn't that far." She was dressed in lawyer clothes: a crisp navy-blue pantsuit with a white silk shell under the two-button jacket. She wore pearls. I'd always heard you could tell real pearls from fake by running them across your teeth, but I wasn't clear what information that was meant to impart. I thought it'd be rude to ask if I could bite her necklace. She had dark eyes, delicately enhanced with a smoky eyeliner, a straight nose where mine was ever so faintly bumpy from having been broken twice. Her dark hair was tastefully highlighted with blond and pulled into a rope at the nape of her neck. I could see a bow of red chiffon peeking into view from the hair clip behind.

It's odd to see someone you know looks like you. The face we see in the mirror is always reversed so that our impression of ourselves is flipped left to right. If you stand in front of a mirror and put your right index finger against your right cheek, the mirror will tell you you're touching left to left. The only way you can see yourself as you appear to others is to hold a mirror to the mirror and check your image in that. What I saw now of Tasha was what others saw of me. Already, I liked her face a lot better than mine. I usually ignore my own looks, not from distaste, but from a sense of despair. So many women have mastered an arsenal of beauty products: foundation, powder, blusher, eye shadow, pencils for lining their eyes, brows, and lips. As a rule, I avoid makeup, having little experience with the selection and application process.

It was clear at a glance that Tasha knew her stuff. I couldn't identify all the kinds of goop on her face, but she'd tinted herself with care. Her skin had a healthy glow, her cheeks showed a hint of pink, and her eyes looked enormous because her lashes were so thick. I could see her assessing me while I assessed her. We smiled at the same time, which only furthered the notion we were looking at ourselves. We had identical teeth.

She said, "After our telephone conversation, I had a long talk with Mom. Her version of events is different."

"Oh, really. How so?"

"She says your parents made that trip to meet with Grand and Granddaddy in hopes of a reconciliation. They were killed on the way. Grand blamed herself. Aunt Gin blamed her, too. Mom says Grand tried to keep in touch, but Gin was having none of it. Finally, Grand gave up, but only after years of trying to make contact."

"Bullshit. I don't believe it."

"I'm not asking you to *believe*. I'm telling you what Mother said."

"Well, of course she'd say that. She's still tied into Grand. How can you afford to think ill of someone who has the power to pull the rug out from under you? You'd do just about anything to see them as good no matter what they've done."

"Kinsey, if you really want to find out what went on back then, you can't start by rejecting the messages you don't want to hear. There are two sides to every story. That's why we have the courts. To settle disputes."

"Oh, right. Compare this to litigation. That'll win you points," I said. "Most people can't stand lawyers. I'm one of the few with any respect for the trade." I stopped. I stared down at the floor for a moment and then shook my head. "I'm sorry. Forget it. I didn't mean to get into it with you again."

Tasha smiled slightly. "I told you we couldn't talk without hassling."

"You set me off."

"That's not my intent."

"I know. The hard part is that neither of us has any concrete proof. We can do this 'Did too! Did not!' routine until the cows come home. It's Grand's word against Aunt Gin's, or my mother's word against your mom's. There is no *fact* of the matter."

"Probably not. Just keep an open mind. That's really all I ask."

"I'm afraid it's too late for that. My mind's been made up since the day I met Liza. I wasn't interested then and I'm probably not interested now."

"At least you use the word 'probably.' That's progress, isn't it? You used to be adamant. Now you're obdurate."

"Which means what?"

"Resistant, but less flinty. It's a big improvement."

The comment seemed patronizing, but I shrugged it off. Why take offense when she might not have actually meant it that way? I said, "It feels like unfinished business and that bothers me. Regardless of how it comes out, I'd like to think I'm doing the right thing."

"That works both ways. We're having to go back and revisit the past, which is good for all of us. The point is, we have time to work this out."

"Thirty-two years of it so far."

"So what's thirty-two more? We can't settle a long-standing quarrel in a few casual talks." She glanced at her watch and then rose. "I have to get back to work. Did you finish the tour?"

I pulled myself up. "Essentially. I hoped I'd remember something, but I'm drawing a blank." The two of us paused simultaneously to brush off the backs of our pants.

We crossed to the front door, our shoes making scratching sounds in the grit that had accumulated on the marble floor. She said, "What do you think of the place?"

"It must have been beautiful in its day."

Tasha turned back, letting her eyes travel across the foyer and up the stairs. "You know Grand moved out shortly after Aunt Rita's death." Rita Cynthia Kinsey was my mother's maiden name.

"I didn't know that."

"Granddaddy Kinsey was fit to be tied, but she finally got her way. That's when they bought the house in town. You remember him at all?"

I shook my head.

"Maybe I can find some family photographs."

"I'd like that. I don't think I've ever seen pictures of anyone. Aunt Gin discounted sentiment as a form of sniveling. She refused to let either of us sink to such depths."

"She was tough."

"That she was."

"Well. I better go."

"Me, too," I said. "I do have one request. I know you've already talked to your mother about me, but please don't bring Grand into this."

"My lips are sealed."

It was 4:35 by the time I reached Santa Teresa. I made a stop at the public library, leaving my car in the adjacent four-story parking structure. My conversation with Roxanne Faught had raised unsettling questions, namely, what did she know and when did she know it? I wondered if there was any way to check. I trotted down the carpeted stairs to the periodicals room, where I asked the reference librarian for the microfilm records of the *Santa Teresa Dispatch* from the week of August 3, 1969. Since the body was found that Sunday, I didn't expect the news to hit the paper for another day or two. Once I had the box of film in hand, I sat down at the machine and unreeled the strip, which I threaded under the lens, catching the sprocket holes. I hand-cranked it until the strip caught properly and then pressed a button and watched the Sunday paper speed by in a blur. My eyes picked up a remarkable amount of information on the fly. I bypassed the sports, the business section, and the classified ads. I slowed now and then just to see what was going on. The oil spill off the Santa Teresa coast was in its 190th day. *Funny Girl* and *Goodbye Columbus* were playing at the local movie theater along with *Planet of the Apes*. There was talk that Don Drysdale's fourteen-year pitching career might be coming to an end because of a recurrent injury, and a Westinghouse 2-Speed Automatic Washer was selling for $189.95.

When I reached Monday's paper, I slowed to a dead stop and scanned it page by page. On Monday, August 4, five column inches were devoted to the discovery of the body near the Grayson Quarry in Lompoc. Con Dolan and Stacey Oliphant were both mentioned by name, but there was little to report. The next day, August 5, in a column called "North County Events," I caught the second squib. By then the autopsy had been done and the cause of death was detailed. The same few physical traits were noted—hair and eye color, height and weight—in hopes of identifying the girl. I cranked the reel forward, through Wednesday and Thursday of the same week. Thursday's paper included a brief follow-up, with the same information I'd read in the initial account. Both gave a brief description of the girl's clothing, detailing the dark blue voile blouse and the daisy-patterned pants. Neither article specified the color of the pants. I knew from police reports that the daisies were dark blue, a red dot at each center, on a ground of white, but if you relied strictly on this data, it would be natural to assume the daisies were "daisy-colored," as Roxanne Faught had so aptly summed it up. Factoring in her certainty about the torn earlobe, the big feet, the big-boned wrists, and the closely bitten nails, I doubted the girl she'd dealt with was actually our Jane Doe. It was always possible, of course. Eyewitness testimony is notoriously shaky, easily influenced, subject to subtle modification with each telling of the tale.

Roxanne had admitted she'd gone back to reread the very clippings I was looking at myself. I didn't wholly discount what she said, but I wondered at its relevance to our investigation. Stacey had hoped to establish a time line, working backward from Roxanne's encounter to Cloris Bargo's sighting of the girl hitchhiking outside Colgate. Now Cloris had recanted and I suspected Roxanne's observations were too tainted to be of use. I fast-forwarded. That same week, on August 9, five people, including film and television actress Sharon Tate, were found slain in a Bel Air home. Two days later, Leno and Rosemary LaBianca were discovered murdered in a manner similar to the Tate slayings. I tracked forward again, but there was no further mention of Jane Doe. I jotted a few notes on my index cards and then made copies of the news stories, paid for them at the counter, and returned to my car.

It was just after 5:00, and Con was doubtless at CC's, knocking back Happy Hour drinks on a two-for-one deal. For my sake, I hoped he hadn't been at it long. I spotted his car as soon as I pulled up in front, but the area was otherwise deserted. Across the street at the bird refuge, two women in sweats were just starting a walk, chatting with animation. Closer to the water, a mother looked on placidly as her five-year-old child fed day-old bread to the gulls under a sign that read: PLEASE DO NOT FEED THE BIRDS.

I went into CC's, pausing in the doorway to let my eyes adjust. A plank of daylight had fallen in the open door, enhancing the contrast between CC's and the outside world. The place was dark. There was no one in the front room except the bartender and a waitress engaged in intimate conversation. Stacey and Dolan were seated in a booth in the rear. Stacey got up when I appeared. He was looking better today. I said, "Hi. Am I late?"

"Not at all," Dolan said. Both had glasses in front of them. Dolan's contained whiskey dark enough to pass for iced tea. Stacey's was empty except for the ice cubes and a wad of freshly squeezed lime. Dolan hauled himself to his feet just as Stacey sat down. "What can I get you?"

"Water's fine for now. I may switch later."

"I'll take another Tanqueray and tonic."

Dolan frowned. "You just had one. I thought the doc didn't want you mixing meds with booze."

"Or else what, I drop dead? Don't worry. I'll take full responsibility. I'd be doing myself a favor."

Dolan gestured impatiently and then moved off to the bar. I slid into the booth and put my shoulder bag on the seat beside me.

He said, "How'd your day go?"

"So-so. I'll tell you about it as soon as he gets back."

Stacey reached into his vest pocket and removed a pipe and a tobacco pouch, then filled the bowl. He fished around in another pocket for a pipe pick and tamped down the tobacco before he took out a wooden kitchen match and slid the head along the underside of the table. I waited while he puffed at the pipe. The smoke was sweet-smelling, like a meadow full of dried hay.

I said, "You're as bad as he is."

Stacey smiled. "On the other hand, suppose I only have a few months left? Why deny myself? It's all in your perspective."

"I guess it is."

We engaged in idle chitchat until Dolan returned, bearing a tray with my water and two fresh drinks for them. He'd added napkins, a bowl of popcorn, and a tumbler of nuts.

"Look at this guy, buying dinner for us," Stacey said.

"Hey, I got class. More than I can say for you."

The air was cool and free of cigarette smoke, which Dolan corrected for as soon as he sat down. I didn't bother to complain. Stacey's pipe tobacco and Dolan's cigarette smoke masked the faint whiff of noxious gases from the excavation site outside. Dolan helped himself to a handful of nuts, popping them in his mouth one by one while he looked at me. "What'd you get?"

"You're not going to like it." I went on with a summary of my travels, starting with Cloris Bargo and the lie she'd told.

Stacey said, "I talked to her twice myself and she never said a word about that."

"It's my charm and finesse."

"Well, shit. I didn't realize she was married to Joe Mandel. He worked with us on this."

"I know. I remembered the name."

Dolan said, "I can't believe she was blowing smoke up our skirts. She actually admitted that?"

"Well, yeah. She said at the time she couldn't see the harm."

Stacey said, "Let's leave that one alone. No sense butting into their business. I tell you what we might do though is ask Joe if he could locate Jane Doe's effects for us. It'd be good to take a look. Might spark an idea. I'll make a call and clear it with the sheriff. Don't think he'd object, but you never know about these things." He made a note to himself and turned back to me. "What else?"

"After I left her, I drove on up to Lompoc, stopping off at Gull Cove, which is closed, by the way." I laid out my conversation with Roxanne Faught, what she'd said, and where the story she'd told me varied from what we knew. I gave them copies of the news clippings to demonstrate my point. "I think she lifted the details from these, which means we can't rely on her. I believe she encountered someone, but it wasn't necessarily our Jane Doe."

"Too bad. It sounds like a dead end," Dolan said.

Stacey said, "Dead ends are a given. That's how these things go. We're bound to run into a few along the way. All that tells us is to back up and look somewhere else. Lucky we found out about it now before we wasted any more time on it."

"Knocks our hitchhiking theory all to hell," Dolan said.

"Maybe so, maybe not. She could have gone to Lompoc by train or bus and hitched a ride from there."

I said to Dolan, "What about the vehicles seen in the area? Any way to check those out?"

"Johanson said something about a hippie van. We could track down that guy—what's his name . . ."

"Vogel."

"Right, him. Why don't we see what he remembers."

"It's a long shot," I said.

"So's everything else we've come up with so far."

Stacey let that remark pass, still fixating on his original point about where the girl had come from. "Another possibility is she bummed a ride to Lompoc with a friend, someone she stayed with 'til she hit the road again."

Dolan made a sour face. "Would you quit obsessing? We went over that before. If she'd had friends in the area, they'd have wondered what happened as soon as she disappeared."

"Not if she'd told 'em she was on her way north. Suppose she stays in Lompoc a couple nights and then leaves for San Francisco. She goes out the door, has a run-in with the Devil, and ends up dead."

"They'd still put two and two together as soon as the story broke."

Stacey stirred irritably. "We're not going to find answers to every question we ask."

"So far we haven't found answers to anything," I remarked.

Stacey waved that aside. "Maybe our mistake is assuming she's from somewhere else. Suppose she's local? Someone kills her and then makes up a story explaining where she's gone. That's why she wasn't reported missing. It's part of the cover-up."

Dolan was shaking his head.

"What's wrong with that?"

Dolan sat back in the booth. "No one exists in a vacuum. She must've had family and friends. She worked, went to school. She did some damn thing. *Somebody* must have wondered. Essentially, this girl dropped off the face of the earth and you're telling me no one noticed? There's something off about that."

I said, "But, Dolan, think of all the kids who disappeared in those days. There must be dozens unaccounted for. Families probably still fantasize they'll show up one day."

Stacey said, "Why don't we forget that angle and come at it from the other direction?"

"Which is what?" I asked.

"What we talked about before, assume Frankie killed her and see if we can find a way to make it stick."

"Based on what? Make that leap and we could end up spinning our wheels," I said.

"We're doing that anyway. The exercise is only pointless if it turns out we're wrong. What do you say, Con?"

"I'm with you on that one. We'd be no worse off. I've always thought Frankie had a hand in it."

Stacey turned to me. I said, "You're the boss."

"My thought exactly. Let me show you what I got."

He opened a manila folder and removed two con-

nected sheets of computer paper with perforated edges. I
peered at the pale print. There, in abbreviated form, was
Frankie Miracle's criminal history, starting with his first
arrest in Venice, California, in January of 1964. Stacey
picked up the paper and began to rattle off the long
string of his offenses. "I love this guy. Look at this. 1964.
Kid's twenty-one years old, arrested for drunkenness and
resisting arrest. Fined twenty-five bucks and put on a
year's probation. Well, okay. No problem. His first contact with the law . . ."

"That we know of," Dolan said.

Stacey smiled. "That's right. But boys will be boys.
They're not going to execute the lad for public drunkenness. In May that same year, he was arrested for burglary
and contributing to the delinquency of a minor. Probably
screwed a thirteen-year-old. That'd be about his speed.
Put on probation. In February of '65, he was arrested for
another burglary. He pleaded guilty; sentence was sixty
days in jail and probation. Judge is really cracking down
on him," he said, tongue in cheek. "June 1965. Burglary
again. This time, his probation's revoked and he's sentenced to state prison, six months to fifteen years; released
after serving six months. December 1965. Drunk and
disorderly, assault, and marijuana possession. Admitted
for psychiatric evaluation and treatment of drug and alcohol dependency." Stacey snorted derisively. "The guy's a
creep. We all know that. April 1966—burglary and escape. November 1966—robbery, kidnapping, attempted
rape. This time they threw in assault and possession of a
dangerous weapon. March 1967—another burglary. Oh,
and here's a good one. I can't believe this guy's back on
the street. In January 1968, Frankie abducted a woman
from a supermarket parking lot. He was later arrested on
charges of kidnap, assault, robbery, oral copulation, sod-

omy, and attempted murder. You better believe she hasn't had a good night's sleep since she ran into *him*. January 1969—attempted kidnap, statutory rape, contributing to the delinquency of a minor. Now we're getting down to business. In March 1969, he was picked up on charges of armed robbery, assault, and attempted murder. Case dismissed. Cops probably beat a confession out of him, and the public defender had the whole thing thrown out. Sometime in June, he met a sixteen-year-old girl named Iona Mathis. He was married to her briefly—six months I think. About as long as some of his jail time, as it turns out. Which brings us to Venice, California, late July, when Frankie killed Cathy Lee Pearse." Stacey shook his head. "God bless the courts. If they'd done their job right, they could have saved her life."

I said, "How'd he manage to get away with all that shit?"

"Easy," Dolan said. He stubbed out one cigarette and fired up the next. "He knew how to work the system. Every time he was charged with multiple crimes, he'd plead guilty to one in exchange for the others being dropped. You haven't met Frankie. He can be as charming as all get out. He had judges and prosecutors bending over backwards, trying to give him a chance to straighten up and fly right."

Stacey returned the report to the manila folder. "Lot of times he was sentenced to state prison under the old indeterminate sentence system. Other times he was released on automatic parole. Longest he ever went between crimes was this period between March of '67 and January of '68."

Dolan said, "Bet you a dollar he just didn't get caught. He hasn't gone that long between crimes since he started out."

"Probably right about that. If you look at the pattern, you can see the stakes go up. Violence escalates. The stretch between crimes starts getting shorter and shorter until he killed Cathy Lee. For that one, he only served seventeen years on a life sentence so he's still lucking out. If I were her parents, I'd be pissed as hell."

I said, "What else do we have?"

Dolan pulled a battered notebook from his jacket pocket and began to leaf through the pages. He clicked his ballpoint pen. "Frankie's cellmates. Turns out there were twelve altogether, but half the last known addresses are incorrect. We got two in state prison and one serving time in a federal prison camp in Yankton, South Dakota. I know the whereabouts of three for sure: Lorenzo Rickman, Pudgie Clifton, and John Luchek."

Stacey said, "Scratch Luchek. He was killed in a two-car accident in 1975. Drunk hit him head on."

"Right. That's the information I have." Dolan drew a line through the name. "Rickman's out on parole. Word has it he's been a real good boy of late, working as an auto mechanic at a place out in Colgate. I got the name here somewhere. Stacey'll stop by Monday to have a chat with him. Which leaves Clifton, who's currently at the tail end of ninety days on a misdemeanor possession. I picked up mug shots on all these guys in case you need something to refresh people's memories. I mixed in some unrelated photos so we can't be accused of biasing the witnesses—assuming we find a few."

"Let's be optimistic. It doesn't cost anything," Stacey said.

Dolan passed one pack of photos to me and one to Stacey, who said, "We'll let Kinsey talk to Pudgie. He's the type who'd respond to her feminine wiles."

"Like I got some."

"Don't underestimate yourself."

Dolan said, "That leaves Frankie."

"You and I can draw straws, but let's hold off on that until we contact the other two." Stacey winced and then stood up abruptly, saying, "Shit! Hang on a sec."

Dolan said, "What's wrong?"

Stacey groaned, then sucked in air through his teeth, his face tense. "Damn back's seizing up. *Jeez, that hurts.* Pain's shooting all the way down my leg."

"What's the doctor say?"

"How do I know? This ain't Death at my door. I told you—I pulled a muscle. I can't call the oncologist for every little thing." He leaned sideways, stretching. After a moment, he stood upright, taking a long, slow, deep breath.

"Better?"

"Much. Sorry to interrupt. Damn thing caught me by surprise."

"Would you quit the self-diagnosis and call the guy?"

"The doctor's a woman, you sexist prick. You ought to give some serious thought to the assumptions you make."

"Quit the bullshitting, Stace. This is all a big smoke-screen. You keep acting like you've only had the back pain for the past two days when you've complained of it for weeks. You should have had the docs take a look while you were in the hospital."

"It wasn't hurting me then."

"Oh, for heaven's sake. You know what? This is called 'denial.' This is you trying to minimize a problem that could be damn serious. Hell, give me the gal's name and I'll call her myself."

"No, you won't."

"Then *you* call."

"I will. I was going to do that."

"Now."

"Con, cut it out! It's past five. She's probably left for the day."

"Then call the service, leave CC's number, and have her paged. We can wait. You don't call her, I will. I'm sick of hearing you bellyache."

"You don't even know her name."

"I'll find out."

"Don't be ridiculous."

"Quit arguing. Maybe she'll give you some Valium to help you sleep at night."

Stacey shook his head. "I hate making a fool of myself because of you." Despite his grumbling and protests, he did go off to find a phone.

Dolan and I sat without looking at each other. I didn't like the sound of it any more than he did. Finally, I said, "Are the two of you okay? You seem testy."

"We're fine. He's just pissing me off. It's not about his back. The man's depressed. He thinks the cancer's spread and that's why he doesn't want to get it checked."

"I missed that, I guess. He seemed fine as far as I could tell. I mean, aside from his back."

"That's because he puts on an act for your benefit. You should've heard him before you showed. The shit's wearing him down. If he'd had a gun on him, he'd have blown his brains out. He's that close." Dolan held up his thumb and index finger a quarter of an inch apart.

"You're not serious."

"I am. He wasn't even going to do the chemo until I talked him into it. As far as he's concerned, this is the end of the line so why play it out? Get the damn thing over with is his attitude."

"But suppose the cancer's moved into his bones?"

"Now, damn it, don't you start. Don't be so negative."

"I'm just saying I can understand where he's coming from."

"Well, keep your opinion to yourself."

"My opinion's not relevant. He can do anything he wants. It's his life."

"Wrong. He could use a pep talk. He needs someone to make him realize how selfish it is."

"To kill himself? How so?"

"People who commit suicide are the ultimate narcissists. What makes him think everything revolves around him? I'm in this, too. Thirty years down the drain and all because he's a cowardly damn chickenshit and won't see this through."

"But what if he's terminal? I don't understand what you want."

"I want him to think about someone else for a change."

"If you don't get to think about yourself when you're dying, when do you?" I said.

Stacey reappeared moments later and we dropped the conversation. He declined to sit, remaining by the table with his fists pressed into the small of his back.

Dolan fired up another cigarette, pausing to cough into his fist. "What'd she say?"

Stacey waved the cigarette smoke away from his face. "She'll see me first thing tomorrow morning; maybe take an X-ray or do a CT scan."

"What's the matter with her? Did you tell her how bad it is? She should see you right now and find out what the hell's going on."

"Goddammit. Quit nagging. This isn't an emergency so lay off that stuff. Anyway, I'm tired and it's time to go home. I can't be sitting here drinking all night like some I could name."

"Sit down. You haven't had dinner yet. You have to eat. It's my treat."

"I got food at my place. You two stay. I can get a cab."

"I'll take you," I said. "My car's right outside."

"You don't have to do that. I can manage on my own."

"Really, I don't mind. I need to get home myself."

I reached for my shoulder bag and took out the keys. Stacey was already moving toward the door as I slid out of the booth.

Dolan stubbed out his cigarette. "I'll take care of it."

In the end, we left at the same time; Stacey in Dolan's car and me in mine. I watched Dolan turn off, heading toward the freeway. I took a right on Cabana Boulevard and followed the road as it wound along the beach. It was not quite dark, but a fog was rolling in off the ocean, enveloping the shore. I parked in Henry's driveway. He'd be home tomorrow in the late afternoon. I let myself into his place where I did a quick tour, making sure all was in order. No broken water pipes, no power outages, and no sign of disturbances. For a moment, I stood in his kitchen, drinking in the lingering scent of yeast and cinnamon—Henry's home-baked sweetrolls. Surely, I could survive one more day.

I was home minutes later, safely tucked away for the night. 5:56 on a Friday evening and I had no plans. I made an olive-and-pimento-cheese sandwich on whole-wheat bread, which I cut into quarters. I poured myself a glass of wine and settled on the couch where I took up the Jane Doe file and started back at page one. Sometimes you work because there's nothing else to do.

8

At 1:35 that morning, I was awakened from a sound sleep: Dolan on the phone, calling from the ER at St. Terry's.

"Stacey's back got worse after I dropped him off. He called me at midnight and asked me to bring him in. They took one look at him and rounded up the doc on call. I'm waiting to hear what the fellow has to say."

"You want me to come over?"

"Hang on a second." He put a hand over the mouthpiece and conducted a muffled conversation with someone else, then returned to the line. "I'll call you back in a bit. Soon as I find out what's going on."

I replaced the handset, now wide awake. If Dolan intended to phone again, there was really no point in going back to sleep. I flipped on the light and fumbled for my running shoes. Given my new efficiency measures, I was fully suited up in sweats and crew socks. I needed only brush my teeth and run wet hands through my mop and I was ready to go.

I parked on a side street across from the hospital

emergency entrance. I love the town at that hour. Traffic is sparse, the streets are empty, most businesses are shut down. The temperature had dropped into the forties and the lights in the emergency room looked inviting. Apparently, the usual weekend traumafest hadn't gotten under way as yet, because the front desk was deserted and all was quiet. I found Dolan reading a magazine in the reception area. He rose when he saw me.

Without even thinking, I gave his cheek a buss. "How's he doing?"

"They're in the process of admitting him. I could have saved you a trip. I tried calling you back, but I guess you'd already left by then."

"Don't worry about it. I was up anyway. What now? Will they let you see him again?"

"They gave him something for the pain and he's out of it. He probably won't know the difference, but I'll feel better if I do. After that, I thought I'd make a run over to his place and pick up some of his things. Toothbrush and comb, stuff like that."

"Why don't I find us a cup of coffee? There's bound to be a vending machine on the premises somewhere."

We sat together for half an hour, sipping treacherous-smelling lukewarm coffee from thick paper cups with handles like flat-folded butterfly wings. He said, "What were you doing home? I was all set to leave a message. I figured you'd be out on a date."

"People don't *date* anymore; at least I don't," I said.

"Why not? What's wrong with it? How else are you going to meet someone?"

"I don't want to *meet* anyone. I'm fine, thanks so much. What about you? You're single. Are you dating these days?"

"I'm too old."

"Me, too," I said, peering over at him. "How long ago did your wife die?"

"Ten months today." He was silent for a moment. "I'll tell you what's been hard. She bugged me for years to go on a cruise. I hated the whole idea. Tahiti. Alaska. She'd bring me color brochures full of these pictures of happy couples, all of 'em thirty years old, standing on the deck, holding champagne flutes. Sunset. Romance. Inside'd be a picture of this mountain of food you could stuff yourself with twenty-four hours a day. Just the sight of it's enough to make your ulcers perforate. I hate being cooped up, and I was worried I'd be stranded with a bunch of fools. Does that sound unreasonable?"

"You think it was a cruise she wanted or just a trip someplace?"

Dolan turned and gave me a look. "I never thought to ask."

I got back to my place at 2:45 A.M. and then slept restlessly until 10:00. The Santa Teresa County Jail is housed in a 25,000-square-foot building, two-stories, 120 beds, designed to be staffed by only two corrections officers, one of whom monitors the state-of-the-art security panel with its bank of television screens.

Still feeling half-dead from lack of sleep, I pulled the VW into one of the slots out front and went through the main entrance doors, where I picked up a copy of the visitation request form. I filled in my name and gave it to the clerk at the counter, then hung out in the lobby area while the word went down to Pudgie that he had a visitor. I could picture his puzzlement, as I was reasonably certain he'd never heard of me. Curiosity (or boredom) must have gotten the better of him because the clerk returned and said he'd agreed to see me. She gave me the booth number where I could meet him.

Ten of us entered the elevator: two lone women and three mothers with assorted small kids. I pressed DOWN, wondering if I looked like the sort of person who'd have a boyfriend in jail. The elevator descended by inches while we all secretly worried about getting stuck. Once the doors opened on the floor below, we spilled into a room that was probably twenty feet by twenty. Molded beige and gray plastic armchairs, chunky and square, were arranged in a double row down the middle of the room, with additional seats around the perimeter. The floor was a glossy beige vinyl tile. The walls were cinder block, painted a matte two-tone beige. A posted sign read KEEP FEET OFF WALL, though there was nothing to suggest how one might accomplish violating such a . . . well, feat. In the visitors room, eight stationary stools, with a handset at each place, were lined up on either side of a large glass-enclosed aisle. I sat down and placed my shoulder bag at my feet. I rested my elbows on the counter, feeling as if I were seated at the lunch counter of an old five-and-dime.

I knew from the police report that Pudgie was born Cedric Costello Clifton in 1950, the same year I was. He had a birthday coming up, June 7, so I'd aced him by a month and two days. The door opened on the jail side and a few inmates straggled in on the other side of the glass, hands linked behind their backs, a requirement any time they were moved from place to place. Pudgie appeared and took a seat on a stool that was a match for mine. His face was moon-shaped, and he wore glasses with big round frames perched on a surprisingly dainty nose. His facial hair was disorganized—rough mustache and a beard that ran from patchy to thick as it drifted across his cheeks. There were miscellaneous whiskers scattered almost to his eyes. His dark hair looked jangled, a texture that on a woman would be attributed to a bad home permanent. He wore the usual jail garb: a white T-shirt, blue cotton elastic-waisted pants, and rubber shoes. I've seen similar outfits on surgical residents in the corridors of St. Terry's. He was bulky through the shoulders, his chest and biceps bulging from years of pumping iron. The hair on his left forearm only partially masked an entire gallery of elaborate tattoos: a spiderweb, a skull wearing a sombrero, and a graphically portrayed sex act. There was also a big-breasted woman with flowing black tresses whose torso was laid out between his elbow and wrist. His right arm seemed to be bare of art. He studied me for a long time. Through sheer effort, I held his gaze without breaking eye contact. Finally, he lifted the handset on his side of the glass and said, "Hey, how you doin'?"

I held the handset loosely against my ear. "I'm good, Mr. Clifton. How about yourself?"

"I'm doing okay. I know you?"

"My name's Kinsey Millhone. I'm a private investigator. I appreciate your seeing me."

"Why don't you skip the 'mister' shit and tell me what you want." Behind the round lenses of his glasses, his eyes were a mild hazel under ill-kempt brows.

"I was wondering if you'd answer a few questions."

A slight smile appeared. "About what?"

"Something that happened in 1969."

"Why ask me?"

"This isn't about you. It's about someone else."

"Goody. And who's that?"

"You remember being arrested in Lompoc in August of '69?"

"Yeah." He replied with all the caution of someone who's not quite sure what he's agreeing to.

"You gave the officer a home address in Creosote, California. Can you tell me where that is? I never heard of it." I'd looked it up on the map, but in the manner of a polygraph, I thought I'd start with baseline questions, whose truth value was easily verified.

"Little town out near Blythe. Two miles this side of the Arizona line."

"How'd you end up in Lompoc?"

"I was traveling to San Francisco. I had a buddy who'd just come back from six months living on the streets up there. He told me you could buy dope right out on Haight. 'Ludes, grass and hash, peyote, acid. Free sex and free clinics to treat crabs and the clap if you picked up a dose. Sounded like a good deal to me. Still does, come to think of it. Anymore, you lay a hand on a chick, she blows the whistle on you."

I glanced at the sheet of paper I'd taken from my bag, though I knew what it said. "According to this, you were picked up for vagrancy and possession of an illegal substance."

He loosened up at that, face creasing into a smile. Apparently, he'd made an entire career out of substance abuse and denial. "What a crock of shit *that* was. I'm standing on the side of the road, thumbing a ride, when this cop car comes by. Couple rednecks in uniform. Fuckin' pigs. These two pull over and pat me down. Turns out I had some pot on me. One fuckin' joint. And for this I'm locked up. I should've sued for harassment and false arrest."

"You'd hitchhiked?"

"I'se nineteen years old. You don't have a car, that's what you do."

"We're interested in anyone who might have seen a young girl hitchhiking in the area. Seventeen, eighteen years old. Dyed blond hair, blue eyes. She was probably five foot three, a hundred twenty-five pounds."

"That's half the girls I knew. All of 'em looked like that except the ones porked up on grass. Ever notice that? Girls'd smoke too much dope and munch themselves up to twice their normal weight. Either that or all the fat ones were on the street in those days, hoping to get laid. Who else would have 'em?"

"That's a wholesome attitude."

Pudgie laughed at that, genuinely amused while I was not.

I said, "Can we get back to the subject?"

"Which is what now? I forget."

"The girl I described."

"Sure. What'd she do?"

"She didn't do anything. Her body was found dumped off the side of the road."

His attitude shifted slightly. "Sorry to hear that. You never said she was dead or I wouldn't have smarted off."

"The point is, she had no ID and her body was never claimed. We'd like to find out who she is."

"Yeah, but 1969? Why worry about it now after all these years?"

"It's someone's pet project. Couple of guys I work with. What about you? What happened when you got out of jail?"

"I had to call my old man to come pick me up. He was royally pissed. Soon as we got home, the shit-head threw me out; flung my clothes in the yard and broke my dinner plate on the porch. Fucking drama queen. Had to make a big scene, make sure all the neighbors knew he'd busted my ass."

"At least he was willing to drive all the way from Creosote."

"Yeah, but not before I'd spent the worst three days of my life in a cell with a bunch of freaks," he said and shrugged. "Worst until then. I've seen a lot worse since."

"You remember Lorenzo Rickman or Frankie Miracle?"

He snorted. "Lorenzo? What kind of name is that? What's the guy, some kind of fruit?"

"You shared a cell with those two and a guy named John Luchek. You remember him?"

"Not especially. I guess. Any reason I should?"

"What about Rickman?"

"Is this about him? Mean, it'd be nice if I knew what you were going for."

"We'll get to that. Did the two of you talk?"

"Jail's a bore. You talk just to keep from going out of your gourd. Food stinks, too, until you get used to it. Here, it's not bad; you know, heavy on the starch. Macaroni and cheese tastes like library paste. You ever eat that stuff?"

I wasn't sure whether he was referring to the jail cuisine or library paste. I'd dined on both, but I didn't think that was any of his business. I wasn't here to compare exotic foods. "What about Frankie? You have a conversation with him?"

"Must have. Why not? I'm a friendly little fuck. Course, I probably wouldn't recognize those guys now if I saw 'em on the street."

"Would it help if you saw pictures?"

"Might."

I shifted the handset from my right ear to my left, tucking it between my cheek and shoulder so I could free my hands. I removed assorted mug shots from the file folder and placed them by twos against the glass in front of him. There were twelve in all; names, aliases, and personal data, wants and warrants carefully blocked out. Pudgie subjected the black-and-white photos to the same careful scrutiny he'd lavished on me. He pointed to Frankie. "That one? That's Frankie. I remember him. Coked up and jumpy. He talked up a storm until the high wore off."

"What about the others?"

"Maybe him. I'm not sure." He pointed to Lorenzo Rickman, his memory better than he realized.

"Anyone else?"

"Don't think so."

"Did Frankie talk about his arrest?"

"What, you mean the chick he whacked? I guess he cut her up bad and then he fucked it up big time."

"Like what?"

"Stole her car, for one thing. What's he think? The cops aren't going to put out a fuckin' APB? Then he takes her credit card and uses that to pay for his entire escape. He left a paper trail a mile wide. Guy's dumb as he is mean. You kill a girl, you ought to have more sense." He stopped and stared. "I bet you know all this stuff, right? What's the story, is he out?"

"You're full of questions."

"How can I help if you won't say what you're after?"

"Did he indicate how long he'd been in Lompoc before his arrest?"

Pudgie smiled. "I don't get your fascination with a little puke like him."

"I'm not fascinated with anything, except the truth."

"Hey, come on. Tell me the game and I can play for keeps."

I broke off eye contact. "Well, thanks for your time.

Actually, I think that's it." I pinned the handset against my ear again while I gathered the mug shots and tucked them in the folder.

"Wait! Don't go. We're not done yet. Are we done?"

I paused. "Oh, sorry. I was under the impression you'd told me everything you knew. I didn't want to waste your time."

"It's like this: I might remember more if we could sit and chat awhile. You know, small talk and like that. Ask another question. Maybe it'll stimulate my brain."

I smiled at him blandly, getting to my feet. "Why don't you get in touch if you think of anything useful?"

"About what exactly? At least put me in the ballpark here."

"I'm not going to feed you lines. If you don't know anything, that's fine. We'll let it go at that."

"Naw, now don't get mad. How's this? I'll think real hard. Meanwhile, you come back later and bring a carton of smokes."

"I'm not buying you cigarettes. Why would I do that?"

"It's the least you can do, compensation for my time."

I glanced at my watch. "Four minutes' worth."

"Smoking helps me think."

I adjusted my shoulder bag, the handset still at my ear. "Bye now."

He said, "Okay. Skip the carton. Three packs. Any kind except menthol. I really hate those things."

"Buy your own," I snapped.

"I'm out tomorrow. I can pay you back."

"Quit while you can. That's my advice."

"What's your name again?"

"Millhone. I'm in the book. If you can read." I returned the handset to the cradle.

"I love you," he mouthed.

"Yeah, right. I love you too."

He winked and wiggled his tongue, a gesture I pretended not to see.

On my way home from the jail, I stopped at the supermarket to pick up items for Henry's return. Traffic permitting, he was due back in town sometime between five and six. He'd left his car in long-term parking at the Los Angeles airport. I'd offered to take them down, but Henry, ever independent, had preferred driving himself. He and Rosie and William had flown to Miami, where they were joined by their older sister, Nell, age ninety-seven, and brothers Lewis and Charles, ages ninety-five and ninety, respectively. This morning, after two weeks in the Caribbean, they'd dock in Miami and three of them would catch a plane to L.A. while the three older siblings returned to Michigan.

I loaded my shopping cart with milk, bread, bacon, eggs, orange juice, bananas, onions, carrots, a four-pound roasting chicken, new potatoes, and fresh asparagus, along with salad mix and a fifth of Jack Daniel's, Henry's beverage of choice. Briefly I considered fixing dinner for him myself, but my repertoire is limited and I didn't think pouring skim milk over cold cereal was that festive. Shopping done, I stopped at a corner kiosk a block from the market and bought a bouquet of zinnias and dahlias, a mass of orange and yellow with a ribbon tied around the stems. I could feel my energy lifting the closer I got to home, and by the time I unloaded groceries in Henry's kitchen and put away the perishables, I was humming to myself. I arranged the flowers in a silver coffee server and set them in the middle of the kitchen table.

I did a quick circuit of the house. His answering machine was blinking, but I figured he could pick up any messages as soon as he came in. I went into his cleaning closet and hauled out the vacuum cleaner, a dust mop, a sponge mop, and some rags. I made a second circuit of the house, dusting and vacuuming. All I needed were the singing mice to keep me company. After that, I scrubbed the kitchen and bathroom sinks and ran the sponge mop across the kitchen floor until it gleamed. Then I went home and took a serious world-class nap.

I woke at 5:25, at first reluctant to leave the cozy swaddling quilt in which I'd wrapped myself. It was still light outside. The spring days were getting longer, and we'd soon have the equivalent of an extra half-day at our disposal. People getting off work still had time to walk the dog or to sit on the front porch with a drink before supper. Mom could take a moment to read the paper. Dad could mow the lawn or wash the family car.

I pushed the covers back and moved into the bathroom, where I peered out the window, angling my face so I could catch a glimpse of Henry's back door. The kitchen light was on and I was energized by the idea that he was home. I put on my shoes, washed my face, tidied my bed, and trotted down the spiral stairs. I went out, locking the door behind me, noting with satisfaction that Henry's station wagon was now sitting in the drive where I'd parked the day before yesterday.

He had his back door open, the screen door latched but unlocked. There was no immediate sign of him, but I knocked on the frame and heard his "Yoo hoo" coming at me from the hall. He appeared half a second later in his usual T-shirt, shorts, and flip-flops. Before he could get the door open, his wall phone rang. He motioned me in and then snatched up the receiver. He had the briefest of conversations and then said, "Let me switch to the other phone. Hang on a minute. Don't go away." He held out the handset and whispered, "Be right back. Help yourself to a glass of wine."

I took the phone, waiting while he went into the bedroom and picked up in there. As soon as I knew he was on the line, I replaced the handset in the wall-mounted cradle. He'd already opened a bottle of Chardonnay, which sat in a frosty cooler with a stemmed glass close by. I poured myself half a glass of wine. I could smell chicken baking and I peered through the oven window. The plump hen I'd bought was already turning brown, surrounded by onions, carrots, and rosy new potatoes. He'd set the kitchen table for four, and I knew it wouldn't be long before William and Rosie popped in. It'd take them a day or two to get the tavern up and running. I wondered if Rosie's Hungarian dishes would take on the flavors of the Caribbean. I tried to imagine her pork stew gussied up with coconut, pineapple, and plantains.

Henry returned to the kitchen moments later and poured a drink of his own. He looked tanned and fit, his cheeks wind-burned, his eyes a lustrous blue. William and Rosie arrived at that point, William in a straw boater, Rosie with a tote made of woven fibers that looked like a cross between corn husks and grass. William was two years Henry's senior and blessed with the same silky white hair and the same lean frame. To my mind, he isn't quite as handsome as Henry, but he looks good nonetheless. William is a recovering hypochondriac who still can't resist a good story about inexplicable illness and sudden death. Rosie, by way of contrast, is stocky and solid, bossy, opinionated, insecure, humorless, and generous at heart. The tropical sun had rendered her dyed red hair a singular salmon hue, but she was otherwise unchanged. While Henry took out lettuce and tomatoes, I asked the newlyweds how they'd liked the cruise.

Rosie made a face. "I din't like the food. Too blend. No taste and what there was is no good."

William poured them each a glass of wine. "You ate more than I did! You were gluttonous."

"But I din't enjoy. That's what I'm say. Is forgettable. I don't remember nothing I ate."

"You forgot that pineapple pie? Delicious! Extraordinary. You said so yourself."

"I make twice as good if I want, which I don't."

"Well, I can't argue with that, but you were there to be pampered. The point of the whole vacation was not having to cook."

"What about activities? What'd you do with yourselves all day?"

William pulled out a chair for Rosie and then took a seat at the table. "It was terrific. Wonderful. We docked at various ports, maybe seven in all. When we weren't off seeing the sights, we had lectures and movies, swimming, shuffleboard, aerobics—you name it. They even had a bowling alley. At night, there was gambling and ballroom dancing. Bridge, chess tournaments. Never an idle moment. We had a ball."

"Good for you. That sounds great. How about the other sibs? Did they enjoy it?"

William said, "Well, let's see now. Charlie finally got his hearing aids adjusted and he's a changed man. You can hardly shut him up. Used to be he kept to himself since he never had a clue what anyone was saying to him. He and Nell played bridge and beat the socks off their opponents."

"And Lewis?"

"You put him around a bunch of women and he's happy as a clam. Men were outnumbered ten to one. He was the cock of the walk."

Rosie held up an index finger. "Not quite." She gave Henry a sly smile. "Tell what you did."

"No, no. Unimportant. Enough about us. What about you, Kinsey? What are you working on? Something interesting I'm sure."

"Come on, Henry. You haven't finished telling me about the trip. I've never been on a cruise. I really want to know what it was like."

"Just what William said. Little bit of everything. It was nice," he said, busy with oil and vinegar and his whisk.

Rosie leaned forward, her tone confidential. "He's pose for calendar and now all the old womens calling him night and day."

"Don't be silly," he said over his shoulder to her.

"What kind of calendar?"

"Oh, you know, the usual. The crew thought it'd be a good way to commemorate the trip. They do this all the time. It's nothing. Just a joke."

Rosie nodded, lifting one brown-penciled brow. "The 'nothing' I agree. Is what he's wearing. Our Mr. February, Kings of Heart."

"He wasn't wearing *nothing*," William said. "You make it sound like he was *nude* when he was no such thing."

She reached in her tote and pulled out a glossy calendar filled with color photographs. "I heve right here. You take a look and see for yourself. The man's got no clothes. Only underpents." She flipped to the month of February and turned the page so I could see it. The candid shot showed Henry on the upper deck, leaning against the rail with his back to the ocean. A distant palm-dotted island was visible to his right. He wore red shorts, no shoes, a white dress shirt hanging loose and unbuttoned down the front. A captain's hat was tilted forward at an angle. His grin was unaffected, showing a flash of white teeth against the tan of his face. The effect was rakish, the perfect combination of charisma and sex appeal. Henry, in the kitchen with us, blushed from ear to ear.

"Ooo, I love this. I have to have a copy of my own," I said.

"Is yours. You keep. I heve more for ladies in the neighborhood."

"Thanks." I flipped through the pages, checking the other entrants. While some of the photographs showed moderately attractive men—all octogenarians, by the look—not one was as dashing as Henry. I laughed with pleasure. "I never knew you were so photogenic. No wonder the phone's ringing. You look fabulous."

"The phone's not ringing," he said.

At that moment, the phone did, in fact, ring.

"I get," Rosie said, heaving herself to her feet.

"No, you won't. That's what machines are for."

We waited out the three additional rings until Henry's answering machine kicked in. From the other room, we heard the outgoing message, followed by the usual beep. "Henry? This is Bella, *'ma petite belle.'* Remember me? I promised I'd call you so here I am. I just wanted to say how disappointed I was we didn't have a chance to visit again before you left the ship. You bad boy. When you have a chance, you can reach me at . . ."

Dinner was punctuated by two additional calls, which Henry ignored. He kept his eyes on his plate, cutting his chicken with a concentration he rarely lavished on his food. The third time the phone rang, he left the table and went into the living room, where he turned off the ringer and lowered the volume on the answering machine. None of us said a word, but Rosie and William exchanged a look as she smirked at her plate. I could see her shoulders shake, though she pretended to cough, a napkin pressed to her lips.

"It's not *funny*," Henry snapped.

9

With Stacey back in the hospital for a second time in five days, I volunteered to take the Monday interview with Lorenzo Rickman. Dolan had offered to do it, but I knew he was eager to be on hand when the doctors talked to Stacey about this latest round of tests. As it turned out, my chat with Rickman was brief and unproductive. We stood in the service bay of an import repair shop that smelled of gasoline fumes, motor oil, and new tires. The floor, work benches, and all available countertops were littered with a jumble of tools and equipment, parts, manuals, blackened spark plugs, cracked cylinder heads, valves, fan belts, drive shafts, alternators, and exhaust manifolds.

Rickman was in his late thirties with an angular face and a neck that appeared too thin to hold his head upright. His dark hair was receding, a few feathers combed down on his forehead to form a fringe of sparse bangs. A beard, closely trimmed, ran along the line of his jaw, and he stroked it reflexively with fingers blackened by oil. His uniform probably wasn't any different than the outfits he'd worn in prison, except for the machine-embroidered name above his left shirt pocket. He made a show of being cooperative, but he had no memory of incarceration with Frankie Miracle.

He shook his head. "Can't help. Name doesn't ring a bell. I was only in jail the one night. First thing the next morning, a friend of mine bailed me out, but only after I promised to join AA. I've been on the wagon—well, more or less—ever since." He smiled briefly while he smoothed his hair toward his forehead. "I still get in trouble with the law, but at least I'm clean and sober—condition of my parole. Right now, I do, you know, five, six meetings a week. Not that I like hanging out with dudes hyped up on coffee and cigarettes, but it sure beats incarceration." He put his hands in his back pockets and then changed his mind and crossed his arms, fingers drifting back to his beard, which he stroked with his thumb.

"What about the other guys in the cell that night? You remember anything about them?"

"Nope. Sorry. I was eighteen years old, drunk and stoned the night they picked me up. My second or third blackout, I forget which. Third, I think. I could've been in with Charlie Manson and you couldn't prove it by me."

I tried priming the pump, claiming we had a witness who was there at the same time and said Frankie'd bragged about a killing. This generated no response. I handed him the packet of photographs, which he shuffled through carelessly. He shook his head and handed them back. "Look like a bunch of thugs."

I tucked the photos in my bag. "I know this is none of my business, but what'd you do to warrant a prison sentence?"

His fingers became still and then he pulled at a thatch of beard growing under his chin. "What makes you ask?"

"No reason. I'm just curious."

"I don't really care to say."

"Ah. My fault. Sorry. It's your business, of course. I didn't mean to step on your toes." I gave him my card, offering the standard line. "Thanks for your time. If you think of anything, will you let us know?"

"Sure."

"Can I ask one more thing? You think you're out for good?"

He considered my question and then smiled to himself. "I doubt it."

I stopped off at the hospital on my way into town. Stacey was back on 6 Central, in another private room located down the hall from the room he'd had before. When I glanced in, his bed was empty. Beside it, a wide window looked out on a view of the ocean, maybe two miles away, across the shaggy treetops. An occasional glimpse of a red-tile roof punctuated the thick expanse of green. The room was airy; spacious enough to accommodate a forty-eight-inch round table and four captain's chairs, where I found Dolan sitting with a tattered copy of *Road & Track*.

"Oh, hi. Where's Stace?"

"In X-ray. He should be back in a bit."

"How's he doing?"

"Don't know yet. What'd Rickman say?"

"Regrettably, not much." I filled him in on my conversation. "I think we can safely write him off. Probably Pudgie as well. He's cagey, but dumb, and I don't trust the combination. So now what?"

Dolan set his magazine aside. He wore a dark blue windbreaker and a Dodgers baseball cap. "Stacey never got a chance to call Joe Mandel to see if he can lay hands on Jane Doe's effects. Soon as he's got a minute, he's going to do that. Meantime, we thought you might have a phone chat with this C. K. Vogel fellow that Arne was talking about. You might try Directory Assistance—"

"Dolan, this is what I do for a living."

"Oh, right. Sorry."

"I'll go down to the lobby and find a public phone. You want anything while I'm there?"

"I don't suppose they sell Camels in the gift shop."

"I don't suppose they do." When I got to the door, I hesitated. "What was Rickman in prison for?"

Lieutenant Dolan picked up his magazine and wet his index finger. He turned the page, paying close attention to a full-page ad for a fuel additive that required the presence of a blonde in a bathing suit. "Well, let's see. Molestation, sodomy, oral copulation, lewd and lascivious acts with a child. I'm surprised he wasn't killed in prison. As a rule, inmates don't have a lot of tolerance for guys like that."

Geez, I'd been picturing a bit of B&E.

I took the elevator down and made my way through the maze of corridors to the lobby. I found a bank of public phone kiosks outside the front entrance, sheltered by a marquee that extended from the lobby door to the passenger loading ramp. While I looked on, a young nurse's aide helped a new mother out of a wheelchair and into a waiting van. I couldn't see the baby's face, but the bundle wasn't much bigger than a loaf of bread. I scrounged around in the bottom of my bag and came up with a handful of coins. Lompoc was in the same area code as Santa Teresa, so I knew it wasn't going to require much. I dialed Directory Assistance while the young husband loaded flower arrangements into the back of the van, along with a cluster of bobbing pink and silver helium balloons.

I got C. K. Vogel's number and made a note of it before I dialed. When he picked up on his end, I identified myself. Judging from the sound of his voice, he was in his eighties and possibly in the midst of an afternoon nap. I said, "Sorry to disturb you."

"No, no. Don't worry about that. Arne called on Friday and said someone might be in touch. You want to know about the van I saw, is that correct?"

"Yes, sir. It is."

"Tell you the truth, I didn't say much at the time. I had a brother-in-law worked for the Sheriff's Department—this was my sister Madge's husband, fella named Melvin Galloway. He's since died. Two of us never did get along. He's a damn know-it-all. Had an opinion about everything and hear him tell it, he's always right. I couldn't abide the man. Might not sound Christian, but it's the truth. I told him twice about that van, but he pooh-poohed the idea, said if he stopped to track down every half-assed theory the John Q. Public volunteered, he wouldn't get anything else done. Not that he did much to begin with. He's the laziest son of a gun I ever came across. After 'while, I figured I'd done what I could and said to hell with him. What struck me afterward was not the hippie van so much as that other car I saw. Snappy-looking red convertible with Arizona plates."

"Arne mentioned the red car, but I got the impression it was the van you thought was suspicious. Did I get that wrong?"

"No, ma'am. I noticed the van on account of the paint job—peace symbols and that sort, in the wildest colors imaginable. It was parked right there in that fork in the road when I first became aware of it."

"I know the location."

"Reason the other car caught my attention was because I later read in the paper they recovered a stolen car matching that description."

"You remember the make?"

"I don't, but I saw that car on three occasions. First time near the quarry, just a little piece down the road, and the second time over town. I was driving to the doctor's office to have a cyst removed and passed the wrecker pulling it up out of the ravine, all banged up. Looked like whoever took the car let the handbrake loose and pushed it down a hill into a bunch of brush. Must have hit a goodly number of trees on the way, judging from all the scratches and dents. Wasn't spotted for a week, but the fella where I take my car for repairs was the one the Sheriff's Department called when they needed it towed. I saw it at the repair shop the next day when I was having work done on my carburetor. That was the third time. Never saw it again after that."

"I remember mention of a stolen car. Was there anybody in it when you saw it the first time?"

"No, ma'am. It was setting on the side of the road just inside the entrance to your grandma's property. Top down, sun beating hard on those fine black leather seats. I slowed as I went by because I wondered if someone'd had engine trouble and had wandered off to get help. I didn't see a note on the windshield so I drove on. Next time I passed, the car was gone."

"Did you tell Melvin about that one?"

"I told Madge and she told him, but that's the last I heard. I didn't want to force my observations on a fella doesn't want to hear. He'd have pooh-poohed that, too.

Trouble with Melvin is he didn't believe a thing unless it come from him. He's the type if he didn't know something, he made it up. If he didn't feel like doing something, he claimed he did it anyway. You couldn't pin the man down. Ask him a question, he'd act like he'd been accused of negligence."

"Sounds like a pain."

"Yes, he was. Madge, too."

"Well. I appreciate the information. I'll mention this to the guys and see if it's something they want to pursue." Inwardly, I was still hung up on the fact that he'd mentioned my "grandma." I never thought of Grand that way. I had a grandmother. How bizarre.

As though reading my mind, he said, "I knew your mama once upon a time."

"Really."

"Yes ma'am. You know Arne Johanson worked for the Kinseys from the age of seventeen. He was sweet on her himself, but Rita wouldn't give him the time of day. He figured it's because he was too old for her and then she up and marries your dad, the same age as him. He got his nose out of joint, I can tell you that. I told him don't be ridiculous. In the first place, she was never going to take up with a cowpoke. Second place, she'd rather die than get stuck where she is. She was wild, that one, and pretty as they come. Restless as all get out. She'd have taken up with anyone to get off the ranch."

"That's flattering," I said. In truth, this was the first concrete image I'd ever had of her. In that careless vignette, he'd captured the entire story of her life. My cousins, Liza and Tasha, had spoken of her in ways that seemed larger than life. She'd taken on the aura of family myth, a symbol of that legendary clash of wills. "I understand she and my grandmother didn't get along."

"Oh, they tangled, those two. Rita was Cornelia's pride and joy. I felt sorry for her in a way . . ."

"Who, my mother?"

"Your grandma. She liked to maintain she didn't have a favorite among the five girls, but Rita was her firstborn and Cornelia doted on her. You know the story, I suppose."

"Well, sure. I heard it once," I said, lying through my teeth. Somehow gossip seems less pernicious if the person telling the tale thinks it's one you've already heard.

"Cornelia married Burton Kinsey when she was seventeen, exactly half his age. That's one more reason she didn't want Rita to marry young like she did. She lost three babies in a row, all of them boys and not a one went to term. Rita was the first of her children to survive. Cornelia's boys were stillborn. Only the girls made it through alive."

"What was that about?"

"I don't think the doctors determined the cause. In those days, medicine was largely good luck and guesswork. People died of diabetes until those two fellows discovered insulin in 1923. Folks died of anemia, too, until liver therapy came along in 1934. Think of it. Eating liver was a cure. We forget things like that; forget how ignorant we were and how much we've learned." He stopped to clear his throat. "Well, now. I didn't mean to run on at the mouth. Trouble with getting old is you lose all the people you tell your stories to. You let me know if that red car turns out to be anything. I'd like to have a laugh at Melvin's expense after all these years."

"Thanks for your time. I'll be in touch."

I replaced the handset in the cradle and headed for the elevator, which I took to 6 Central. The doors slid open and I stepped off just as Dolan approached, having exited Stacey's room. He took a seat on a couch positioned under a window. The area wasn't designated as a waiting room, but it probably served as a getaway for friends and family members who needed a break. He rose when he caught sight of me.

"Don't get up," I said. "What are you doing out here? I thought you'd be down the hall with Stace."

Dolan sat down again on the couch. "The doctors are in there. Oncologist, radiologist, and another specialist nobody bothered to introduce."

"What's going on?"

"Beats me. All three had on those long medical faces so the news couldn't be good. How'd the phone call go? Did you talk to Vogel?" He scooted over on the couch to make room for me. "Here. Have a seat."

I perched on the near arm and propped my hand on the back of the couch. "For starters, in the small-world department, it turns out C. K. Vogel was Melvin Galloway's brother-in-law." I went on, summarizing the information C. K.'d given me about the red convertible.

"He could be confused. Frankie's car was red."

"I know, but he was very specific about it's being a convertible with black leather seats."

"Let's run that by Stacey and see what he says. It can't hurt to check."

Out of the corner of my eye, I saw the three doctors emerge from Stacey's room. I pointed in their direction as they rounded the far corner and disappeared. "Looks like they're done. You want to go down and find out what they said?"

"No. But I will."

I let Dolan take the lead as we entered Stacey's room, thinking that if Stace was upset, I could ease out without calling undue attention to myself. He was in bed, having cranked up the head so he could see the view. He had his knit cap off and I was disconcerted by the sight of his bare head. His hair was wispy, a cross between duck down and baby fuzz, scarcely half an inch long. The watch cap had given him an air of manliness. Without it, he was just a sick old man with a scrawny neck and ears that protruded from the bony shell of his skull. He turned from the view with a smile that came close to merriment unless you knew him. "Never let it be said God doesn't have a sense of humor."

Dolan said, "Uh-oh."

"It's really not too bad. No meningioma or neurofibroma; in other words, there're no metastatic tumors along my spine. The business with my back's benign. Probably a herniated disc, which is the result of degenerative changes not uncommon in a man my age. I'm quoting the doc here just in case you think I've started talking strange. The treatment of choice is bed rest, which is something I'm already well acquainted with. Analgesics, a mild tranquilizer, possibly Valium as you suggested. That doesn't work, they go to plan B, which they haven't laid out as yet. I'm guessing surgery, but they haven't actually said as much. Doctor did suggest exercises to strengthen my back once the pain subsides. Fair enough. Unfortunately, the very same X-ray that showed my back problem's no more than a pain in the ass also revealed a lesion. I'm supposed to be in remission, free and clear."

"What's he think it is?"

"She, goddammit! And don't interrupt. I was just getting to that. Doc says it could be scar tissue, it could be the remains of a dying tumor, or it might be our old friend lymphoma cropping up again. They can't tell from the film. So first thing tomorrow morning, I'm scheduled for a biopsy. Lucky I'm here is how they put it to me. Lucky my back feels like shit, they said. Without back pain, no X-ray. Without the X-ray, this whatever I've got would have gone undetected until the next follow-up appointment, which isn't on the books for months." He pointed at Dolan. "And don't say 'I told you so' because I don't want to hear it."

"I'd never say that—though I'll admit I did mention it."

I thought he was pushing his luck, but Stacey laughed. Dolan said, "So when do you get out?"

"They haven't told me yet. Meantime, I'm not lying here idle. I put in another call to the Sheriff's Department. Joe Mandel's made detective so I'm hoping he'll let us take a look at the Jane Doe evidence."

"Kinsey and I can do that."

"Not without me. You want to keep me alive, you better do what I say."

"Bullshit. That's blackmail."

"That's exactly right. So tell me about Rickman. I could use a good laugh about now."

I had dinner that night at Rosie's, so grateful to have her home I could have kissed the hem of her muumuu. Since the tavern had been closed for two weeks, the smell of beer and cigarette smoke had nearly faded from the air. In her absence, she'd had a cleaning crew come in and scrub the place down. Floors now gleamed, wood surfaces were polished, and the mirror behind the bar reflected the rows of liquor bottles with a sparkle that suggested expensive handblown glass. The crowd that night was light, the usual patrons perhaps still unaware that the restaurant was open for business again.

William stood behind the bar, pulling beers and pouring drinks for the smattering of customers. Henry sat at his usual table, amusing himself with a book of anagrams.

At his invitation, I took a seat across from him. I looked over as Rosie emerged from the kitchen with an armload of what appeared to be slim binders. She crossed the room, heading in our direction, clearly pleased with herself. She handed a binder to me and a second to Henry. I thought they might be picture albums, but I opened the front cover and found myself staring at a handwritten menu done in a calligraphic script.

"This is different," I remarked.

"Is new menu. So I don't hef to tell every dish what I'm cooking. William wrote by hand and then went to photo copy shop and hed them print. You order anything you want and what you can't say in Henglish you point." She stood and looked at us expectantly. Since she'd returned from the cruise, her Henglish seemed to have gotten worse.

Henry surveyed his menu, a curious expression crossing his face. I glanced at mine, running my gaze down the page. The dishes were listed first in Hungarian, complete with letter combinations and accent marks I'd never seen before. Under the Hungarian name for each dish there was the translation in English:

Versenyi Batyus Ponty
Carp in a Bundle

Csuka Tejfeles Tormaval
Pike Cooked in Horseradish Cream

Hamis Oztokany
Mock Venison

Diszno Csülök Káposztával
Pig's Knuckles and Sauerkraut

I couldn't wait to see what the crowd of softball rowdies was going to think about this.

"You've outdone yourself, Rosie," Henry said.

"Really," I said. "I can hardly choose."

She seemed to wiggle with pleasure, order pad in hand. For a minute I thought she intended to lick her pencil point.

Henry smiled at her blandly. "Why don't you give us a few minutes? This is a lot to take in."

"You keep and I come beck."

"Good idea."

She moved away from our table and began to circle the room, distributing a menu at each booth and table along the way. Henry stared after her with something close to wonderment. "I guess this is what happens when you take someone on a cruise. She's come home inspired. If I didn't know her better, I'd say she was putting on airs."

I set my menu aside. "That's the least of our worries. What are we going to do? I don't want to eat a pig knuckle with sauerkraut. That's disgusting."

He looked at his menu again. "Listen to this one. *'Mazsolas es Gesztenyés Borjunyelv.'* You know what that is? Calf's Tongue with Chestnuts and Raisins."

"Oh, that can't be true. Where do you see that?" I peered over at his menu, hoping it was somehow completely different.

He pointed at an item under a column entitled "Specialities of the House." "Here's another one. Lemon Tripe. I forget what that is. Could be stomach or bowel."

"What's the big deal with organ meats?"

Rosie had completed her circuit and she now headed back to our table. "I hef idea. I prepare for you special. Big surprise."

"No, no, no," Henry said. "I wouldn't want to put

you to any trouble. We'll just order from what's here. My goodness. So many interesting dishes. What are you having, Kinsey?"

"Me? Oh. Well, actually on a night like this, I'd love a nice big bowl of soup and maybe noodles on the side. Could you do that for me?"

"Easy. Of course. I give Shepherd's Soup. Is already make," she said, pausing to pencil an elaborate note on her order pad. She turned to Henry.

"I think I'll hold off for now. I just had a bite before I came over here."

"Little plate of dumplings? Jellied pork? Is fresh. Very good."

"Don't tempt me. Maybe later. I'll just keep her company for now," he said.

Rosie pursed her lips and then shrugged to herself. I thought she'd insist, but apparently decided to let him suffer. Neither of us said a word until she'd disappeared.

I leaned forward. "Why didn't you tell me you were doing that? I could have said the same thing."

"I blurted out the first thing that occurred to me. You were quick about it, too. Soup and noodles. That's safe. How can you go wrong?"

My gaze strayed toward the kitchen. Mere seconds had passed, and Rosie was already using her backside to push her way through the swinging kitchen doors into the dining room, bearing a wide tray that held a shallow bowl of steaming soup.

I said, "Oh, geez. Here she comes. I hate service this quick. It's like eating in a Chinese restaurant. You're in and out on the street again twenty minutes later."

She crossed the room, setting the tray on the adjoining table, then placing the bowl in front of me. She tucked her hands under her apron and looked at me. "How you like?"

"I haven't tried it yet." I fanned some of the steam toward my face, trying to define the odor. Burnt hair? Dog hide? "Gee, this smells great. What is it?"

She peered at my bowl, identifying some of the diced ingredients. "Is parsnip, ongion, carrot, kohlrabi—"

"I love vegetable soup!" I said, with perhaps more enthusiasm than I'd ordinarily express. I tipped my spoon down into the depths, bringing up a rich cargo of root vegetables.

She was still peering. "Is also head, neck, lungs, and liver of one lamb."

The spoon was already in the air by then, soup sailing toward my mouth as though of its own accord. As the spoon reached my lips, I caught a glimpse of porous gray chunks, probably minced lobe of lung, along with some floaters of something I was too fearful to ask about. I puckered my lips and made a slurping sound, sucking up the broth while deftly avoiding the little knots of offal. I made insincere *Mmm* noises.

"I come right beck with noodles."

"Take your time."

As soon as she left, I put my spoon down, craning to check all four corners of the room. "I wonder if I have time to scoot to the toilet and put this back where it belongs. She doesn't even have planters where I can dump the stuff."

Henry leaned closer to the bowl. "Is that a nostril? Oh no, sorry. It's probably just a little cross-section of heart valve. Head's up. Here she comes again."

Rosie was returning to the table with a dinner-sized plate in hand. I made a big display of stirring my soup and wiping my mouth with a napkin as she set the noodles in front of me. I patted my chest as though overwhelmed, which I was. "This is filling. Really rich."

I stole an apprehensive look at the dish as she placed it on the table beside my soup bowl, experiencing a flash of relief. "What's that, manicotti?"

"Is call *palacsinta tészta*. Like what you call crêpes."

"Hungarian crêpes. Well, that sounds wonderful. I can do that."

"I fill with calf's brains scrembled with egg. Very dainty. You'll see. I can teach you to make."

"Okay then, I'll just chow down," I said. She stood by the table, as though prepared to monitor my every bite. I leaned to one side, focusing my gaze on the far side of the room. "I think William's calling you. It looks like he needs help."

Rosie crossed to the bar where she and William engaged in a baffled conversation. Meanwhile, I'd grabbed up my shoulder bag and I was rooting through the contents. Earlier that day, I'd spotted an outdated grocery list done on a sheet of yellow legal paper. I kept one eye on Rosie while I folded the note paper into a cone, pointed at the bottom with a wide mouth at the top. I turned the pointed bottom up to form a seal. I forked up crepes in rapid succession, ignoring the gnarly bits that fell back on the plate. I folded the top down, wrapped the cone in a paper napkin, and shoved the bundle in my purse.

By the time Rosie glanced in my direction, I was bent over my plate, making fake chewing motions while trying to look entranced. Another couple entered the bar and her attention was distracted. I put a twenty on the table near Henry's plate. "Tell her I was called away on an emergency."

Henry pointed to my soup, most of which was still in the bowl. "I'll have her put that in a jar and bring it over to you later tonight. I know how you hate to see food go to waste."

10

I was home earlier than I'd intended, concerned that calf brain would leak out of the makeshift container and contaminate the interior of my shoulder bag. As I passed Henry's garbage can, I removed the bundle from my purse and dumped it. I lifted my head, alerted by the dim ringing of a phone somewhere. I banged down the lid and hurried to my front door, unlocking it in haste. Three rings. Four. I slung my bag on a kitchen chair and snatched up the receiver. My answering machine had already kicked in and I was forced to override my own voice, singing, "It's me. I'm here. Don't go away. I'm answering."

"Kinsey?"

The caller was male and he spoke against the dull murmur of background conversations. I put a hand against one ear. "Who's this?"

"Pudgie."

"Well, hi. This is a surprise. I didn't think I'd hear from you. What's up?"

"You said call if I thought of something, but you have to promise you won't let this get back to him."

I found myself straining to hear. "Back to who?"

"Frankie. You ever meet him?"

"Not yet."

"He's a crazy man. You can't tell it right off because he's good at faking it . . . like he's normal and all, but believe me, you don't want to mess with him."

"I didn't realize you knew him."

"I don't, but it doesn't take a genius to figure out the guy's a freak."

"Is that why you called, to say how nuts he is?"

"Nuhn-uhn. I'll get to that, but lemme ask you something first. Suppose someone tells him I called you?"

"Come on. I can't control that. Besides, who's going to tell? I can promise not a word of this will come from me."

"You swear?"

"Of course."

I could hear him cup a hand over the mouthpiece, lips so close to the phone I thought he'd slobber in my ear. "He talked about stabbing some chick to death."

"Oh, for heaven's sake, Pudgie. That's why he went to prison. For killing Cathy Lee Pearse."

"Not her. Another one. This was after he killed her."

"I'm listening."

"He's bragging about what happens to any bitch tries to cross him. He said he picked up this chick in a bar. She had some dope on her and the two of them got loose. They go out to the parking lot to play grab ass, but she turns all sour on him and starts giving him a hard time, which pisses him off. When she refuses to put out, he offs her and sticks her in the trunk of Cathy Lee's car. He drives around with her two days, but he's worried she'll start to stink, so he dumps her when he gets to Lompoc."

"Where'd he pick her up?"

"What bar? Don't know. He never said. He didn't mention the town, either. I'd guess Santa Teresa. It had to've been before he hit Lompoc because that's where he got caught."

"What about the dump site? Did he say where that was?"

"Some place outside town where she wouldn't be found. I guess they managed to nail him on Cathy Lee, but nobody knew about the other one, so he was free and clear on that."

"What made you suddenly remember? This doesn't sound like something that would slip your mind."

"It didn't 'slip my mind,'" he said, offended. "You're the one came to me. I never offered to snitch. I didn't 'suddenly' do anything. I remembered the minute his name came up."

"Why didn't you tell me then?"

"We'd only just met. How'd I know I could trust you? I had to think about that."

"What made you decide to tell me?"

"I probably should've kept my mouth shut if it comes right down to it. Frankie's a bad-ass. Word leaks out and my sorry butt is fried. He's not a guy you fuck with and expect to live."

"Fair enough," I said. "Did he say anything else?"

"Not that I remember offhand. Time, I didn't pay much attention. Jail, everybody brags about stuff like that. It's mostly bullshit, so I didn't attach anything to it. I mean, I did, but then that's the last I ever heard of it. Now you're saying some girl's body was dumped and right away I think about him."

"You're sure about this."

"No, I'm not *sure*. He might've made the whole thing up. How the hell should I know? You said call and I did."

I thought about it briefly. This could be a hustle, though for the life of me, I couldn't see what Pudgie was getting out of it. "That's not much to go on."

"Well, I can't help you there."

"How'd he kill her?"

"Knife, I guess. Said he stabbed her, wrapped her up, and stuck her in the trunk. Soon as he got to Lompoc, he pitched her off the side of the road and hightailed it out of there. By the time the cops picked him up he figured he was safe. All they cared about was nailing him for Cathy Lee."

"Did he know the girl?"

"I doubt it. He didn't talk like he did."

"Because I'm curious about his motive."

"You gotta be kidding. Frankie doesn't need a *motive*. She could've looked at him funny or called him a pencil dick. If she knew he was on the run, she might've threatened to turn him in."

"Interesting," I said. "I'll have to give this some thought. Where are you calling from?"

"A place I hang out in Creosote. My sis drove up from the desert and brought me back to her house."

"Is there any way I can reach you if I need to get in touch?"

He gave me a number with an area code.

I said, "Thanks. This could be a big help."

"Where's Frankie now?"

"I'm not sure. We've heard he's in town."

"You mean the fucker's *out*?"

"Sure, he's been paroled."

"You never said that. Oh, shit. You have to swear you won't tell him where you heard this. And don't ask me to testify in court because I won't."

"Pudgie, you couldn't testify in court. This is all hearsay. You didn't see him do anything so quit worrying. I'll tell the two cops I'm working with, but that's the end of it."

"I hope I haven't made a mistake."

"Relax. You're fine."

"You buy me those cigarettes?"

"No, but I owe you a bunch."

Dolan picked me up at the office Tuesday morning at 10:00. I'd managed my usual 6:00 A.M. run, after which I'd showered and dressed. I had coffee and a quick bowl of cereal, making it into the office by 8:35. By the time I heard Dolan's car horn, I'd finished catching up on all the odds and ends on my desk. Dolan had the good grace to toss his cigarette out the window as soon as I got in. Stacey's biopsy had been scheduled for 7:45, but neither of us wanted to talk about that. After I'd wrenched open the car door on the passenger side and hauled it shut again, I told Dolan about Pudgie's call.

He said, "Don't know what to make of it. What do you think?"

"I'd love to believe him, but I'm not sure how credible he is for a jailhouse snitch. He did seem to have a couple of the details right."

"Like what?"

"Well, he knew she'd been stabbed and he knew she'd been wrapped in something at the time she was dumped."

"It's possible he took a flyer, guessing at the fine points to make himself seem important."

"To me? Why would he care?"

"Because he's flirting with you. Gave him an excuse to call."

"Is that it? Well, I'm thrilled."

"Point is, what he says is useless. It's all air and sunshine."

"And hearsay as well."

"Right."

The next stop was Frankie's to see what we could shake loose from him. Dolan had talked to Frankie's parole officer, Dench Smallwood, who'd given him the address.

On our way across town, Dolan told me he'd gone through the murder book again. Early reports had made reference to three stolen vehicles, one of which was the red 1967 Chevrolet in which Frankie'd been stopped. Melvin Galloway had been asked to follow up on the other two, but gauging from the paperwork, it was impossible to tell what he'd actually done. Miracle was a fugitive and his arrest was a feather in Galloway's cap. Given his reputation for laziness, the routine aspects of the investigation probably didn't have much appeal. It was possible he'd simply claimed he'd handled the query when he'd let the matter slide. The red convertible C. K. Vogel had seen turned out to be a 1966 Ford Mustang, owned by a man named Gant in Mesquite, Arizona, just across the California line. Stacey had asked Joe Mandel to run the VIN and license plate to see where the vehicle was now. If Mandel could determine the current whereabouts, it might be worthwhile to track it down and take a look.

The room Frankie rented was located in the rear of a frame house on Guardia Street. We picked our way down the drive, avoiding a cornucopia of spilled garbage from an overturned can. Surrounding orange and red hibiscus shrubs had grown so tall that the narrow wooden porch was cold with shade. Dolan knocked on the door while I stood to one side, as though worried I'd be fired on through the lath-and-plaster wall. Dolan waited a decent interval and knocked again. We were on the verge of departing when Frankie opened the door. At forty-four, he was baby-faced and clean-shaven. He wore a T-shirt and loose shorts, with a sleep mask pushed up on the top of his head. His feet were bare. He said, "What."

"Mr. Miracle?"

"That's right."

Dolan moved his windbreaker aside, exposing the badge on his belt. "Lieutenant Dolan, Santa Teresa Police Department. This is Kinsey Millhone."

"Okay." Frankie had mild brown wavy hair and brown eyes. His gaze was direct and tainted with annoyance. I was surprised to see he had no visible tattoos. He'd been in prison for the past seventeen years and I expected him to look as though he'd been rolling naked and wet across the Sunday funnies. He wasn't overweight by any means, but he looked soft, which was another surprise. I picture prison inmates all bulked up from lifting weights. His eyes caught mine. "I suit you okay?"

I declined a response.

Dolan said, "You have a late night? You seem cross."

"I work nights, if it's any of your business."

"Doing what?"

"Janitorial. The Granger Building on the graveyard shift. I'd give you my boss's name, but you already have that."

Dolan smiled slightly. "Matter of fact I do. Your parole officer gave it to me when I talked to him."

"What's this about?"

"May we come in?"

Frankie glanced back across his shoulder. "Sure, why not?"

He stepped away from the door and we crossed the threshold. His entire living quarters consisted of one room with a linoleum floor, a hot plate, an ancient refrigerator, an iron bedstead, and little else. In lieu of a closet, he had a rack made of cast iron pipe on which he'd draped his clothes, both dirty and clean. I could see a cramped bathroom through a door that opened off the rear wall. In addition to an ashtray full of butts, there was a tumble of paperback books on the floor by his bed, a mix of mystery and science fiction. The room smelled of ripe sheets and stale cigarette smoke. I'd have killed myself if I were forced to live in a place like this. On the other hand, Frankie was used to prison, so this was probably an improvement.

There was no place to sit so the two of us stood while Frankie crawled back in bed and pulled the sheet across his lap. The ensuing conversation seemed bizarre, like a visit with Stacey in his hospital room. I'd never seen anyone other than the chronically ill opt to be interviewed prone. It suggested a wary sort of self-confidence. He straightened the sheet and folded the top over once. "You can skip the small talk. I'm working again tonight and I need my sleep."

"We'd like to ask you about the time you spent in Lompoc before you got picked up."

"What about it?"

"How you got there, what you were doing before your arrest?"

"Don't remember. I was stoned. I had shit for brains back then."

"When the officers pulled you over, you were six miles from the spot where a young girl's body was found."

"Wonderful. And where was that?"

"Near Grayson Quarry. You know the place?"

"Everybody knows Grayson. It's been there for years."

"It seems like quite a coincidence."

"That I was six miles away? Bullshit. I have family in the area. My dad's lived in the same house forty-four years. I was on my way to visit."

"After killing Cathy Lee."

"I hope you aren't here coughing up that old hair ball. I'll tell you one thing, they never should have nailed me for murder one. That was strictly self-defense. She came at me with a pair of scissors—not that I need to justify myself to you."

"Why'd you run? Hardly the actions of an innocent man."

"I never said I was innocent. I said—oh hell, why should I tell you? I was in a panic, if you want to know the truth. You do meth, you don't think straight. Temper runs hot and you think everybody's after you."

"No need to be defensive," Dolan said.

"Please forgive me. I beseech you. People wake me up, I get cranky sometimes."

Dolan smiled. "You get cranky, you fly off the handle, is that it?"

"You know what? I've done my time. Not a mark on my record in seventeen years. Credit for time served, good behavior, the whole shootin' match. Now I'm out, I'm clean, and I'm gainfully employed so you can go fuck yourself. No offense."

"Prison did you good."

"Yes, it did. See that? Rehabilitation works. I'm living proof. Went from bad to good and now I'm free as a bird."

"Not quite. You're still on parole."

"You think I don't know that? All the fuckin' rules they lay down? Tell you something, you won't catch me in violation. I'm way too smart. I'm willing to play fair because I don't intend to go back in. And I mean, ever."

"You know the problem with you, Frankie?"

"What's that, Lieutenant? I'm sure you'll spell it out in great detail."

"You may be righteous today, but back then you didn't know enough to keep your big mouth shut."

"Come on. What *is* this?"

"I told you. We have an unsolved homicide with circumstances similar to Cathy Lee's."

"Yeah, well, I can't help you there. I don't know jack about that. You want anything else, you can talk to my attorney."

"And who's that?"

"Haven't hired one yet, but I'll let you know. Where's this horseshit coming from, or is that classified?"

"We got somebody willing to put the ju-ju on you."

"Ju-ju, my ass. What have you got, some ex-con having lunch on my expense account? I didn't kill the chick. You're full of shit."

"That's not what our witness says. He says you bragged about it afterward."

"You're blowin' smoke and you know it. You had anything on me, you'd've showed up with a warrant instead of this hokey song-and-dance routine."

Dolan shook his head. "I don't know, Frankie. I figure you had a hard-on for the girl and when she wouldn't put out, you lost control of yourself."

"Yeah, yeah, yeah." Frankie made a gesture like he was whacking off.

"Why don't you own up to it? You could really help us out. Show your heart's in the right place now that you've turned over this new leaf."

Frankie smiled, shaking his head in disbelief. "You think I'd be dumb enough to sit here and confess? To what? You got nothing on me. I don't even know who the fuck you're talking about."

"I'm not here to hassle you."

"Good, because I'm trying not to lose my cool. You want a urine sample, I'll piss in a cup. You want to search the place, have at it. Whatever it is, just be quick about it. Otherwise we're done. Pull the door shut behind you on your way out." He slid the mask down over his eyes and turned his back to us.

"Well, that was unproductive," I said when the two of us were back in the car again.

"I wanted you to have a look at him. It's always best if you know the players firsthand. Besides, it's good to let him sweat a bit, wondering what we have."

"That won't take long. We don't have anything, do we?"

"No, but he doesn't know that."

Dolan was going to go back over to St. Terry's as soon as he dropped me at the office, but when we pulled onto Caballeria Lane, we caught sight of Stacey sitting on the curb in front of my place, a brown paper bag at his feet. He wore his red knit watch cap, short-sleeve shirt, chinos, and shoes with no socks. His perforated plastic hospital bracelet still encircled his wrist. His arms were bone thin, his skin translucent, like the pale tissue overlay on a wedding invitation. Dolan parked two cars away. While we walked back to Stacey, Dolan took out a pack of cigarettes and his matches and paused to light up. He tossed the match aside and drew deeply, sucking smoke down as though he were using an asthma inhaler. "How'd you get here?"

Stacey shaded his eyes, looking sideways at him. "Called a cab. They do that. Pay 'em money, those guys'll take you anyplace you want."

"I didn't think you'd be released until they ran more tests."

Stacey waved that notion aside. "Hell with 'em. I got tired of waiting for the doc to pull a thumb out. I packed my things and took a hike. I don't have time for nonsense. It won't change anything. Meantime, I got a call from Mandel and he says come on out. He's pulled the Jane Doe evidence and we can take a look. Speaking of which, what'd our friend Frankie have to say for himself?"

"Don't change the subject. How'd the biopsy go?"

"Piece of cake. They've stuck me so often, it's like a bug bite."

"How soon do you get the results?"

Stacey's hand was so small he managed to ease his bracelet off without breaking it. "Day or so. Who cares? We got work to do. Now give me a hand here. My age, you get down, you can't get up again. Tell me about Frankie."

"He's completely innocent."

"Of course. We should have known."

Dolan extended a hand and pulled Stacey to his feet. He seemed to totter fleetingly and then he regained his balance. Dolan and I exchanged one of those looks, which Stacey caught.

"Quit that. I'm fine. I'm tired is all. I've been in bed too long."

The Santa Teresa County Sheriff's Department is located near Colgate off El Solano Road in the same general vicinity as the county dump. I guess land out there is cheap and there's room to expand. Behind the building, I could see rows of black-and-whites, county cars, and assorted personal vehicles belonging to the Sheriff's Department personnel. The one-story structure is a creamy beige and white stucco, with a series of arches across the front. The main jail is just across the road. We parked and went in the front entrance, letting Stacey lead the way. I could tell he missed working. Just the sight of the facility seemed to give him strength.

To the left, in the tiny lobby, was a counter with a glass partition, probably bulletproof, though it was impossible to tell. The civilian clerk, a woman, looked up when we came in. Stacey said, "We're here to see Sergeant Detective Joe Mandel."

She pushed a clipboard across the counter. "He said he'd be right out."

All three of us signed in and she gave us each a visitor's badge, which we fastened onto our shirts. There were three chairs available, but we elected to stand. Through the locked glass door, I could already see someone approaching from the far end of the corridor. He pushed the door open from his side and let us in. There were the usual introductions and a round of handshakes. From the flicker in his eyes, I could tell he recognized me from our meeting in his kitchen, but if he thought it odd, he never let on. He knew Stacey well, but I gathered he hadn't seen Dolan for many years. They exchanged pleasantries as he held the door open and let us into the corridor.

We turned left and followed him down a long hallway, a dogrun of beige carpeting and beige walls, with offices opening up on either side. Joe introduced us to Sergeant Steve Rhineberger, in the Sheriff's forensics unit. He unlocked a door and showed us into a room that looked like a tract-housing kitchen without the stove. There were counters on three sides and some sort of ventilation apparatus at the rear. A large battered-looking brown paper bag sat on the table in the center of the room.

Sergeant Rhineberger opened a lower cabinet door, tore off a length of white paper from a wide roll inside, and took out a pair of disposable latex gloves. "I asked the coroner's office to send over the mandible and maxilla. I thought you might want to look at those, too."

He placed the sheet of protective paper on the table, pulled on the gloves, and then broke the seal on the evidence bag. He removed the folded tarp and various articles of clothing, which he spread on the paper. Mandel removed a handful of disposable gloves from the cardboard dispenser on the counter. He passed a pair to Stacey, a pair to Dolan, and a pair to me. The guys had been chatting about department business, but we all fell into a respectful silence. Eighteen years after the violence of her death, there was only the crackle of white paper and the snap of gloves.

It was strange to look at items I'd only seen before in faded photographs. The shirt and daisy-print pants had been cut from the body and the garments seemed sprawling and misshapen laid out across the tabletop. The fabric was soiled and moist, as though permeated with damp sand. The bloodstains resembled nothing so much as smudges of rust. Her sandals were leather, decorated with brass buckles linked with leather bands. A narrow thong would have separated her big toe from the remaining toes on each foot. The sandals looked new except for faint stains on the sole where her heel and the ball of her bare foot had left indelible marks.

Rhineberger opened a container and removed Jane Doe's upper and lower jawbones. Her teeth showed extensive dental work, sixteen to eighteen amalgam fillings. When he set the maxilla on the mandible, matching the grooves and worn surfaces where they met, we could see the extent of her overbite and the crooked eyetooth on the left. "Can't believe nobody recognized her by the description of the teeth. Charlie says it was all probably done a year or two before she died. You can see the wisdom teeth haven't erupted yet. He says she probably wasn't eighteen." He placed the bones back in the container, leaving the lid off.

Her personal effects scarcely covered the tabletop. This was all that was left of her, the entire sum. I experienced a sense of puzzlement that any life could be reduced to such humble remnants. Surely, she'd expected far more from the world—love, marriage, children, perhaps—at the very least a valued presence among her friends and family. Her remains were buried now in a grave without a headstone, its location marked by lot number in the cemetery ledger. In spite of that, she seemed curiously real, given the sparse data we had. I'd seen the black-and-white photograph of her where she lay on the August-dry grass, her face obscured by the angle of her body and the intervening shrubs. Her midriff, a portion of her forearm, and a section of her calf were all that were visible from the camera's perspective, her flesh swollen, mottled by decomposition as though bruised.

I picked up the plastic bag that contained a lock of her hair, which looked clean and silky, a muted shade of blond. A second plastic bag held two delicate earrings, simple loops of gold wire. The only remaining evidence of the murder itself was the length of thin cable, encased in white plastic, with which her wrists had been bound. The tarp was made of a medium-weight canvas, the seams stitched in red, with metal grommets inserted at regular intervals. It looked like standard-issue—a painter's drop cloth, or a cover used to shield a cord of firewood from rain. In one corner, there was a red speck that looked like a ladybug or a spot of blood, but on closer inspection I realized it was simply a small square of red stitches, where the thread had been secured at the end of the row. From these few tokens, we were hoping to reconstruct not only her identity but that of her killer. How could she be so compelling that eighteen years later the five of us would assemble like this in her behalf?

Belatedly, I tuned into the conversation. Stacey was laying out our progress to date. Apparently, Mandel had gone back and reviewed the file himself. Like Stacey and Dolan, who'd actually discovered the body, he'd been involved from the first. He was saying, "Too bad Crouse is gone. There aren't many of us left."

Dolan said, "What happened to Crouse?"

"He sold his house and moved his family to Oregon. Now he's chief of police in some little podunk town up there. Last I heard he was bored to tears, but he can't afford to come back with housing prices here. Keith Baldwin and Oscar Wallen are both retired and Mel Galloway's dead. Nonetheless, it's nice to have a chance to revisit this case. You have to think after all these years, we might shake something loose."

Stacey said, "What's your take on it? You see anything we missed?"

Mandel thought about that briefly. "I guess the only thing I'd be curious about is this Iona Mathis, the gal Frankie Miracle was married to. She might know something if you can track her down. I hear she came back and sat through the trial with him. She damn near married the guy again she felt so sorry for him."

Stacey made a pained face. "I don't get the appeal. I can't even manage to get married once, and I'm a law-abiding citizen. You have an address on her?"

"No, but I can get you one."

11

Dolan dropped me off at the office before he took Stacey home. Stacey's energy was flagging and, in truth, mine was, too. As I unlocked the door, I noticed a Mercedes station wagon parked in the narrow driveway that separated my bungalow from the next in line. The woman in the driver's seat was working on a piece of needlepoint, the roll of canvas resting awkwardly against the steering wheel. She looked up at me and waved, then set her canvas on the seat beside her. She got out of the car, reached into the rear seat, and pulled out a shopping bag, saying, "I was beginning to think I'd missed you."

I waited while she locked the car door and headed in my direction. She looked familiar, but I couldn't remember how I knew her. I placed her in her early sixties, trim, attractive, nicely dressed in a lightweight red wool suit. Her hair was medium length, tinted a deep auburn shade and brushed loosely off her face.

I hesitated on the threshold, still scrambling through my bag of memories, trying to connect a name to the face. Who was this? A neighbor? A former client? "Are you waiting for me?"

She smiled, showing a row of square even teeth. Before she managed to say another word, I felt a silvery note of fear pluck at the base of my spine, like a sandcrab picking its way erratically across guitar strings. She held out her hand. "I'm your aunt Susanna."

I shook hands with her, trying to compute the term "aunt." I knew the meaning but couldn't for the life of me figure out what to do with it.

"Tasha's mother," she added. "I hope I didn't catch you at a bad time. She did tell you I'd stop by, didn't she? How embarrassing for me if she forgot."

"Sure. Of course. Sorry I drew a blank, but I was thinking of something else. Come on in and have a seat. You want coffee? I was just about to put a pot on for myself."

She followed me through the front door and into the inner office. "Thank you. I'd like that." She set down her shopping bag and took a seat in the client chair across the desk. Her eyes were hazel like mine. The air around her was scented with cologne. The fragrance suggested citrus—grapefruit, perhaps—very fresh and light.

"How do you take it?"

"I'm not fussy. Black's fine."

"It'll take me a minute."

"I'm in no hurry," she said.

I excused myself and went through the outer office and into the kitchen, where I leaned against the counter and tried to catch my breath. I'd been faking composure since the moment she'd announced herself. This was my aunt, my mother's sister. I was acquainted with Tasha and Liza, the oldest and youngest of Susanna's three daughters. The third girl, Pam, I'd heard about but never met. My introduction to the family had been thoroughly disconcerting as I'd known nothing of their existence. A fluke in an investigation three years previously had turned them up like a nest of spiders in the pocket of an old overcoat. In the absence of my parents and Aunt Gin, Susanna had to be one of my closest living relatives.

I patted myself on the chest. This was so bizarre. I don't remember my mother and I've never had a concrete image of her. Even so, I sensed the kinship. All the Kinsey women bore a strong resemblance to one another, at least from what I'd heard. I certainly looked like Tasha, and she'd told me that she and her sister Pam looked enough alike to be mistaken for twins. I looked much less like Liza, but even there, no one could deny the similarities.

I picked up the coffeepot and filled it with water, which I poured into the reservoir of the machine. Filter paper, coffee can. I couldn't see my hands shake, but the counter near the coffeemaker became gritty with grounds. I grabbed a sponge, dampened it, and wiped the surface clean. I set the pot in the machine and flipped the button to ON. I didn't trust myself to talk to her, but I couldn't hang out here until the coffee was done. I took a couple of mugs from the cabinet and set them on the counter. If I'd had brandy on the premises, I'd have downed a slug right then.

I walked back to my office, trying to remember what "normal" felt like so I could imitate the state. "It'll be ready in a minute. Hope you didn't have to wait for me long. I was tied up on business."

She smiled, watching me take my seat across the desk from her. "Don't worry about that. I'm always capable of amusing myself." She was pretty; a straight nose, only the slightest touch of makeup to smooth out the palette of her complexion. I could see sun damage or faded freckles and a series of fine lines etched around her eyes and mouth. The red suit was becoming, the jacket set off by the white shell underneath. I could understand where Tasha had developed her taste in clothes.

She held up a finger. "Oh, I nearly forgot. I brought you something." She leaned down and reached into her shopping bag, coming up with a black-and-white photograph in a silver frame. She held it out and I took it, turning it over so I could see what it was. "That's me with your mother the day of her coming-out party, July 5, 1935. I was nine."

"Ah." I glanced down, but only long enough to take in a flash of the eighteen-year-old Rita Cynthia Kinsey in a long white dress. She was leaning forward, laughing, her arms around her youngest sister. My mother looked unbelievably young, with dark curly hair falling across her shoulders. She must have worn dark red lipstick because the black-and-white photo made her mouth look black. Susanna was done up in a long frothy dress that looked like a miniature version of Rita's.

I felt my face get hot, but I kept it averted until the rush of feeling passed. The pain was sharp, like the lid of a box being slammed on my fingertips. I wanted to howl with surprise. By sheer dint of will, I put myself in emotional lockdown. I smiled at Susanna, but my face felt tense. "I appreciate this. I've never had a photograph of her."

"That's my favorite. I had a copy made so that one's yours to keep."

"Thanks. Are there any pictures of my father?"

"I'm sure there are. If I'd thought of it, I could have brought the family album. We have everyone in there. Maybe next time," she said. "You know, you look like your mother, but then so do I."

I said, "Really," but I was thinking, *This is all too weird*. In my dealings with Tasha, it was easy to keep her safely at arm's length. We used words to hack at each other, establishing a comfortable distance between us. This woman was lovely. For ten cents, I'd have scampered around the desk and crawled up in her lap. I said, "From what I hear, all the Kinsey women look alike."

"It's not the Kinseys so much as the LeGrands. Virginia had some of Daddy's features, but she was the rare exception. Grand's features dominate. No surprise there since she dominates everywhere else."

"Why do you call her Grand?"

She laughed. "I don't know. We've called her that ever since I can remember. She didn't want to be 'Mummy' or 'Mommy' or any of those terms. She preferred the nickname she'd always had and that's how we were raised. Once we got to school, I became aware that other kids called their mothers 'Mama' or 'Mom,' but by then it would have seemed odd to refer to her that way. Maybe, on her part, it was a form of denial—ambivalence about motherhood. I'm not really sure."

The smell of coffee began to permeate the air. I didn't want to leave the room, but I got up and circled the desk. "I'll be right back."

"You want help?"

"No, I'm fine."

"Just yell if you need me."

"Thanks."

Back in the kitchen, I was businesslike, though I noticed, pouring coffee, I was forced to use both hands. How was I going to pass her the mug without spilling coffee in her lap? I took a deep breath and mentally slapped myself around. I was being ridiculous. This was a virtual stranger, a middle-aged woman on a mission of goodwill. I could do this. I could handle it. I'd simply deal with her now and suffer the consequences later when I was by myself again. Okay. I picked up the two mugs, my gaze fixed on the coffee as I walked. I really didn't spill that much and the rug was so gross it wouldn't show, anyway.

Once in my office, I placed both mugs on the desk and let her claim hers for herself. I took my seat again and reached for my mug, sliding it toward me across the desk. I wondered briefly if I could just lean down and slurp instead of lifting it to my lips. "Can I ask you something?"

"Of course you can, sweetie. What do you want to know?"

Sweetie. Oh dear. Here came the tears, but I blinked them back. Susanna didn't seem to notice. I cleared my throat and said, "Liza mentioned nephews the first time we met, but that's the last I've heard of them. Arne told me Grand had three sons, all stillborn, but wasn't there a boy who died in infancy? I thought Liza made reference to that."

She made that dismissive gesture so familiar to me. I'd used it myself and so had my cousin Liza on the day we met. "She never gets that right. Really, family history isn't her strong suit. Technically, it's true. Mother had three boys before Rita was born. The first two were stillbirths. The third lived five hours. All the other boys in the family—nine nephews—are part of the outer circle. Maura's husband, Walter, has two sisters, and they both have boys. And my husband, John, has three brothers, with seven boys among them. I know it's confusing, but since most of those peripheral family members also live in Lompoc, they're included in all the Kinsey gatherings. Grand doesn't like to share us with our husbands' fami-

lies, so at Thanksgiving and Christmas she makes sure
her doors are open and the celebrations are so lavish no
one can resist. What else do you want to know? Ask me
anything you like. That's why I'm here."

I thought for a moment, wondering how far I dared
go. "I've been told you and Aunt Maura disapproved of
my mother." The topic made me feel mean, but that was
easier than feeling frail.

"That was Maura and Sarah, both of whom were
older than me. Maura was twelve and Sarah fifteen when
the 'war broke out,' for lack of a better term. Both sided
with Grand. I was the baby in the family so I could get
away with anything. I just pretended I didn't know what
was going on. I always adored your mother. She was so
stylish and exotic. I think I mentioned I was nine when
she made her debut. I was always more concerned about
my Mary Janes than the larger family issues. I like to
think I'm independent, but I'm not the maverick your
mother was. She took Grand head on. She never shied
away from confrontation. I use diversionary tactics myself—charm, misdirection. For me, it's more effective to
conform on the surface and do as I please when I'm outside Grand's presence. It might be cowardice on my part,
but it makes life easier on everyone, or that's what I tell
myself."

"But why did Sarah and Maura object to my mother's
marriage? What business was it of theirs?"

"Well, none. It really wasn't the marriage so much as
what that did to the family. Once the battle lines were
drawn, Grand was unyielding, and neither your mother
nor Virginia would give in."

"But what was that about? I still don't get it. It's not
as if my father was a bum."

"I don't think Grand had any personal objections to

your father. She saw the age difference as a problem. He was what, thirty-five years old to your mother's eighteen?"

"Thirty-three," I said.

Susanna shrugged. "Fifteen years. That really doesn't seem like much. I think Grand's problem was Rita's marrying on impulse. Grand did that, too—married Daddy on a whim the day she turned seventeen. He was twice her age, and I think they'd known each other less than a month. I suspect she may have regretted her haste, but divorce wasn't an option in those days, at least for her. She never likes having to admit she's wrong so she stuck it out. They were devoted to each other, but I'm not sure how long her infatuation survived. I know it's an old story, but I suspect Grand was hoping to express an unlived part of her life through Rita."

"I can understand that. What you're saying makes sense."

"What is it that bothers you? That's part of what I'd like to address."

"I'm thirty-six years old . . . thirty-seven in three weeks. I've lived all my life without a clue about this stuff. From my perspective, it sure seems like somebody could have let me know. I've said this before to Tasha and I don't mean to harp, but why didn't anyone ever get in touch? Aunt Gin's been dead now for fifteen years. Grand didn't even come down for the funeral, so what's that about?"

"I'm not here to argue. What you're saying is true and you're entirely correct. Grand should have come down here. She should have sent word, but I think she was afraid to face you. She didn't know what you'd been told. She assumed Virginia turned you against her, against the whole family. At heart, Grand's a good person, but she's proud and she's stubborn—well, face it, she can be impossible sometimes—but Rita was stubborn, too. The two of them were so much alike it would have been comical if it hadn't been so destructive. Their quarrel tore the family to shreds. None of us have ever been the same since then."

"But Grand was her mother. She was supposed to be the grownup."

Susanna smiled. "Just because we're old doesn't mean we're mature. Actually, Grand did reach out. I can remember half a dozen times when she made a gesture toward your parents only to be ignored or refused. From what I understand, your father stayed out of it as nearly as he could. The fight was Rita's, and while he was certainly on her side, she was the one who kept the game alive. Virginia was even worse. She seemed to relish the split, and I'm really not sure why. She must have had issues of her own. In my experience, any time someone makes such a big deal about autonomy, it's probably a cover for something else. So, Grand tried to include them, especially after you were born, but they'd have nothing to do with her. If she and Daddy were out of town, the three of them would come to visit and, of course, they'd bring you, but there was always a stealthy feel to it. I remember thinking they enjoyed it, sneaking around behind her back."

"Why?"

"Because it forced the rest of us to declare ourselves. Every time we welcomed them—which we did on numerous occasions—it put us squarely in their camp. Maura and Sarah felt guilty about deceiving Grand. She'd come home from a trip and none of us would say a word. Sometimes I have to wonder what she knew. She has her network of spies, even to this day, so someone must have told her. She never let on, but maybe that was her way of making sure there was contact even if she couldn't enjoy it herself."

I thought about it for a moment, turning her comments over in my mind. "I'd like to believe you, and I guess I do in some ways. I know there are two sides to every story. Obviously, Aunt Gin took it seriously enough to maintain silence on the subject until the day she died. I never knew any of this until three years ago."

"It must be difficult to cope with."

"Well, yes. In part because it's been presented to me as finished business, a done deal. To you, it must be old news, but to me it's not. I still have to figure out what to do with my piece of it. The breech had a huge impact on how I turned out."

"Well. You could have done worse than having Virginia Kinsey for a role model. She might have been an odd duck, but she was ahead of her time."

"That about covers it."

Susanna looked at her watch. "I really should go. I don't know about you, but I find conversations like this exhausting. You can only take in so much and then you have to stop and digest. Will you call me sometime?"

"I'll try."

"Good. That would make me happy."

Once she was gone, I locked the office door and sat down at my desk. I picked up the photo of my mother and studied it at length. The picture had been taken at the ranch. The background was out of focus, but she and her sister were standing on a wooden porch with railings like the ones I'd seen at the Manse. By squinting, I could make out a group of people standing to one side, all holding champagne flutes. The young men wore tuxedos and the girls were decked out in long white dresses similar to the one Rita Cynthia wore. In many ways, hair and clothing styles hadn't changed that much. Given any formal occasion, you could lift these people out of their decade and set them down in ours without dramatic differences. The only vintage note was the white shoes my mother wore with their open toes and faintly clunky heels.

My mother was slim, and her bare shoulders and arms were flawless. Her face was heart-shaped, her complexion smooth and clear. Her hair might have been naturally curly—it was hard to tell—but it had been done up for the occasion, tumbling across her shoulders. She wore a white flower behind one ear, as did Susanna, who was loosely encircled by my mother's arms. It looked like my mother was whispering some secret that both of them enjoyed. Susanna's face was turned up to hers with a look of unexpected delight. I could almost feel the hug that must have followed once the picture was snapped.

I placed the frame on my desk, sitting back in my swivel chair with my feet propped up. Several things occurred to me that I hadn't thought of before. I was now twice my mother's age the day the photograph was taken. Within four months of that date, my parents would be married, and by the time she was my age, she'd have a daughter three years old. By then my parents would have had only another two years to live. It occurred to me that if my mother had survived, she'd be seventy. I tried to imagine what it would be like to have a mother in my life—the phone calls, the visits and shopping trips, holiday rituals so alien to me. I'd been resistant to the Kinseys, feeling not only adamant but hostile to the idea of continued contact. Now I wondered why the offer of simple comfort felt like such a threat. Wasn't it possible that I could establish a connection with my mother through her two surviving sisters? Surely, Maura and Susanna shared many of her traits—gestures and phrases, values and attitudes ingrained in them since birth. While my mother was gone, couldn't I experience some small fragment of her love through my cousins and aunts? It didn't seem too much to ask, although I still wasn't clear what price I might be expected to pay.

I locked the office early, leaving the photo of my mother in the center of my desk. Driving home, I couldn't resist touching on the issue, much in the same way the tongue seeks the socket from which a tooth has just been pulled. The compulsion resulted in the same shudder-producing blend of satisfaction and repugnance. I needed to talk to Henry. He'd offered counsel and advice (which I'd largely ignored) since the Kinseys had first surfaced. I knew he'd be quick to see my conflict: the comfort of isolation versus cloying suffocation; independence versus bondage; safety versus betrayal. It was not in my makeup to imagine emotional states in between. I saw it as all or nothing, which is what made it difficult to risk the status quo. My life wasn't perfect, but I knew its limitations. I remembered Susanna's comment about a passion for autonomy serving as a cover for something else. When she'd said it, I'd been too startled to wonder what she meant. She'd been referring to Aunt Gin, whose hard heart I'd assimilated as a substitute for love. Had she been alluding to me as well?

Once I reached my neighborhood, I spotted an Austin Healy parked in my favorite place. I did a U-turn and found a space across the street. I pushed through my squeaking gate and down the driveway to Henry's backyard. He'd hauled his lawn furniture out of storage, hosed off the chairs, and added a set of dark green cushions with the tags still attached. Two glasses and a pitcher of iced tea rested on a small redwood table, along with a plate of homemade oatmeal cookies with raisins. At first I thought he'd meant them for me, but then I spotted him in the far corner of the yard, showing off his garden to a woman I'd never seen. The tableau bore an eerie similarity to an earlier occasion when a woman named Lila Sams had waltzed into Henry's life.

He smiled when he saw me, gesturing me over so he could make the introductions. "Kinsey, this is Mattie Halstead from San Francisco. She stopped off to see us on her way to L.A." And to Mattie, he said, "Kinsey rents the studio . . ."

"Of course. Nice to meet you. Henry's talked quite a bit about you."

"It's nice meeting you, too," I said, with a sly glance at him. He'd had his hair trimmed, and I noticed he was wearing a white dress shirt and long pants. I didn't think he'd ever gotten that spiffed up for a woman before. Mattie was easily his height and just as trim. Her silver hair was cut short and layered in a windblown mop. She wore a white silk shirt, gray slacks, and stylish low-heeled shoes. The jewelry she wore—matching earrings and a bracelet—were custom-made, hammered silver and amethysts.

She regarded me with intelligent gray eyes. "I was afraid he might be away so I called from Carmel when I arrived there last night. I'm taking my time, stopping to see friends as I travel down the coast."

"Is this business or pleasure?"

"A little bit of both. I'm delivering some paintings to

a gallery in San Diego. I could've crated them for shipping, but I needed a break."

"You were on the cruise Henry took?"

"Yes, but I'm afraid that was work. This is my time off."

"Mattie teaches drawing and painting, and she lectures on art. Nell took her watercolor class and ended up doing quite well."

"Better than Lewis," Mattie said, with a smile. "I felt so bad for him. I've never seen anyone quite so enthusiastic."

"He was flirting," Henry said reprovingly before turning to me. "Why don't you join us? We were just about to sit down and have a glass of iced tea."

"I better pass on that, thanks. I've got some reading to do and then I thought I'd sneak in a run. My schedule's been horsed up and I owe myself one."

"What about supper? We're heading up to Rosie's at six."

"No way. I don't intend to go until she gets off this kick of hers. Gourmet entrails. Did Henry mention that?"

"He warned me, but I'm actually a fan of liver and onions."

"Yeah, but the liver of what beast? I won't risk it myself. You ought to have him do the cooking. He's terrific."

She smiled at him. "Maybe another time. I've been looking forward to reconnecting with William and Rosie. They were dear."

"How long will you be here?"

"Just one night. I have a reservation at the Edgewater, my favorite hotel. My husband and I used to come here for anniversaries," she said. "I'll take off in the morning as soon as it's light. With luck, I can avoid the rush-hour traffic through Los Angeles."

"Well, it's too bad we won't have time to chat. Do you plan to stop by on the return trip?"

"We'll see how it goes. I don't want to be a nuisance."

"Maybe you can talk him into cooking for you then."

I let myself into the apartment, tossed my bag on the kitchen counter, and headed up the stairs. I didn't have any reading to catch up on and I'd done my three-mile run at six A.M. I told those tiny fibs to make sure Mattie and Henry had some time alone. I peered out the bathroom window, taking in the truncated view of the two of them down below. It was not quite four o'clock. I managed to kill an hour and a half and then thought about where to go for supper that night. I was serious about boycotting Rosie's until she abandoned her newfound passion for animal by-product cookery. As it was currently Happy Hour, I knew Dolan would be at CC's. I could have joined him, but I didn't want to sit and count his drinks while inhaling his secondhand smoke. I returned to the bathroom window and peered down at the backyard. Henry and Mattie were gone, but their two lawn chairs remained, pulled slightly closer together than they'd been when I'd first arrived home. I could see the lights on in his kitchen, so they were probably fortifying themselves with Black Jack on ice before braving Rosie's food.

Now that the coast was clear, I grabbed my shoulder bag and a jacket and scooted out the front door. I retrieved my car and drove to the McDonald's on lower Milagra Street. I'm at the drive-through lane so often, the take-out servers recognize my voice and deal with me by name. On impulse, I ordered extras and went to Stacey's house. In my opinion, there's no condition in life that can't be ameliorated by a dose of junk food.

When I knocked on his screen door, I could see him perched on a cardboard carton in the living room. His desk drawers were open and a shredder was plugged into an extension cord that trailed across the room. He motioned me in.

I held up the white bag. "I hope you haven't eaten supper. I've got Cokes, french fries, and Quarter Pounders with cheese. Very nourishing."

"I don't have much appetite, but I'll be happy to keep you company."

"Fair enough."

I left the bag on the desk and moved into the kitchen where I found a package of paper plates and a roll of paper towels. I returned to the living room, put the dinnerware on the floor, and hauled over two boxes from the stack against the wall. I sat on one box and used the second as a table that I arranged between us. I unpacked Cokes, two large cartons of fries, packets of ketchup and salt, and a paper-wrapped QP with cheese for each of us. I squeezed ketchup on the fries, salted everything in sight, and then downed my QP in approximately eight bites. "I'm going for the land speed record here."

Stacey lifted the top of his bun and eyed his burger with misgivings. "I've never eaten one of these."

I paused in the midst of wiping my mouth. "You're joking."

"I'm not." He tried a cautious bite, which he chewed with suspicion, letting the flavors mingle in his mouth. He wagged his head from side to side. With his second bite, he seemed to get the hang of it, and after that he ate with the same dispatch I did.

I reached into the bag and took out another burger that I passed to him. This time, halfway through, a nearly subliminal moan escaped his lips. I laughed.

"Where'd you get that?" I asked, pointing to the shredder with a french fry.

"Fellow next door," he said, pausing to swallow his bite. "I'm cleaning out my desk. Can't quite bring myself to shred my receipts. I don't intend to file a tax return. I figure I'll be dead before the IRS catches up with me. Even so, I worry about an audit without the proper paperwork on hand." He licked his fingers and wiped his mouth. "Thank you. That was great. I haven't had an appetite for weeks."

"Happy to help."

He gathered all the trash and put it back in the bag, then turned and made a free throw, tossing it in the wastebasket. He reached into the bottom drawer and took out a cardboard box filled with black-and-white photographs. He set the box in his lap, picked up a handful, and fed them to the machine.

I watched while six images were reduced to slivers. "What are you *doing*?"

"I told you. Cleaning out my desk."

"But those are family photographs. You can't do that."

"Why not? I'm the only one left."

"But you can't just *destroy* them. I can't believe you'd do that."

"Why leave the job for someone else? At least if I do it, there's a personal connection." He sang, "Good-bye, Uncle Schmitty. Bye Cousin Mortimer . . ." Two more images were converted to confetti in the shredder bin.

I put a hand on his arm. "I'll take them."

"And do what? You don't even know these folks. I

can't identify the better half of 'em myself. Look at this. Who's he? I swear I never saw this guy before in my life. Must have been a family friend." He touched the edge of the photo to the shredder teeth and watched it disappear before he picked up the next.

"Don't shred them. Aren't those your *parents*?"

"Sure, but they've been dead for years."

"I can't stand this. Give me those. I'll pretend they're mine."

"Don't be ridiculous. You're alone just like me. If I let you take 'em, someone else will end up throwing them in *your* trash."

"So what? Come on, Stace. Please."

He hesitated and finally nodded. "Okay. But it's dumb."

He handed me the box of photos, which I placed near my bag out of his reach. I was worried he'd change his mind and shred someone else. He turned his attention to a file folder marked AUTO INSURANCE and fed its contents into the shredder. Idly, he said, "I almost forgot to mention, Joe Mandel called with an address for Iona Mathis. She's living in the high desert, little town called Peaches."

"Which is where?"

"Above San Bernardino, off Highway 138. There's no phone in her name so she might be bunking in with someone else. Did I tell you Mandel got a line on the red Mustang? This guy Gant, the original owner, died about ten years ago, but his widow says the car was stolen from an auto upholstery shop in Quorum, California, where he'd taken it to get the seats replaced. Gant had the car towed back from Lompoc, but it was such a mess he turned around and sold it to the guy whose shop it was stolen from—fellow named Ruel McPhee. According to our sources, the car's now registered to him. I've left him four messages, but so far I haven't heard back. Con thinks it's worth a trip down there just to see what's what."

"Where's Quorum? I've never heard of it."

"Well, neither had I, but Con says it's just south of Blythe near the Arizona line. Now here's the kicker on that. Turns out Frankie Miracle grew up in Quartzsite, Arizona, which is just a few miles from Blythe in the same neck of the woods. Con wants to take a detour through Peaches and talk to Iona Mathis on his way to Quorum."

"When?"

"Tomorrow morning he says. I thought I better warn you in case you want to make up an excuse."

"Not at all. I'll go. I could use a change of scene. What about you? Are you feeling up to it?"

"You two go on. I'll wait and see what the doc has to say. They may want me back in the hospital for the third time this month. Talk about tedious."

"How're you holding up?"

"I'm not thrilled with this new development, but I don't see that I have much choice."

"I'll hold good thoughts for you."

"I could use a few," he said. He hesitated. "This may be out of line, but I'm wondering if Con's told you about his wife's suicide."

"I knew she had cancer, but he never said a word."

"That's why he gets so pissy on the subject. He thinks he could have saved her."

"Could he?"

"Of course not. When it comes right down to it, you can't save anyone except yourself. Sometimes, you can't even do that. Anyway, I thought you should know."

He smiled to himself for reasons I suspect were unrelated to me. I watched while his army discharge papers disappeared into the shredder with a grinding sound.

12

My packing for the trip took all of five minutes. At most, I figured we'd be gone for two days, which meant a toothbrush, toothpaste, two clean T-shirts, a sweatshirt, two pairs of socks, four pairs of underpants, and the oversized T-shirt I sleep in. I shoved it all into a duffel the size of a bolster pillow. Since I was wearing jeans and my Sauconys, the only other items I'd need were my running sweats, my windbreaker, and my little portable Smith-Corona. Dolan had opted for an early start, which in his terms translated to a 9:30 departure. This gave me time to sneak in a three-mile run, followed by a supersetting weight session at the gym. I was racking up virtue points in case I didn't have the chance to exercise while I was on the road.

By the time Dolan pulled up, I was sitting on the curb, reading a paperback novel with my shoulder bag, typewriter, and duffel. At my side, I had two rubber-band-bound stacks of index cards in my bag. He must have run his vehicle through a car wash because the exterior was clean and the floorboards were free of gas receipts and discarded fast-food wrappers. Now that we were cohorts, he didn't feel required to escort me around the car and let me in. I hauled the door open, while he reached over the seat and shoved his suitcase to one side. "You can put your things back there with mine unless you'd rather leave 'em in the trunk."

"This is fine." I tucked my Smith-Corona on the floor, tossed my duffel in the rear seat, and got in. I tried hauling the door shut, but the hinges responded sluggishly and refused to budge. Dolan finally reached across me and gave the door a yank. It closed with a thunk. I wrestled with the seat belt, jerking until I'd pulled sufficient length to reach the catch and snap it down. I spotted a fresh pack of cigarettes on the dash. "I hope you don't intend to smoke."

"Not with the windows closed."

"You are so considerate. You have a map?"

"In the side pocket. I thought we'd go the back way. I'd take the 101 to the 405 and hit the 5 from there, but with my bum ticker, I don't want to risk the freeway in case I die at the wheel."

"You're really making me feel good about this."

Dolan turned onto the 101 heading south while I flapped at the California map and refolded it into a manageable size. By my estimate, Peaches was ninety miles away, roughly an hour and a half. Happily, Dolan didn't like chitchat any more than I did. I sat and stared out the window, wondering if love would blossom between Henry and Mattie.

The coastline looked smoky. There was a harsh light on the ocean, but the surf was calm, advancing toward the shore in long, smooth undulations. The islands were barely visible twenty-six miles offshore. Steep hills sloped down to the highway, the chaparral a dark mossy green, flourishing after a wet autumn and the long damp winter months.

In many sections of the hillside, the vegetation had been overtaken by thick patches of cactus shaped like Ping-Pong paddles, abristle with thorns. I've always thought California prisons could discourage escape by seeding the surrounding landscape with vicious plants. Missing prisoners could be located by their howls of dismay and could spend their stay in solitary confinement picking thorns out of their heiniebumpers.

After twenty minutes, I glanced at Dolan. "You have kids?"

"Naw. Grace used to talk about it, but it didn't interest me. Kids change your life. We were fine as is."

"Any regrets?"

"I don't spend a lot of time on regrets. How about you? Are you planning to have kids?"

"I can't quite picture it, but I won't rule it out. I'm not exactly famous for my relationships with men."

At Perdido, we caught the 126 heading inland. The power lines disappeared. There was a dusting of snow on the distant mountain peaks, an odd contrast to the vivid green in the fields below. In the citrus groves, oranges hung on the trees like Christmas ornaments. The roadside fruit stands were boarded up, but they'd be open for business in another month or so. We passed through two small agricultural communities that hadn't changed in years. This section of the road was known as Blood Alley: only two lanes wide with an occasional passing lane in which the fiery crashes usually occurred. I kept a close eye on Dolan in the event he was on the verge of conking out on me.

He said, "Quit worrying."

At Palmdale, we turned east off Highway 14, picking

up the 18. Ancient, cranky-looking billboards indicated land for sale. I saw a sign for 213th Street with a dirt road shooting off to a vanishing point. We passed a hand-painted sign that read PAIRALEGALS AVAILABLE: WILLS, CONTRACTS, DIVORCES, NOTER REPUBLIC. According to the map, the road we were on skirted the western border of the Mojave Desert at an altitude of 4,500 feet.

I checked the map again and said, "Wow. I never understood the size of the Mojave. It's really big."

"Twenty-five thousand square miles if you include the portions in Nevada, Arizona, and Utah. You know much about the desert?"

"I've picked up the occasional odd fact, but that's about it."

"I've been reading about scorpions. Book claims they're the first air-breathing animal. They have a rudimentary brain, but their eyesight's poor. They probably don't perceive anything they can't actually touch first. You see two scorpions together, they're either making love or one of them is being eaten by the other. There's a lesson in there somewhere, but I can't figure out what. Probably has to do with the nature of true love."

I don't know why, but the information made me smile. We passed a sign that read PEACHES, POP. 897. The town was marked by a scattering of Joshua trees and was notable for its abundance of abandoned businesses. The San Gabriel Mountains loomed on our right, antiqued with snow, which had settled into all the crevices, defining them in white. Timbers formed a windbreak along the crest, while below them, I could see stands of evergreens laden with white. A freak spring storm had left mounds and patches of aging snow on the ground. Five cars had pulled over and parked on the berm where five sets of parents stood by chatting while their respective children played in the drifts. Most of the kids looked un-derdressed. As with the ocean, they'd frolic in the elements until their teeth were chattering and their lips had turned blue.

We passed a Liquor Mart that sold gas, tires, beer, and sandwiches. There were two cafés, one saloon, and no motels that I could see. There was a cluster of six single-wide trailers surrounded by chain-link fence and two real estate offices in double-wides with empty asphalt parking lots out front. What possessed people to move to Peaches in the first place? It seemed mysterious to me. What dream were they pursuing that made Peaches, California, the answer to their prayers?

Dolan did a U-turn, using the wide apron of gravel beside a service station, its gas pumps missing and its plate glass windows boarded up. The ground glittered with broken glass. Forlorn tatters of plastic wrap were caught in the bushes along the road. He backtracked as far as the enclave of mismatched trailers, which had the letters *A, B, C, D, E,* and *F* on small painted signs in front. A sign announced PEACH GROVE MOBILE HOME PARK, which was actually not a "park" so much as two rows of trailers with space remaining in the event a seventh trailer decided to pull in. Dolan nosed his car into a graveled area near a row of battered mailboxes and the two of us got out. I waited while he went through the ritual of tucking his gun in the trunk. "Looks like F's down that way," he said.

I followed him along the rutted two-lane dirt drive. "Wonder what she's doing up here?"

"We'll have to ask."

The door to F stood open, with a flimsy sliding screen across the frame to allow fresh air to circulate. A small handmade plaque said NAILS BY IONA with a telephone

number too small to read in passing. A faded width of
awning formed a covered porch, complete with bright
green indoor-outdoor carpeting underfoot. The trailer
was old and small. Two women were seated in the kitchenette, one on a banquette and the other on a chrome
dinette chair pulled close to a hinged table that was supported by one leg. Both turned to look at us. The
younger of the two continued to paint the older woman's nails.

Dolan said, "Is one of you Iona Mathis?"

The younger said, "That's me." She went back to
brushing dark carmine polish on the thumbnail of the
other woman's left hand. On the table between them, I
could see an orange stick, emery boards, a bottle of cuticle remover, cotton balls, a nail brush, and a plastic
halfmoon bowl filled with soapy water. To the right of
the older woman, there was a pack of Winstons, with a
book of paper matches tucked under the cellophane. The
ashtray was filled with butts.

The older woman smiled and said, "I'm Iona's mom,
Annette."

"Lieutenant Dolan with the Santa Teresa Police Department. This is Miss Millhone. She's a private detective."

Iona slid a look at us before she started work on her
mother's index finger. If she was sixteen when she married Frankie, she'd be close to thirty-five now, roughly
my age. Oh, hey, I was a little older, but who was keeping track? I tried to put myself in her place, wondering
what might persuade me to live here and make my living
nipping someone else's cuticles and massaging their toes.
She was just shy of pretty. I watched her with interest
through the softening haze of the screen door, trying to
figure out where her looks fell short. Her hair was a lus-

trous brown, wavy, shoulder-length, and in need of a trim. She kept it parted in the center, which made her face look too long. She had full lips, a strong nose, brown eyes, and dark brows that were a shade too thick. She had a mole on her upper lip and one on her left cheek. In many ways, she still looked sixteen—lanky and round-shouldered. Her feet were bare, and she wore faded knee-ripped jeans and an India-print tunic in shades of rust and brown.

Annette leaned toward her daughter and said, "Baby, if you're not going to ask the man I will." When Iona made no response, she looked back at Dolan. "Hon, I wish you'd tell us why you're here because you're scaring me to death." Iona's mother, surely in her fifties, looked closer to thirty-five than Iona did. She had the same strong nose, but she'd had hers surgically reduced to something thinner and more sunken. Her hair, which she wore pulled up in a ponytail, was the same shade of brown, but of a uniformly intense hue that suggested she was dyeing it to cover gray. A sleeveless white knit top emphasized her big boobs, cantilevered over a thick waist and slightly rounded tummy. She wore red shorts and red canvas wedgies. Her toenails had been polished in the same red Iona was using on her fingernails. I thought she'd have been wise to cover more of herself than she had.

Dolan said, "We have a few questions about Iona's ex. You mind if we come in?"

"Door's open," Annette said.

Dolan slid open the screen door and stepped into the trailer, then sidestepped to his left so I'd have room to enter. Once inside, I moved to the right and perched on the near end of the blue plastic-padded bench where Annette was sitting. There was a long padded cushion across the back of the bench, and I was guessing at the presence of a mechanism that would allow the couch to level out into a double bed once the hinged table had been flattened against the wall. Did the two women share the trailer, or did Mom have her own? Dolan and I had agreed that he'd conduct the interview as it was confusing to have questions lobbed from two directions at once. I was there primarily to observe and to take mental notes.

Beyond the kitchenette, I could see a sliding door on the right that I assumed was the bathroom. Dead ahead, I saw the double bed that filled the only bedroom. I'm a sucker for small spaces, and I wouldn't have minded living in a place like this, though I'd have held out for something clean. I did love the diminutive sink and the half-size oven, the four-burner cooktop, and the wee refrigerator tucked under the counter. It was like a playhouse, designed for dollies, tea parties, and other games of make-believe. I focused my attention on Iona, whose bad posture was probably a side effect of hunching over her table all day.

Annette said, "You haven't said which ex, but if you're a police lieutenant, you must be talking about Frank. Her second husband, Lars, never broke the law in his life. He wouldn't even cross the street without a crosswalk. He drove Iona crazy. Here, she went out and found a fellow as different from Frank as you could possibly get and then it turns out he's worse. He suffered from that obsessive-compulsive syndrome? Shoot. Everything he did, he had to repeat six more times before he'd allow himself to move on. Getting anything accomplished took hours. I about went insane." She peered closely at her pinkie. "Baby, I think you got outside the line there. You see that?"

"Sorry." Iona used her thumb nail to eradicate the line of red that had encroached on Annette's cuticle.

Dolan said, "Mind if I smoke?"

Annette's eyes flicked briefly to Lieutenant Dolan's left hand. He wasn't wearing a wedding ring and it must have occurred to her that he might be a bachelor. "Only if you light one for me," she said. "Iona has a fit if I mess up a nail before she's done with all ten."

Dolan reached over and picked up Annette's pack of Winstons. He shook one free and placed it between her lips. She rested her hand seductively on his while he lit her cigarette. He then extracted and lit one from his own pack, apparently scorning her brand.

Annette inhaled deeply, blew a stream of smoke upward, and then removed the cigarette and placed it on the ashtray, being careful with her fingertips. "Lord, that tastes good. It just bores me to tears people get so tense about smoking these days. What's the big whoop-dee-do? It's no skin off their nose." Her eyes slid to me. "You smoke?"

"I did once upon a time," I said, hoping I didn't sound quite as pious as I felt.

To Dolan, she said, "What's Frank up to? We haven't heard from him in years, have we, baby?"

Iona ignored her mother and concentrated on her work.

Dolan said, "You know he's out on parole."

Annette made a face as though afflicted by a mildly spasming bowel. "I guess it was bound to happen. I never did care for the man myself. I hope you're not going to tell us he knows where she is."

"We talked to him yesterday and he didn't mention her."

"Well, thank god for that."

"Are you worried he'll make contact?"

"I wouldn't say 'worried,' but I don't like the idea."

Dolan focused on Iona. "When did you see him last? Do you remember the date?"

Annette stared at her daughter and when Iona failed to speak up, she said, "Iona, answer the man. What's the matter with you? I didn't raise you like that."

Iona shot a dark look at her mother. "You want me to mess these up or not?"

Annette smiled at Dolan. "She felt sorry for him. Frank's parents disowned him. His father's an oral surgeon, makes big bucks cutting on people's gums, but he's a stick-in-the-mud. His mother isn't much better. They had three other boys who did well, so naturally Frank lost out by comparison. Not that he wasn't a little shit from birth. Iona always said he was sweet, but you couldn't prove it by me. I thought he was kind of clinging, if you want to know the truth. He certainly became possessive toward the end of their marriage. Six months."

"Why'd the two of you break up?"

"I don't have to answer that," Iona said.

"He ever knock you around?"

This time when Iona declined to answer, Annette seemed happy to fill in. "Only twice that I know of. He was stoned all the time back then—"

"*Most* of the time, not *all*, Mom. Don't exaggerate."

"Oh, pardon. I stand corrected. He was stoned *most of the time* and when he was, he got mean. She told him if he didn't straighten up his act she'd kick his butt out the door. They were living in Venice then, right on one of the canals down there. All these little baby ducks. Didn't smell so nice, but they were cute as could be. Frank kept on drinking and he refused to budge, so I sent her the money to get out."

"Is that when he connected with Cathy Lee Pearse?"

"Oh, that was awful, wasn't it?" Annette said. "I still get the shivers when I stop and think of it. He'd only known her a week before the incident."

"Is that what you call it, *an incident*?" Dolan asked. I could tell he was trying to suppress the outrage in his voice.

Iona put the brush back in the polish bottle and screwed the top shut. "You don't have to take that tone. For your information, Cathy Lee came onto him. She was a gold digger, pure and simple. All moody and temperamental. Frankie said she was violent, especially when she drank, which she'd been doing that night. She turned on him just like that." Iona snapped her fingers. "Came at him with a pair of scissors, so what was he supposed to do, let her jam the blades through his throat?"

Dolan's expression was bland. "He could have grabbed her wrist. It seems somewhat excessive to stab her fourteen times. You'd think once or twice would have done the job."

Iona began to tidy up her work space. "I don't know anything about that."

"Did you know Cathy Lee yourself?" Dolan was clearly working to maintain the contact now that she'd decided to talk.

"Sure. Frankie'd picked up a job painting this house for a friend of his so we'd moved in next door to her the week before. She was a tease, hanging out in her bikini, shaking her tits at him when he was out in the yard. Frankie felt terrible about what happened. He said he wished he could undo it, but by then it was too late."

"I heard you went back to him when the case went to trial. What was that about?"

"He needed me, that's what. Everybody else turned their backs on him."

"Iona's just like me. Can't resist a wounded bird. Lars was the pits. Had to count everything. He was great for chopping onions—one, two, three, four, five . . ."

"Is that it, Iona? You see Frankie as a wounded bird?"

"He's a good person when he's sober and off drugs."

"Did he ever talk to you about what happened after Cathy Lee was killed?"

"Like what?"

"I'm wondering what he did between the time he killed Cathy Lee and the time the cops picked him up. There's a two-day gap when we don't know where he was."

Iona shrugged. "Beats me. Frankie and I were busted up by then."

Annette said, "Shortest marriage on record. Divorce took six times longer, didn't it?"

Iona declined a response, speaking to Dolan instead. "I don't know what he did or where he went after I moved out."

"Baby, I thought you said he ended up at your place. 'Member that? You'd moved into that studio apartment in Santa Teresa . . ."

"Mom."

"Well, why can't you tell him that if it's the truth? Believe me, Lieutenant, Iona knows better than to aid and abet. She fed him a meal and let him stay the night and then said he had to hit the road. I begged her to call the sheriff, but it was no, no, no. She was scared if she turned him in, he'd come back and retaliate."

"Mother, is there any way you could just shut the fuck up?"

"I'm trying to be helpful. You might think about that yourself. Now what's this about, Lieutenant?"

"We think he had contact with a young girl hitchhiking in the Lompoc area. It's possible he picked her up on his way to see his dad."

"Oh my lord. You don't mean to tell me he killed someone else?"

"That remains to be seen. Her body was dumped in a quarry on the outskirts of town. Right now, we're trying to find out who she is."

Iona stared at him. I thought she was on the verge of volunteering information, but she seemed to catch herself. "Why didn't you ask him, if you saw him yesterday?"

Dolan smiled. "He said he couldn't remember. We thought he might've said something about her to you."

Iona focused her attention on her mother's nails. "First I've heard."

When it was clear she wasn't going to say more, Dolan glanced at Annette. "I'm curious how the two of you ended up in Peaches."

She took another drag of her cigarette. "Originally, we're from a little town out near Blythe. Iona's grandparents—I'm talking now about my mom and dad—invested in sixty acres; must have been 1946. What we're sitting on right now is the only parcel left. I was the one had the idea for a trailer park after they passed on. It seemed like a smart move since we already owned the land. We each have our own place and the four other tenants pay rent. I work part-time over at the café; Iona has this business, so the two of us get by."

"What town?" I asked.

She looked at me with surprise, as though she'd forgotten I was there. "Come again?"

"What town are you from?"

"Oh. Little burg called Creosote. You probably never heard of it. Two miles this side of the Arizona line."

"You're kidding. I met someone else from Creosote just two days ago. A guy named Pudgie Clifton."

Iona's dark gaze strayed to mine.

Annette perked right up. "Oh, Iona's known Pudgie since elementary school. Isn't he the fella you dated before Frank?"

"We didn't *date,* Mom. We hung out. There's a big difference."

"Looked like dating to me. You went off and stayed weekends with him if memory serves." When Annette reached for her cigarette again, her hand brushed against the edge of the ashtray, dinging her freshly painted nail. "Oh, shit. Now lookit what I've done."

She held her hand out to Iona, who studied the smudge. She wet her index finger and rubbed it lightly on the smear of red polish, effectively smoothing it out.

Dolan said, "You must have known Pudgie well."

"He mostly messed around with kids from somewhere else."

"Except for weekends when he went off with you," he said.

She looked up sharply. "We took some road trips, okay? He liked driving my car. Doesn't mean I screwed him. We were friends."

"Did he and Frankie know each other back then?"

"How would I know? I'm not in charge of either one of them."

There was a tap at the door. "Iona, honey? Sorry to interrupt." A woman stood on the porchlet, peering in at us.

Iona said, "My next appointment. I hope you don't mind."

"Not at all. We'll wait and talk to you when you get off work."

Annette scooted over from behind the table, her bare thighs creating fart sounds against the plastic seat. I stood up to make room for her while Dolan stepped outside. Annette was already chatting with Iona's client, wagging her fingers in the air. "Hey, sugar, take a look. This is called Cherries Jubilee. The shade would look gorgeous with your coloring."

The other woman, in her forties, didn't seem that excited by the prospect, as her coloring was blah.

Annette clomped down the trailer step on her canvas wedgies and tucked her hand through Lieutenant Dolan's arm. "Iona won't be long. I'm working lunch today. Why don't you walk me over to the Moonlight and have a bite to eat. It's on me."

I said, "Great. Let's do that. What hours do you work?"

She said, "Usually lunchtime on. We're open from five in the morning until ten at night. The only other restaurant is the Mountain View so people go back and forth, depending on their mood."

The three of us walked down the rutted driveway and across the two-lane road. Once in the café, we had our pick of the empty tables. Annette said, "It's mostly drinks and cold sandwiches. I can fry up some burgers if you want something hot."

"Sounds good to me. How about you, Kinsey?"

"Fine."

"What about something to drink? We have coffee, tea, Coke, and Sprite."

Dolan said, "Coke, I guess."

"Make that two."

Annette took her place behind the counter. She turned on the gas burner under the griddle, removed two hamburger patties from the refrigerator, and slapped them on the grill. "It'll just be a minute."

Dolan said, "Things slow today?"

"Things are slow every day."

She made a quick return trip with a dish of celery, carrot sticks, and green olives. She'd tucked a bottle of ketchup and a squeeze bottle of yellow mustard in her apron pocket and she placed those on the table as well. By the time she got back to the griddle, the patties were done and she assembled our plates. "I forgot to ask how you wanted these," she said as she unloaded her tray.

"This is fine," I said. I was busy doctoring my burger with mustard, ketchup, pickle, and onion. Not up to QP standards, but it would have to do.

Dolan said, "What are the chances she's been in touch with Frank?"

"You think he might've had something to do with that young girl's death?

"I have no idea. We were hoping Iona could help us fill in some blanks."

Across the road at the trailer park, we could see a car pull onto the highway, turn left, and speed off with Iona at the wheel. Annette leaned toward the window, frowning slightly to herself. "Wonder what that's about?"

Dolan bit into his burger. "Guess she doesn't want to talk to us."

13

We left the tiny town of Peaches at 2:00, when it finally became apparent Iona wouldn't return. The ever-loquacious Annette had nattered away, answering every question we asked, though most of the information consisted of her own attitudes. It was clear she was no friend of Frankie's, and I was reasonably certain she'd told us as much as she knew. Iona, on the other hand, had clearly left the vicinity to avoid being pressed. Annette wanted to believe she was done with Frankie Miracle, but I wasn't so sure.

From Highway 14, we took Highway 138 as far as the 15, then angled our way down to the eastbound 10, otherwise known as the San Bernardino Freeway. Despite Dolan's worries about his heart, there is quite literally no other way to get to Blythe. This 175-mile stretch of highway extends from the eastern edges of Los Angeles and crosses the state line into Arizona at Blythe. For close to three hours, Dolan kept his foot pressed to the accelerator while the road disappeared beneath us. The scenery became monotonous, the typical urban sprawl of tract housing, billboards, industrial plants, shopping malls, and railroad tracks. The highway was lined with palms, evergreens, and eucalyptus trees. We passed recreational vehicle "estates," an RV country club, and an RV resort and spa. This was a long stretch of land where no one intended to put down roots. We stopped once for gas in Orocopia and I picked up a copy of the *Mobile Home Gazette*; sixteen pages of coupons for discount dinners, cruise specials, golf lessons, custom dentures, and early-bird bingo.

After Palm Springs, the land flattened and the color faded from the landscape. For mile after mile, there was only sand and rock, chaparral, power lines, and passing cars. On either side of the road, at the horizon, the land rose to a fringe of foothills that confined the view. Everything was beige and gray and a pale dusty green. California deserts consist, in the main, of pale soils—fawn, cinnamon, sepia, and pink. We passed the state prison, its presence underlined by signs that advised us not to pick up hitchhikers. The speed limit was seventy, but the landscape was so vast that we scarcely seemed to move. Aside from the Salton Sea to the south of us, the map showed only dry lakes.

I said, "How does anything manage to grow out here?"

Dolan smiled. "The desert's a marvel of adaptability. California desert has one rainy season where southern Arizona has two. The rest of the year, you have drought. If you had seeds that germinated right after the rains, the young plants wouldn't survive the hard sun and heat. Lot of seeds are covered with wax that prevents them from absorbing water until a period of time has passed. Once the wax wears off, they germinate, and that's where the food chain originates. Rabbits and desert rats turn the vegetation into animal flesh and that provides dinner for the predators. Snakes eat the rodents and then the bobcats eat snakes."

"Very nice," I said.

"Efficient. Like crime. Everybody's busy eating someone else."

He went on in this fashion, regaling me with the mating and egg-laying habits of various desert insects, including the black widow, the brown widow, and the tarantula hawk, until I sang, "I'm getting sick here." That shut him up.

At Blythe, we turned south, taking the two-lane state road that ran twelve miles to the community of Quorum, population 12,676. On the map, the town was little more than a circle. Dolan slowed as the outlying residential properties began to appear. The houses were plain and the yards were flat. We reached the central business district less than a minute later on a main street six lanes wide. Buildings were low, as though by hugging the ground, the inhabitants could escape the penetrating desert sun. Palm trees seemed to flourish. There were numerous motels along the thoroughfare, most with wistful-sounding names, like the Bayside Motor Court and the Sea Shell Motel. Among the commercial establishments, many seemed travel-related: gas stations, car dealerships, tire sales, car washes, camper shells, and automotive repair. Occasionally, I'd catch sight of a locksmith or a beauty shop, but not much else. Here, as in Peaches, there were numerous boarded-up businesses; signs with the glass punched out, leaving only the frame. Jody's Café, Rupert's Auto Radiator, and a furniture store were among those that had failed. Glancing to my right, I could see that even the secondary streets tended to be four lanes wide. There was clearly nothing out here but space.

As we drove through town, we made a brief detour, stopping in at the Quorum Police Department and the Riverside County Sheriff's substation, which were next door to each other on North Winter Street. I waited in the car while Dolan talked to detectives in both agencies, letting them know he was in the area and what he was working on. Technically, neither visit was required, but he didn't want to step on any toes. It was smart to lay the groundwork in case we needed local assistance later. When he got back in the car and slammed the door, he said, "Probably a waste of time, but it's worked in my favor often enough to make it worthwhile."

It was close to 5:30 by then and the afternoon temperatures were dropping rapidly. Dolan's plan was to find a motel and then cruise the town, looking for a place to eat. "We can have supper and turn in early, then scout out the auto upholstery shop first thing in the morning."

"Fine with me."

Most of the motels seemed equivalent, matching rates posted on gaudy neon signs. We settled on the Ocean View, which boasted a pool, a heated spa, and free TV. We checked in at the desk, and I waited while Dolan gave the clerk his credit card, picking up the tab on two rooms and a key for each of us. We hopped back in the car, driving the short distance so he could park in the slot directly in front of his room. Mine turned out to be right around the corner. We agreed to a brief recess during which we'd get settled.

I let myself into my room. The interior smelled like the Santa Teresa beach, which is to say, faintly of damp and less faintly of mildew. I placed my shoulder bag on the desktop and my duffel on the chair. I christened the facilities, shrugged into my windbreaker, and met Dolan at his door. Not surprisingly, his goal was to find a restaurant with a cocktail lounge attached. Failing that, he'd opt for a decent bar somewhere, after which we could eat pizza in our rooms. We stopped in the motel office, where the desk clerk recommended the Quorum Inn, two blocks down, on High Street. I'd miscalculated the chill in the desert air at night. I walked with my arms crossed, hunched against the brisk wind whipping down the wide streets. The town seemed exposed, laid open to the elements, low buildings the only hope of shelter from the desert winds.

The Quorum Inn was already packed when we arrived: the late-afternoon martini crowd firing up cigarettes, alternating bites of green olives with the mixed nuts on the bar. The walls were varnished pine and the booths were upholstered in red Naugahyde. The free-standing tables were covered with red-and-white checked cloths. Most of the menu choices were either steak or beef. The side dishes were french fries, fried onion rings, and batter-fried zucchini. You could also order a foil-wrapped baked potato smothered in butter, sour cream, bacon, and/or cheese.

We sat at the bar for the first hour while Dolan downed three Manhattans and I sipped at a puckery white wine that I diluted with ice. Once we retired to a table, he asked for a well-done twenty-two-ounce sirloin and I settled for an eight-ounce filet. By 8:00, we were back at the motel, where we parted company for the night. I read for a while and then slept the way you do with a tummy full of red meat and a shitload of cholesterol coursing through your veins.

At breakfast, I had my usual cereal while Dolan had bacon, eggs, pancakes, four cups of coffee, and five cigarettes. When he pulled out the sixth, I said, "Dolan, you have to quit this."

He hesitated. "What?"

"The booze and cigarettes and fatty foods. You'll trigger another heart attack and I'll be stuck doing CPR. Haven't you read the Surgeon General's report?"

He gestured impatiently. "Nuts to that stuff! My granddaddy lived to ninety-six and he smoked hand-rolled cigarettes from the time he was twelve until the day he died."

"Yeah, well I'll bet he hadn't had two heart attacks by the time he was your age. You keep ragging on Stacey and you're worse than he is."

"That's different."

"It is not. You want him alive and that's exactly what I'm bugging *you* about."

"If I'm interested in your opinion, I'll be sure to ask. I don't need a lecture from someone half my age."

"I'm not half your age. How old are you?"

"I'm sixty-one."

"Well, I'm thirty-six."

"The point is, I can do anything I want."

"Nah, nah, nah. I'll remind you of that next time Stacey threatens to blow his brains out."

Dolan crushed out his cigarette butt in the ashtray. "I'm tired of jawing. Time to go to work."

McPhee's Auto Upholstery was located on Hill Street in the heart of town. We parked across from the shop and took a moment to get our bearings. The morning was filled with flat, clean sunlight. The air felt pleasant, but I was guessing that by afternoon the heat, while dry, would feel oppressive. By the time the sun went down, it'd be as cold as it had been the night before. Behind the shop, we could see a small lot where six cars had been parked, each shrouded in an automobile cover. That part of the property was enclosed by heavy chain-link fence topped with razor wire. The building itself was constructed of corrugated metal with three bays on one side, the doors rolled up to reveal the shop's interior. It looked like a gas station, surrounded with the usual cracked asphalt. We could see two men at work.

"You really think the car we're after is the one C. K. saw?"

"That's what we're here to find out," he said. "We know it was stolen from here."

"If it was parked near the quarry, then what?"

"Then we'll see if we can establish a connection between the car and Jane Doe."

We got out and crossed the street to the front entrance. Under the big plate glass window, a large concrete planter sat empty except for packed dirt. To the right of the shop there was a lumberyard; to the left, a long-distance hauling company with a lot full of tractor rigs and detached semitrailers. This was a commercial neighborhood made up of businesses that catered to customers in pickups and vans.

The showroom was an extension of the shop area out back. The floor was done in black-and-white vinyl tile. Behind a glass case filled with service manuals, there was a metal desk, metal file cabinets, and a Rolodex. The top surface of the glass case was piled high with sample books showing automobile and marine vinyls, "Performance-rated fabrics for heavy-duty application." Rear and side camper windows in a variety of styles had been mounted on pegboard and hung on the wall. We picked our way through a cluster of bench and bucket car seats still exhibiting their torn upholstery. A display board was set up to show the leather/vinyl match for Ford, GM, Chrysler-Jeep Eagle, Honda, and Toyota interior upholstery. You could order any number of convertible tops, tonneau covers, floor mats, and glass or plastic window curtains.

An open door led from the showroom into the first of the three connecting bays, where one of the two men looked up. I pegged him in his mid-thirties. He was medium height, clean-shaven, his complexion ruddy. His hair had the kind of blond streaks that women pay money for. He wore it parted in the middle with strands falling loosely on either side of his face. Most of his teeth were good. There were creases around his mouth where his smile had made inroads. His hands were dirty, his nails permanently underlined with black like a lady's French tip manicure in reverse. Blue-plaid flannel shirt, jeans, desert boots. He was built like a high school football player—which is to say, some guy who'd get creamed if he played football today. I tried to decide whether I'd have been attracted to him when I was sixteen. He looked like the type I'd have had a crush on from a distance. Then again, most guys in high school were like that as far as I was concerned.

He was using a crescent wrench and a pair of pliers to dismantle a car seat that was propped up in front of him. The workbench, which extended the length of the wall behind him, was stacked with bolts of vinyl, hoses, coffee cans, sheets of foam rubber, toolboxes, cans of latex paint, tires. Two fans were blowing, thus circulating the smell of synthetics. Beside him there was a garbage bin full of scraps. A second ripped and cracked auto seat sat on a counter nearby. He was smoking a cigarette, but he put it out casually before he spoke to us. "Help you?"

Dolan put his hands in his pants pockets. "We're looking for Ruel McPhee."

"That's my dad. He's retired. Who are you?"

"Lieutenant Dolan, Santa Teresa Police Department. This is my colleague, Ms. Millhone. I didn't catch your name."

"Cornell McPhee. Are you the one who left the phone message?"

"That's my partner, Detective Oliphant. As a matter of fact, he left four and says your father never called him back."

"Sorry. I didn't realize it was urgent. I gave Dad the messages and he said he'd take care of it. I guess it slipped his mind."

The second man in the shop was older, possibly in his fifties. He'd returned to his work as soon as he figured out the conversation had nothing to do with him.

"Your dad still in town?"

Cornell put down his crescent wrench and wiped his hands on a rag. "Sure. What's this about?"

"We're hoping to track down a vehicle stolen from his shop in 1969."

Cornell's brow shifted slightly. "That car was recovered. It belonged to a guy in Arizona."

Dolan smiled briefly. "We know about him. DMV says the car's now registered to Ruel McPhee."

"What brought this up again?"

"We're looking at the possibility of a link between the car and a homicide back then."

"A homicide?"

"That's right," Dolan said. "We're taking another run at it."

"I'm still not clear why you want to talk to him."

"We have a witness who says he saw a red Mustang in

the area shortly before the body was found. We're wondering if the vehicle's the same one stolen from his shop."

"You can ask him if you want. He and Mom live on Fell. 1520. It's just a few blocks away. You go down two blocks, take a left at Ruby. You'll find Fell five blocks down. You want me to call and make sure he's there?"

"That's fine. We can swing by later if he's out somewhere," Dolan said. He indicated the seat Cornell was working on. "How long's it take to do a job like that?"

"Couple of days. Depends on the condition. You have some work you need done?"

"Might."

"What kind of car?"

"Chevy. 1979."

"Leather seat?"

"No, cloth."

Cornell smiled. "Throw a bedspread over it. You'd be better off."

"That's my idea. I just wondered what you'd say. Appreciate your help."

"Sure, no sweat. I wish you luck."

The house at 1520 Fell was a redbrick ranch with a detached two-car garage on the right-hand side of the drive. Behind the house, at a distance, I caught sight of the rear of an outbuilding that looked like a large storage shed or second garage. A basketball backboard was still planted in concrete on a wide asphalt apron set aside for guest parking. Cornell probably spent his leisure time in high school practicing his free throws. I imagined him lettering in three sports, elected pep king or treasurer of his senior class. A check of the yellow pages had indicated that McPhee's was the only game in town, so he must be doing well financially even if his job lacked glamour and pizzazz.

Dolan parked at the curb out in front and we made our way along the walk to the porch, where we rang the bell. The door was opened by a girl who was probably six years old, judging by the number of missing teeth. Her hair was still a white blond that would probably darken over time. She wore glasses with pink plastic frames and a pair of barrettes with a row of pink and blue flowers. Her dress was pink-and-blue plaid with rows of white smocking across the bodice.

Dolan said, "Hey there, young lady. Is your grandpa at home?"

"Just a minute." She shut the door and a moment later her grandmother opened it, wiping her hands on a kitchen towel. A mild, vanilla-smelling breeze wafted out from behind her. She was heavy-set and wore small rimless glasses and a knee-length striped apron over a loose floral-print housedress. Her gray hair had a fringe of curls around her face while the rest was cut short. "Yes?"

"Good morning. We're looking for Ruel McPhee. Cornell, over at the shop, gave us this address."

"Ruel's out back. Won't you come in? I'm Edna, his wife."

She opened the door for us. We did a round of introductions that included the McPhees' granddaughter, Cissy, who skipped on ahead of us in her Mary Janes. Edna led us through the house, saying, "We're about to frost cupcakes for Cissy's birthday. Six years old today. She's having a little party with her kindergarten class this afternoon."

Cissy said, "My grammaw made me this dress."

Dolan said, "Well, that's real cute. I like that."

As usual, I played the silent sidekick, prepared to fly into action if Edna or the child suddenly went berserk.

Cissy had climbed onto a kitchen chair and was now perched on her knees, inspecting the baking project. On the table, there were two muffin tins, each containing twelve freshly baked cupcakes in paper liners with little golden-brown domed heads. I could see the yellow-cake mix box on the counter by the sink where the mixing bowl sat.

The room was decorated in a patriotic flurry of red, white, and blue. The kitchen paper was done in Revolutionary War motif, a repeating pattern of battle scenes, complete with cannons, ships, and soldiers in various heroic poses. The woodwork was white, the counters red, and a window seat built into a side bay was filled with plump pillows and a neatly folded quilt, all in coordinating hues.

Crayon and fingerpaint projects were fixed to the refrigerator with magnets shaped like fruit. There were also school pictures of two additional girls, ages about eight and ten, who might have been Cissy's sisters. All three had the same blond hair and features reminiscent of Cornell's. Cissy lowered her face, her nose a mere centimeter from a cupcake.

Edna said, "Cissy, don't touch. You wait until they're cool and don't pick at them. Why don't you take these nice folks to see Grandpa? I'll have the frosting ready as soon as you get back."

That job would be quick. I could see the container of ready-to-use fudge frosting on the table with a photo of a shiny chocolate swirl, like an ocean wave, on the side. As a kid, I'd imagined that's what real grannies did— sewed and made cakes. Aunt Gin always said, "I'm not the cookie-baking type," as though that excused her from cooking of any kind. Now I wondered if that's why I was so bent—because I lacked the homely services she'd so proudly repudiated.

Cissy got down off the chair and took Dolan by the hand. Behind Edna's back, he shot me a look that said, *Help*. I trailed after them, crossing a section of grass that butted up against the garages. A side door stood open and Cissy took us that far before scampering back to her post.

Ruel McPhee sat on a wooden desk chair inside the door. A small color TV set had been placed on a crate and plugged into a wall-mounted outlet. He was smoking a cigarette while he watched a game show. Ruel was half the size of his wife, gaunt-faced and sunken-chested, with narrow bony shoulders. He wore a broken-rimmed straw hat pushed back on his head while his bifocals were pulled down on the bridge of his nose. He smelled a teeny, tiny bit like he hadn't changed his socks this week. Dolan handled the introductions and a quick explanation of why we were there. At the sight of Ruel's cigarette, Dolan was inspired to take out one of his own.

Ruel was nodding, though his attention was still fixed on the television set. "That was years ago."

"DMV tells us the vehicle's registered to you."

"That's right. Fella from Arizona brought it over here to have the seats redone. I had it parked behind the shop. Someone must have broken in and hot-wired the ignition because when I came to work Monday morning, it was gone. Don't know when it was taken. Saw it Friday afternoon, but that's the last I know. I reported it right off and it wasn't but a week later someone called from the Sheriff's Department up north to say it'd been found. This fellow Gant, who owned the car, paid to have it towed back but it was worthless by then. Car looked like it'd been rolled—doors all messed up, front banged in.

Gant was pissed as hell." He flicked me an apologetic look for the use of the word. "I told him to file a claim with his insurance company, but he didn't want anything more to do with it. He'd already been in a couple fender-benders and the engine froze up once. He was convinced the car was jinxed. I offered him a fair price, but he wouldn't take a cent. He said good riddance to bad rubbish and signed it over to me." Ruel's gaze returned to the screen where contestants were pressing buttons while the prize money they'd racked up was being flashed on monitors. I couldn't answer even one of the questions they responded to with such speed.

Dolan said, "What happened to the car?"

"Someone pushed it down a ravine is what I heard."

"I mean, where is it now?"

"Oh. It's setting right out back. Cornell and I intend to do the restoration as soon as we have time. I guess you met him. He's married with three girls, and Justine lays claim to any spare time he has. We'll get to it in due course."

"Justine's his wife?"

"Going on fifteen years. She's difficult to get along with. Edna has more patience with the situation than I do."

"You have any idea who might have stolen the car?"

"If I did, I'd've told the police back then. Joyriders is my guess. Town this size, it's what the kids do for fun. That and throw paint balloons out the back of their trucks. Not like when I was young. My dad would've pounded me bloody and that'd've been the end of that."

"You ever had a car stolen from the shop before?"

"Not before and not since. I put up a fence with concertina wire and that took care of it." He turned his attention from the TV. "What's your interest?

Dolan's expression was bland. "We're cleaning out our files, doing follow-up on old crime reports. Most of it's administrative work."

"I see." Ruel stepped on his cigarette and then placed the flattened butt in a Miracle Whip jar that was nearly filled to the brim. He held the jar out to Dolan who stepped on his cigarette and added it to the collection. Ruel was saying, "I'm not allowed to smoke inside, especially when the granddaughters visit. Justine thinks it's bad for their lungs so Edna makes me come out here. Justine can be moody if she doesn't get her way."

"Why'd you hang on to the car?"

Ruel drew back and made a face as though Dolan were dense. "That Mustang's a classic. 1966."

"Couldn't have been a classic then. The car was only three years old."

"I told you I got the car for free," he said. "Once we finish the restoration, it'll be worth somewhere in the neighborhood of fourteen thousand dollars. Now I'd call that a profit, wouldn't you?"

"Mind if we take a look?"

"Help yourself. I got five of them back there; one sweet little GT Coupe, silver frost with the black vinyl top torn up. Doesn't run yet and the body needs work, but if you're interested, we could talk money and maybe make a deal."

"My car's fine, thanks."

Dolan lit another cigarette as the two of us trooped through high grass to a rutted dirt lane overgrown with weeds that led to the second of Ruel McPhee's garages. The entire area had been undercut by gopher tunnels, and my foot occasionally sank into a softly crumbling hole. The garage was positioned so that its backside was to us, its double doors facing a flat field beyond. We could see the faintly defined path where the lane had originally been laid out, possibly in anticipation of a second house on the property. Three additional vehicles were visible in the area immediately in front of us. We checked those cars first, lifting their respective car covers like a series of ladies' skirts. The two I peeked at were in poor shape, and I didn't think they'd ever amount to more than yard ornaments. While we made our inspection, I said, "You think someone used the vehicle to drive the body to Lompoc?"

"Hard to say. She could have been alive when she left, assuming she was ever in Quorum at all. Just as likely someone stole the car and picked her up along the way."

"But what if she was killed here? Why drive the body all the way up there to dump? Seems like it'd be easier to go out in the desert and dig a hole."

Dolan shrugged. "You might want to put some distance between the body and the crime scene. It'd make sense to take off and go as far as you could. Then you'd have to find a place to pull off and unload, which's not as easy as you'd think. If the body was in the trunk much more than a day, it'd start to decompose and then you'd have a big problem on your hands. You'd have to figure the car'd been reported stolen, which means you couldn't risk a traffic stop in case the officer became curious about what you had back there. At least Lompoc's off the main highway and if you found an isolated spot, you'd dump her while you had the chance."

"What about the original owner? How do we know he didn't have a hand in it?"

"It's always possible," he said, "though Gant's been dead the last ten years. Ruptured abdominal aneurysm, according to the information I received."

When we reached the garage, Dolan tried the side

door, but a combination of warping and old paint had welded it shut. We went around to the double doors in front. Both were closed, but there were no locks in the hasps. Dolan gave the one on the right a hefty yank and the three-section door labored up, trailing spider webs and dead leaves. Sunlight washed in, setting a cloud of dust motes ablaze. The two cars inside were both covered with canvas tarps and the space was crammed with junk. In addition to old cars, McPhee apparently saved empty cans and jars, stacks of newspapers bound with wire, wood crates, boxes, shovels, a pickax, a rusted tire iron, firewood, sawhorses, and lumber. The garage had also been made home to an ancient mower, automotive parts, and dilapidated metal lawn furniture. The air smelled stale and felt dry against my face. Dolan paused to extinguish his cigarette while I raised a corner of the nearest tarp. "This looks a lot like the tarp the body was wrapped in."

"Sure does. We'll have to ask McPhee if one was taken the same time the car was."

I looked down, catching sight of the battered right rear fender of the red Mustang. "Found it."

Together we removed the car cover and folded it like a flag. To my untutored eye, the car looked as though it hadn't been touched since the day it was hauled out of the ravine back in '69. At best, the exterior had been hosed off, but dried dirt still clung to the underbelly of the car with its scraped and dented right side and its banged-in driver's door. Both sides were rumpled. A portion of tree branch was caught under the left rear fender. Something about it made my heart thump. Dolan took out a handkerchief and gingerly pressed the trunk lock. The lid swung open. Inside, the spare tire was missing from the mount. A couple of dusty cardboard boxes filled with old *National Geographic* magazines had been shoved into the space. Dolan removed the boxes and set them aside. The exposed matting looked clean except for two large dark smudges and two smaller ones near the back. Dolan peered closer. "I think we better call the local Sheriff's Department and get the car impounded."

He crossed to the single door and tested it again. Satisfied that it was frozen shut, he said, "Wait here. I'll be back in a minute."

I stood just outside, staring at the untilled pasture with its tangle of wildflowers while Dolan headed off toward his car. I noticed he steered a wide path around the backside of the garage, where I assumed McPhee was still sitting. I couldn't see the old man, but the occasional drift of frenetic music suggested he'd remained in his wooden chair, watching TV. I returned to the Mustang and circled it, hands behind my back, peering in the windows with their cracked and broken glass. The black leather seats, while gray with dust, seemed to be in good shape.

Dolan returned six minutes later carrying a Polaroid camera, his pant legs covered with burrs. He handed me the camera while he took out a pen and a packet of seals he'd retrieved from his car. He jotted his initials, the date, and the time on four seals and affixed one across each of the two doors, one to the hood, and the remaining seal across the trunk opening. Then he clicked off a series of Polaroid shots while he circled the car. As each photograph emerged from the slot, Dolan handed it to me. I waited for the image to appear and then wrote a title across the bottom. Dolan added his name, the date, and the time, and tucked them in an envelope he placed in his jacket pocket.

I said, "Does McPhee know we're doing this?"

"Not yet."

"What now?"

"I'll go back to the motel and call Detective Lassiter. He can send out a deputy to secure the car until a tow truck arrives. I'll also put in a request to the Santa Teresa Sheriff's Department to send down a flatbed as soon as possible. They can load the car at the local impound lot and tow it back."

"How long will that take?"

Dolan checked his watch. "It's ten-thirty now. They should be able to get someone here by six tonight. Meantime, I'll call Judge Ruiz in Santa Teresa and ask him to issue a telephonic warrant. We'll return the affidavit with the Mustang and have Stacey file the paperwork up there. I'll be back within the hour."

14

I hadn't sat surveillance for ages and I'd forgotten how long an hour could feel. At least the car wasn't going to move. I took off my watch and slipped it in my pocket so I wouldn't be tempted to keep peeking at the time. I settled in the shade, leaning against the garage while I added a few notes to my index cards and then slipped the paperback from my shoulder bag and found my place.

Half a chapter later, I heard a car door slam, and when I peered around the corner, I saw Cornell getting out of a white truck. He was crossing the parking pad, heading for his parents' back door, possibly to have lunch. I was starving and had to take my nourishment in the form of an ancient Junior Mint I'd tossed in the bottom of my shoulder bag. I figured the fuzz on it would supply my quota of fiber.

The day had warmed up considerably and the air smelled of wildflowers and weeds. An occasional bumblebee lumbered by, a black-and-yellow gumball in flight. A swarm of gnats danced in the light and a horsefly zipped around, looking for a place to land. This was entirely too much wildlife for my purposes. I'm an indoor kind of person, and I prefer my contact with Nature reduced to the front of a picture postcard.

I heard someone trampling through the grass. I got to my feet, dusted off my jeans, and tucked the book back in my bag. I was expecting to see Dolan. Instead, Cornell appeared, smoking a cigarette he'd cupped in the palm of his hand. He didn't seem all that happy to see me. His gaze shifted to the open garage door, where the Mustang sat in plain view, its tarp removed, a seal affixed across the opening of the hood.

I said, "Hi. I'm Kinsey. We met this morning." I flicked a look toward the driveway, hoping to see the deputy arriving, but no such luck.

"I know who you are. What's all this?"

"A sheriff's deputy should be here shortly. Lieutenant Dolan thinks this might be the vehicle used to transport our victim. He wants to have it checked."

"What's that mean?"

I put a casual shrug in my voice. "It's no big deal. He wants the evidence technicians to go over it."

"And Dad knows about this?"

"I'm assuming so," I said, lying through my teeth. "I'm not sure what the lieutenant told him. You'd have to ask him."

Cornell frowned. He dropped his cigarette and stepped on it. "How long's this going to take?"

"Probably no more than a couple of days." I was hoping it wouldn't occur to him we'd be removing the Mustang from the premises. Also, hauling it north where he probably wouldn't see the car again for months. I didn't want to deal with him if he raised a big stink.

He hunched his shoulders. "The law allows you to just waltz in this way? You're on private property out here, same as the house. My dad owns everything as far as that fence."

I turned and followed his gesture. "I wasn't aware of that. Lot of land," I said. "Actually, we had a chat with your father and asked to see the Mustang. He told us to help ourselves."

"I don't think he understood what you meant. He didn't mention it to me."

"Is that a problem?"

"Well, no. Not at all. It just seems weird."

I looked down at the ground, snubbing the tip of my right Saucony in the dirt. "I don't know what to tell you. Maybe Lieutenant Dolan can explain it when he gets back. He asked me to secure the car until the deputy arrives. Did you need something out here?"

"I came out to see what was going on. Dad saw you head in this direction, but then you never came back. Where's Lieutenant Dolan?"

"Ah. I guess he went around the other way. He probably didn't want to bug your dad while he was watching his show." I let a silence settle. I didn't want to manufacture small talk and I wasn't interested in continuing the conversation on its present course.

"I better let Dad know. He's not going to like it, but that's your look-out."

"Go ahead. Do anything you like."

Cornell backed up a step and then took off for the house. By the time he reached the driveway, a black-and-white unit was pulling in. When the deputy got out, he and Cornell shook hands. I watched the two men confer, joined moments later by the old man himself. He had his straw hat set square on his head, the rim shading his face. Even from a distance, I could see he'd taken on the air of a bandy rooster whose barnyard was under siege. The conversation continued with a lot of hand waving on Ruel's part. The three faces turned in my direction. Behind them, Lieutenant Dolan pulled up and parked at the curb. The three of them waited for Dolan and then another discussion ensued, at the end of which the four of them formed a little ragtag parade and trudged toward me.

Dolan introduced the deputy, whose name was Todd Chilton. He seemed to be acquainted with Ruel, and I gathered their relationship predated the current meeting. Chilton was in his late thirties, with dark hair clipped short on the sides and curling slightly on top. He'd loosened his tie, and he took a moment to rebutton his collar before the two of us shook hands.

Ruel peered at me and then turned to Lieutenant Dolan. "This the technician you were talking about?"

"She's a private investigator. We'll tow the car to Santa Teresa and do the evidence search up there."

Ruel turned and stared. "You mean to take the car *away?*" He looked from Dolan to the deputy in disbelief. "He can't do that, can he?"

"Yes, sir."

"But I hold title to that car and it's registered in my name. He never said what he was up to or I'd've told him to get lost."

Chilton said, "We understand that, Mr. McPhee, and I'm sure Lieutenant Dolan appreciates the inconvenience."

"Inconvenience, my foot! That car's been setting out there for the past eighteen years. If the cops thought it was so all-fired important, they should have taken it back then."

Dolan said, "The information came in a week ago. That's the first we'd heard of it, or we'd have done just that."

"This's private property. The car belongs to me. You can't sashay in here and walk off with what's mine." He turned to the deputy. "I want him out of here."

Chilton said, "I can't help you with that. He has the right to take it."

"Then you clear off, too! What good's that gall-dang badge of yours if you can't protect us any better than this?"

Chilton's manner was beginning to shift. Where at first his tone had been conciliatory, now it was turning flat. "Excuse me, sir, but that car's considered evidence in a criminal investigation. You don't have a choice. Techs don't find anything, you get the vehicle back and there's no harm done."

"I'm calling my lawyer."

Lieutenant Dolan said, "Mr. McPhee, we have a legitimate search warrant. You can call anyone you want, but it won't change what's happening. No disrespect intended, but you might as well save your breath."

"I'm entitled to one call."

"That's only if they put you in jail," Chilton said, exasperated. "No one's proposing to arrest you. It's the car he wants. He's talking about a homicide. You interfere here and you're only making trouble for yourself. None of us want that."

Cornell said, "Let it go, Dad. Come on. They're going to do it anyway."

Ruel gave way suddenly. He took his hat off and slapped his thigh with it. "People been telling me we live in a police state, but I never thought I'd see the day. It's a damn shame when a law-abiding citizen gets treated like dirt."

He walked away from the group. Cornell glanced back with a dark look and then followed his father to the house.

We heard a quick horn toot at the street and saw the local towing company with a flatbed truck idling at the curb. Chilton whistled to catch the driver's eye and then gestured him in our direction with a series of arm rolls. The driver shifted gears, pulling the truck forward. He then backed into the driveway and eased up the long dirt lane toward the garage where we were standing.

Dolan and I acted as sideline supervisers while the chain was attached to the Mustang's front axle and the car was winched up the ramp. Cornell's truck was gone by then and there was no sign of Ruel. Once the Mustang was loaded, we tagged after the moving tow truck as far as the street. The driver waited while we got in Dolan's car. We followed him, keeping the Mustang in view.

I said, "By the way, you talked to Stace? What's he heard about his biopsy and X-rays? They must know something by now."

Dolan looked at me blankly. "Completely slipped my mind. He wanted to come down here and I was so busy trying to talk him out of it I forgot to ask."

"He's joining us?"

"Not if I can help it. I'd rather have him up there where he can do some good."

At the impound lot, we waited while the Mustang was unloaded and the rolling gate was locked. Dolan took care of all the paperwork and then he returned to the car. We headed for the motel. He was whistling idly to himself, tapping out a rhythm on the steering wheel.

"You seem chipper."

"I am. I got a good feeling about this."

"How long until the forensics guys can get back to us?"

"Soon, I hope. Things are quiet at the moment, so Mandel said he'd ask them to get right on it."

"And in the meantime, what?"

"Nothing. If they can connect our victim to the Mustang, we'll use her dental chart to canvas the local dentists. Teeth that bad, someone might remember her."

"Can't we do that while we wait? I hate sitting around. We know someone stole the car and drove it up to Lompoc. C. K. spotted it near the quarry . . ."

"We still don't know for sure this is the car he saw. It could've been something similar; some guy stopping near the quarry to take a leak. Don't be so quick off the mark."

"But suppose this *was* the car, doesn't it seem safe to assume it was used to move the body?"

"Where do you get that, unless they find trace evidence?"

"Oh come on, Lieutenant . . ."

"I'm serious. Even if we're right about the car, it still doesn't prove the girl was from Quorum. Killer could have picked her up and stabbed her when he was on the road."

"Okay, I'll grant you that one. So what now, we just sit?"

"Yep."

"But it could take *days.*"

"I can put you on a bus and send you home," he said mildly.

"That's not what I'm getting at."

"Then what?"

"Why don't you do the sitting while I start nosing around."

He shook his head. "There's no point going off half-cocked."

"How about this? I'll work with the meter off, but keep a running tab of my hours. If I manage to track her down, pay me, and if I don't, oh well."

Dolan thought about it, taking up his finger tapping as he studied the street ahead. "Maybe."

"Come on, Dolan. Please, please, pretty please with sugar on it? Let me take a crack at it. I'll be good. I swear."

"Begging's unbecoming. You're not the type." He stopped tapping. "I suppose I could borrow your typewriter and catch up on the paperwork. I want to get some of this down while the details are fresh."

"Good. I'm glad. Makes it a lot more fun."

Once in my room again, I opened the bed-table drawer and took out the pint-sized Quorum phone book, looking for the address of the public library. The Quorum Branch of the Riverside County District Public Library was on High Street. According to the minimap in the front of the directory, it was only five blocks away. I tucked the book into my bag, left my typewriter with Dolan, and then headed off on foot.

At the library, I went straight to the reference room and pulled the city directories for 1966, '67, '68, and '69. I took the phone book from my shoulder bag and turned to the yellow pages under the heading "Dentists." There were ten listed. I checked the current names against those of dentists in practice during the years in question. Two past dentists, Drs. Towne and Nettleton, had disappeared, which I was guessing meant they'd retired, died, or left the area. Four names carried over and six were new. Most seemed to be generalists, judging from their full-page ads, which trumpeted crowns, dentures, fillings, periodontal work, bridges, root canals, cosmetic dentistry, and oral surgery. With my dental phobia, this was making my palms sweat. Already I favored the fellow who offered "Nitrous oxide: Dentistry while you sleep." I wouldn't be opposed to postponing my next appointment 'til I was dead.

Of the carryovers, the fourth dentist, Dr. Gregory Spears, had listed himself twice, once under the general heading and again under the listing for orthodontists, of which there was one, namely him. The word "straightening" had been added in parentheses for those who didn't know what an orthodontist did. I jotted down the four names and addresses, returned to the city map, and charted my route. Given the size of the town, it was no big deal to walk from the library to the first dentist on my list.

Spears's office was located in a storefront on Dodson. There was no one in the waiting room. His front office "girl" was in her sixties, a Mrs. Gary, according to her name tag. Her desktop was orderly and the surrounding office space was laid out with efficiency; charts filed on the vertical. A random band of color-coded labels formed an irregular line across the flaps. A small sign in cross-stitch hung on the wall: PLEASE PAY AT TIME SERVICES ARE RENDERED. I was sure she'd be sympathetic when she heard your front cap came off in the middle of a ladies' lunch, but she probably wouldn't take any guff from you if your check should bounce.

When she opened the sliding glass window that separated her office from the waiting room, I placed a copy of my PI license on the counter. Dolan had given me the file containing Jane Doe's dental chart, showing the number and location of her fillings. I placed that on the counter as well. In the background, I could hear the high-pitched squealing of a drill, a sound that was sometimes sufficient to cause me to pass out. I ran a dampened palm across the seat of my pants and said, "Hi. I'm hoping you can give me some information."

"I can certainly try."

"I'm currently working with two Santa Teresa homicide detectives on a Jane Doe case that's been on the books since 1969. This is a chart of her dental work. There's an off chance she lived in this area and we're wondering if she might have been a patient of Dr. Spears's. She was most likely a minor when the work was done."

She glanced at the file. "He's with a patient right now. Can you come back in half an hour?"

"It's easier if I just wait," I said. "How long have you worked for him?"

"Since he opened his practice in 1960. What did you say the patient's name was?"

"I don't know. That's the point. She was never identified. She had numerous fillings and the forensic odontist who examined the maxilla and mandible thought the work was probably done in the two years before her death. It's a long shot, I know."

"I doubt we'd have a chart on someone we haven't seen in nearly twenty years."

"What happens to the old charts? Are they destroyed?"

"Usually not. They're put on inactive status and retired to dead storage. I'm not sure how far back they go. You're talking about hundreds of patients, you know."

"I'm aware of that. The charts are here in town?"

"If you're suggesting a hand search, that's something you'd have to talk to Dr. Spears about. I'm not sure he'd agree to anything without a court order."

"We'll only be in town for two days and we were hoping to avoid delay."

"Wait and see what he says. It isn't up to me."

"I understand."

I took a seat in the corner, where I sorted through the magazines. I chose the current issue of *Architectural Di-*

gest and entertained myself trying to imagine a color spread on my studio apartment, all eight hundred and fifty feet of it.

Fifteen minutes later, a woman with a puffy lip emerged, pausing at the desk while she wrote out a check for services. I waited until she'd left and then set the magazine aside and returned to the counter.

"Shall we try again?"

Mrs. Gary went into the examining room. I could hear the murmur of voices as she explained my request.

Dr. Spears came out to meet me, still wearing his white coat, wiping his hands on a paper towel he then tossed in the trash. He was gray-haired and blue-eyed and after we shook hands, mine were left smelling like soap. While he seemed to appreciate my problem, he wasn't much help.

Before I could even get through the details, he was shaking his head. "I couldn't do that without a name. Inactive charts are filed alphabetically. I've got hundreds of them. From what Mrs. Gary's said, the girl was a minor, which further complicates matters. I don't see how you'd find her."

"She had tons of fillings, buckteeth, and a crooked eyetooth on the left," I said.

"Most of my patients have crooked teeth. I'd like to help, but what you're asking is impossible."

"That's too bad. I'd hoped for more, but I can see your point. What about the other dentists in the area back then? Can you tell me anything about Dr. Towne or Dr. Nettleton? I noticed both were in practice in the late sixties."

"Dr. Towne died two years ago, but his widow might be willing to help if his records are still in her possession. Dr. Nettleton's over ninety. He's reasonably sharp, but I doubt you'll get much." He turned to Mrs. Gary. "You know the family, don't you? Where's he living these days?"

"With his daughter. She goes to my church."

"Why don't you give Miss Millhone the information. Maybe he'll remember. It's worth a try, at any rate."

"Thanks. I'd appreciate that."

Mrs. Gary checked her Rolodex and made a note of the daughter's name and address. From her expression, I was guessing I'd be lucky if Dr. Nettleton could remember how to tie his own shoes.

I left the office, pausing on the sidewalk out front. I consulted my map and my list, moving on to the next name. I repeated the same conversation, with variations, in my chats with the three remaining dentists. The response was polite but discouraging. They seemed willing to help, but all of them were busy and no one was interested in searching dead files on the off chance of finding her. Not only was I unable to supply them with a name, but I couldn't prove she'd ever lived in Quorum or that her dental work was done there. My only hope had been that the meager facts in my possession might have triggered a recollection. I did have Dr. Nettleton's address, but I was too tired by then to pursue the point.

It was close to 6:00 by the time I walked the ten blocks back to the motel where Dolan waited. I hated admitting I'd bombed out, but that's what I did as soon as he answered his door.

He seemed unusually magnanimous. "Don't worry about it. You covered a lot of ground."

"For what it's worth."

"Let it go for now. Start again tomorrow. You might have better luck. Right now, it's time for drinks and dinner. Are you up for that?"

"Sure, but you'll have to give me half an hour. I want to check in with Henry and then I'm grabbing a shower. If you're going to the Quorum Inn, I'll meet you there."

"Good."

My call caught Henry just as he was going out the door. I gave him a hasty summary of the trip and the lack of progress, and he was properly consoling. "By the way, you received a package from Lompoc. It was on your doorstep this morning. I brought it in."

"Who's it from?"

"Doesn't say."

"What's it look like?"

"About the size of a shirt box, two pounds. Probably not a bomb. I'm holding it to my ear and it doesn't tick."

"Now you've got me curious. Open it and peek."

"I refuse to open your mail. I'll keep it 'til you get back."

"If you change your mind, I'm giving you permission to see what's there," I said. "How's Mattie?"

"She's fine. She ended up staying an extra day so she could hike Diamondback Trail. There's a hot springs up there she used to visit with her husband. She's thinking about a painting of the scene if she can find it again."

"Sounds like fun. Did you go?"

"No, no. My knees wouldn't take it so I sent her on alone. Besides, I'd agreed to do a tea for Moza and I ended up making finger sandwiches and cookies all day." Henry had been a commercial baker during his working life, and he was still smitten with the process. He catered the occasional luncheon or tea and worked a deal with Rosie, trading homemade breads for occasional free meals.

"I liked her. She seems nice."

"I hate to cut this short, but I'm late as it is. When will you be home?"

"I'm not sure yet. I'll let you know."

I hung up the phone, stripped off my clothes, and hopped in the shower, thinking *Late for what?* He'd been in a hurry to get off the phone, but I couldn't tell if it was me he was avoiding or the subject of Mattie. I'd hoped to find out if he was interested in her and she in him. She and Henry had been cute together and I was feeling proprietary. I'd thought it was a good sign she stayed the extra day, but then the mention of her husband didn't sit well with me. I'd assumed she was a widow, but she might be divorced. In either case, she'd referred to her husband twice, so maybe she was still emotionally connected to him. Not a good sign.

15

At breakfast, drinking my second cup of coffee, I said, "I'll track down Dr. Nettleton this morning to get some closure on that." I watched Dolan eat his eggs Benedict. The yellow of the sauce was suspiciously bright, suggesting that the "chef" had used a packet of powdered Hollandaise.

He mopped up a puddle of poached egg with a fragment of buttered sweetroll. "I thought you covered all the dentists when you were out yesterday."

I shook my head. "Didn't get to him. This guy's retired. I got his address from Dr. Spears but haven't been there yet. Are you interested in coming?"

"Sounds like something you can handle on your own. Why don't you drop me at the Sheriff's Department. I asked them to go through their dead files looking for any missing-persons reports that might sound like our girl. After that, I'll walk back to the motel, see if we've heard from Mandel. I talked to him late last night and he said the guy who picked up the Mustang did a quick turnaround and headed right back. He and his wife were leaving on vacation this morning so that worked in our favor. Mandel said the evidence techs'll get on it first thing this morning. He'll call as soon as he has anything to report. I don't hear soon, I can call him again."

"Sounds good. I'll report in after I've talked to Dr. Nettleton."

Once back from the Sheriff's Department, Dolan put the car in neutral and pulled on the emergency brake, then slid from the driver's seat while I emerged from my side, went around the front, and took his place at the wheel. He'd fired up a cigarette before I could get my bearings. He fished his key out of his pocket and let himself into his room. I spent a few seconds adjusting the seat and the rearview mirror, trying to get a feel for the old Chevy, which had the bulk of a tank after my snub-nosed VW. As soon as I was set, the engine conked out on me. I turned the key in the ignition and pressed the gas pedal lightly, coaxing and cajoling until the engine caught hold again. I felt like a little kid. I peered down the length of the hood, wishing I were perched on a New York City telephone book, though my feet barely touched the pedals as it was.

I pulled my bag onto my lap and checked my notebook for the address I'd been given, then consulted the minimap. The town of Quorum was roughly twenty-five streets wide, transected by five big boulevards that ran east and west. A series of smaller east-west streets further defined a grid that made navigation easy. Dr. Nettleton's daughter lived on Banner Way in a small subdivision on the northern outskirts. I released the hand brake and backed out of the space with caution, then eased the car through the lot and onto the main drag. Drive time was approximately four minutes.

The house number I was looking for turned out to be another one-story brick ranch set among full-grown trees. The two-car garage had been incorporated into the main structure, and I was guessing it now served as guest quarters. Large tubs of pink begonias were lined up across the porch with its wide overhang.

I rang the bell and waited. The door was opened by a woman in her late forties. I'd caught her in the middle of her morning exercise, pink-faced and out of breath. In the background, I could see Jane Fonda doing leg lifts.

"I'm looking for Dr. Nettleton. Are you his daughter?"

"That's right. I take it you're the private detective. Alana Gary told me you might be stopping by. Come on in."

"I'm Kinsey Millhone."

"Vonda Landsberg," she replied. "Dad's in his room down the hall, the last door on the right. If you don't mind, I'll let you find your own way."

"Sure. Is he expecting me?"

"Hard to say. His mind is sharp, but his memory comes and goes. He can still beat the pants off my husband at chess, but he's easily exhausted, so please don't stay long."

"Fifteen minutes tops."

Vonda returned to her exercise mat while I went down the hallway to the back bedroom. The door was ajar. I pushed it open. Dr. Nettleton was sitting in a bentwood rocker, staring out the window, which was open about six inches. On the sill outside, someone had scattered sunflower seeds. A squirrel was perched up on its haunches peering in at him.

The old man looked ninety; frail and bent, hunched in his chair with a shawl across his knees. His face was long and his earlobes drooped like melting candle wax. Most of his hair was gone, but what he had was pure white and clipped close to his head. Flesh-colored hearing aids filled his ear cavities like flattened wads of bubble gum.

"Dr. Nettleton?"

Rheumy-eyed, he turned in my direction and cupped a hand behind one ear. "What say?" His voice was powdery and dry, as though dust had accumulated on his windpipe.

"May I join you?"

"Are you the visiting nurse?"

"I'm a private detective." I spotted a small wooden desk chair that I pulled close to his. I sat down. He seemed perfectly accepting of my appearance on the scene. Perhaps at his stage in life, he'd given up the notion of personal boundaries and privacy. In a slightly elevated voice, I explained who I was and what I needed from him. As I talked, Dr. Nettleton kept his head tilted, his trembling right hand cupped behind his ear. "Come again?"

I pulled my chair closer and went through it again, speaking louder this round. I could see the intelligence in his eyes, though I wasn't at all certain he was following me. When I finished, the ensuing silence went on so long I wondered if he'd caught any of what I'd said. The squirrel picked up a sunflower seed and nibbled rapidly, cracking the shell, tail twitching. Dr. Nettleton smiled with such sweetness I nearly wept.

"Dr. Nettleton?"

He turned his head. "Yes?"

"I was wondering about the girl. Did you ever have a patient like her?"

He pulled himself upright, staring at a spill of sunlight on the floor. "The last year I had my practice, there was one girl fits that description. I was forced to retire when

I was seventy-five. Hands weren't steady and I couldn't take standing on my feet all day. I forget her name now, but I remember the fuss I made when I saw her teeth. Told her, 'Cavities like that can undermine your health.'"

I blinked at him. Maybe he'd misunderstood. "She had the buckteeth I mentioned?"

"Oh, yes. Occlusion was pronounced and her upper left cuspid was pointed anteriorly and slightly outward. That's this one right here," he said, pointing to his eye-tooth. "Left third molar hadn't yet erupted and I warned her she might have a problem with it if it didn't come through shortly. She had considerable plaque, of course, and her gums tended to bleed. Teeth spoiled her looks. Pleasant-looking girl otherwise, though if I remember rightly, she had behavioral problems."

"Like what?"

"Not sure. Something off about her. She'd been taken from her natural parents and placed in foster care. Must've had their hands full with her. Boisterous. Inappropriate. I believe she had a tendency to take things that weren't hers. She'd come in for an appointment and the next thing we knew, the stapler'd be missing or the paper clip dispenser. I took care of her fillings and then referred her to Dr. Spears for orthodontic evaluation. Don't know what happened to her after that. Doubt she had the work done. Didn't seem the type. Pity, if you ask me."

"Can you remember the name of the foster family?"

His focus shifted to the wall. "Not offhand. They weren't patients of mine. I forget now who they went to."

"What about the girl? Do you remember her name—first, last? Anything that might help?"

He gave his head a shake like a horse irritated by a fly. "I had to sedate her to get the work done and that affected her badly. Sometimes happens. Made her wild. I did one quadrant at a time, but she fought me every step. Novocaine didn't seem to take either. I must have stuck her four times for every tooth I filled."

I wiped my damp palm casually against my jeans, my dental phobia and my needle phobia having collided midair. "Did she attend the local high school?"

"Must have. State law. Pretty girl I'd say until she opened her mouth. Bad teeth spoil your looks and I told her so. Uncooperative. Missed two appointments and she came late for the ones she made. My hygienist could have told you the name, but she died. Can't believe I outlived her. Fit as a fiddle; worked for me thirty-two years and never took a sick day."

"What'd she die of?" I said, sidetracked.

"Heart. Weeding a pansy bed and toppled over sideways. She was out like a light. Yard work'll do that. Wretched way to spend time. I prefer indoors. Always have."

"Anything else about the girl?"

He squinted at me, shifting in his chair. "What's that?"

I said, "Anything else about the girl?"

He studied his hands, which seemed to move of their own accord, plucking at the shawl. "I remember the foster mother raised a fuss about the bill. Sent to her in error; a simple clerical mistake. You should have heard her carry on. Had my office girl in tears. I never liked the woman after that. She'd bring the girl in, but I wouldn't go out to greet her like I did everyone else. Figured she could sit there by herself. My hygienist was the one who said the woman drank. Can't understand how Social Services considered her fit. She wasn't, in my opinion, but then they never asked me what I thought." He was silent for a moment. "That's all."

I touched his arm. "Thanks so much. This has been a big help. I'll leave my phone number with your daughter. You can have her call me if you think of anything else."

His wandering gaze met mine. "You play chess?"

"I don't, but I hear you're good at it."

"I should be. My pa taught me when I was seven and now I'm ninety-three years old. Son-in-law plays badly. Hasn't got the head for it, if you know what I mean. Requires you to think. You have to plan in advance, maybe ten to fifteen moves. I'd be happy to teach you if you have a desire to learn."

"I'm afraid not, but thanks."

"All right." He was silent briefly and then pointed a dancing index finger at a jar on the chest of drawers. "You might fetch a few more sunflower seeds for that squirrel. Good company for me. More personality than some folks I've known and he's easily amused."

I sprinkled a handful of seeds on the ledge. Dr. Nettleton was already sinking, the energy fading from his face. As I opened the door, he said, "Don't remember your name, but I thank you for the visit. I enjoyed the conversation and hope you did, too."

"Believe me, I did." I wanted to put him in the car and take him with me. I waved from the door, but I don't think he caught the gesture.

I headed back to the motel. Surely we were on the right track. While Dr. Nettleton couldn't supply the name, the details he'd given me were consistent with what we knew. A thought struck me—a quick stop I could make before I reconnected with Dolan. I slowed the car and then pulled over to the curb. I picked up my map and looked for a small black square with a tiny flag on top. I did a U-turn on Chesapeake and drove back in the direction I'd been coming from.

Quorum High, which was part of the Unified School District, occupied a flat, two-block stretch of land on the northeast side of town. The grass looked patchy and the flagpole was bare. The classrooms were dispersed among a number of low-slung outbuildings that appeared to be prefabricated, with walls you could probably pierce with an X-Acto knife. I counted six trees on campus; not enough to pass for landscaping, but sufficient to offer the occasional shallow puddle of shade. The administration building looked like the first story of something far more grand. Maybe the school was in the process of raising funds, driving everyone insane with endless telethons on the local TV station. People will pay big bucks to get their regular programs back: sitcoms and soaps instead of all those amateur rock bands playing songs they've written without training of any kind.

I parked in the lot in a space marked VISITOR. I locked the car and trotted across the flattened grass to the entrance, pushing through the double glass doors and into the main corridor. It was dead quiet, though there must have been students somewhere on the premises. The portable classrooms outside weren't large enough to house the auditorium or the gym. I was guessing that a goodly number of classes were held in this building as well. I could smell sweat and hair spray, hormones and hot gym shoes—the scents of teen misery. Bad skin, no power, too few choices, too much sexual pressure, and not enough wisdom to see you through until you reached eighteen. How many lives were out of whack by then? Girls pregnant, guys dead in cars before the beer cans had quit rolling across the floorboards.

Ahead of me, down the hall, I spotted a sign indicating the principal's office. I could feel my anxiety mount as it had every day of my life during my high school years. I'd been so out of it, such a dork. I'd survived by rebelling—smoking dope and hanging out with other misfits like me. Here I was again, only all grown up (allegedly), crossing the threshold voluntarily, looking for answers to questions I'd never even dreamed of when I was young.

The school secretary was in her early thirties with brown eyes and short silky hair the color of pecan shells. A gossamer array of freckles lay across her nose and upper cheeks. She was casually dressed: beige slacks, short-sleeve brown sweater, and flat-heeled shoes. Her laminated name tag read ADRIANNE RICHARDS, and under that, in smaller letters, ADMINISTRATIVE ASSISTANT. She got up when she saw me and came to the counter. "May I help you?"

"I hope so," I said. "I'm a private investigator from Santa Teresa. I'm working with a couple of police detectives trying to identify a homicide victim, who died in August of '69."

"You mean here?"

"We're not sure." I took a brief time-out, giving her a verbal sketch of the girl we were trying to identify. "We've been down here talking to local dentists, hoping to locate her through her old dental records. I just talked to Dr. Nettleton. He thinks she was a patient, but he can't remember her name. I thought if I could talk to a couple of teachers, my description might ring a bell. Do you have any idea who was on the faculty back then?"

She stared at me blankly. I could almost see her compute the possibilities. I thought she might speak, but her expression shut down and she dropped her gaze. "You'd

have to talk to Mr. Eichenberger. He's the principal. All
our student records are confidential."

"I don't want her *records*. I just want to know her
name."

"Mr. Eichenberger doesn't allow us to give out information like that."

"You mean you know her?"

Her cheeks had begun to color. "Of course not. I'm
talking about school policy."

I stared at her, annoyed. Maybe as administrative assistant she was unaccustomed to people talking back. I'd
be lucky if I didn't end up in detention myself. "I don't
understand the problem."

"Mr. Eichenberger's the only one authorized to discuss the students' files."

"Fine. Is he available?"

"I'll check, but I'd have to see proper identification
first."

I removed my wallet from my shoulder bag and
opened the flap to show the photocopy of my license. I
passed it across the counter.

"May I take this?"

"As long as I get it back."

"Just a moment."

She crossed the office, approaching a closed door that
bore the nameplate, LAWRENCE EICHENBERGER, PRINCI-
PAL. She knocked once and went in. After perhaps a minute, the door opened and Mr. Eichenberger emerged
with Adrianne Richards right behind him. She handed
me my wallet and then returned to her desk, where she
busied herself with paperwork so she could eavesdrop
without appearing interested.

Mr. Eichenberger was a man in his early sixties with
sparse, soft-looking white hair, glasses, and a bulbous

nose. His complexion looked sunburned, and I picked up the scent of his aftershave, which smelled like incense. He wore a vivid blue dress shirt, a dark sweater vest, and a hand-tied bow tie. His manner was officious, his expression suggesting he was hell-bent on thwarting me. "I understand you have a problem with one of our students."

"Not quite," I said. Mentally, I could feel my eyes cross. No wonder I'd hated high school, where I'd been wholly at the mercy of guys just like him. I went through my entire explanation again, feigning a patience I didn't really feel.

Mr. Eichenberger said, "Ms. Millhone, let me make something clear. I've been here since the mid-sixties. As a matter of fact, I'm retiring in May. I came to the job when I was forty and I've enjoyed every minute of it. I don't mean to brag, but I remember just about every student who's come through those doors. I make it my priority to know who they are and what they're about. That's what these kids need—not a buddy or a pal, they need guidance from adults with their best interests at heart. We're in the business of getting these kids shaped up to face the real world. They need skills—reading and writing primarily—all in preparation for productive, well-paid work. If they're not college material, we make sure they find trades. Truancy, gangs, drug problems—we don't see much of that here, despite our proximity to Los Angeles."

I flicked a look over my shoulder. Were we being filmed? It's not that his sentiments weren't admirable, but the spiel sounded canned and had nothing to do with me. "Excuse me, but is this relevant?"

He seemed to collect himself, as though recovering from a momentary lapse of consciousness. "Yes. Well.

You were talking about a student. It would help if you'd give me the details. I can't be of assistance without that."

Ever obliging, I repeated my tale while his assistant moved papers randomly across her desk. Before I could finish my account, Mr. Eichenberger shook his head. "Not here. Not during my administration. You might try Lockaby. That's the alternative high school."

"Really. I didn't know there was one."

"It's over on the Kennedy Pike; a white frame building across from the town cemetery. You can't miss it."

"Is there someone in particular I should ask for?"

"Mrs. Bishop is the principal. She might be able to help."

"You didn't know the girl yourself?"

"If I had, I'd say so. I wouldn't withhold information in a murder investigation."

"What about your assistant?"

"Mrs. Richards wasn't working here back then."

"Too bad. I thought it was worth a try," I said. I took out a business card and made a note of the motel number on the back. "I'm at the Ocean View for the next couple of days. I'd appreciate a call if you think of anything that might help."

"You mentioned a foster family. I'd try Social Services."

"Thanks. That's a good suggestion. I'll do that."

I decided not to make another move until I'd brought Dolan up to speed. For the second time that morning, I was headed back to the motel. I left the car in the parking space in front of his room and gave a rap at his door. From inside, I caught the muffled sounds of the blaring television set. Dolan must not have heard me because he didn't answer my knock. Head tilted against the door, I waited and then tried it again. No deal. I turned and stared off across the parking lot toward the office. I let my eyes stray to the alcove that housed the soft-drink and Coke machines. No sign of him. I knocked again, this time sounding like the ATF at the outset of a drug raid. Maybe he was in the shower or otherwise indisposed.

I crossed the parking lot to the office and poked my head in the door. The desk clerk, a girl in her twenties, was sitting on a swivel stool, flipping through a copy of *People* magazine. I'd interrupted her in the middle of an article about Princess Di. The clerk was dark-haired, pretty in a sulky sort of way, with a mouth way too wide. Her lipstick was dark red and her lashes were so thick I thought they must be false. She was wearing a navy skirt and white blouse, topped by a smart red blazer with a phony crest on the patch pocket. The outfit must have been provided by the motel because it didn't look like anything she'd have worn without the threat of being fired. To compensate, she'd shortened the skirt and left the top three buttons of her blouse undone. She was chewing gum, a habit I'd been warned against when I was in tenth grade. My French teacher swore it made you look like a cow and I haven't chewed gum since. I hadn't even liked the teacher, but the admonition stuck.

I said, "Sorry to bother you, but I'm wondering if you've seen the fellow from room 130? I know he's expecting me, but he doesn't answer his door."

She leaned over and checked the register, flipping back a page. While she did this, she pushed her tongue through the wad of gum until it bulged like a small pink lung being extruded through her lips. "You're talking about the old guy?"

"He isn't *old*," I said, offended.

"Yeah, right. The day he checked in? He got an AARP discount. Fifteen percent off. You can't get that unless you're old. You have to be fifty at least."

"I'm fifty myself."

She said, "Far out. You look forty." She blew a bubble and popped it to punctuate her point. She looked at me. "Oops, sorry. You were kidding, right?"

"Never mind. I asked for that," I said. "Did he leave the motel for some reason?"

"He went out for cigarettes, but I saw him come back."

"How long ago was that?"

"Hour. He stopped by to pick up messages and then he went to his room."

"Had any calls come in?"

"Ask him yourself, you're such a pal."

"Ring his room for me, okay?"

"Sure." She picked up the phone, blowing another bubble as she punched the number in. It must have rung fifteen times. "He must have gone out again. Lotta old people get antsy. Too much energy. Have to be on the go or it drives 'em nuts."

"I appreciate your assessment. Can you come with me to his room and use your key?"

"Nope. I'm here by myself and I can't leave the desk. Why don't you go around the back and bang on his bathroom window? He might be on the pot."

I didn't like this at all. I returned to his room and knocked again about as loudly as the villagers at Frankenstein's castle door. Nothing. I circled the building, counting off the intervening rooms until I reached one I assumed was his. All the bathroom windows were too high off the ground to do me any good. I went back to his front door and stood there, undecided, while I thought about life. Why wasn't he answering? I reached for my shoulder bag and pulled out my wallet. In the windowed compartment under my driver's license, I keep a simple set of lock picks. This was not the battery-operated device I own that opens just about anything. I'd left that one at home, primarily because if I happened to get caught with it, the cops would take a dim view. What I had in hand was a set of the old-fashioned picks, a little hook and a tiny torque wrench, for occasions such as this. In my bag, I also carry a pin light and a folding screwdriver, neither of which would be necessary for to-day's B&E.

I knocked one more time and called Dolan's name in bullish tones. The guy in the next room opened his door and stuck his head out. "Hey! Keep it down, for cripes sake? And while you're at it, you can tell that jerk to turn off his TV set. It's been blasting since ten o'clock and I'm sick of it. Some of us have to work."

"Sorry. He's handicapped," I said, and tapped my ear. "Severe hearing deficit, the poor guy."

The man's expression shifted from annoyance to something less. "Oh. I didn't realize . . ."

"That's okay. People treat him badly all the time. He's used to it."

I waited until he'd disappeared and then I set to work. In movies, thieves tend to pop the locks in no time flat, often with the use of a credit card, a method I avoid. I don't trust the process. I knew a guy once whose credit card snapped off in the door he was trying to open. A neighbor spotted him breaking in and called the cops. When he heard the sirens approach, he hightailed it out of there, leaving half his card behind. The cops picked up his surname and the last six digits of his account. He was busted within a day.

In reality, picking locks takes practice, great patience, and no small measure of dexterity. Though most lock mechanisms are similar, there are variations that would drive the novice burglar insane. It usually takes me a few tries. I manipulated my little torque wrench with one eye on the parking lot. If Dolan was out, I didn't want him to catch me breaking into his room. And I was not all that keen on having the cops called if one of the other occupants was watching me from behind the drapes. At the same time, if he was in there, it was time to find out what was going on. I felt the last gate give way. I turned the knob, pushed the door open, and stepped in. "Lieutenant Dolan?"

He was lying on the bed, fully dressed, his shoes off. He turned toward me. His breathing was shallow and his face was a pasty gray. I flipped off the TV and crossed the room.

His voice was hoarse and raspy. "Heard you knocking, but I was in the bathroom being sick. I'm not doing so good."

"I can see that. You look awful. Are you having chest pains?" Up close, I could see a fine sheen of clammy sweat on his forehead and cheeks.

He shook his head almost imperceptibly. "Tightness across here. Hard to breathe. Feels like an elephant sitting on my chest."

"Oh, shit." I picked up the phone and dialed 911.

16

The Emergency Medical Services crew seemed to take forever, though in truth it was no more than six minutes. I alerted the front desk and then waited in the parking lot so I could flag them down. I heard the sirens before I saw the Fire Department Rescue van speed into view. I waved and the vehicle veered toward me and pulled in with a chirp of brakes. The woman driver and two other EMS techs emerged, wearing bright yellow jackets with FIRE DEPARTMENT written across the backs. They carried their equipment with them as they followed me into Dolan's room.

I stood to one side, watching as the two guys moved the furniture aside, clearing space to work. Their manner was efficient but conversational, taking care not to further alarm Dolan, who was doubtless already aware of the depth of trouble he was in. One tech loosened his shirt and then placed a stethoscope against his chest. He took Dolan's pulse and jotted notes on his clipboard, then attached a blood pressure cuff, pumped it, and took a reading, his gaze fixed on the dial. He asked Dolan a series of questions designed to assess the symptoms and events preceding the episode. I was surprised to hear Dolan admit he'd experienced something similar the night before, though the feeling had been less pronounced and had passed within minutes. The woman tech stepped in. She administered two sublingual tabs of nitroglycerin, and then started an IV line while the third technician secured an oxygen cone across Dolan's nose.

I went outside. A minute later, the crew emerged from the room. Dolan had been loaded onto a gurney. They rolled him as far as the back doors of the ambulance, which they opened to slide him into the rear. A few people passing through the parking lot paused to stare, but most moved on as soon as they realized what was happening. I appreciated their discretion. It's hard enough to be ill without feeling as though you've made a spectacle of yourself.

One tech climbed into the van with Dolan. The rear doors were slammed shut. The hospital was seven blocks away. I got directions from the second tech before he got in the cab of the van on the passenger side. The woman took the wheel again. She backed out and made a beeline for the street, sirens warbling, bar light flashing. I made sure Dolan's motel room door was locked and followed in his car.

When I arrived, the ambulance had already pulled into the emergency entrance. I parked in the main lot and by the time I entered the waiting room, he'd been rolled into the rear. I spoke to the desk clerk, telling her who I was. She asked me a few questions about Dolan, making me aware how little I really knew about him. I told her he had insurance coverage through the STPD and she said she'd pick up the remaining data from him. She got up and left her desk, clipboard in hand, indicating that the ER doctor would be out as soon as she was finished with him.

I took a seat in the waiting room, which was spare and reasonably pleasant: pale green carpet, fake plants, and piles of tattered magazines. An assortment of children's toys was scattered on the floor. Lines of interlocking chairs had been arranged, cotillion-fashion, around the edges of the room. In the corner, the face of a television set was blank. Someone had brought in Easter decorations; a basket filled with plastic eggs nestled in impossibly green paper grass. I wasn't even sure when Easter fell this year, but it was doubtless coming up soon, unless these were left from last year. Two patients came in while I was waiting: a man with superficial contusions and abrasions from a bike accident (judging from his shaved legs and his bun-hugging Spandex shorts), and a woman with her right ankle sandwiched between ice packs. Both were taken into examining rooms in the rear, but probably placed on hold while the doctors dealt with Dolan.

Outside, the sun was shining and the town of Quorum was going about its business as though nothing unusual had occurred. It was odd having a medical emergency in the middle of the day. Somehow, in my life, crises of this sort always seem to happen in the dead of night. I couldn't tally the number of times I'd been sitting in waiting rooms like this one while outside, city streets were deserted and shrouded in darkness.

Restless, I left my seat and wandered into the hall, where I asked a passing nurse for the nearest pay phone. I was directed to the hospital lobby, two long corridors away. I dialed Stacey's home number, charging the call to my credit card. Two rings later, he was on the line and I was filling him in.

"How's he doing?"

"Don't know. I haven't talked to the doctor yet. I wish I'd busted into his room when I first got there. I'm telling you, Stacey, his face was gray. He should have dialed 911 himself, but I think he was in denial. You know him."

"This is ridiculous. You can't do this alone. I'm coming down."

"Don't be silly. You're not well yourself. Just stay where you are. I've got enough on my hands."

"I'm fine. Didn't Dolan tell you? The docs showed my X-rays to some big muckety-muck and she says the shadow's insignificant. I forget now what they call it, but it's bullshit. Biopsy came back negative too so I got a clean bill of health."

"Are you serious?"

"Of course. Why would I lie about a thing like that? I'm in remission. At least for now."

"Lucky you didn't blow your brains out last week. Wouldn't you be pissed?"

"I just wish I hadn't gotten rid of my all personal possessions."

"I could have told you as much."

"Speaking of which, I'd like to have my family photos back."

"Forget it. Find another bunch. Those are mine."

"Come on now, Kinsey. I'll get duplicates made."

"Quit wheedling. I don't want duplicates. I want those. Anyway, you shredded Cousin Mortimer and he was my favorite."

"You never even met him."

"I know, but he had a good face."

"You're tough."

"A deal's a deal."

"How about joint custody. Shared visitation. One week on, one week off."

"Maybe," I said. "You shouldn't have been in such a hurry."

"At least I had the good sense not to shred my tax returns. I could be in jail for life, however much of it I got left."

"What about your clothes?"

"Those went last week. I'll have to scour the Goodwill thrift store and buy 'em back."

"Oh ye of little faith. Dolan swore you'd be fine. You should have listened to him."

"What does he know? The man's a mess. Didn't I tell you he was heading for another heart attack? Talk about a time bomb."

"I know. I told him the same thing, but there was no stopping him. What about you, are you really feeling okay?"

"Terrific. Full of beans. I'm determined to come down. Don't know how I'll get there, but I'll find a way."

"The doctor's letting you drive?"

"Of course. It's no business of hers. Problem is, I sold my car and let my license lapse."

"Oh, no."

"Well, I didn't want to take the test again. I was sure I'd be dead."

"What about the lease on your house?"

"Shit, I'd forgotten about that. Healthy, but homeless. What a turn of events. By the way, did Dolan tell you what happened here?"

"We never had a chance to talk."

"Triple homicide this morning—woman, her boyfriend, and her kid shot to death. The ex-husband's fled into the backcountry, where he's hiding out. All the SO guys have been pulled into the search. This guy's a wilderness expert, a paramilitary type. No telling how long it's going to take to flush him out. Forensics is still at the crime scene, which means they won't get to us again until they wrap that up. Could be days."

"So why hang around down here? Once Dolan's out, I can drive us home in his car and that'll save you the trip."

"No way. I'm bored to tears up here. I got cabin fever so bad, I'm about to go insane. Besides, if you two come home, we'll just have to turn around and go back again."

"Assuming there's a link between the Mustang and Jane Doe," I said.

"Trust me, it's there and Dolan thinks so, too. You been in business as long as we have, you develop a feel for these things. We're getting close."

"Actually, I'd agree. I talked to a dentist this morning who remembered her—someone like her, at any rate. He thinks she was one of the last patients he treated before he had to retire. The guy's ninety-three now and couldn't give me the name, but everything else he says seems to fit. I checked with the principal at Quorum High and he referred me to the alternative high school for problem kids. I haven't had a chance to deal with that—I'd just stopped by the motel to give Dolan the news when I found him in the throes of this heart attack."

"You hang on 'til I get there. Then we'll put our heads together and decide what's next. How will I find you?"

"I'll be around somewhere. If I'm not at the motel, you can try me here. You know Dolan's car. Just keep an eye out for that. This town's so small you can hardly miss."

"Let me get a pencil and paper and you can give me that address. As soon as I find wheels, I'll be on my way."

I gave him the name and address of the motel.

He said, "Do me a favor and reserve a room in my name."

"Why not take Dolan's? He's already forked out the bucks for it."

"Good plan. Let's do that."

"While we're at it, I need you to do me a favor. Could you stop by my apartment and pick up my leather jacket before you hit the road? It's hanging in my downstairs closet. I'll tell Henry to let you in and he can show you where it is."

"It's that cold?"

"To me it is. You better be prepared." Out of the corner of my eye, I saw a woman in scrubs come out of the treatment area with a manila folder in hand. "I think the doc just showed. I'll call you back if there's anything to report."

Dr. Flannery, the ER physician, was in her late forties, small, with short, pale brown hair, a broad forehead, thin lips, and deep lines in her face. Her nose was a raw pink, as though she'd blown it a few times since she'd applied her makeup. She had a tissue in her pocket and she dabbed at it before she held her hand out. "Sorry. Allergies. I'm Dr. Flannery. Are you Mr. Dolan's friend?"

We shook hands. "Kinsey Millhone. It's actually Lieutenant Dolan."

She checked his chart. "So it is."

"How's he doing?"

"He's been stabilized, but he has a serious left coronary arterial blockage. We'll be admitting him as soon as his paperwork's done. I've spoken to his cardiologist in Santa Teresa and he's suggested a cardiac surgeon he knows in Palm Springs. Dr. Bechler's on his way now. As soon as he's seen the patient and reviewed the EKG, the two of them will talk. I'm guessing they'll insert a stent. The choice is Lieutenant Dolan's, but that's what I'd do if I were in his shoes."

I made a face. "They'll open his chest?"

The doctor shook her head. "They'll run a catheter through a small incision in his left inguinal area and go up through the vein."

"How long will he be in?"

"That depends on his progress. Not as long as you'd think. Two days."

"Can I see him?"

"Of course. I've plugged him full of morphine so he's feeling no pain. The effect is about the same as a four-martini lunch."

"Not unusual for him."

"So I gathered. We had a little chat about that. I told him the smoking and heavy drinking would have to stop. He has to clean up his act around food as well. If you eat like he does, you should do the same yourself. QP's with cheese?"

"He ratted me out?"

She smiled. "Make sure we know how to reach you. He's listed you as next of kin, which means you're cleared for visits if you keep it brief. You want to follow me?"

I tagged after her as she pushed through the door and padded down the highly polished corridor. When we reached Dolan's cubical, she pulled aside the curtain on its overhead track. "I have a visitor for you."

Dolan mumbled a reply. Dr. Flannery held up five fingers, signaling a five-minute visit. I indicated I understood and she withdrew. I looked down at Dolan. "How're you feeling?"

His eyes were closed and he had a goofy smile on his face. His color had improved. He was stretched out on

the table, his upper body draped with a cotton coverlet.
His shoes were off and the toe of one sock was pulled up
to form a little cap, which made him look like a kid. He
was still on oxygen; attached to a bank of machines that
monitored his vital signs. He had an IV line in each arm.
A bag of clear liquid had been hung on one pole and I
counted fifteen drips. He began to snore.

I took his hand, wagging it. "How're you doing?"

He opened his eyes. "I'm good."

"You were in big trouble, you dork. You should have
called for help."

"Heard you knock. Couldn't move. Glad you got in."
He spoke carefully, as though his lips had been injected
with novocaine.

"Me and my little key picks. Don't tell."

His eyes closed again and he put a finger to his lips.

I said, "I put a call in to Stacey and told him where
you were. He says his X-rays are clear and he's coming
down."

"Said the same to me. No point arguing."

"Tell me about it. I tried to talk him out of it, but he
was adamant. I figured as long as you're stuck in here, he
might as well pitch in. We can't do much for now, but
maybe we can stir things up. I'm hoping Forensics will
come up with something good. I think we'll put him in
your room if I can have the key."

"Hang on." Dolan revived himself long enough to
fumble in his pants pocket and extract his key. I tucked it
in my shoulder bag, thinking I'd stop by and pick up my
typewriter before Stacey arrived.

The desk clerk appeared at the curtain with a plastic
hospital bracelet and a sheaf of documents affixed to a
clipboard. "I have your jewelry, Lieutenant Dolan. I just
need your signature and you'll be on your way."

He roused himself, lazily gestured her in. "Sign away my life." He turned to me. "You okay on your own?"

"Don't worry about me. You take care of yourself and get some rest. I'll stop by this evening. You behave."

"Good deal."

Before I left Quorum General, I put a call through to Henry. He was out. I left a message on his machine, telling him about Dolan's heart attack. I also mentioned that Stacey'd be stopping by. I told him where my jacket was and said I'd call later when there was more to report. It was 1:35 when I emerged from the hospital and returned to the parking lot. I hadn't realized how tense I was until I'd unlocked the car door and slipped behind the wheel. I took a good deep breath and did a neck roll. Anxiety was roiling through my body now that I was on my own. I hadn't realized how dependent I'd become on Dolan. It was nice to compare notes, nice to share meals, even fun to knock heads. My attachment didn't contain a shred of romance, but it did trigger a longing to be connected to someone. I'd trained with two old guys, who'd taught me the business many years before. Maybe it was them I missed.

I flipped through my note cards. The next obvious move was to chat with the principal at the alternative high school. I wished Dolan were on hand so he could handle it. Though I hated to admit it, he'd be subjected to a lot less guff. *Mano a mano*. Once he flashed that badge of his, people tended to respond. I picked up my minimap and located the Kennedy Pike, then fired up the Chevy and pulled out of the lot. On the way down Main Street, I detoured into a filling station and pumped gas into the tank. I stood there clutching the pump, watching the gallons go in while the total sales price went up. The process took so long I thought the tank must have sprung a leak. I'm accustomed to my VW with its gas tank the size of a bucket of paint. $29.46 later, I nosed out of the station and turned right.

Once I reached Kennedy Pike, I drove west, scanning for sight of the cemetery and the white frame structure across the street from it. This section of Quorum was made up of endless flat, empty fields stitched together with lines of trees that served as windbreaks. When I finally spotted the cemetery, it looked as flat as the fields around it. There was only a smattering of visible headstones. Most were laid flat in the ground. I could see a few concrete benches and a sparse assortment of plastic bouquets that had been left near graves. The surrounding fence was iron and without ornament. Square brick support posts appeared at fifteen-foot intervals. There were seven full-sized trees of an indeterminate type, but the branches hadn't leafed out yet and the limbs looked frail against the April sky.

Just beyond the cemetery entrance and across the street, I saw the Lockaby Alternative High School. I wondered if the students made the same melancholy association: from Youth to Death with only a stone's throw between. When you're of high school age, the days go on forever and death's little more than a rumor at the end of the road. Dolan and I knew death was just a heartbeat away.

I parked in the lot and followed the walkway to the front porch, up a flight of wide wooden steps. This must have been a farmhouse once upon a time. It still carried an air of small rooms and cramped hopes. I let myself into the foyer, where eight kids were sprawled on the floor with sketchbooks, doing pencil drawings of the

staircase. The teacher glanced up at me and then continued moving from student to student, making brief suggestions about perspective. From upstairs, I could hear
another class in progress. Laughter trickled down the
treads like leaking water. I don't remember anything
funny from my high school days.

To my right, the former parlor served as the main office, complete with the original fireplace. The hearth and
surround were dark redbrick and the whole of it was
topped with a dark mahogany mantelpiece. There was no
counter separating the reception area from the office secretary, whose desk had been arranged facing the wide
bay window. She interrupted her typing to turn and look
at me. She seemed pleasant; dark-haired, plump, probably in her forties, though it was hard to tell. When she
said, "Yes, ma'am?" several dimples appeared in her
cheeks. She pulled out a chair and patted the seat.

I crossed the room and sat down, introducing myself.
"I'm looking for Mrs. Bishop."

"She's in district meetings all day, but maybe I can
help. I'm Mrs. Marcum. What can I do for you?"

"Here's the problem," I said, and launched into the
tale. I'd told it so often that I had it down pat; the search
for Jane Doe's identity in fifty words or less. For the
umpteenth time, I described Jane Doe and the series of
interviews that had led me to Lockaby. "Do you remember anyone like that?"

"Not me, but I've only been here ten years. I'll ask
some of the teachers. Mrs. Puckett, who teaches typing,
doubles as the guidance counselor. She'd be the one
who'd recognize the girl if anyone did. Unfortunately,
she's out today—we all get a mental-health day every
couple of months. She'll be in first thing tomorrow
morning if you want to come back."

"If she does recognize the girl, would you have her records somewhere?"

"Not going back that far. We had a fire here eight years ago. Between the smoke and water damage, we lost the majority of our files. It's a wonder the whole place didn't go up in flames. The fire department saved us. They were here in seven minutes and knocked it down in thirty before it had a chance to spread."

"How'd it happen?"

"Fire chief said electrical. We had wiring that dated from the original construction—1945. He said it was a wonder it hadn't happened before. Now we have smoke detectors, heat detectors, and a sprinkling system—the works. We're lucky we weren't wiped out. Happily for us, there weren't any injuries or loss of life. Paperwork, who cares? It accumulates faster than I can file it."

"The kids like it here?"

"They seem to. Of course, we're a magnet for the troublemakers—dropouts, truants, delinquents. We get them when everyone else gives up. We only have a handful of teachers and we keep the classes small. Most of our students do poorly in an academic setting. Basically, they're good kids, but some are slow. Short attention spans. They're easily frustrated and most of them suffer from poor self-images. With a regular high school curriculum, they lose heart. Here the emphasis is practical. We cover the basics—reading, writing, and math—but we teach them how to write a résumé, how to dress for a job interview, simple etiquette. Art and music, too, just to round them out."

"Sounds like something every school should do."

"You'd think so, wouldn't you?"

The phone on her desk rang, but she made no move.

"You want to answer that?"

"They'll try back. I'm often out of the office and they've learned. You have a business card?"

"Sure."

"Why don't you give me a number. I'll try to reach Betty Puckett and have her give you a call."

"That'd be great." I took out a card and jotted down the name of the motel, the phone number, and my room number on the back. "I appreciate this."

"I can't swear she'll know the girl, but if she was ever a student here, I promise you, Betty dealt with her."

"One more question: Dr. Nettleton seemed to think this girl was in a foster home, so I'm wondering if Social Services might help?"

"I doubt it. They closed that office years ago, and I have no idea how you'd locate the old files. It'd be Riverside County, but that's as much as I know. You'll have a battle on your hands. They're worse than schools are about access to records, especially on a juvenile."

"Too bad. I had hopes, but I guess not."

"Sorry."

"I'll figure it out eventually. It's just a question of time."

When I left Lockaby, I was no better informed, but I was feeling encouraged. Once in the car again, I sat for a moment, beating out a little rhythm on the steering wheel. Now what? In the confusion of the moment, I hadn't thought to ask Dolan what he'd learned from the Quorum PD and the sheriff's office about the old missing-persons reports. I'd ask him when I went to visit. I did a mental check of our list. The only item we hadn't covered yet was the issue of the tarp and whether one had been stolen at the time the Mustang was taken. I started the car and backed out of the slot, took a left on the Kennedy Pike, and returned to town.

The McPhee's redbrick ranch house looked deserted when I arrived—doors shut, curtains drawn, and no cars in the drive. I passed the house, cruising slowly, and at the next intersection, did a U-turn and drove back. I parked across the street. I disliked the idea of seeing Ruel again, but who else could I ask about the tarp? While I'd remained largely in the background during the impounding of the Mustang, he'd still associate me with his loss of face.

I sat and studied the house, wondering if I could handle the question by phone. Chickenshit idea. Where possible, it's always better to deal in person. I was on the verge of taking off, postponing the visit until later in the day, when an approaching car slowed and turned into the drive. Edna.

Once she turned off the engine, I could see her fussing in the front seat, gathering packages. After a bit of maneuvering, she got out with her purse over her shoulder, a grocery bag in one hand, and two department store carryalls clutched in the other. She pushed the door shut with one hip and moved to the rear of the car, setting down the carryalls while she opened the trunk. She placed her purse and the grocery bag on the driveway, reached into the trunk, and removed several additional grocery bags. I could see her debate whether she could manage everything in one trip or if she'd be forced to make two. I took the opportunity to get out of my car and cross the street at a trot. "Hi, Edna. Kinsey. Can I give you a hand?"

She looked up with surprise, coloring slightly at the sight of me. "I can manage."

"There's no sense in making two trips. Why don't I take these and you can handle the rest?" I leaned forward and picked up her purse, one grocery sack, and the two large paper carryalls. "You must have spent all morning running errands."

"The family's coming for supper and I'm running late. I want to get a pot roast in the oven." Her demeanor had softened, though she seemed ill at ease. Good manners apparently took precedence over any discomfort she felt at my reappearance on the scene. Ruel would have cut me dead, but the removal of the Mustang had little to do with her. It'd been sitting in the garage for years, anyway, and she was probably tired of his procrastination. His collection of classic cars must have seemed like a lousy investment since he'd apparently made no effort to restore even one of them.

I followed her along the driveway to the back gate and then, since she didn't protest, I continued up the porch steps and through the back door. I put her purse on the Formica counter, waiting to see where she wanted the other bags. The red, white, and blue color scheme was like a tone poem to Americana. I took the time to let my gaze rest on every surface. "What time will Ruel be home?"

She'd placed her bags on the kitchen table. "Soon, I'd guess. The rest of them—Cornell and his wife and kids and my daughter—are supposed to come at six. You can put those over there," and she gestured toward the window seat.

I left the grocery sack on the kitchen table and crossed to the window seat, where I placed the department store carryalls. I moved aside a couple of pillows and the patchwork quilt and perched, uninvited. I glanced at my watch. "It's almost two now. Do you mind if I wait?"

"I'm not sure that's a good idea. Ruel's been upset and I don't want anything to set him off again." She began to put groceries away, leaving out the items she intended to use: a mammoth cellophane-wrapped chuck roast that looked like the whole back end of some unidentified beast, onions, carrots, potatoes, fresh green beans, brown-and-serve rolls. She looked at me. "Did you need him for anything in particular? You know he's madder than spit. There's nothing he hates more than someone trying to put one over on him. You and that detective should have told him the truth."

"We told Cornell why we were here. He could have mentioned it himself. We're talking about a murder. What difference does it make if Ruel's mad?"

"Nonetheless."

"Nonetheless, what?"

"He won't be happy if he finds you here."

"Maybe you can help me and I'll be on my way."

"What do you want?"

"We're wondering if someone took one of his tarps at the time the car was stolen."

She paused to think about that and then shook her head. "Not that I recall. He never said anything. I suppose I could ask him and get in touch with you later on."

"You'd be doing him a service, especially if it turns out the Mustang was used to abduct the girl."

Edna laid a hand against her chest. "You can't seriously believe he had anything to do with it."

"It's not up to me." Her anxiety was infectious. I stood up, suddenly eager to be gone. As I picked up my shoulder bag, my glance fell on the red, white, and blue quilt folded neatly on the seat. The pattern consisted of a series of patches stitched together in a traditional log cabin pattern. In repeat rows, running along the diagonal, the fabric was a print of dark blue daisies, a dot of red in each center, on a white background.

I must have made a sound because Edna looked at me, saying, "What?"

"Where did you get this?"

"That was given to me by Justine's mother, Medora—Cornell's mother-in-law. Why?"

"I need to talk to her."

17

I stood on the front steps of Medora Sanders's house, a modest stucco box with a shallow overhang that served to shield the small concrete porch. The exterior was painted dark gray. The wood trim had shed flakes of white paint, like dandruff, on the shrubs planted along the foundation. At the end of the dirt drive there was a detached single-car garage with its door padlocked shut. Edna had allowed me to borrow the quilt and I carried it draped over one arm. The daisy-print fabric had been pieced into the quilt in seven adjoining sections. While it was true that the fabric might have been sold across the country, the coincidence was too striking to imagine it was unrelated.

I couldn't find a bell so I opened the wood-framed screen and knocked on the glass pane in the front door. A moment passed and then a woman peered out. She was thin and unkempt, with pale green eyes and pale flyaway hair. Her cheeks and the rim of her nose were patterned with spider veins. She smoothed her hair with a knobby-fingered hand, tucking a loose strand into a disordered chignon before she opened the door a crack. "Yes?"

"Mrs. Sanders?"

She wore faded jeans and a red nylon sweater with a runner up one sleeve where a loop of yarn had come loose. I could smell whiskey fumes seeping through her pores like toxic waste. She hesitated, apparently unwilling to confirm or deny her identity until she knew why I asked. "I don't buy door-to-door," she said.

I held up the quilt. "I'm not selling anything. I came to talk to you about this."

Her gaze shifted, though her manner remained fuzzy and her eyes were slightly out of focus. She looked like someone chronically inebriated. "Where'd you get that?"

"Edna McPhee let me borrow it. I'm returning it later, but I have some questions for you first."

"Why'd she send you over here?"

"She said since you made the quilt, you might have some information. May I come in?"

Medora thought about that briefly, probably wishing I'd go somewhere else. "I hope this won't take long. I got other things to do."

She opened the door and I stepped directly into the living room, which was small and cramped, with an acoustic-tile ceiling and a stingy-looking brick fireplace. On the mantel there was a cluster of statuettes: angels, milkmaids, and coy-looking kids with the toes of their shoes turned in.

Medora closed the door, saying, "That Edna's a pill. I don't know how Justine manages to put up with her."

"The two of you don't get along?"

"I never said that. Edna's a good person and I know she means well, but she's holier-than-thou. You know the type—doesn't drink, doesn't smoke, and doesn't hold with those who do."

"Cornell smokes."

"Not around his mother. He's pure as the driven snow," Medora said. "She disapproves of cards, too. Devil's handiwork, she says. Granddaughters come here, we play Canasta, War, Fish, Slap Jack. Doesn't seem like the Devil's work to me."

She returned to the couch and sat dead center, causing the cushions to rise on either side of her. A crocheted green-and-black afghan was bunched haphazardly at one end. There was an ashtray full of butts on the coffee table, a cluster of prescription pill bottles, a fifth of Early Times, and a highball glass half-filled with melting ice cubes. Many surfaces looked sticky, and there was a fine haze of dust over everything. "I was taking a little nap. I haven't been feeling well the last couple days. What's your name again?"

"I should have introduced myself. I'm Kinsey Millhone."

"Medora Sanders," she said, "but I guess you know that. What's your connection to Edna? I hope it's not through her church. She's always trying to get me roped in."

"Not at all. Mind if I sit?"

She waved me into a chair. I moved aside a stack of newspapers and took a seat, keeping the quilt on my lap. There were a number of crafts projects in the room, most from kits, by the look: a wall-hung quilt, embroidered pillows on the couch. In front of the hearth there was a hand-hooked rug bearing the image of a Scottie. There were several framed cross-stitched pieces voicing corny sentiments. She followed my survey. "I used to do a lot of needlework until my joints flared up." She lifted her right hand, displaying a twisted thumb and fingers that did a slow curve outward. It looked like she'd been tortured for information she'd refused to give. "I don't quilt anymore in case you want one for yourself."

I folded a section of the quilt until the daisy-print fabric was foremost. "Actually, I'm curious about this fabric. Do you remember where you got it?"

She glanced at the print. "I used to make clothes for my daughter." She reached for a pack of Camels and extracted one. She flicked her lighter, but it took her two tries to make the flame touch the tip of the cigarette. "That was a remnant. Cheaper to buy that way. I used to check the bin at the fabric shop in town. It's gone out of business now so you can save yourself a trip. Same time I bought that, I picked up six yards of royal blue taffeta that I offered to run up for Justine's prom dress. She about had a cow. Said she'd kill herself before she wore anything homemade. She insisted on store-bought, so I made her pay for it. It's like I told her, 'Money doesn't grow on trees, Justine.' Kids these days don't appreciate that."

"They're embarrassed," I said. "They want exactly the same clothes every other teenager has. That's how they express their unique individuality."

"I guess. I had to make do with precious little once her dad ran out."

"When was that?"

"Summer of 1969, somewhere around in there. Who keeps track? Fellow wants to take a hike, it's good riddance." She reached for one of her pill bottles and shook out a white tablet that she placed on her tongue. She picked up her highball and took a swallow, frowning slightly when she realized how watered down it was. "I'm on pain medication. Whiskey gives the codeine a little boost. Any rate, what's this in relation to?"

"I'm trying to identify a young woman who was murdered during that same period. When the body was found, she was wearing home-sewn pants made of this same daisy print."

Medora's laugh was like a cough, hacking and full of phlegm. "I don't know about a murder, daisy print or no, but I can tell you one thing. You got a big job ahead. Company must've made thousands of yards of that print."

"I'm sure you're right, but I thought it was worth a shot. The girl I'm referring to would have been somewhere between fifteen and eighteen. This was late July, early August, of 1969. About five foot four, a hundred and twenty-five pounds. Brunette hair she probably dyed blond. She had prominent teeth and the eyetooth on this side was twisted. She'd had a lot of dental work done."

Her smile had begun to fade.

"Does any of that sound familiar?"

Medora crossed her arms and squinted against the smoke, cigarette held close to her face. "Years ago, I had a girl living with me sounds like that. Name was Charisse Quinn."

I felt my heart thump twice from the hit of adrenaline that shot through my veins. I'd run across the name before, but I wasn't sure where. "What happened to her?"

"Nothing as far as I know, except she flew the coop. I went in her room one morning and found her bed hadn't been slept in and half her stuff was gone. She'd helped herself to my best suitcase, too. Of course, she stole just about anything wasn't nailed down."

"The murdered girl I'm talking about was found in Lompoc. You know the area?"

"Up near San Francisco?"

"Not that far north. Closer to Santa Teresa."

"Couldn't prove it by me. I don't travel. Used to, but now I prefer to stay put."

"Why was she living in your home?"

"I was a foster mom—something like that. Reason

she ended up with me is I had this woman lived next door asked if I'd help. She'd had a whole string of foster kids trooping through her place. County wanted her to take Charisse, but her husband wasn't well and it was more than she could manage. She asked if I could open my home—that's how she put it—'open my home to someone less fortunate than myself.' What a joke. Wilbur barely gave me enough to cover all the household expenses. At any rate, my neighbor told me Social Services paid close to a hundred and eighty dollars a month, so that's why I agreed. Doesn't sound like much, but every little bit helped."

"How'd the arrangement work out?"

"Not that good. Girl was foul-mouthed and disrespectful, though, at that age, I'll be the first to admit, Justine was the same. Her and me had troubles enough without Charisse sticking in her two cents' worth."

"How long was she was with you?"

"Five, six months, I'd guess. I believe she came here early March."

"Can you remember the date she disappeared?"

Medora made a sour face. "I never said she disappeared. I said she took off."

"Sorry. That's what I meant. When did she take off?"

"July, I'd say. Doesn't surprise me to hear she came to a bad end. She's a wild one, that girl. Had a bad case of hot pants. Picked up boys every chance she got. Out until all hours. She'd come waltzing in here three in the morning, smelling like crème de menthe and marijuana. I warned her and warned her, but would she listen to me?"

"What happened to her parents?"

"Don't know. I never laid eyes on that pair. Must've been druggies or something if the State had to step in."

"How old was Charisse?"

"Seventeen. Same as Justine. Girls were both seniors. Of course, Charisse got kicked out of regular high school and sent over to Lockaby. That's the school for dummies and delinquents."

Bemused, I thought back to my conversation with Eichenberger, the principal of Quorum High, who'd sworn up and down he remembered every student who'd ever passed through his doors. What a pompous old windbag. Charisse had not only been there, but she'd caused enough trouble to get tossed out.

"You have other children?"

"Just the one."

"And you were living here at the time?"

"I lived here ever since Wilbur and I got married in 1951. We only have the two bedrooms, so the girls had to share. Imagine how popular that was."

"Must have been hard."

"Oh, they went through every kind of conflict—spats over clothes and boyfriends—the two went round and round like alleycats, spitting and hissing, fur flying. You never heard the like. Justine didn't want Charisse hanging out with her friends and I could see her point. Always had to raise a fuss. Always had to have her way."

"Not much of a charmer from the sound of it."

"She could be charming once she put her mind to it, but only if she wanted something."

"What about your husband? Where was he?"

"Well, he lived here in theory, but he was gone half the time."

"What sort of work?"

"He hired on at Sears in major appliances—dishwashers, refrigerators, things like that. Worked nights, weekends, and every holiday. Never got us a deal,

SUE GRAFTON

but that was him in a nutshell. You'd think he could've got me a portable dishwasher at the very least. I had to do everything by hand. Probably why my joints went bad. Made my back hurt, too."

"So he left about the same time she did?"

"I suppose so, though I never thought of it like that." She frowned at me, taking a drag of her cigarette. "I hope you're not saying he went off with *her*."

"I don't know, but it does seem odd. If she was so hot for guys, why not him?"

"He was close to fifty years old, for one thing. And I can't think why he'd take an interest in someone her age. He never paid any attention to her as far as I could see. He's a skunk, that's for sure, but I can't believe he'd sink *that* low. That's—what do you call it?—statutory rape."

"Did he give you any explanation when he left?"

She took another drag of her cigarette. "None. He went off to work one day and he never came home. He left before she did, now I think of it. I remember because he missed seeing Justine in her prom dress and that was June fourteenth."

"What'd you do when he left?"

"Nothing. Gone is gone," she said.

"What about Charisse? Did you talk to the police when you realized she'd left?"

"I went to see them that day. Police and the sheriff. I got county funds for her and I knew the social worker would have a fit otherwise. As it was, I had to return the next month's check and with Wilbur gone, I came up short on the bills. Justine tried to tell me Charisse wasn't to blame, but it was typical of her. She'd do anything she could to screw it up for someone else."

"But you did file a missing-persons report?"

"I told you, that day, though the deputy didn't offer

much encouragement. He found out she'd run off half a dozen times before. And like he said, with her eighteenth birthday coming up she'd be on her own, anyway. Said they'd do what they could, but he couldn't promise much. He as good as told me to go home and forget about her."

"Which you did."

"What else could I do? I didn't even know her mother's name. I guess the social worker called the mother."

"You think that's where she went, back to her mom?"

"Don't know and didn't care. With Wilbur gone, I had my hands full just trying to make ends meet. In case you intend to ask, I never heard from her again. Him either. Far as I know, we're still married, unless he's dead. That'd be something, wouldn't it?"

"You have reason to think something might have happened to him?"

"I'm saying, if he's alive, you'd think he could have dropped us a card. Thirty-six years married, that's the least he could do."

"What about Charisse's social worker? What was her name?"

"Don't remember. It's been too many years. Tinker, Tailor—something along those lines. I called and talked to her, and you know what she said? Said she never expected the arrangement to last; Charisse was such a pain. Not those words exactly, but that's the gist of it. I thought, Oh, thanks. Now she pipes up, after all I went through."

"You must have felt terrible."

She coughed a thick laugh into her fist, pausing then to cough in earnest. She took a sip of watery bourbon and then recovered herself. "Especially when I found out Wilbur'd emptied all the bank accounts. Excuse me, are you about done here? Because if not, I intend to fix myself another drink—see if I can get some relief from this cough. That was my mother's remedy—whiskey and honey—though you ask me, it wasn't the honey that helped."

"Just a few more questions and then I'll let you get some rest. How did Charisse travel? Do you have any idea?"

"Wasn't by bus. I know because police checked on that. I suppose she hitched a ride with one of those hoodlums she ran around with once she got to Lockaby."

"You remember any of their names?"

"Couldn't tell one from the other. They were all the same—skanky-looking boys with bad skin."

"You heard about the car that was stolen from the back of Ruel's shop?"

"Everybody heard. He was fit to be tied."

"Is there any chance Charisse took it?"

"I doubt it. She didn't drive. Never passed the test. I offered to help her get her license, but she didn't get around to it. Afraid to fail, you ask me; worried she'd end up looking like a fool."

"How'd she get around if she didn't drive?"

"Bummed rides with Justine and Cornell and everyone else. That's another thing got on people's nerves. She was a mooch."

"Did she work?"

"Her? That's a laugh. I couldn't even get her to pick up after herself."

"I know I asked you this before, but is there any way you could pinpoint the date she left?"

Medora shook her head. "I was just glad to have her gone. Does seem queer to think she's been dead all these years. I pictured her married with kids. That or living on the street. Wonder who killed her."

"That's what we're trying to find out. Do you have a photograph by chance? I'd be interested in seeing how she looked."

"I don't, but you might ask Justine." She paused, coughing again with such vigor it brought tears to her eyes. "I can't stand it. My throat's killing me. You want a drink?"

"No, thanks."

I watched Medora pour herself some whiskey, her hands shaking so badly she could scarcely lift the glass to her lips. She swallowed with relief and then took two deep breaths. "Whoo! That's better. Whiskey'll cure just about anything."

"Well, I guess that's it. I can't tell you how much I appreciate your help."

"You want my opinion, whatever happened to her? She brought it on herself."

I was on my way down her walkway, heading for Dolan's car with the quilt over my arm, when I noticed a sedan had pulled in and parked at the curb. The door on the driver's side opened and a woman got out. She tucked her keys in her purse and she was halfway up the walk when she caught sight of me and stopped. Her gaze flicked to the quilt and then back to me. This had to be Justine. She and Medora shared the same body type and the same pale flyaway hair. Though their features were unremarkable, I could see the resemblance; something in the shape of their narrow chins and their pale green eyes. Like her husband, Cornell, she appeared to be in her mid-thirties.

"Excuse me. Are you Justine McPhee?"

"Yes?"

"My name's Kinsey Millhone. I'm a private detective—"

"I know who you are. I believe we have you to thank for the foul mood my father-in-law's been in." Her manner was an odd mixture of composure and agitation, her tone giving vent to something prickly lurking under the surface.

"I'm sorry about that, but it couldn't be helped."

She glanced toward the house. "What are you doing here?"

"I was just chatting with your mother about Charisse."

Her expression was vacant for an instant and then I could see recognition spark. "Charisse?"

"That's right. I don't know if Cornell mentioned this, but we're investigating a murder . . ."

"That's what he told me, but surely you're not talking about her."

"We don't have a positive ID yet, but it does look that way."

"I don't believe it. What happened?"

"She was stabbed and her body was dumped outside of Lompoc. This was August of '69. The sheriff's detectives worked the case for months without progress. Now they've decided it's time to try again."

"But what brought you to Quorum? She was only here a few months."

"Following our noses. We were lucky to get some breaks."

"Like what? I'm sorry for all the questions, but none of this makes sense."

"I know it's tough to absorb," I said. "When I was at

Edna's, I spotted the quilt and realized the dark blue daisy print was a match for the victim's home-sewn pants. Edna told me your mother made the quilt, so I came to see her. You thought she'd run away?"

"Well, yes. It certainly didn't occur to me the poor girl was *dead*. I'm sure Cornell and his dad would have helped you if they'd known who it was."

"Let's hope that's true. At this point, we're trying to pin down events between the time she took off and the time her body was found."

"When was that again?"

"August third. Your mother said she left in July, but she couldn't remember the exact date."

"Charisse came and went as she pleased. I didn't even realize she was gone until Mom started screaming about her suitcase. The pants you mentioned must've been the pair my mother made for me."

"Did you give her the pants or did she take those, too?"

"I wouldn't have *given* them to her. She always helped herself to my stuff."

"What about the other items she stole?"

"I don't remember anything specific. She had no scruples at all. She didn't care who she hurt as long as she got what she wanted. The kids at Quorum didn't want to have anything to do with her." She adjusted the watchband on her wrist, glancing at the time as she did.

"You have to go?"

"I'm sorry, but we're due at my in-laws for supper and I still have to pick up the girls. I stopped by to see Mom because she hasn't been feeling well."

"What about tomorrow? I'd love to talk to you again."

"Oh, I don't think so. I wish I could help, but Ruel's mad enough as it is. He'd have a fit if he knew I'd even said this much."

"You said he'd've been cooperative himself if he'd known it was her."

"I meant if he'd known about it up front. He's hard to predict, especially now that he thinks you've made a fool out of him."

"Well, give it some thought and let me know."

"I'd have to talk to Cornell. He's pissed off, too, because his dad blames him about the car."

"That's dumb. Ruel's the one who took title and let it sit all those years."

"True, but I don't want to give him reason to come down on me. He complains enough as it is. He thinks I'm controlling. Ha. Like he's not."

"He doesn't have to know. That's entirely up to you. I don't want you getting into trouble on my account."

"Trust me. I won't. You have to watch your backside around him. He might seem harmless, but he's a snake."

"Well. I better let you go. I'm staying at the Ocean View. I'd appreciate your calling once you've talked to Cornell. He might have something to contribute even if you don't."

"I doubt it. He really only knew Charisse because of me."

"Speaking of that, your mother told me Charisse hung out with a bunch of hoodlums at Lockaby. You might ask if Cornell remembers anyone in particular. We could use a few names."

"You really expect to find her killer after all these years?"

"We've made it this far," I said. "I hope to hear from you."

"I can't promise anything, but I'll do what I can."

*   *   *

I went back to the motel and put a call through to Dr. Spears. I told Mrs. Gary, his assistant, what I'd learned from Medora Sanders. She remembered Charisse Quinn as soon as she heard the name. She made a note and said she'd pass the information along to him. She assured me that if he had time, he'd search the dead storage boxes for her chart. If he couldn't do it himself, she promised she'd pitch in. I thanked her profusely. Once I hung up, I sat on the edge of the bed, grinning from ear to ear, finally allowing myself a moment to celebrate. I couldn't wait to tell Dolan. A match on dental records would confirm my hunch. I was convinced this was her, but we needed concrete proof.

18

I went in through the front entrance of Quorum General and asked the volunteer at the reception desk for directions to the CCU. The facility wasn't large, but it seemed up-to-date, at least judging by the portions of it I saw en route. As it turned out, Dolan had been taken into surgery by the time I reached the floor. The Palm Springs cardiologist had blown in an hour before, and he'd kicked butt in six directions getting the procedure under way. I got a cursory briefing from the charge nurse, who checked with the OR. She assured me everything was going fine, though it'd be a while before Dolan was out of post-op. She suggested I call her at 7:00 to make sure he'd returned.

Leaving the hospital, I could feel my exhilaration fade. It was 4:30 by then. I had no access to Dolan and no way to know when Stacey Oliphant would appear. At best, I wouldn't hear from Justine until some time the next day, if I heard from her at all, which left me with no one to talk to and nothing to do. I retreated to the Ocean View. I parked the car in the motel lot and bought a can of

Diet Pepsi from the vending machine. I used Dolan's key to let myself into his room, where I retrieved my Smith-Corona. Once ensconced in my own room, I set up a minioffice, using the motel desk. I typed up my notes, a process that took the better part of an hour and a half.

At 6:15 I opened the phone book and consulted the yellow pages for the nearest pizza joint. I called and ordered a medium sausage-and-pepperoni pizza with jalapeño peppers and extra cheese on top. Given Dolan's diet restrictions, there was no way I'd be able to eat such fare in front of him. As a courtesy, I decided to indulge now. While I waited for delivery, I popped out to the vending machine and bought another Diet P. I ate supper sitting on my bed, my back propped against the pillows, watching the news and feeling completely decadent.

I called the hospital shortly after 7:00 and talked to the ward clerk in CCU. She said Dolan was in his room if I wanted to visit, which, of course, I did.

It was fully dark outside and the temperature had dropped precipitously by the time I emerged from my room and headed back to the hospital. Despite the halo of light pollution hovering over the town, the stars were as distinct as pinpricks in black construction paper, light shining through from the other side. The moon hadn't yet risen, but I could see where the darkness would lift and the desert would glow like a silver platter once it mounted the sky. I parked in the hospital lot and walked through the entrance doors for the second time that day.

All of the interior lights were ablaze, and it lent the premises a warm, cozy air. The lobby was filled with evening visitors. I passed the gift shop and the coffee shop and continued to the elevators, heading for the second floor. In all the semiprivate rooms I peered in, the curtains were drawn and the corner-mounted television sets were tuned to reruns. Dinner had probably been served at 5:30 or so, and the trays were now in the meal carts that still sat in the corridor. I caught glimpses of partially consumed foodstuffs: canned green beans and Salisbury steak (which is a fancy name for meatloaf) and countless packets of saltines still secured in cellophane. Plastic cups of taut red Jell-O squares sat untouched, and I suspected the hospital dietitian would find herself in a state of despair. These meals, like those in elementary schools, look better on paper than they do to the hapless participants. Half the items end up in the trash.

CCU was quiet and the lights were subdued. Dolan was in a private room attached by tubes and wires to a bank of monitors. His vital signs were flashed on a digital read-out, like the time and temperature bulletins outside a bank. The decor had been designed to minimize stress. The color scheme consisted of restful blues and pale, soothing greens. There was a bank of windows and a wall-mounted clock, but no television set and no newspapers trumpeting the day's quota of economic woes, murders, disasters, and fatal accidents.

One of Dolan's IV lines had been removed and I could see the bruising in the crook of his arm. His one-day growth of beard already looked like the splayed white bristles on a toothbrush used to clean the bathroom grout. Two clear-plastic oxygen prongs extended from his nose. That aside, he was alert, his color was good, and some of his friskiness had been restored. He seemed tired, but he didn't look half-dead. Any minute now, he'd get cranky about the absence of booze and cigarettes.

"Hey, Lieutenant, you look great. How're you feeling?"

"Better. Almost human, as a matter of fact."

There was a murmur behind me and I turned to find a nurse standing in the doorway. She was in her forties, with dark eyes and shiny brown hair streaked with gold. She wore civilian clothes, but her shoes were crepe-soled and her name tag announced her as CHRIS KOVACH, RN. She said, "Sorry to bother you, but there's a fellow at the nurses' station claiming he's related to you. I checked your chart, but you don't have him listed as an emergency contact or your next of kin."

Dolan's face went blank.

Chirpily, I said, "It must be your brother, Stacey. When I called and told him about your heart attack, he said he'd hop in the car and head right down." I turned to Ms. Kovach. "I know the lieutenant's not supposed to have more than one visitor at a time, but his brother's just finished chemo for non-Hodgkin's lymphoma, and it'd be great if we could be together after all these months."

I thought the medical angle was a nice touch, but the look she gave me indicated she heard tales like that, on average, three times a day. "His brother? I don't see the family resemblance."

"That's because he's bald. With his hair grown in, they look enough alike to be mistaken for twins."

"And you're *his* daughter," she said, indicating Dolan with a tilt of her head.

"Uh-huhn."

"So the fellow in the hall is your uncle Stacey, is that correct?"

"On my mother's side."

She wagged a warning finger. "Just this once, but not for long. I've got my eye on the clock. No cheating on the time."

Piously, Dolan said, "Thank you, Nurse."

His tone was what finally netted us the smile she'd been trying to suppress.

Stacey appeared in the doorway moments later. I was happy to see he'd doffed his watch cap, exposing an endearing patchwork of bald spots and fuzz. At least the nurse would know I hadn't lied about that.

Dolan said, "How'd you get here? I thought you sold your car."

"Rented one—a spiffy little Ford I drove like a bat out of hell. I'm surprised I didn't get a ticket. How are you?"

"Especially driving without a license."

Stacey pulled over a chair, offering it to me. "You want to sit?"

"You take that. I prefer to stand."

Since the visit was being limited, we truncated polite talk in favor of a Jane Doe update. I said, "I think I may have a line on her." I told them about the quilt with the daisy-print patches that led me to Medora Sanders. "From what Medora says, the girl's name is Charisse Quinn. She was apparently a ward of the State, fostered out through Riverside County Social Services. Both Medora and her daughter said she was a pain in the ass: dishonest, promiscuous, and foul-mouthed. According to Medora, she lived with 'em five months or so and then took off without a word. This was in the summer of '69. I should also mention that Wilbur Sanders, Medora's husband, disappeared at about the same time. I asked if the two events could be related, but she hated that idea. Let's hope Dr. Spears can confirm the ID when he pulls her old chart."

"You know the date this girl left?"

"I'm still trying to pin that one down. The timing's close enough to work, or so it appears. I hope to talk to

Justine again and maybe she can narrow the frame. By the way, she's married to Ruel's son, Cornell, if that's significant."

Stacey piped up. "The auto upholstery guy?"

Dolan said, "That's him. The Mustang was recovered from his shed."

Stacey was squinting. "And this runaway. You're sure the name's Charisse Quinn?"

"Fairly sure," I said. "Why?"

"Because she shows up in one of the old reports. You can check for yourself. Her mother called the Sheriff's Department here a week or so into the investigation. She'd heard her daughter'd been reported missing and wanted us to know she was alive and well."

"I remember now. You're right. I knew I'd read the name, but I couldn't think where."

Dolan said, "Well, she couldn't be Jane Doe unless she rose from the dead. You said she called in a week or so after the body was found."

"The caller *said* she was Quinn's mother. Might have been someone else," Stacey said.

"I don't guess those old phone records still exist," I said.

"Probably not," Dolan replied. "Too much time's elapsed. All we can hope is the deputy took down her number when the call came in."

Stacey said, "Let's see what this dentist says. If the records match, then we know the victim's Quinn and the call's a fake."

"Any word on the Mustang?" Dolan asked.

Stacey smiled, holding up three fingers. "Three blond hairs caught in the hinge of the trunk. Characteristics are similar to Jane Doe's hair. Not conclusive, of course, but it shores up the theory she was stowed in the Mustang for transport. Someone made an effort to wipe the car clean, but the techs picked up a few latent fingerprints, including a partial palm print on the jack. The guy must have moved it when he was clearing space in the trunk."

I said, "What about the stains, were those blood?"

"We sent the carpet to the DOJ lab in Colgate, but we won't get results on that for weeks. We're lucky we have the technology now we didn't have back then. The blood might be all hers, or we might have some of the killer's mixed in."

"Seems like the other question is whether the stains in the trunk match the ones on the tarp. A bloody stabbing like that, she might have put up a fight," I said.

Stacey's tone was dubious. "Maybe so, but don't forget, her hands were bound and the coroner's report doesn't make mention of defensive wounds."

Dolan said, "Even so, the guy might have been nicked."

"Let's hope. Problem is, we don't have a suspect for comparison."

"Correction. We don't have a suspect *yet*."

I raised my hand. "Could one of you ask Ruel about the tarp? I want to know if it was his."

Dolan snorted. "Why should *we* ask? Why not you?"

"Come on. You know he's going to yell at me. He'd never yell at the two of you."

"Chickenheart."

"What a wuss."

I smiled. "I thought that's what you tough guys were for. To do the dirty work."

"I'll tackle him," Stacey said. "He won't pick on a guy as sick as me."

Dolan said, "Wait a minute, Stace. Don't pull rank. You said you were well. I'm the sick one. Lookit where I am."

"So you can ask him. Who cares? Point is, we ought to see if we can find out where the tarp came from."

"How're you going to do that? Damn thing doesn't even have a tag with the manufacturer's name. Besides which, I don't see the relevance."

I said, "The killer might have been a long-distance hauler. They sometimes use tarps to secure a load." I stopped. "Uh-oh."

"Uh-oh, what?"

"I just had a flash."

"Of what?"

"If the victim turns out to be Charisse and the body was transported in the Mustang, then your theory about Frankie Miracle is really screwed."

Dolan frowned. "How you figure that?"

"We know Frankie stole Cathy Lee's Chevy. So how could he have driven two cars, one from Quorum and one from Venice, and have both arrive in Lompoc at the same time?"

I could see him calculate. "He could have made two trips."

"Oh, please. What's he do—he kills Charisse, drives the Mustang to Lompoc, dumps the body, abandons the car, and then hitchhikes to Venice so he can stab someone else?"

"So he had an accomplice," Dolan said.

"To do what? There's no link between the two murders, unless I missed a beat somewhere."

Stacey said, "Dolan hates the idea Frankie's innocent."

"I don't hate the idea, it's Frankie I hate," Dolan said, irritably. "But what you say makes sense. How'd you come up with that?"

"I don't know. It's like one of those thought problems in high school math. The minute I'd see that sentence about the two trains, one leaving Chicago at sixty miles an hour, and the other blah, blah, blah, I'd start blacking out. I abandoned math the minute I was allowed."

"You didn't believe 'em when they said math would be useful later in your life?"

"Not even a little bit."

In the doorway, Chris Kovach cleared her throat and pointed to her watch.

"We're just going," Stacey said, rising from his chair.

"You can come back tomorrow, but only one at a time."

Stacey followed me to the motel in his rental car and we parked in adjoining slots. I walked with him to Dolan's room and gave him the key. He unlocked the door and put his duffel on a chair. The room had been made up and the furniture was back in place. It was 9:25 and I was ready to say good-night, assuming he was tired and wanted to hit the sack. "If you like, we can have breakfast together. What time do you get up?"

"Not so fast. I drove straight to the hospital after hours on the road. I haven't had my dinner yet. Wasn't that an Arby's I saw out on Main?"

"Sure, but the Quorum Inn's still open. Wouldn't you prefer a regular sit-down meal?"

"Arby's has tables. I've never had an Arby-Q. Isn't that what they're called? Now you've introduced me to fast food, I have some catching up to do."

I sat with Stacey, watching him plow through an Arby-Q, two orders of curly fries, and a roast beef sandwich, oozing a yellow sauce that was rumored to be cheese. He looked as if he'd picked up a few pounds in the days since I'd seen him last. "You do this often?"

"Couple times a day. I found a cab company that delivers fast food, sort of like Meals on Wheels. Geez, this is great. I feel like a new man. I never would have known if you hadn't turned me on to this stuff."

"Happy to be of help. Personally, I never thought of junk food as life-affirming, but there you have it."

Stacey wiped his mouth on a napkin. "Forgot to mention this to Con. I got a call from Frankie's PO. Dench says he may be in violation. Looks like he left the county without permission."

"When was this?"

"Yesterday."

"That surprises me. To hear Frankie talk, he knew all the rules and regs and wasn't going to be caught out. Wonder what set him off?"

"Might have been your visit. Con said he seemed cool, but you never know about these things. What's on for tomorrow?"

"Let's talk to Ruel. I've got the perfect excuse. I still have Edna's quilt. We can ask him about the tarp when I take it back it to her."

Stacey leaned forward. "Kinsey, we're cops. We don't need excuses. That's for them to give us."

Sheepishly, I said, "Oh. You've got a point."

When we reached the motel again it was 10:15. The wind had kicked up and I had my arms crossed, trying to protect myself from the cold.

Stacey said, "Hang on a minute. I have your jacket in my trunk."

I stood by his rental car while he opened the trunk and extracted my bomber jacket, along with a bulky mailing pouch he handed to me. "What's this?"

"Henry sent it. He said he found it on your doorstep and didn't think you'd want to wait. What is it?"

I turned the package to the light. "Beats me. Postmark's Lompoc, which means it's probably something from my aunt Susanna."

"I didn't think you had folks."

"I don't. Well, sort of. The jury's still out."

"Got it," he said. "I'll leave you to open it. Good-night."

"'Night," I said.

In the privacy of my room, I turned on the light and set my jacket aside. I left my shoulder bag on the chair and then I sat on the bed, turning the mailing pouch over in my lap. On the back, there was a pull tab that opened a seam along one edge. I pulled the strip and peered in. I removed the leather-bound album she'd sent. I remembered her mentioning family pictures, but never imagined she'd actually send them to me. I leafed through page after page of heavy black paper on which black-and-white photographs had been mounted by means of paper seals affixed to the corners and glued into place. Some of the pictures had come loose and the photos were tucked into the spine of the book. Under each, someone had written in white ink, identifying the subject, the date, and the circumstance.

There they were. All of them. My mother. Various uncles and aunts. The wedding of my grandfather Kinsey and my grandmother Cornelia Straith LeGrand. Babies in white christening dresses that trailed to the floor. Group photos, complete with cousins, servants, and family dogs. In most, the faces were solemn, the poses as stiff as paper dolls assembled on the page. A Christmas at the ranch with everyone gathered in front of an enormous pine tree laden with ornaments, garlands, and lights. A summer picnic near the house, with wooden harvest tables set out on the grass. Long dresses, pinafores, straw hats with wide brims freighted with artificial flowers; women looking buxom and broad-shouldered, their waists pinched by corsets that made their ample hips look twice as wide. Two men had been photographed in the army uniforms of World War I. One of the two appeared at later family gatherings while the other was never seen again. Sometimes the men were in shirt sleeves, dark vests, and black bowlers; sometimes striped summer jackets and white straw boaters. I could see the passing years reflected in women's rising hems, their arms increasingly bare. Thanksgiving of 1932, suddenly all the little girls were decked out like Shirley Temple. Nothing of the Great Depression seemed to have touched the house or its occupants, but time did march on.

Many of these people were dead by now. The adults had grown old. The children had married and given birth to children of their own. There was my mother in that long white dress again at her coming-out party, July 5, 1935. There were other snapshots of the occasion. In one, I could have sworn the photographer caught my father in the background, his eyes fixed on her. I'd never actually seen a picture of him, but I felt I'd recognized him nonetheless. After that, the pages were abruptly blank, the entire last third of the album empty. That was odd. I thought about it, puzzled that the family history so carefully recorded up to that point should suddenly be abandoned.

Oh. Could that be right?

My parents had eloped. I'd seen a copy of their marriage license dated November 18, 1935. My grandmother had been horrified. She'd had her heart set on Rita Cynthia's marrying someone she considered worthy of her firstborn daughter. Instead, my mother had fallen in love with a common mail carrier, who was moonlighting as a waiter on the day of her debut. There was apparently no Thanksgiving that year. And precious little in the way of celebrations since.

19

Saturday morning after breakfast, Stacey and I drove to the McPhees'. The day was clear and sunny. The wind had died down and the desert stretched out in a haze of beige and mauve. Cactus, mesquite, and creosote bushes grew at neatly spaced intervals, as though planted by an arborist. Out there, unseen, the bobcats, foxes, owls, hawks, and coyotes were feeding on the smaller vertebrates. I'd read that jackrabbits constitute half the diet of breeding coyotes, so that when hard times reduce the rabbit population, the coyote population shrinks, as well, thus maintaining the balance in nature's culinary scheme.

We paused briefly on the street and I pointed across the pasture to the shed where we'd found the Mustang. Stacey said, "I wonder why he got himself in such a lather when the car was impounded?"

"Territorial, I guess. You'd do the same in his place."

"I'm not so sure about that. Sounds like a man who knows more than he's letting on."

"Maybe he's just another cranky old geezer, used to having his way."

"Nothing wrong with that."

"Stace, I wasn't talking about you."

I rang the bell and the two of us stood on the porch, waiting for someone to respond. From the backyard, I could hear children giggling and shrieking while a dog barked.

When Edna finally opened the door, she seemed somewhat taken aback. "Oh. I didn't expect to see you here again," she said. She averted her gaze politely from Stacey's patchy head.

"Hi, Edna. How are you? This is Detective Oliphant from the Santa Teresa Sheriff's Department. Have we caught you at a bad time?"

"I have my Baptist Church Auxilliary Committee here and we're busy."

I held out the quilt. "We won't take long. I wanted to return your quilt."

She took it, murmuring, "Thank you," and then moved to shut the door.

I put a restraining hand on the frame. "We were hoping to see Ruel. Is he here?"

"He's in the garage."

"Mind if we talk to him?"

With a tiny flicker of irritation, she gave in. "You might as well come through the house and I'll send you out the back. It's quicker than going all the way around."

The two of us stepped inside while she closed the door and then we followed her down the hall.

She said, "Did you talk to Medora?"

"I did. She was great. Thanks so much."

In the kitchen, there were five women sitting at the table, which was stacked high with flyers and long white envelopes. All five glanced up at us, smiling expectantly as we moved toward the back door. Edna did a brief detour, returning the quilt to its place on the window seat. I noticed she didn't stop to introduce us, probably reluctant to explain the arrival of an out-of-town sheriff's detective and a private eye.

On the counter, she'd set up a big Thermos of coffee, a plate of sweet rolls, and a pile of paper napkins. The one empty chair was clearly hers. Two women folded the flyers, while another two stuffed them in the envelopes. The last woman in line licked the flaps and applied the stamps. I recognized this one: the light brown hair, brown eyes, the sprinkling of freckles across her nose. I'd seen her at Quorum High, where she worked as Mr. Eichenberger's assistant.

I paused, saying, "Hi. How're you?"

"Fine."

"I'm Kinsey Millhone. I'm sorry, but I've forgotten your name."

"Adrianne Richards."

Edna hesitated and then said, "Adrianne's my daughter."

"Ah. Well, it's nice seeing you again. This is Detective Oliphant," I said, thus forcing a round of introductions. I really hate to be pushy, but what's a poor girl to do?

One of the women piped up and said, "I'm Mavis Brant. This is Chalice Lyons, Harriet Keyes, and Adele Opdyke."

Stacey tipped an imaginary hat, which the ladies seemed to like.

I smiled at them briefly, my attention returning to Adrianne. "You're Cornell's sister? I didn't realize that. Small world."

"Isn't it?" She offered me a thin smile before she turned to the woman at the end of the table. "Excuse me, Harriet, could you pass me some envelopes?"

Harriet handed a batch of envelopes to Adele who passed them on to Adrianne, who was busy being busy. She must have been married, because if her office name tag had read "McPhee," I'd have asked if she was related. She flicked a look in my direction and then engaged the woman next to her in conversation.

"Well, we don't want to hold you up," Edna said to us, ushering us on.

Stacey and I went out the back door and trooped down the stairs, heading for the garage. Edna's grand-daughter, Cissy, and her two older tow-headed sisters were racing across the yard in the throes of hysteria, a little yappy dog bouncing after them, nipping at their heels. As we watched, the dog caught a mouthful of Cissy's sock. Growling, he tugged, trying to dig in his paws while she dragged him across the grass. I envisioned dog bites, blood, and tetanus shots later in the afternoon. There was no sign of Justine, so I was guessing the girls had been parked with the grandparents while she was off somewhere.

I smelled Ruel's cigarette before we caught sight of him. He was in the same wooden desk chair with the same straw hat pushed to the back of his head. He looked small and harmless, and I could sense that Stacey was perplexed that I'd expressed any uneasiness about him. He was close to Stacey's age, in his early seventies I'd guess. He was watching another television show with all the concentration of a kid. This time, it was a cartoon so completely asinine that even the little girls preferred be-ing chased and bitten by a dog.

Without looking up, Ruel said, "Back again, I see. Who's your friend?"

Stacey stepped forward, extending his hand. "Stacey Oliphant, Mr. McPhee. I'm a homicide detective with the Santa Teresa Sheriff's Department. Nice to make your acquaintance."

Ruel gave him an obligatory handshake. "Suppose you're here to confiscate something else. It's a damn shame you can walk in and take anything you want."

"I can understand your point. Then again, the law's the law. We don't make it up; we just carry it out," Stacey said.

"True enough," Ruel said. "Nothing I can do about it now. You just be sure that car comes back without a scratch."

I said, "Wait a minute. How's that supposed to happen? The car was banged up to begin with."

Ruel rolled his eyes with annoyance. "I meant, no damage aside from that."

Stacey eased back in. "Mr. McPhee, I only drove in last night so I'm new on the scene. If it's not too much trouble, I wonder if I can ask you to bring me up to speed."

"Ask her, she's so smart. I got better things to do."

"She tells me you made quite a deal on that car."

Like a recording, Ruel recited the details of his good fortune. "I got that Mustang free of charge back in 1969. Fella left it at the shop to have the seats repaired. Car was stolen and once it came back, he didn't want anything to do with it."

"Is that right? Good deal," Stacey said, as though impressed. "And what inspired you to keep the car all these years?"

"My son and I intended to restore it, though now they've as good as told me it was used in some kind of criminal enterprise. Homicide, is that right?"

"Yes, sir. Naturally, we're interested in taking a closer look."

"You ought to talk to the previous owner. Feller name

of Gant. He could've stolen the car himself. Have you ever thought of that?"

"I don't believe we have. Wonder why he'd steal his own car and then turn around and give it to you?"

"Why does anyone do anything? Man might've been nuts."

"Always possible. Happens he's dead now."

"Too bad. Otherwise, you could pester him instead of me," Ruel said. He paused to light a cigarette with a wood match that he dropped in his jar. "Point is, I don't know beans about a murder and my son knows less. Cornell should be here shortly to fetch the girls and that nasty dog of theirs. Talk to him yourself. Waste of time, you ask me."

"That could well be. Police work, we pursue a lot of lines that don't pan out. For instance, we've been curious about a tarp that was dumped with the girl's body. Anybody mention that?"

"What kind of tarp?"

"Canvas. Looks like a car cover or a drop cloth. Ms. Millhone saw a couple tarps at the shop and wondered if one of yours might've come up missing at the time."

"Nope. Can't help. Happens I own a bunch of tarps, but I never had one taken and couldn't care less if I did. Tarps are cheap. Take a stroll through the Kmart, if you doubt my word."

"What about a car cover? You remember if there was one on the Mustang when it was taken?"

"I already answered that. All my tarps and car covers are accounted for."

"You buy those in town?"

"You think I send off with box tops? Two of you are like dogs, chasing your own tails. Try something new. I'm tired of tarps."

Stacey and I exchanged a look while Ruel returned his attention to the TV set. Stacey shifted his weight. "Do you happen to remember a young woman in town by the name of Charisse Quinn? Same age as your kids, so you might have met her through them."

"Doesn't sound familiar. She the one who got killed?"

"Yes, sir."

"I don't remember things like that."

I touched Stacey's arm, leaning close so I could murmur a question of my own. He nodded, saying, "What's the story on Justine's father? Medora told us yesterday the man deserted her."

"Poor specimen of a fella, if you want to know the truth."

"We heard he was a womanizer."

"Everybody knew that . . . except his wife. Not to speak ill of the woman, but she has a serious drinking problem, has had for years. Edna and I, we don't hold with hard liquor or spirits of any sort. It's one thing Justine's always appreciated about us."

"You were talking about her dad's womanizing. What's the story on that?"

"He used to drive up to Palm Springs to meet the ladies. He'd tell Medora he was working late and go keep company with floozies."

"You know this for a fact or was that just the gossip around town?"

"He told me so himself. Wilbur was as fond of drink as Medora, and once he imbibed, he had a tendency to brag about himself. Homely as a monkey, but he must've had his ways. Claimed he could walk into a bar and the women'd fall all over him. Married or single didn't matter to him. He'd order a drink and offer to buy one for the gal sitting next to him. Once she said yes, he'd pull out his wallet and all he'd have on him was a hundred dollar bill. She'd end up paying, assuming he'd pony up by the end of the evening. Next thing you know he'd be getting in her panties and she'd be out that, too. I never figured women for such nitwits, but that's how he told it."

"This Quinn girl I mentioned was a ward of the court. A social worker placed her with the Sanderses."

Ruel turned and stared at Stacey. "That who you mean? Well, I'll be. I hadn't thought of her in years. Quinn. That sounds right. You should have said so in the first place."

"We heard her name for the first time yesterday. How well did you know her?"

"I knew her to speak to, but not otherwise. Cornell said she fooled around with any boy she met. 'Free with her favors' is how he put it. She'd take 'em up to the Tuley-Belle and misbehave."

"The Tuley-Belle?"

"Construction site outside town. Big condominium complex some fellas started building in 1968. Leon Tuley and Maurice P. Belle. Got it half-done and went bankrupt so the place's sat there since. Kids like it because in parts there's a roof overhead and the walls are up. Plumbing and electrical are torn out, but given what they're up to, I guess you don't need that."

"Wilbur Sanders ever say anything to you about the Quinn girl?"

"I didn't know him well, except as Justine's dad. Cornell was dating her and the families would get together every now and then. Medora wasn't often sober. I felt sorry for Justine. She'd sit there trying to cover up her shame and embarrassment. Meanwhile, Wilbur would excuse himself, come out here, and bend my ear about his sexual exploits. Ask me, he should have paid more attention to his wife."

"And Charisse?"

"I don't know anything about that. Hear Wilbur tell it, he was too much the gent to mention names. Minute they arrived, he'd make excuses and head out here. Always brought a flask of dark rum and we'd smoke our cigarettes. Once he got talking, you could hardly shut him up. Best of my knowledge, he kept his escapades to Palm Springs so Medora wouldn't get wind."

"If she was drinking so much, would she have cared?" I asked.

"Of course she'd have cared! Infidelity doesn't sit well with the ladies. They're apt to tear your head off."

I heard a car pull into the driveway and I turned in time to see Cornell park his white pickup. As he came through the back gate, his three daughters made a run at him and piled into his legs, the pup bouncing along behind them like a basketball. Much squealing and hugging, punctuated by the dog's shrill barks. Cornell extracted himself and headed in our direction, combing his hair with his fingers, tucking in the tail of his shirt where the girls had pulled it loose. He said, "Hey, Dad," with some enthusiasm. To me, he said hi in a tone as flat as a tumbler of two-day-old Coke.

I introduced him to Stacey and the two men shook hands. Stacey said, "We've just been chatting with your dad about Charisse."

Cornell seemed embarrassed by the subject. "Justine told me about that. I was sorry to hear."

"Was she a friend of yours?"

"Well, no, but I'd see her at school. This was before she got kicked out and went over to Lockaby."

"Did she have a boyfriend?"

"She never went steady with anyone I knew. She dated quite a few guys, various classmates of mine."

"Who would you say offhand?"

Cornell thought about it briefly. "I guess Toby Hecht and George Baum. You might start with them."

Stacey made a note of the names while Cornell peered over his shoulder and pointed. "That's *B-A-U-M*, not *B-O-M-B*."

"Got it. And how could I go about getting in touch with these birds? They still around somewhere?"

"George is your best bet. He sells new and used cars over in Blythe. Toby, I don't know about. I haven't talked to him in years."

Ruel had been following the conversation, but now he rose to his feet. "You fellers will excuse me, I got to go see a man about a dog. Nice talkin' to you."

"Same here," Stacey said, touching his head as though tipping his hat.

Ruel took off across the grass, heading for the house while Stacey was saying to Cornell, "How about Wilbur Sanders? You ever see her with him?"

Cornell shifted his weight. He reached in his shirt pocket and took out a pack of cigarettes. He shook one loose and lit it, glancing back to make sure neither Edna nor Ruel was watching him. "I'm sorry, but I don't want to say anything bad about my wife's dad."

Stacey said, "We're not asking you to tell tales. I'm sure he's a fine man."

Cornell didn't seem prepared to go that far. "All I know is she doesn't want to think ill of the man even if he's gone."

"Good point. She doesn't want to think what, that Wilbur cheated on her mom?"

"Now I never said that. He put up with a lot."

"You're talking about Medora's drinking? That'll certainly throw a family into disarray. At the same time, people have been telling us Charisse was so interested in men, we can't help but wonder was she interested in him?"

"I think I've said enough. If I were you, I wouldn't mention this to Justine. She gets touchy on the subject."

After that, Cornell stubbed out his cigarette, resisting any further attempts to probe. I watched Stacey come at the matter from a number of directions, but, try as he might, he couldn't weasel anything more out of him.

Later, with Stacey at the wheel of the rental car, I said, "What was that about? Talk about resistance."

Stacey shook his head. "I can't decide if he was lying about something and doing a piss-poor job, or trying not to tattle and making a sore botch of that."

"How could he be lying? He didn't say anything."

"Maybe you should talk to Justine—you know, woman to woman."

I rolled my eyes. "Oh yeah, right. Like she'd break down and confide in me."

"Well, she might. Meanwhile, I think we better go by the hospital and see Con. First day without a smoke, he'll be climbing the walls."

"What about you? I haven't seen you light your pipe since you arrived."

"I gave it up; part of the deal I made, hanging on to life."

The CCU nurse we'd been dealing with the night before was off duty and wouldn't be back on the floor until 3:00. Winsome as we were, the current charge nurse, Meredith Snow, couldn't be persuaded to let us break the rules. I sat in the waiting area, with its bare end table and four upholstered chairs, while Stacey went in to Dolan's room for the requisite ten-minute visit. In the absence of magazines, I amused myself by cleaning all the woofies, loose hair, and tatty tissues from the bottom of my shoulder bag. In the process, I came across the Quorum phone book that I'd been toting around for days. I sat and thought about the tarp, wondering how to figure out where Ruel bought his. As the entire phone book, white and yellow pages combined, was about the thickness of a modest paperback, I tried the obvious, looking under "Tarpaulins" first. There were two sub-headings: "Renting" and "Retail." I wasn't sure anyone would rent a tarpaulin to wrap up a corpse, but I suppose stranger things have happened. Dolan's theory about the killer involved haste and improvisation, so it was always possible a rented tarp was the closest at hand. Ruel didn't rent his, but someone else might.

"Tarpaulins—Renting" referred me to "Rental Service Stores" and "Yards." Of the seven companies listed, four offered heavy equipment: lifts, loaders, backhoes, hand tools, paint sprayers, scaffolding, generators, air compressors, and related items. The remaining three companies were devoted to party supplies, including canopies and tents. I turned a corner of the page down, thinking I might check into them later.

Under "Tarpaulins—Retail," there was one company listed, Diamond Custom Canvas. The boxed advertisement went on at some length in the teeniest print imaginable, listing their products, which included: asphalt, lumber, lumite, mesh, polyethylene, steel haulers, vinyl-coated polyester, vinyl laminates, tarps, welding curtains, screens, blankets, roll systems, and drop cloths. The address was on Roberts, one block over from Main. I was still staring at the ad when Stacey reappeared.

I tucked my finger in the book to mark my place. "You were in there ten minutes? It didn't seem that long."

"Lady came in with a tray to draw blood so I high-tailed it out of there." He noticed the phone book. "Good reading."

"Actually, it is," I said. "Are you going back in?"

"Nah, he's grouchy as all get out. I knew he'd turn sour if he didn't get his fix. I think I'll take a little trip to Blythe and see if I can find this Baum fellow. Shouldn't take long; it's twelve miles. You want to come along?"

"Nah, I'm going to try something else. Why don't you drop me at the motel and I'll pick up Dolan's car? If you're finished by noon, we can hit the Burger King in town and pig out on Whoppers."

"Sounds like a good plan to me."

Diamond Custom Canvas was part of a block of two-story brick buildings, constructed with shared walls, that ran between Twenty-third and Twenty-fourth. There were several warehouses, an abandoned furniture whole-saler, and a discount clothing outlet. Some of the businesses were padlocked shut and the few that were open looked as though they'd fallen on hard times. Diamond was the single exception. Though the location wasn't a magnet for the walk-in trade, both phones were busy. I stood at one end of the counter, listening idly to one of the two clerks, who was engaged in a lengthy discussion about the volume discount on a shipment of lumite as-phalt solid tarps. The second clerk finished her conversa-tion, got up, and disappeared through a side door. While I waited for assistance, I took a visual tour of the place.

The interior was one vast, gloomy room, twice as long as it was wide. The pressed-tin ceiling was two stories high, with long banks of hanging fluorescent lights. On the left, an ornate wooden stairway, painted an odd shade of turquoise, curved upward to the second floor. Across the back wall, two courses of glass blocks let in a muted light. I could see water marks streaking down the wall, some long-ago plumbing leak or possibly a hole in the roof.

I picked up and studied a pamphlet that listed the part numbers, cut size, UPC codes, and weights of various twelve-ounce olive-drab tarpaulins. The twenty-by-thirty weighed seventy-nine pounds—tough to tote around, I thought. The tan ten-ounce tarps seemed to be lighter, but I was already worried they wouldn't hold up as well.

The second clerk came out of the back room. Glancing up, she spotted me and crossed to the counter. "May I help you?"

She was probably in her fifties, with heavy eye makeup and dyed black hair that she'd pulled up in a swirl on top. She wore jeans, a sweatshirt, and a pair of black spike-heel boots. Her fingernails were long, perfect ovals, painted dark red with a thin white stripe across each. I was reminded briefly of Iona and I wondered if she'd developed an expertise in nail art.

I said, "I know this is a weird request, but I hope you'll bear with me." I told her about Jane Doe and the tarp that was found when the body came to light. I did a quick summary of our reasons for believing the victim was local and our suspicion that the murder and/or abduction might have taken place down here. "I keep thinking if we could find out about the tarp, we might get a line on the guy."

"You mean what kind of work he did?"

"Something like that. If he did painting or drywall . . ."

"Not drywall," she said. "Those guys usually use a big

roll of paper. It would help if I knew the material the tarp was made of. Are you talking about duck, cotton, acrylic, or a blend?"

"Well, I don't really know and that's the point. Looking at this brochure, I can see you make hundreds of tarps, so the question's probably absurd."

"Not really. Many of our products fall into other categories, like cargo control—lumber tarps and steel haulers. I don't think you'd mistake either for a painter's drop cloth. They're too big. Too bad you don't have it with you. At least I could tell you if it's one of ours."

"Sorry. They've got it in the property room up north, under lock and key."

"In that case, let's think how else we might help. Most drop cloths are standard, though we do make two grades—eight- or ten-ounce natural. If I showed you, do you think you'd recognize the difference?"

"I could try."

"My name's Elfreida."

"I'm Kinsey. I appreciate your time."

I followed as she came out from behind the counter and *clip-clopped* across the bare concrete floor to a big worktable where two stacks of folded canvas tarps were sitting side by side. She grabbed a tarp from each stack and opened both across the tabletop, flapping them like bedsheets to shake the folds loose. "Look familiar?"

"It's that one, I think," I said, pointing to the lighter of the two.

"Here's the trick," she said. She held up one edge, showing me the red-stitched seam with a tiny square of red in the corner. "This is not a trademark per se, but we use it on everything."

"Oh, wow. I remember that red square from the tarp we have."

"It's actually not a square. It's a diamond."

"The company name," I said.

She smiled. "Of course, that doesn't tell you anything about where it was purchased. Might have been here in Quorum or it might have been somewhere else. Problem is, we distribute to paint stores and hardware stores all across the country, plus places like Target and Kmart. There's no way you'd ever track the outlet. We don't code for things like that."

"Who buys them?"

"Painting contractors, for the most part. The average homeowner usually buys a plastic tarp he can dispose of when he's finished. Makes the job easier. You toss it in the trash and you're done. Do commercial or residential work, you need something you can use more than once. These things are sturdy. They last for years." She went on talking, but I found myself snagged again on the issue of painting contractors. Where had I run across mention of a paint contractor? I was sure I'd seen it in one of the county sheriff's reports. She said, "Looks like I lost you back there."

"Sorry. I'm fine. I just remembered where I'd seen mention of a painting contractor. I should go check that out. Thanks so much. You've been more help than you can know."

20

After I left Diamond's, I returned to the motel. The housecleaning cart was parked on the walk outside my room. The maid had stripped off my sheets and she was using the pile of soiled linens to prop the door open while she went about her work. I peered in, trying to get a sense of where she was in the process. My plastic-covered mattress was bare and a flat stack of clean sheets rested at the foot of the bed. I could hear her in the bathroom with her portable radio tuned to a Spanish-language station. On the night table the message light was blinking on my phone. I heard the toilet flush and the maid emerged with my damp towel across her arm. She toted her carryall of cleaning products.

I said, "Oh, hi. Sorry to interrupt. How much longer will you be?"

She smiled broadly and nodded, saying, *"Hokay. Sí. Una momento."*

"I'll come back," I said. I trotted across the parking lot to the office and went in.

The desk clerk was perched on her swivel stool, still

chewing bubble gum, her skirt hiked up, swinging one foot while she read the inner pages of the *National Enquirer.*

"My message light's blinking. Can you tell me who called?"

"How should I know? Pick up the phone and dial 6."

"The maid's in my room so I'm here to ask you."

The look she gave me said she was feeling put-upon. "What room?"

"125."

With exaggerated patience, she set the paper aside, swiveled her stool to face her computer, tapped on the keyboard, and read from the screen. She chewed her gum briefly and then her face brightened. "Oh, yeah. I remember now. You got a call from a dentist, Dr. Spears. What's the problem with your teeth?"

"Did he leave a number?"

She blew a bubble and curled it back into her mouth on the end of her tongue, waiting to pop it after she'd closed her lips. "He did, but I didn't bother to write it down. It's in the book."

"When you first took this job, did they train you?"

She stopped chewing. "To do what?"

"Simple clerical skills, phone etiquette, manners—anything like that?"

"Nah. Know what I'm paid? Minimum wage. Three dollars and thirty-five cents an hour. Besides, I don't need manners. My uncle owns the place. My name's Geraldine, in case you feel like filing a complaint."

I let the matter drop.

I went out the office door and turned right, moving to the bank of pay phones I'd seen near the ice machine. I opened my bag and fished out the Quorum phone book and a handful of change. I looked up the dentist's number and dialed, receiver tucked between my shoulder and my tilted head while I put the directory back in my bag.

When Mrs. Gary picked up, I said, "Hi, Mrs. Gary. Kinsey Millhone here. I can't believe I caught you in the office on a Saturday."

"I'm just catching up on insurance claims. This is about the only time I have."

"Dr. Spears left me a message. Is he there by any chance?"

"He's off playing golf, but I can tell you why he called. He found the chart you asked about. I've got it sitting on my desk."

"Tell him I'm in love."

"He'll be thrilled to death," she said.

I laughed. "Could you do me a favor? Could you slip it in a manila envelope and mail it to Sergeant Detective Joe Mandel at the Santa Teresa County Sheriff's Department? He'll talk to the forensic odontologist and they'll handle it from there." I gave her the address, adding my copious thanks to her and to Dr. Spears. I hung up the phone, offering up small, fervent prayers.

I had to believe that a comparison of his records with the Jane Doe maxilla and mandible would confirm Charisse Quinn's identity. At the same time, I knew reliance on such records could prove inconclusive. A chart might contain errors, or it might be incomplete if details of previous or subsequent dental work had been omitted for some reason. A positive ID might take weeks, but once it was confirmed, the guys could chase down the paperwork on Charisse's birth parents through Riverside County Social Services. In the meantime, I was feeling good. We seemed to be making progress in spite of the odds.

When I returned to my room, my door was closed and the maid's cart was halfway down the corridor. I let myself in and tossed my purse and jacket on the bed. I retrieved my duffel from the closet and took it over to the desk, digging deep to the bottom, where I'd stashed my copy of the murder book. I sat and went through it page by page. I knew what I was looking for, but not where it was. Twenty pages in, I came across the report, dated August 1, 1969, detailing the arrest of Frankie Miracle, who'd given the deputy his home address in Blythe, California. No mention of Venice, where the murder had taken place. Under occupation, he'd classified himself as a handyman/helper. For his employer, he'd listed Lennie Root, R&R Painting, with an address and phone number in Hazelwood Springs. I turned down a corner of the page and moved on. I was curious about the purported call from Charisse's mother that Stacey'd mentioned earlier.

Fifty pages further on, I found the follow-up report, dated 8-9-69/Approx. 1400 hrs., in which Deputy Joe Mandel had entered information about a call he received from the Riverside County Sheriff's substation in Quorum. A Detective Orbison had contacted the Lompoc substation in response to the teletype regarding the Jane Doe homicide victim whose description matched that of a missing juvenile named Charisse Quinn. She'd left home on July 27. The Riverside County Sheriff's Department noted her DOB as 4-10-52; height: 5'3"; weight: 120 lbs. Blond hair, blue eyes, pierced ears, and extensive dental work. Her foster mother was listed as Medora Sanders, at the address where I'd had my conversation with her. According to Orbison, she'd come in the morning of August 9, to file the missing-persons report.

After Orbison's call, Mandel had made two attempts to contact Medora without success. Then on 8-11-69/ Approx. 1855 hrs., RCSD phoned again, this time telling Mandel they'd received a call from a woman who stated she had a daughter named Charisse Quinn, whom she understood was believed to be a murder victim. She wanted to let them know the girl had come home and she was alive and well. She gave the Riverside County Sheriff's deputy a phone number where she could be reached, and Orbison passed the number on to Mandel. In his typed account, Mandel indicated that he'd attempted contact, but the number was listed as out of service. If he'd tried tracing the party, there was no notation of the fact. I continued leafing through the book, but I found no other reference to Medora or Charisse. I made a few notes and then sat, playing idly with my index cards, laying them out randomly in rows.

It was odd to see how the pieces realigned. When Dolan had first given me my copy of the murder book, I'd read these same reports, many of them more than once. The entry about the missing girl had been only one of a number of items that had meant nothing outside the current context. The name itself didn't seem significant until Stacey remembered it. It was the same with Frankie Miracle's place of employment. In early readings, the note had seemed incidental. Now the information fairly leapt off the page.

Three things struck me: First, in filing the missing-persons report, Medora hadn't been quite as prompt as she'd led me to believe. She'd implied she'd gone straight to the police, when she'd actually waited more than a week. I'd have to go back and ask her about the delay. Secondly, Charisse's July 27 departure from Quorum would place her in easy range of Frankie Miracle's road trip after the murder of Cathy Lee Pearse on July 29. I still couldn't figure out how the Mustang ended up in Lompoc, unless Charisse had stolen it herself. Despite Medora's claim that she had no license, she might have known how to drive. If so, she might have gone as far as Lompoc, abandoned the vehicle, and tried hitching a ride from there. And finally, I wondered who'd made the call pretending to be Charisse's mother. If Frankie'd had anything to do with Charisse's murder, Iona could have made the call to cover for him. By August 11, when that call came in, Charisse's body had been discovered and attempts were under way to determine who she was. What better way to eliminate the link than to claim the missing girl was home? As nearly as I could tell, that call had effectively removed Charisse's name from the loop.

I put the murder book and my index cards in the desk drawer and pulled out my trusty pint-sized phone book, which covered Quorum, Blythe, Mesa Verde, Hazel-wood Springs, Palo Verde, Ripley, Creosote, and eight towns in Arizona. I flipped to the yellow pages and found the listing for paint contractors. There were only four in the area—two in Blythe, one in Palo Verde, and one in Hazelwood Springs. According to his boxed ad, Lennie Root of R&R Painting was a residential painting special-ist who also did condominiums, apartments, and com-mercial accounts. He was insured, bonded, and state licensed, promising reasonable rates, prompt work, and free estimates. There was a phone number, but no street address, which probably meant he operated on an an-swering machine from his home. I checked the white pages under "Root" and, sure enough, there he was. I was becoming quite fond of these small towns for the ease of access to its citizens. Big-city paranoia with its unlisted phone numbers only made my job tougher. I had ways of acquiring the information, but not as readily as this. I picked up my bomber jacket and got in the car.

When I got to the Burger King it was 12:15 and Stacey's rental car was already parked in the side lot. I went in, scanning the crowd until I spotted him at a table on the far side of the room. Even here, there were Easter decorations—big posterboard eggs and posterboard Easter bunnies. Stacey waved when he saw me.

I slid in across from him, saying, "Sorry to keep you waiting."

"Who said anything about waiting? I already had a Whopper and an order of fries."

"Well, good for you. I hope you don't mind sitting while I grab a bite myself."

"Oh, I'll be eating again. The Whopper was good, but it didn't fill me up. I've been thinking we should do a study—purely scientific—a side-by-side tasting, a Whopper and a Big Mac, to see which we prefer. Or go vertical—McDonald's hamburger, cheeseburger, a QP with cheese, and a Big Mac. What do you think?"

"You sit. I'll go. You want a Coke with that Whopper?"

"I'd prefer a chocolate shake."

Over lunch (my first, his second), I brought Stacey up to date on my visit to the canvas shop and my review of the murder book with its reference to Lennie Root. "How was your interview with George Baum?"

"What a pain," he said. "He's the consummate sales-man—all capped teeth and phony charm. He tried talking me into a BMW, but I nixed that idea. Point is, when I asked him about Charisse, he sidestepped the whole subject. He thought he was being slick; like I never heard a guy equivocate. I'm guessing he diddled her, but now that he knows she was murdered, he'd like to distance himself. He nearly shit when I told him where I got his name. He's maneuvering like crazy, doing anything he can to get me off his back, so he gives me some information I think you'll find interesting. He tells me Charisse and Cornell's *sister* were thick as thieves."

"Well, that's a new one."

"Isn't it? He says he used to see the two of them all over town. He swears Charisse had the hots for Cornell and sucked up to Adrianne to get close to him."

"Kind of makes you wonder why Adrianne didn't speak up. To hear Cornell tell it, he barely knew Charisse. Justine certainly gave me that impression."

"It's worth a chat with Adrianne if not the other two."

"You want to do that while I talk to the painting contractor?"

"I'd rather you take care of both. My energy's running low. I need a nap. As soon as you finish, stop by the motel. I should be up, and if not, feel free to wake me. We'll go back to the hospital and let Dolan know what's going on."

Once Stacey and I parted company, I sat in my car debating which interview to do first. At the moment, I was more interested in hearing about Adrianne's friendship with Charisse than I was in talking to Justine, Cornell, or the painting contractor. However, when I consulted the phone book, there were eight "Richards" listed, and Adrianne didn't seem to be among them. I had no idea what her husband's name was. Since it was Saturday, I knew she wouldn't be at the school. *Quelle bummeur.* This brought the matter down to a toss-up between the painting contractor and the younger McPhees. Again, according to the phone book, I was only four blocks from Cornell and Justine's, so they won by default.

Their house turned out to be a bright yellow board-and-batten, with white trim and diamond-paned windows flanked by dark green shutters. Pink geraniums grew in flower boxes across the front. The yard was enclosed by a white two-board fence. The two-car garage stood open, and I could see six-year-old Cissy and her two older sisters arranged in a cluster around Cornell's workbench.

I parked in front and approached, moving up the driveway past a tangle of bikes. Cornell looked up, greeting me without interrupting his work. "Hey, how're you?"

"I'm great. Is that a doghouse you're building?"

"You bet, and I'm almost done as soon as I finish this roof. Girls are all set to paint it. You meet my daughters?"

"I met Cissy on Thursday. I saw all three of them at your parents' house this morning."

"Oh, that's right. So you did. This is Amelia and Mary Francis."

I said, "Hi." I couldn't tell which was Amelia and which was Mary Francis, but it probably didn't matter. Most children seem interchangeable to me, anyway. "Is Justine at home?"

"Doing laundry. You can go in through there. Utility room's just inside the door. Cissy, why don't you show her where it is."

I hesitated, tempted to ask him about Charisse before I broached the subject with Justine, but with his children present, it didn't seem like a good idea. Cissy was tugging at my hand so I allowed her to lead me through the rear of the garage and into the utility room. She skipped back to her dad and his Saturday-morning project.

I found Justine in her sock feet, wearing an olive green sweatsuit. Her back was to me and she was cramming filthy blue jeans and work shirts into the washing machine. Beside her, the dryer was already in service, filling the room with a rich, damp heat while a garment with buckles clattered endlessly as it tumbled in the drum. I said, "I hope you don't mind my dropping by without notice."

She jumped and gave a yelp. "Shit, you scared me to death. I didn't hear you come in."

"Sorry. I didn't mean to sneak up on you. Cornell suggested I come in this way. I guess he figured you'd never hear me if I rang the front bell."

"What are you doing here?"

"The usual. I'm nosing around. Mind if we talk?"

"I've already told you everything I know."

"Indulge me, okay?"

She stared at the floor, curbing her annoyance, but I could see her relent, albeit unhappily. "Let me finish this and we'll go into the kitchen."

She shoved in the last of the load of clothes, added liquid detergent and bleach, then closed the lid and set the program knob. She pushed the Start button. She washed her hands at the utility sink, drying them on a terry cloth towel she retrieved from the pile of soiled linens.

I followed her into the kitchen, which was immaculate, a far cry from her mother's house with its grunginess and knickknacks. I don't know how women with active kids manage to keep a house picked up. She offered me coffee, probably to atone for her snappishness. I accepted with an eye to stringing out the visit. She poured me a mug and popped it in the microwave to heat. She was not a pretty girl. There was something washed-out about her looks, as though vital blood supplies had been suppressed for years, leaving her pale and depleted. The green sweatsuit added more color to her eyes than I'd seen before, but it still wasn't much. The microwave pinged and she removed the mug.

When she set it in front of me, a wave of coffee slopped over the rim. She handed me a paper napkin. "Did you want something in particular? We haven't eaten lunch. I need to go to the market to pick up some bread."

"This shouldn't take long," I said, busy cleaning the spill. I decided to take an indirect route getting to the subject of Adrianne and Charisse. "Did you have a chance to talk to Cornell?"

"About what?"

"You were worried he'd get mad at you if you talked to me."

"He got over that. He said he saw you at his dad's so I guess all's forgiven. Lucky you," she said. She brought sugar and half-and-half to the table and then sat down, tucking her hands under her thighs.

"That's because Detective Oliphant was there. He and Ruel seemed to hit it off. Did you meet Stacey?"

She shook her head. "I heard there was a second detective in town, but I haven't met him yet. They must be going all-out."

"They are. They're very serious about this."

"Well, good, though I don't get why it matters after all these years."

"Cops are funny that way. They never really give up. They just wait."

"Look, I don't mean to be rude about it, but I really have to scoot. The kids'll get cranky."

"Sorry. I'll get down to it," I said. "This morning, when Stacey spoke to Cornell, he mentioned a high school classmate of yours named George Baum."

"Sure, I know George. Why was he talking about him?"

"Cornell seemed to think he was involved with Charisse."

"Involved?"

"That's a dainty way of saying he screwed her."

"Oh, for heaven's sake. He did not. George had a girl-friend, a cheerleader named Swoozie Franks. They went together for years, since junior high at least. They got married a month after graduation."

"Swoozie?"

"It's a nickname. I forget her real one."

"Maybe Swoozie wouldn't put out so George got re-lief from Charisse instead."

Justine made a face. "That's a tacky idea."

"Why? You've all been saying what a slut she was."

"Well, yes, but I can't believe George would do some-thing like that. Did he admit it?"

"Not as far as I know, but he did tell Stacey that Cha-risse and Adrianne were close. I was curious why no one mentioned that to us."

"That's not true at all. Why would he say that? He's crazy."

Dubiously, I said, "I don't know, Justine. He says Charisse had a crush on Cornell and hung out with Adri-anne to have access to him. You'd think Adrianne would've volunteered the information as soon as she heard Charisse was dead."

"You said you weren't even sure it was her."

"Well, the ID isn't positive, but now we have her den-tal records so we're getting close. I would have mentioned it this morning, but it didn't seem appropriate in front of Edna's church group. Besides, that was the first time I realized who Adrianne was. You can imagine my surprise. I see her at Quorum High. I find out she's Cornell's sister, and then I hear she and Charisse were such good pals."

"They weren't *pals*. George doesn't know what he's talking about. Charisse's so-called pals were a bunch of losers from Lockaby. They were more her speed."

"Really. Your mother said she made a real pest of herself, wanting to hang out with the two of you."

"We took her with us sometimes, but she was an embarrassment."

"Did you know Charisse was so smitten with him?"

"Oh, please."

"Why would George lie to us?"

"I didn't say he *lied*. I said he got it wrong. The guy's a dimwit. Besides, even if she had a crush on Cornell, what difference did that make? A lot of girls had crushes. He was the most popular guy in our high school class."

"But how'd you feel about it? Didn't it bother you?"

"I knew we'd end up together, so who cared about them?"

"I mean Charisse in particular."

"She was nothing. A pig. I couldn't have cared less about her."

"Geez, that's amazing. When I was in high school, I was insecure. You must have had a lot more self-confidence."

"I wouldn't say that. It just seemed like fate. The minute I saw Cornell, that was it for me. That was grade school. We went to different junior high schools and reconnected in high school in our senior year."

"Love at first sight."

"Right."

"So really, it didn't matter if Charisse and Adrianne were friends—in terms of its effect on you."

"Charisse could do anything she liked. No skin off *my* back." She glanced at her watch, signaling time was up. She could have been a shrink, given her skill in silent communication.

I held up a hand. "Just one other thing and then I'll let you go. Doesn't it seem a trifle coincidental that your father disappeared just about the same time she did?"

Justine stared at me. "I don't get what you mean."

"Come on, Justine. You're not that naive."

"You're implying the two of them went off *together*?"

"Didn't it ever cross your mind?"

"Of course not. Daddy left in June. She was with us for months and months after that."

"Actually, it was only until the end of July. Maybe six weeks or so. What if they were having an affair?"

Justine laughed. "Oh, that's gross. I don't like to think he had sex with my mother, let alone with someone like her. That's disgusting."

"Disgusting to you perhaps, but in the annals of human history it's not exactly a first. I said the same thing to your mom. Charisse was promiscuous, so why not him?"

Justine clamped her mouth shut, staring at the floor. Agitated, she tucked a strand of pale hair behind one ear.

I said, "Look, I'm not making any claims here. None of us have the facts. This is purely speculation."

"Well, it's in bad taste," she said. She stood up.

"I guess I better let you go. Maybe I should have a chat with Cornell."

"I'm not sure he's interested."

"He didn't seem opposed to my talking to you."

"He was being polite."

"A quality I've always admired in a man. Anyway, you needn't fret because I can't do it now. I have something else to do."

Hazelwood Springs on my California map was a microdot on Highway 78 ten miles south of Quorum. The town turned out to be so small that I drove straight through without realizing it. I made a three-point turn, using the next convenient driveway, and then doubled back. The entire town consisted of a minimart, two side roads, a scattering of houses, and a two-pump gas station of the old-fashioned variety, where some guy actually came outside, filled your tank, cleaned the windshield, and passed the time of day. I ended up putting another twenty bucks' worth of gas in Dolan's boat, but in return, the fellow was kind enough to point out Lennie Root's place, which was just across the road.

Lennie Root's small white frame house sat on pylons of raw cinder block, thus creating the crawl space he used to store his miscellaneous painting equipment. There was a flowery ceramic plaque affixed to the wood frame above the front door that read THE ROOTS, MYRA AND LENNIE.

Lennie responded to my knock. He was a man in his sixties with a narrow, sagging face and heavy bags beneath his eyes. His bushy gray hair was peppered with tiny specks of dried red paint. Over his chinos and white T-shirt he wore a full-length apron with a ruffle around the bib. He held a wrinkled white dress shirt like an errant tomcat he intended to boot out the door.

"Mr. Root? My name's Kinsey Millhone. I'm hoping you can answer a few questions about a former employee. You remember Frankie Miracle?"

"What makes you ask? Because if you're working for OSHA or state disability insurance, I want it on record—the injury was fake."

"I'm not here about that. I'm actually a private investigator, doing follow-up on a homicide investigation. This was August of '69. Frankie says he worked for you shortly before that."

He blinked. "How much do you know about ironing?"

"Ironing?"

"My wife's out of town at her mother's until next Monday and I'm supposed to be at my daughter's for supper tonight. I need to iron this shirt, but I don't know how. My wife always sprinkles 'em with water and leaves 'em in a wad, but I never paid attention to what comes next. You show me how to do this and I'll tell you anything you want to know."

I laughed. "Mr. Root, you're in luck. You got a deal."

He handed me the shirt and I followed him through a modest living room to the kitchen at the rear. There were dirty dishes piled in the sink, and the counter was littered with additional glasses, flatware, and plates. On the breakfast table, there was a large broken-rimmed plastic basket piled with freshly laundered clothes. The door to the utility room stood open and Lennie crossed the kitchen to retrieve an ironing board with a floral padded cover and scratched metal legs. When he opened it, the sustained screech of metal on metal sounded like the mating call of an exotic bird. He plugged in the iron. I moved the setting to Cotton and waited for the iron to heat.

"My aunt Gin taught me to do this when I was seven years old, primarily because she hated to do the ironing herself." I licked an index finger and touched it to the hot iron. It made a spatting sound. "Watch this." I took the dampened shirt by the yoke, holding it between my hands, and straightened the puckered seams with one efficient snap.

"That's first?"

"Unless your shirt doesn't have a yoke. Then you start with the collar." I placed the shirt on the ironing board and explained the strategy: the yoke, followed by the collar, then the cuffs, the two sleeves, and finally the body of the garment.

He watched with care until I'd finished the shirt and buttoned it onto a wire hanger. I handed him a second shirt from the basket and had him try his hand. He was slow and a bit clumsy, but he did a credible job for his first time out. He seemed pleased with himself, and I had a brief vision of him whipping through the entire basket of ironing as the afternoon wore on. He turned off the iron, moved the basket aside, and gestured me into a chair.

As soon as we were seated, he said, "Now. What can I tell you about Frankie, aside from the fact he's the biggest punk who ever lived?"

"How long did he work for you?"

"Six months. Drunk most days; incompetent the rest."

"Did you hire him or did your business partner?"

"I don't have a partner."

"I thought your company was called R&R Painting. I figured it was your brother, your son, or your dad."

"No, no. It's just me. I put that other R in there to reassure the public. One-man painting company, people worry you don't have the manpower to get the job done. This way I give the estimate and get the contract signed and then when it turns out it's just me, well, what's it to them. I'm fast, I'm thorough, and I'm meticulous."

"How'd you end up hiring Frankie?"

"Did someone a favor. Biggest mistake I ever made. This fellow knew Frankie's brother and he asked me if I'd give him a job. He'd just gotten out of jail and no one else would take a chance. I wasn't all that crazy about the idea myself, but I'd just taken on a big project and I was desperate for help."

"What year was this?"

"Between Christmas of '68 and the summer of '69. He claimed he had experience but that was a lie. Worst excuse for a helper you ever saw, him and that friend of his. It's people like that give prison a bad name."

"What friend?"

"Clifton. Big guy. Had a funny first name . . ."

"Pudgie."

Lennie pointed at me. "Him."

"I didn't realize Frankie and Pudgie were such buddies back then."

"Were when they worked for me."

That was an unexpected nugget of information. I couldn't wait to tell Stacey, though for the moment I wasn't sure what it meant—if anything. "From what you said earlier, I gather Frankie filed some kind of worker's comp claim. Was he injured on the job?"

"Said he was. Oh, sure. Said he fell off a scaffold, but he was working by himself and it was bull. I got notice of the claim and next thing I knew, he was back in jail, this time on a murder rap. Is that the homicide you mentioned?"

"This was a second murder—a young girl stabbed to death within days of the first. Her body was dumped in Lompoc, which is where he was arrested. You remember when he left your employment?"

"June. How I know is because Myra's and my twenty-fifth wedding anniversary fell on the fifteenth and he was gone by then."

"How'd he end up in Venice?"

"I heard he got a job in Blythe, doing landscape work—in other words, a grown man cutting grass for minimum wage. He met some sixteen-year-old girl and three weeks later, the two of them got married. He was fired from that job so they moved up to Venice, where he did some painting for a friend."

"Got it."

"That other homicide you mentioned, is he a suspect in that?"

"Let's put it this way. The cops have been taking a long, hard look at him. Unfortunately, at this point, there's no proof he even knew the victim and nothing to link him to the crime itself."

"How'd you end up at my door?"

"A drop cloth at the scene was made by the Diamond Custom Canvas Company in Quorum. I was over there a while ago looking at their tarps when I remembered mention of a painting contractor on his arrest sheet. He listed you as his employer."

"Nah, he was long gone by then. I was all set to fire his butt if he hadn't quit, which I'm sure he knew. Shortly afterward, the project I was working on went belly-up. It was a bad year for me."

"I don't suppose you'd recognize the drop cloth if you saw it again."

"Should. I've used the same ones for years. I buy them in Quorum at the hardware store on Main. You have it with you?"

"I wish I did. It's in the property room at the Santa Teresa County Sheriff's Department."

"Well, you might have 'em check for paint spots.

During the time Frankie worked for me, the only exterior color we used was something called Desert Sand. I forget the company—Porter most likely, though it might have been Glidden. Get a match on the paint and it might help tie the tarp to him. I'd be willing to testify."

"Thanks. I'm impressed. You've got a good memory."

"Desert Sand turned out to be a bad luck color. Biggest job I ever bid. At least to that point," he said. "I'd've made thousands if the complex hadn't gone in the tank."

I felt a minor jolt in my chest. "Are you by any chance talking about the Tuley-Belle?"

"How'd you hear about that?"

"Ruel McPhee mentioned it earlier today."

"Oh, I know Ruel. I've done many jobs for him over the years."

"Where is this place? I'd like to take a look."

"You passed it on your way in. It's on 78, halfway between here and Quorum. On the west side of the road. From a distance, it looks like a prison. You can't miss it."

21

The faded billboard on the side of the road read THE
TULEY-BELLE LUXURY CONDOMINIUMS—TOMORROW'S
LIVING FOR TODAY. The project had been ambitious, accompanied by hype designed to create a buying frenzy.
The banner pasted across one corner of the sign trumpeted ONLY TWO UNITS LEFT UNSOLD! If true, the law-
suits were doubtless still in the courts. I slowed and
turned off the highway, following the deteriorating four-
lane blacktop that was divided by concrete planting beds
as empty as the surrounding landscape. The builders
must have intended to create a lavish entrance with lush
grass and palm trees lining the parkway, but the project
had been abandoned long before the plans were exe-
cuted. Vegetation was minimal. The flat terrain gave way
to foothills stretching upward to form the Palo Verde
Mountains. Distances were deceptive, the clear, dry air
apparently functioning as an atmospheric zoom lens.
The complex, which appeared to be a short quarter mile
away, turned out to be closer to a mile and a half.

When I finally pulled into the dirt parking area and

cut the engine, the silence enveloped the car like an in-
visible shield. In the harsh afternoon light, the partially
constructed buildings looked as bleak as cliff dwellings.
Piles of trash had blown up against the edifices. The surrounding acreage was flat and still. Dolan had told me
that despite torrential desert rains, the runoff is usually
swift and results in little saturation. Even from the car, I
could see numerous deep channels cut into the porous
soil, where flash floods had carved runnels, baked now to
the hardness of poured concrete.

I got out and slammed the car door. The sound was
muffled, as though absorbed by the very air itself. The
subdivision was sprawling. Some portions had been
completed; others had been framed in and deserted
where they stood. Farther out, I could see where a series
of foundations had been poured but the slabs remained
untouched. There were numerous tire tracks, and I pictured a steady stream of teenagers slipping through the
darkness, escaping from the raw night into the relative
warmth of insulated walls. Out here, the wind was constant—a strong, whistling presence that whipped my hair
across my face. Behind me, sand gusted across the road.

Two hundred feet away, a gaunt gray dog was
stretched out on its belly, lazily tearing flesh from the
carcass of a recent kill. It took me a moment to realize I
was looking at a coyote. He regarded me without interest, but he did rise and pick up his prized bone before he
trotted off. His coloring was so close to the muted desert
hues that he vanished like a wraith.

I turned back to the nearest building and went in.
The windows were gone and the doors had been removed from their hinges. The squatters hadn't penetrated far. In what must have been intended as a lobby,
mattresses now lined the walls like a hospital ward. Some

sported ratty blankets, but most were bare. Cardboard boxes had been carted in and now served as bed tables for an assortment of ashtrays, drug paraphernalia, and empty beer cans. I toured, checking out the pharmaceutical fare. These kids were doing grass, hash, and cocaine, but the addiction of choice was still nicotine, with cigarette butts outnumbering the roaches four to one. A used rubber, draped across the toe of a lone high-top basketball shoe, just about summed it up. I tried to imagine the poor teenaged girls whose introduction to sex took place under such sorry circumstances. Maybe they were too drunk or too stoned to care what they were doing or what was being done to them.

Outside, I heard a racket like a flock of birds lifting into the air. I listened, struggling to identify the noise. It sounded like plastic flapping, as though a dust barrier had torn loose and was being blown by the wind. The rattle was unsettling, like someone shaking open a fresh garbage bag after taking out the trash. I crossed to the nearest doorway and ventured down the corridor, peering in all directions. There was no sign of the errant sheeting, only rooms opening off rooms, filled with merciless sunlight. I stopped, my senses acute. It occurred to me then what I should have realized right away: The Tuley-Belle was the ideal setting for a murder. The cries of the victim wouldn't carry a hundred yards. If the killing took place outside, any blood could be concealed by turning the soil under with a spade. And if the killing took place inside, the floors could be swabbed down and the rags subsequently buried like strange soil amendments.

The Tuley-Belle reminded me of grand and ancient ruins, as though some savage civilization had inexplicably come and gone. Even in broad daylight, I could smell defeat. I knew I was alone. Because of the isolation, anyone approaching by car would be visible for miles. As for vagrants, they might be anywhere on the premises. There were countless places to hide, ways to remain concealed if the necessity should arise. I retraced my steps, trying not to run, scarcely drawing a breath until I'd tucked myself safely in the car. Stacey had to see this.

When I got back to the motel, he was pacing up and down in front of my door. I figured he was ready for another fast-food binge because I couldn't think what else would generate such excitement. The minute he saw me, he scurried to the car. I rolled down my window. He leaned on the sill while he grinned and pointed to his face. "Well, am I glad to see you! I thought you'd never get here. Know what this is? This is me being as happy as I'm ever going to get."

"What's up?"

He stepped back, opening the car door so I could emerge. "Joe Mandel called. The fingerprint techs are working overtime. I told you, it looks like someone made an effort to wipe down the Mustang? Well, it turns out the job wasn't very thorough because the techs picked up two sets of prints: one on the emergency brake, the gas cap, the inner rim of the spare tire, and the outside of the glove compartment. Looks like the driver leaned over to get something out and then pushed it shut. They lifted the second set of latents from a California road map shoved under the front seat."

"They managed to get good prints after all these years?"

Stacey gestured dismissively. "These guys can do anything. It helps that the car's been out of circulation and locked in that shed."

"Whose prints?"

Stacey's expression was pained. "Quit being so pushy and let me tell it my way. They compared both sets of prints with Charisse's, but no luck on that score. It's my theory she was already dead and in the trunk by then. The spare tire had been removed, probably stowed in the backseat to make room for her. Whoever wiped down the car actually did us a favor. All the incidental prints were eliminated and the ones he overlooked were as clear as a bell. Mandel got a pop on the first set within minutes. Guess who? You'll never guess. This is so good."

"Frankie Miracle."

"That's what I said, but I was wrong. Guess again."

"Stacey, if you don't spit it out, I'm going to fall on you and beat you to death."

"Pudgie."

I felt myself blinking. "You think Pudgie was involved?"

Stacey laughed. "I don't know yet, but there's a good possibility. When Mandel first told me, I nearly dropped my teeth. However, if you think about it, it does make sense. When you talked to Pudgie at the jail, he must have started to sweat. He probably assumed the business was forgotten, but eighteen years later, it's coming up again. He couldn't have been sure how much we knew or how close we'd come to establishing his connection. He must have pondered his options and decided it'd be smart to implicate someone else. That's how he knew the little details to seed into the tale. Doesn't mean he killed her, but I think he knows who did."

I said, "He was subtle about it, too. I remember when he mentioned that the body had been wrapped, he was so offhand about it, I thought it was just a minor part of Frankie's jailhouse talk. The same with the fact she'd been stabbed."

"You didn't mention it yourself?"

"Of course not. He was fishing for information, but I never gave him that. No wonder he was so worried about word getting back. Frankie'd go berserk if he thought Pudgie pointed a finger at him. I take it the second set of prints wasn't Frankie's."

"Nah, what a pisser. I felt bad about that."

"Me, too. I just talked to the painting contractor, a guy named Lennie Root. He says Frankie and Pudgie both worked for him in early '69. After six months, Frankie quit—this was approximately mid-June. Apparently, after that, he worked in Blythe for three weeks. That's where he met and married Iona Mathis."

"What about Pudgie? Where was he?"

"Don't know, but I can go back and ask. I was focusing on Frankie."

"So Root puts him in Quorum at the same time as Charisse?"

"Not Quorum, but Blythe, which is close enough," I said. "By the end of July when she disappeared, Frankie'd moved to Venice, a five-hour drive. Here I was, just about to swing over to your view, thinking Frankie's our guy, and now Pudgie surfaces, so there goes that."

"Not necessarily. They could've been in it together. Pudgie told you they didn't know each other, but that was clearly horseshit."

"Yeah, right. Pudgie knew Iona, so why wouldn't he know Frankie? She could have introduced them," I said. "Or maybe it was the other way around and Pudgie was the one who introduced Iona to Frank."

"Well, it doesn't make much difference since the second set of prints wasn't his. Personally, I hate to see him off the hook for this."

"Well, someone was in the Mustang with Pudgie. Iona maybe?"

Stacey frowned, scratching at the underside of his chin. "Well now, wait a minute. Hold on. That's a leap we can't make. We're putting Pudgie in the Mustang when the girl was killed, but the prints might have been sequential instead of simultaneous. Did Pudgie know the McPhees?"

"If he stole the car it wouldn't matter if he knew them or not."

"Problem is, if Pudgie knew Cornell or any one of them, he might've had legitimate access to the vehicle. The car came back in poor condition. Ruel might have asked him to move it into the shed or hose it down. Or he and Cornell might have gone out to the shed to sneak a smoke. There could be all kinds of explanations for his prints being there."

I said, "Assuming they knew each other."

"Right."

I thought about that briefly. "Pudgie did grow up in Creosote, which is only sixteen miles south. I think it's down below Hazelwood Springs."

"That's my point."

"But even if they knew each other, it still could've been Pudgie who stole the Mustang. When he was arrested in Lompoc, he was thumbing a ride. He could have stolen the car, driven it to Lompoc, dumped the body, and pushed the car into that ravine."

"Why don't we ask him? You said his sister brought him down here after he got out of jail. You have an address for her?"

"No, but we can probably get one."

We picked up Pudgie's home address from the administrator at the Santa Teresa county jail. We decided to take the rental car since Dolan's smelled like cigarette smoke. Driving south on Highway 78, I pointed out the Tuley-Belle, telling Stacey what I'd seen. As I'd predicted, he was interested in seeing it and we decided to stop off as soon as time allowed.

Creosote wasn't as big as Quorum, but it was ten times larger than Hazelwood Springs, which we passed through en route. The sign said POP. 3,435, but the Chamber of Commerce might have been inflating the facts. Given its close proximity to the Arizona state line, the town had opted for a Western look and resembled nothing so much as a cheap movie set where, at any moment, a cowboy might be shot and sail, tumbling, from the roof of the saloon. The commercial properties on the narrow main street were all wood frame, two- and three-story structures built side by side, with tall, fake facades, steep outside wooden stairs, and plank walkways between buildings instead of the usual sidewalks. It might have been an actual mining town or it might be masquerading as a place with a more interesting history than it had.

Stacey'd donned his red knit watch cap, claiming his head was cold. I suspected he was suffering a rare moment of vanity, but I could have been wrong. Pudgie's sister's house was on A Street near the corner of Third, a small, square box set on a square patch of lawn. Three concrete steps led to a small porch. From inside, we could hear a vacuum cleaner droning away. Stacey rapped smartly to no particular effect. He knocked again, and this time we could hear the vacuum cleaner being turned off. A woman opened the door, barefoot, dressed in jeans and a T-shirt, with a dust rag hanging from a belt loop. She was a tall, big-boned redhead with a blue bandanna tied around her head, Cinderella-style. Her eye makeup was dramatic. Both her upper and lower lids were lined with kohl. A fringe of false lashes set off the blue of her eyes. "Yes?"

"We're looking for Felicia Clifton. Is that you?"

"Yes."

"I'm Stacey Oliphant, with the Santa Teresa Sheriff's Department, and this is Kinsey Millhone . . ."

Felicia closed her eyes. "If this is about Cedric, I'll kill myself. I swear to god, I will."

"He's not in trouble, Ms. Clifton—at least as far as I know—but we'd like to have a word with him if he's here."

"Well, he's not. He went out late last night or first thing this morning. I'm really not sure which. He didn't even leave a note about where he was going or when he'd be back."

"Would you mind if we stepped into the house?"

Felicia hesitated, scanning the street as though the neighbors might be peering through their curtains at us. "I guess I can't have you standing in the yard."

We found ourselves stepping directly into the living room, which was probably ten feet by ten. We could see the kitchen from where we stood, and I was guessing the rest of the house consisted of two small bedrooms with a bath between. The air was scented with cleaning products. I could see where she'd swabbed a wet mop across the kitchen floor, leaving residual streaks of Pine-Sol. I picked up whiffs of Pledge furniture polish, Comet, Lysol toilet bowl cleaner, and perhaps a soupçon of household bleach.

"Have a seat," she said.

Stacey settled on the couch while I chose a bright yellow molded-plastic chair to his left. Felicia couldn't quite settle down, and I wondered if she cleaned to calm her anxieties, as I sometimes did. She'd worked hard to make the place attractive though the furnishings seemed to be an odd assortment of seconds, thrift shop finds, and discount sales.

"What sort of work do you do?" Stacey said, trying to strike a friendly tone.

"I manage a dry-cleaning establishment. My whole life's about that—cleaning up other people's messes."

Stacey said, "I imagine Cedric's been a problem."

"Oh, go ahead and call him Pudgie. Everybody else does. I don't know why I insist on 'Cedric.' It's ridiculous given the sort of person he is." She perched on a plastic chair that was a mate to mine. She reached out and straightened a stack of magazines, then idly, took out her dust rag and ran it around the table, picking up unseen particles of dust.

Stacey cleared his throat. "Is it just the two of you?"

"Just us. He's been a source of aggravation as long as I remember. Our parents split when he was only eighteen months old. Mom ran off with this guy who sold galvanized pipe. Daddy drank himself to death a little over two years ago. I was eight when my brother was born. Daddy was useless by then so I raised him myself. You can imagine how that went."

"Tough job at that age."

"You can say that again. I must not've done too good a job because Cedric's been in trouble since he was nine. I know I should quit coming to his rescue, bailing him out, trying to get him on his feet again. It doesn't do any good. His only talent is avoiding work; plus he sometimes steals cars."

I said, "What's he been doing since he got out of jail?"

"Same thing he always does. Drinks, smokes, borrows money from me, and lies around on his butt. Occasionally he helps out, but only if I scream loud enough. Then he'll sometimes do dishes or he'll grocery shop. I guess I've been waiting for the other shoe to drop."

"Has he been looking for work?"

"Says he has, but in this town, there isn't much to do. There's an opening at the Dairy Queen, but he thinks that's beneath him. I don't know where he got that. He's down so low, there's nothing under him as far as I can see. It's only a matter of time before he blows it again. I don't get how that works. Every time a guy screws up, there's always some gal around to feel sorry for him. In this case, it's me."

"I know one of those," I said, thinking of Iona.

"It's guilt," Stacey said.

"Is that it? Well, I guess. He always seems so sincere. Every time I look at him, I see him at nine. He got caught when he stole two silver picture frames from a neighbor lady across the street. What in hell did he want with two silver picture frames? Then he cried like a baby and swore up and down he'd never do it again."

"How long did that last?"

"About a month. I forget what he stole next— something equally useless. I can lecture him all I like; scream and yell. He knows exactly what to say to reel me in again. He's not dumb by any stretch, but he's lazy as all get out. He does whatever works in the moment without a thought in his head about the consequence. I'm sorry, I don't know how I got off on that. You want me to have him call you when he gets back?"

"If you would, that'd be great," Stacey said, taking out a ballpoint pen. "You have a piece of paper? I can give you the number."

"You can write it on the cover of that *Cosmopolitan*. I never throw those out."

Stacey jotted down the name of our motel, the number, and our two room numbers on the cover of the magazine.

"You might write your names down so I don't forget," she said, meaning that she already had.

Stacey scribbled our names, then clicked his pen and tucked it away. "When he goes out, do you have any idea where? We'll be happy to scout around and see if we can find him ourselves."

"There's a tavern—just a little hole-in-the-wall—over on Vine. You might try there. I can't think where else he might be, unless he drove into Blythe."

"Who's he hang out with?"

"No one that I know. He's been in jail so many times, he doesn't have many friends left. He did get a couple of phone calls Thursday night. The first, I don't know about. He took that himself. The second time I answered and it turned out to be a woman he dated years ago . . ."

"Not Iona Mathis," I said.

"That's exactly who. You know her?"

"I met her a few days ago."

"She's nice. I like her. Too bad he didn't end up with her. I hear she married someone else."

"Why'd she call him?"

"I don't know, but she must have been pissed because I heard him backpedaling like crazy, swearing up and down he didn't do whatever it was she was so aggravated about. Then some guy got on the line and it started all over again."

"Frankie Miracle?"

"Could be. I think so. I wasn't paying that close attention. Phone's in the kitchen. The call came during my favorite TV show, so after a few minutes of his yammering, I got up and shut the door."

"After the call, he didn't say anything about going out last night?"

"No, but then it's not like he tells me half of what he does."

"You think he might have gone off to meet Iona?"

"Oh god, no. I sincerely hope not. As mad as she was? He'd be smart to keep his distance."

"I don't like the sound of that," I said when Stacey and I were in the car again. "Why don't you find a gas station and we'll see if there's a pay phone."

"Who're you going to call?"

"Annette up in Peaches. Iona's mom."

There were two gas stations on the main drag; a Chevron at the corner of First and Vine and an Arco station at the corner of Hollywood and Vine. Somebody had a sense of humor here, at any rate. Stacey pulled in at the Arco. The two of us emptied our pockets and came up with a handful of change. He waited in the car while I dialed Directory Assistance and got the number for the Moonlight Café. Within minutes, I had Annette on the other end of the line.

"Hi, Annette. This is Kinsey Millhone. Lieutenant Dolan and I . . ."

"I remember you," she said. "How's that lieutenant? I forget his first name . . ."

"Conrad. People call him Con. As a matter of fact, he had a heart attack yesterday. He's in the hospital in Quorum."

"Well, forevermore. I'm so sorry to hear that. The poor man. How's he doing?"

"Well, he's got good doctors and they seem to think he'll be okay."

"Thank goodness. You tell him I intend to keep him in my prayers."

"I'll do that. In the meantime, I have a question for Iona. Is she working today?"

"Honey, don't I wish. She left Peaches shortly after you did and drove straight to Santa Teresa. She called later that same day to say she was at Frank's. I can't believe my own flesh and blood's so dumb. I told her to stay away from him, but would she listen? Of course not."

"How'd that happen? Last I heard he didn't even know where she was."

"Baby, that was daydreaming on my part. Now I find out she was in touch with him the whole time he was in prison. They're on the phone with each other just about every day."

"What sent her running to him?"

"You don't know how protective she is where he's concerned. She's worse than a mama bear. She's sure he didn't have anything to do with that other poor girl's death—you know, the one you were here asking about? If he did, she'd be first in line volunteering an alibi for him."

"Could she do that?"

"Do what?"

"Provide him an alibi for the two days after Cathy Lee's death? She was awfully vague on that score."

"Iona's convinced there's an explanation, but so far I haven't heard a word of it. I think that's why she went, to find out where he was for that two days. I know she was fretting about the quarry where the girl was dumped."

I held the receiver out and squinted at the mouthpiece. "Why would Iona fret about that?"

"Oh, she knows the place well. She used to play there

as a kid. She has a couple cousins—this is my sister's two kids. Iona stayed with them every summer for two weeks. They'd ride their bikes over to the quarry and have rock fights."

"In Lompoc?"

"What did I just get through saying to you?"

"Why didn't you tell Lieutenant Dolan?"

"I must not've been thinking or I'd have spoken right up."

"Are you sure it's the same one? There must be others in the area."

"I guess that's what Iona's trying to find out."

"Did she mention Pudgie at all?"

"In regard to what?"

"I'm wondering if she said anything to Frankie about him?"

"Well, she must have. You know Pudgie and Frankie were in jail together right around that same time. If anybody pointed a finger, it almost had to be him. She figures Pudgie threw Frankie's name in the hat, hoping to make some kind of deal for himself."

"Oh geez, that's not true. There wasn't any deal," I said. "Look, do me a favor. If she gets in touch, will you have her call me? I'm in Quorum at the Ocean View Motel, room 125."

"I don't expect to hear from her, but if I do, I'll be happy to tell her. Of course, you're closer to her than I am."

"Excuse me?"

"Well, hon, she's in Creosote. I told you that. After she left Santa Teresa, she went looking for Pudgie to see if she could straighten this out."

"Did Frankie come with her?"

"Lord, I don't know. I hope not. She never said."

I didn't actually groan, but I probably should have. "Let's don't worry about that now. Thanks, Annette. You've been a big help."

"Honey, you tell Lieutenant Dolan I'm sending him a big old sloppy kiss."

"I'll do that. Just please have Iona call me if you hear from her. You don't know where she's staying?"

"Of course not. I'd have said if I did."

"Great. I thought I better check in case I missed that part."

22

We cruised Vine, which was the main street of Creosote and all of ten blocks long. There was only the one tavern, done up in the ubiquitous Western theme. We parked and went in, pausing to get our bearings: low ceilings supported by heavy beams, a wooden floor dense with sawdust, rough-hewn log walls chunked with stucco or its equivalent. There was a long, polished mahogany bar with the requisite brass foot railing, eight tables with captain's chairs, and a Foosball table. The place was deserted, so it didn't take long to figure out that Pudgie wasn't there. At one end of the bar, there was an old Orange Julius machine with a perpetual fountain of juice laving the square, glass tank. Behind the bar, there was a rotisserie where old-fashioned hot dogs on skewers circled past a heat source, throwing off an irresistible cheap scent.

Stacey and I made a beeline for the bartender, ordering and consuming two hot dogs each, decorated with a squiggle of mustard, and piled high with a nasty sweet pickle relish and onions minced so fine our eyes were watering. Neither of us said a word until the last bite of bun had been munched and swallowed. I was gratified to hear Stacey making the same low whimpering sounds that accompanied most of my meals.

He chased his lunch down with a Coke and then used a paper napkin to scrub his mouth and fingers. "I'll be burping weenies for the rest of the day, but it's worth it. Don't know how I worked up such an appetite."

"Well Stacey, we haven't eaten since noon and it's after three o'clock."

"Can I get you anything else?" The bartender was a man in his late fifties, with an egg-shaped face, balding head, and a gap between his two front teeth.

Stacey said, "We're looking for Pudgie Clifton. His sister, Felicia, thought he might be here."

"Haven't seen him today. He usually shows up at eleven when we open the place. He'll be in later. Happy Hour for sure. He never misses a chance to get his two for one."

"When he comes in, would you have him get in touch with us? We're out running around, but he can reach us later at the Ocean View Motel in Quorum." Stacey made a note on a paper napkin, which the bartender set on the ledge of liquor bottles behind him. I waited while Stacey paid for lunch (my second, his third) and then we returned to the car.

Heading north again on Highway 78, I pointed out the hazy outlines of the Tuley-Belle in the distance, off to the left. "You want to do the tour now or come back?"

"No time like the present."

Stacey turned into the paved four-lane entrance, noting as I had its deteriorating state. We drove the mile and a half, the desert stretching out on every side of us. When we reached the complex, he parked and we got out. It was still afternoon, and the sun overhead was like a pitiless spotlight, revealing every crack and flaw in the abandoned site. Somehow in my memory, I'd tidied it up a bit, forgetting the garbage and blowing sand, the gaping windows and ruts in the surrounding dirt parking area. I sensed movement and shifted my gaze. I reached out and put a hand on Stacey's arm and both of us stood stock still. Two coyotes had appeared at a trot. Both were pale gray and scrawny, bony-legged, taller than the average German shepherd, but with the same prominent ears. The first coyote stopped and regarded us with a certain leisurely arrogance. These were desert coyotes, smaller than the ones we saw in Santa Teresa. There, when the drought years eliminated small rodents and ground game, coyote packs were forced down out of the foothills into urban neighborhoods. I'd heard them calling to one another, chilling, high-pitched yelps, when they'd cornered their quarry and were closing in on the kill. I'd seen countless handmade signs stapled to telephone poles, usually displaying photographs and phone numbers, offering plaintive appeals for the return of "lost" cats and small dogs. I knew where they were. In dawn light, in my travels around town, I'd spotted the occasional lone coyote crossing the road with a bundle in its jaws. Out here in the desert, where the heat was extreme and even less rain fell, coyotes ate anything: lizards, insects, carrion, snakes.

The second coyote had trotted on, but now circled back to the first. This must have been the female of the pair, her sides rounded by a litter of pups. The two animals stared up at us with an eerie intelligence. I was aware of their cold yellow eyes and the fathomless round, black pupils. I had no sense that they feared us. This was their territory, sparse and untamed, and their survival rates would always be better than ours out here. Stacey clapped his hands and the two continued on to the road at the same unhurried pace. He turned and watched them, as I did, until they disappeared from view.

The wind picked up. Despite the sun and even in my bomber jacket, I found myself huddled against the cold. "Let's go inside before I freeze to death."

We wandered the empty corridors. With Stacey close by, I was willing to venture farther afield. We explored together at first and then separated. While he inspected the partially completed condominium next door, I stumbled across an unfinished wood staircase and picked my way carefully to the second floor. I crossed to a wide, frameless window and looked out at the land; mile after mile of scrub dotted with tumbleweeds. Again, the sound of rapidly flapping plastic. I leaned out, peering to my right. At ground level, I could see a cloudy corner of the sheeting dance forward and back from beneath a pile of rocks. Ghost stories originate from such phenomena. I was surprised the locals hadn't already generated legends about the place.

Across the way, Stacey emerged from the adjacent building into full sunlight. He saw me and waved. I returned his wave, watching as he rounded the corner of that building and disappeared again. I left the window and joined him down below.

It was close to 4:00 when we pulled in at the motel. I felt we'd done enough for one day and I voted for a break. Stacey said he'd go back to the hospital and spend time with Dolan. Once he dropped me at the room, I changed into my sweats and Sauconys and went jogging. My last run had been Wednesday, before Dolan and I left town. As this was now Saturday, I thought it was high time I did something in my own behalf. For once I was happy about the chilly desert air. Humidity was low and I managed to do the entire three miles scarcely breaking a sweat.

Back again, I found the message light blinking on the face of my phone. I dialed 6 and the operator told me I had a message from Betty Puckett. I wrote down the name and number, but it took me a beat to remember her—the guidance counselor slash typing teacher at Lockaby Alternative High School. I thought about showering but decided to place the call before I got myself cleaned up.

When she picked up on her end, she was already sounding most annoyed with me. "I'm sorry to be peevish, but I've called you three times and I expected a call back."

"Mrs. Puckett, my apologies, but this is the first and only message I've ever had from you. When did you call before?"

"Twice yesterday afternoon and again first thing this morning."

"It must be the desk clerk. She's terrible with messages and just about everything else. Believe me, I'd have called you if I'd known."

"Well. I suppose these things happen," she said, mollified. "Patsy Marcum called me shortly after you left the office yesterday. I don't think I can help, but Patsy thought I should get in touch."

"We've actually made some progress since I talked to her. It now appears possible our murder victim is a girl named Charisse Quinn. Do you remember her?"

"That name doesn't ring a bell. When was she at Lockaby?"

"This would have been April or May of 1969. She started at Quorum High in March, but she got expelled fairly soon from what I've heard. She must have transferred to Lockaby close to the end of the school year."

"I was afraid you'd say that. I was out during that period on medical leave. I know because I went back through my records and checked my calendar for that year. Otherwise, I'd have done the intake interview."

"So you didn't meet with her."

"I didn't. I wish I could help."

"I do, too. We've been hearing a lot about her, but most of it's derogatory. I was hoping to get something more objective from you."

"Sorry to disappoint. Was the family local?"

"Not as far as I know." I took a moment to explain the situation with Medora Sanders and her fostering of Charisse.

"I do know the Sanderses, or I should say I did. I'm not familiar with Medora's current circumstances, but in those days, she had a serious drinking problem."

"How much to you know about Wilbur?"

"Well, I knew him to speak to. We went to the same church, at least when Medora was sober enough to attend."

"She says he left her mid-June and she hasn't heard from him since. We've been wondering if there's a link between Charisse's disappearance and his."

"Oh, I wouldn't think so. He did run off with someone, but it wasn't her. This was a woman he worked with at Sears."

"How do you know that?"

"Rumors were flying. That's all anybody ever talked about."

"I can't believe Justine and Medora didn't know," I said.

"I guess no one was willing to be the bearer of bad

news. I heard just recently—and I forget now who told me—that Wilbur married that woman and he's living in Sacramento under a fictitious name. Sandy Wilburson, or some variation."

"Really. That's interesting, because Medora thinks he's dead."

"To all intents and purposes, he is."

"One more thing while I have you on the line. This is probably a long shot, but I'm wondering if you remember a kid named Cedric Clifton. He's originally from Creosote, but he's been in trouble since he was nine and he might well have ended up at Lockaby."

"Yes, I know Cedric, though it's odd you should ask. He was a student of ours in 1968, a year before the period you were talking about."

"What's odd about that?"

"Well, you mentioned the Sanderses. He dated their daughter. He was older than she—probably nineteen or so to her sixteen."

"Justine and Pudgie Clifton? I don't *think* so. Didn't she date Cornell McPhee?"

"Yes, but she dated Cedric first. The two of them broke up after she started dating Cornell and 'set her cap for him,' as they used to say. They were both in my daughter's class at Quorum."

"Oh for heaven's sake," I said. "What's the deal around here? Everybody knows everybody."

Betty Puckett laughed. "Welcome to Smalltown, America. What else can I tell you about Cedric?"

"Did he ever do time for grand theft auto?"

"Oh, sure. Among other things," she said.

"Such as what?"

"Theft by deception, forgery, bad checks."

"Not violent crime?"

"Not while he was at Lockaby. I have no way of know-ing what he's done since then."

"Thanks. You've been a big help. Sorry you had so much trouble getting through to me," I said.

I showered and washed my hair, wishing I could rinse off my confusion as easily with the water running down the drain. All the little bits and pieces, the subterranean links. It was like looking for a pattern in the Milky Way. After I was dressed, I sat down at the desk, where I hauled out a pack of index cards and started making notes. Once I'd jotted down everything that seemed relevant, I orga-nized the cards in roughly chronological order, set the Smith-Corona on the desk, and typed up a report. Both Stacey and Dolan were capable of doing the same work and would have done so if pressed, but I was eager to see how the facts would arrange themselves. I could see the connections form and separate, though they made no particular sense: Pudgie working with Frankie; Frankie married to Iona; Pudgie dating Justine before her mar-riage to Cornell. Iona had grown up in the same town as Pudgie and had hung out with him in her youth. Cor-nell's sister, Adrianne, had been friends with the mur-dered girl, always assuming, of course, that Charisse and Jane Doe were one in the same. Then there were Pud-gie's fingerprints on the stolen car. Now that was an in-teresting development. I sat and stared at the cards, thinking about the players.

It occurred to me that in 1969, I was only two years older than these "kids" were then. I'd fumbled my way through high school without once achieving academic excellence. I was never elected to class office, never played a sport, and never participated in extracurricular activities. I wasn't a member of the band, the pep squad, or the chorus. Mostly, I walked around feeling glum and disenfranchised. I made unremarkable to mediocre grades, smoked dope, and hung out with other low sorts, undistinguished and unnoticed. Had I attended Quorum High School, Pudgie would more likely have been a friend of mine than Justine or Cornell. While Cornell was no longer a varsity hero, he was a decent, hard-working guy with a wife and kids to support. Justine was a full-time wife and mom; Adrianne now worked as an administrative assistant in the very high school she'd attended. And Pudgie was still busy getting sent to jail. As for me, I was now a (more or less) respectable, law-abiding citizen who shunned illegal drugs and refused to place burning objects of any sort between my lips. I wondered how Charisse had figured into the grand scheme of things. At least the rest of us had enjoyed the option of making better choices in later life than we'd made in our teens. All of her opportunities had ended in 1969, and one of the decisions she'd made had been her last.

Once I finished typing the report, I sat and shuffled the cards, playing the little game I always play. I laid them out randomly, then like a hand of Solitaire, watching to see how events would look when the chronological order became jumbled. The truth isn't always immediately apparent, especially when it comes to murder. What appears to be a logical series of incidents might look entirely different when the sequence is turned on its head. The police are always working backward from the homicide itself to events leading up to the fatal blow. Except for random killings, which have become increasingly common these days, murders happen for a reason. There is motive—always motive. In nine cases out of ten, if you know why something happens, you'll know the "who" as well.

I sorted through the cards again just to see if I'd missed anything. Of course, I'd forgotten to go back to Medora and ask why she'd waited a week to file the missing-persons report on Charisse. I placed that card on top of the stack, turning it upside down as a reminder to myself before I secured them with a rubber band. The point was minor and there was probably an explanation, but it was still a question that needed covering.

At 5:00, I tossed the pack of index cards in the drawer on top of the murder book, stacked the pages of my typed report, tucked them in a folder, and drove them to the local print shop, where I had two copies made. On my way back to the motel, driving east on Main Street, I caught a glimpse of Adrianne Richards heading for the local supermarket. She'd just parked her car and was walking from the side lot to the front entrance. I braked, glancing belatedly in the rearview mirror in hopes the car behind me wouldn't climb up my tailpipe. I made a hard left-hand turn to the annoyance of several motorists, one of whom shook his fist at me and mouthed a naughty word. I made a sheepish gesture and blew him a kiss.

I parked and went in. I did a quick walking survey, canvassing the store aisle by aisle. I finally spotted her in the produce section, grocery list between her teeth while she picked through a display of cantaloupes. In her cart, she had a plastic basket of cherry tomatoes, two bunches of green onions, and a cauliflower that looked like a brain wrapped in cellophane.

I said, "Hi. I've been hoping to talk to you, but I didn't know how to get in touch. What's your husband's first name?"

"Peter. We're divorced. He's in Reno."

"Mind if I tag along?"

"Fine with me," she said. She was wearing jeans, tennis shoes, and a twinset of smoky blue cashmere. Her hair was pulled back at the nape of her neck, secured with a barrette. She selected a cantaloupe, sniffed it, and then tucked it in her cart. She moved on, pausing at the dairy case to check the expiration date on a carton of skim milk, which she then placed in her cart. "What can I help you with?"

"Well, I'm curious. When I showed up in the office at Quorum High, didn't it occur to you I might have been talking about Charisse?"

"Not at all. Why would it? She's been gone for years."

"I heard you were good friends."

"I don't know about 'good' friends. We hung out together some."

"Did she say anything to you about leaving town?"

"I didn't even know she was gone. It's not like I saw her every day."

"But once you figured it out, didn't you worry about her?"

"Not particularly. I figured she could take care of herself."

"Did you ever hear from her again?"

"No, but I didn't expect to. That's not how it was. I was a couple of years younger and we didn't have much in common. I've lost touch with a lot of classmates I was closer to than her. Such is life."

"You don't seem upset about the murder. Doesn't that bother you?"

"Look, I'll be honest. I'm sorry for what happened, but I'm not *sad*. Why would I be? I knew her four months at best."

"Tell me about the friendship, such as it was."

"I don't know what to say. I thought she was funny. She didn't care what she said and she really didn't care what other people thought. I was feeling rebellious. She did things I didn't have the nerve to do. I was a good girl. She was bad. I guess opposites attract."

We turned left, ambling down an aisle stocked with canned vegetables, dried pasta, white and brown rice, and dried legumes. She picked up a package of lentils.

I said, "Do you know Pudgie Clifton?"

"Sure. He dated Justine."

"How long did they go together?"

"A year or so, less. Personally, I thought he was a bum, but she liked him. Even after they broke up, they stayed friends."

"He seems like an odd choice for her."

"You should have seen the guy I dated. Talk about a misfit."

"Did Pudgie know Cornell?"

"We all knew each other."

"What about Frankie Miracle and Iona Mathis?"

"I've heard the names, but I don't know either one."

"Did Pudgie spend much time at your house?"

She seemed mildly baffled. "A fair amount. What makes you ask?"

"Do you think he could have stolen the Mustang from your father's shop?"

I could see her consider. "It's possible. He stole other cars back then." She moved over to the shelves, choosing a can of tomato sauce and two cans of pork and beans.

"Did you suspect him at the time?"

"It might have crossed my mind."

"Did you ever mention that to your dad?"

"No. I didn't *see* Pudgie do it so why get him in trouble when I didn't know for sure. I figured he was trying to impress Justine."

"Hadn't they broken up by then?"

"Well, yes, but he was hoping to get her back."

"Did she know he took the car?"

"*I* don't even know that. It's just a guess on my part. I don't understand what you're getting at."

"I think he not only stole the car, but drove up to Lompoc with Charisse." I didn't mention "dead in the trunk."

"So what?"

"You never asked him if he knew what happened to her?"

"I'm sure if he'd known something he would have spoken up."

"Didn't anybody seem concerned?"

"Not really. Medora reported her missing so we all assumed the police would take care of it. I'm sorry if that sounds mean."

By now she'd turned onto an aisle lined on both sides with freezer cases: ice creams, frozen pies, pizzas, and bags of frozen vegetables. Adrianne opened a glass door and removed a bag of baby peas.

I studied her with puzzlement. "Why do I have the feeling you know something you're not telling me?"

"I'm sure I know lots of things I haven't told you."

"About Charisse."

"I don't want to make trouble. I told you that before."

"Who would you be making trouble for?"

"I'm speaking in generalities, not about anyone specific."

"Let's hope that's true. Thanks for your time."

She moved on and I remained where I was, watching the efficiency with which she went about her business.

I stopped by the motel. Stacey's car was gone. He hadn't left me a note, so I figured I'd catch him later. I drove on over to Quorum General, where I found Dolan sleeping, his dinner tray pushed to one side. I tiptoed to his bedside and tucked one copy of the report, sealed in a manila envelope, under the edge of the blanket folded at his feet. On my way past the nurses station, I had a quick chat with Ms. Kovach, who told me he was being transferred out of CCU and onto a regular medical floor. I told her to tell him I'd been in and had left him an update at the foot of his bed.

"I'll be sure and tell him," she said.

As I eased out of the parking lot, Stacey was just pulling in. We both rolled down our windows and had a chat, car to car. I passed him the second copy of the notes I'd typed and included a quick account of my conversation with Adrianne, plus the gossip I'd picked up from Betty Puckett regarding Wilbur Sanders's decampment and his subsequent bigamy.

Stacey said, "Sorry to hear Pudgie spent so much time at the McPhees'. I hate rooting against the guy, but we could use a break about now."

"So what if he knew them? He still could have stolen the car, don't you think?"

"How're we going to prove it? I thought the prints would turn out to be significant," he said. "Oh, well. I'll ask the boys to get to work on Wilbur. Shouldn't be hard to track him down. Might as well cook his goose while we're at it."

"Yeah, Medora's in bad shape. It'd be nice to see him taking some responsibility. Meanwhile, where were you? I stopped by the motel and you were gone."

"I went over to the sheriff's office and talked to a couple of detectives. They said they'd take a set of elimination prints on the McPhees if I can talk them into it."

"You think they'll agree?"

"I can't think why not. By the way, I want you to go to the Baptist Church with me. It's Easter and Edna tells me the McPhees will all be there. Two services tomorrow, but I think the nine o'clock's our best bet. Afterward, they're going back to Edna's for a big Sunday dinner. Easter, I bet she does a spiral-cut ham."

"What makes you say that?"

"She's just like my mother. We had ham every Easter, along with yams and green beans. We'll follow them to the house and have a quick chat with them while they're all there together."

"I don't know, Stacey. Maybe you should go alone. I'll only end up irritating Ruel."

"I want you with me. I promise we'll keep it brief."

A car pulled up behind me and the driver gave a quick, polite beep of his horn.

I said, "I'll catch you later at the motel."

"Give me fifteen minutes."

We ate supper in Dolan's room, which Stacey had by now adopted as his own. Both of us sat on the king-size bed, sharing a bucket of franchised fried chicken, mashed potatoes, gravy, and watery corn on the cob. Once we finished, I gathered the chicken bones, empty cartons, and used plasticware and tossed everything in the trash. Stacey wanted me to stay and watch a movie, but I was ready for a break. I'm not accustomed to spending so much time in the company of others. "If you need me, I'll be in my room. Otherwise, I'll see you in the morning."

"Great. I'll knock on your door at eight. That'll give you time to shower and get dressed."

"Oh shoot. I just remembered. The only thing I have with me are blue jeans."

"No problem. We don't have to go in. We can wait in the parking lot and follow them home."

"Why not go straight to the house?"

"What if they change their minds and decide to go out for Sunday lunch? This may be the only chance we have to talk to them together."

"You think she'd give up the chance to cook her big Easter dinner?"

"Probably not, but I want to see the congregation all dressed up," he said. "We used to do that as kids."

"You're not going to let me get out of this, are you?"

He smiled benignly. "Enjoy your evening."

23

The phone was ringing as I unlocked my door. I dropped my bag and plucked the handset from the cradle on what must have been the fourth or fifth ring. A woman said, "Is this Kinsey?"

"Sure, who's this?"

"Iona. My mom said you called looking for me."

"Where are you, in Creosote?"

"Peaches. I just got in. What do you want?"

"Did you talk to Pudgie Clifton Thursday night?"

"I might have called him," she said, cautiously. "Why do you ask?"

"Did you make arrangements to see him?"

"Why would I do that? He's a lowlife punk."

"His sister said you were pissed at him. What was that about?"

"None of your business. That's between him and me."

"All right. Let's try this one. Your mother tells me you spent time in Lompoc as a kid. I'm wondering if you told Pudgie about the quarry up there."

Dead silence.

"You remember telling him about that? I'm talking about the one where the girl's body was found."

"How would I know where the body was found?"

"Oh come on, Iona. Don't play games with me. I don't care if you told him. I just want the information."

"I might have."

"You might have, or you did?"

"All right, I did, but that was years ago. I even took him to see it once when we were out on the road."

"Did you know Charisse Quinn?"

"No."

"Aren't you going to ask who she is?"

"I'm not stupid. I assume she's the dead girl they found after Cathy Lee was killed. I asked Frankie about that and he says he had nothing to do with that. He didn't even know her."

"You know, he's not stupid, either. If he killed the girl, he's hardly going to tell you."

"Why are you so against him? Can't you give the guy a break? He hasn't done anything to you."

"This isn't about me, Iona. It's about Charisse. Is Frankie there by chance? I'd like to talk to him myself."

"He took off Friday morning. He was scheduled to work Friday night and had to get back."

"Short visit, wasn't it?"

"So what?" she said, annoyed.

"What'd you tell him about Pudgie?"

Another silence, during which I could hear her breathing in my ear.

"Iona?"

"If you must know, I told him Pudgie's a fuckin' snitch. He knew somebody had pointed a finger at him. The minute you mentioned Pudgie, I figured it was him."

"Is that why you were so pissed at him?"

"I'm not the only one. Frankie's pissed about it, too. Pudgie cut a deal for himself by blaming Frankie for what happened to that girl."

I felt a whisper of fear, like a millipede, running down my back. "Where'd you get that?"

"Well, it's true, isn't it?"

"No."

"Yes it is, because Frankie checked it out. He knows this guy at the county jail who's serving thirty days? The guy told him Pudgie had a visitor—this woman private eye, who was asking about the murder—that was you, right?"

"Of course, but Pudgie never made a deal."

"Yes, he did. You know how I know? He got out of jail the very next day. The guy said."

"Because his *sentence* was up. He'd served his time and he was released."

"Nuhn-un. No way. Pudgie went back to his cell block and bragged to everyone. He said you were doing something special for him. Next thing you know, he got out."

"He asked me for cigarettes and I said *no*. That's all it was. There wasn't any *deal*."

"Ha, ha, ha. Tell me another one."

"Would you listen to me? Iona, think about this. I don't have the authority to get him out. How would I do that?"

"That's not what the guy said."

"Well, the *guy* got it wrong. I don't have the power to make a deal with anyone. I'm not a cop. I'm a private citizen just like you."

She said, "Oh."

"Yeah, '*oh*,'" I snapped. "Next time you talk to

Frankie, would you set him straight? If he needs to hear it from me, he can call. In the meantime, lay off Pudgie. He didn't do a thing."

Exasperated, I returned the handset to the cradle. All we needed was Frankie Miracle on a rampage. I had to admit I was really splitting hairs on this one. Pudgie had most certainly pointed a finger at Frankie, but not in order to make a deal for himself. He was hoping to divert our attention, which he'd succeeded in doing, but only temporarily. Now that his fingerprints had shown up on the stolen vehicle, the focus had shifted back to him. His attempt to implicate Frankie only made his own behavior the more suspect, so in the end, his scheme backfired. Unfortunately, I didn't credit Frankie with an appreciation of the finer points of finking. To him, a rat was a rat. I checked my notes and picked up the phone again, dialing Felicia Clifton's number in Creosote. I didn't even hear the line ring on her end before she said, "Hello?"

"Felicia? Kinsey Millhone. How are you?"

"Not good. Cedric hasn't come home and I'm worried sick about him."

"He hasn't been gone that long, has he? You said he left the house this morning. That's only a few hours."

"Or he could have gone out last night. All I know is he wasn't here when I got up. Either way, he should have checked in by now. This is not like him."

"Did you call the tavern? The bartender said he was always there for Happy Hour."

"Jerry hasn't seen him either. I don't know where he could have gone."

"Maybe he met a girl and went home with her."

"I don't think so. I didn't give him any money so he didn't even have enough to buy drinks. My car's still here so he has to be on foot. He could have walked to the tavern, but not anywhere else. You've seen this town. We're out here in the middle of nowhere and everything shuts down at six."

"Have you tried the police?"

"I suppose I could do that," she said reluctantly. "I tried the two hospitals—the one in Quorum and the other one in Blythe—but neither has a record of him."

"Well, that's good news, isn't it?"

"I guess."

"Would he skip town without telling you?"

"You mean take off for good? Why would he do that?"

"Ah. He's in a bit of trouble with Frankie Miracle, Iona's ex."

"Shit. Does Pudgie know that?"

"I'm sure he's well aware of it. So maybe he decided to lay low."

"Without any money, where could he go?"

"Good question. Look, why not try the police? Maybe he was picked up. For all you know, he's sitting in jail."

"Trust me, if that was true, he would have hit me up for bail."

"Well, I hope he shows soon, but if he doesn't, let me know. Maybe we can come up with another idea."

"You really think he's okay?"

"I'm sure he's fine, but I agree it's worrisome," I said. We chatted briefly, trying to boost each other's confidence. Once I hung up, I thought, *Who am I trying to kid?* I couldn't believe Frankie would risk jail time on a charge of assault and battery (or worse), but he wasn't exactly famous for his impulse control. Now that Iona had set him off, who knew what he'd do?

*   *   *

Sunday morning at 8:45, Stacey and I were staked out in the parking lot of the Quorum Baptist Church. It was Easter and most of the women and children we'd seen were decked out in pastel suits and floral dresses, wearing fresh corsages, their hats atremble with artificial flowers. The McPhees pulled into the church parking lot in three separate cars. We'd been there for half an hour, the rental tucked discreetly behind a three-foot hedge. I was still arguing it made more sense to go straight to the house, but I think Stacey preferred the drama of doing it this way. The elder McPhees arrived first. They parked and got out, waiting while Adrianne turned in behind them and parked her car close by. Shortly afterward, Justine and Cornell arrived with their three girls. Dressed in their Sunday best, the eight of them looked like a picture-book family. Edna wore a hat. Ruel's hair was slicked down with gel, and his light-blue suit was only slightly too big. The three girls, in matching outfits, complete with hats and white cotton gloves, bypassed the sanctuary and went into the Sunday School building attached at one end.

Stacey and I remained where we were. Some of the church windows were open, and we were treated to organ music and an assortment of hymns. The sermon itself didn't carry that far. Stacey had bought a copy of the *Palo Verde Valley Times,* and while the service went on, we occupied ourselves with the local news. He said, "What'd you hear from Pudgie?"

"Not a word. I called last night, but Felicia said he hadn't showed. I'll call again this afternoon. With luck, he'll be back and we can talk to him. I'll bet you money he has a story cooked up to explain his prints on the Mustang."

I read the front section and the funnies, and Stacey entertained himself by reading aloud ads for cheap desert real estate. I looked up. "You ought to do it, Stacey. Now that you're a homeless person, you could live down here."

"Too hot. I've been thinking to ask Dolan about moving in with him."

"Hey, I like that. He needs someone to ride herd on his profligate lifestyle."

"I'd have to sneak out for junk food. That's the only thing worries me." With a rattle, Stacey flipped the page, his attention shifting to sports.

"It wouldn't hurt you to cut down."

"Speaking of which, what would you like to try next? Taco Bell, Long John Silver's, or Jack in the Box?"

"I thought we were going to McPhee's."

"I'm talking about later. A fella has to eat."

After the church service ended, we waited until the family headed out, and we followed them to the house. Ruel and Edna turned off a block early. "What's that about? Are they ducking us?" I asked, peering back at them.

"They do that every week—visit a shut-in before Sunday lunch."

"You're too much," I said. "Is there anything you don't know?"

Justine let us in. She and Adrianne were apparently in charge of the kitchen until Edna got home. The house smelled of the baked ham she must have put in the oven before she left for church. I detected whiffs of pineapple and brown sugar and the burnt sugar smell of baking sweet potatoes oozing sap onto the oven floor. Justine's girls had settled at the coffee table in the living room, playing a board game with only minor squabbling. I could see their Easter baskets on the floor where they'd left them. Judging from the bits of crumpled foil, it looked as though the girls had already begun to sample the hollow chocolate bunnies and foil-wrapped chocolate eggs. All three had received bright yellow plush ducks. The dining room table had been set with the good china. The centerpiece was an enormous arrangement of Easter lilies I could smell from where I stood.

Justine proceeded down the hall ahead of us. "We're out here in the kitchen putting the finishing touches on lunch."

"No problem," Stacey said as we followed her.

The kitchen was densely heated, in part by the kettle of green beans simmering on the stove. Of course, I was starving, hoping to get on with this so Stacey and I could hit the junk food circuit. I'd already decided it wasn't my job to help Stacey reform. I'd set him on this path so I might as well keep him company while he stuffed himself.

Adrianne stood at the counter, twisting plastic ice cube trays so the cubes dropped neatly into a big clear-glass pitcher. She passed each empty tray to Cornell, who refilled it after she handed it to him. He delivered the last tray to the freezer and then picked up a dish towel and dried his hands. In the meantime, Justine was setting out salad plates, arranging a lettuce leaf on each. She opened the refrigerator and removed a Tupperware Jell-O mold, which she ran briefly under hot water at the sink. Over her shoulder she said to Stacey, "What did you want?"

"I was hoping your parents would be here so I wouldn't have to repeat myself. I don't know if Lieutenant Dolan mentioned this, but we're going to need a set of fingerprints from each of you. Detective Bancroft at the Sheriff's Department said she'd look for you first thing tomorrow morning."

Cornell leaned against the counter and crossed his

arms. He'd taken off his sport coat and loosened his tie. "What's this about?"

"Elimination purposes. Any one of you might've left prints on the Mustang. This way, if we come up with latents, we'll have something to compare 'em to. Saves time and aggravation."

"We're supposed to get inked and rolled like a bunch of criminals?" Cornell asked.

"Well, no sir. Not at all. This is strictly routine, but it's a big help to us. Lieutenant Dolan would have told you himself, but he ended up at Quorum General. I suppose you heard about that."

Cornell wasn't to be distracted by Dolan's medical woes. "What if we say no?"

"I can't think why you would. It's common practice."

"Well, it's not common for me."

Adrianne looked at him. "Oh, just do it, Cornell. Why are you kicking up a fuss?"

"He's not *kicking up a fuss*," Justine said. "He's asking why we have to agree to this crap."

"I wouldn't go so far as to call it 'crap,'" Stacey said. "Left up to me, I'd let the matter slide, but Dolan seems to think it's a good idea. He's the boss on this one. Only takes a couple minutes and the place can't be any more than ten blocks away. If you want, I'll drive you over and bring you back when you're done."

"It isn't that," Cornell said.

"Then what?" Adrianne said. "Why are you acting like this?"

"I wasn't talking to you. I want your opinion, I can ask."

"Excuse the heck out of me."

"Look, I'll go down there, okay? I just don't like being told what to do."

Stacey said, "Tell you what. I've got an inkless pad in the car. Inked prints are superior, but I can see your point. We can take care of it right now if you'd prefer."

"Skip it. I'll go. It just bugs me, that's all."

"We appreciate that. I'll tell the detective the family's coming in."

"Wait a minute. Mom and Dad have to go, too?"

"Since the vehicle belongs to your dad, it wouldn't be unusual to find his prints on it. It's the same with your mom. No point in chasing our tails if there's an obvious explanation."

"Oh, for Pete's sake," Cornell said. He tossed the dish towel on the counter and went out the back door, letting it bang shut behind him. I'd have bet serious money he'd be lighting a cigarette to calm himself.

His sister stared after him. "What's his problem?"

"Just drop it. He's in a bad mood," Justine said.

Adrianne caught my eye briefly and then looked away.

Stacey and I went to Long John Silver's for lunch, this time swooning over crisp-fried fish and chips doused in puckery vinegar the color of iced tea. Afterward, we stopped by Quorum General to visit Dolan. I hadn't seen him since Friday night and I was amazed at his progress. He was out wandering the hall, wearing a pair of paper slippers and a light cotton robe over his hospital gown. He was freshly showered and shaved, his hair still damp and neatly combed to one side.

As soon as he saw us he said, "Let's use the waiting room at the end of the hall. I'm sick of being cooped up."

I said, "You look great."

"I'm lobbying the doc to let me out of here." Dolan

seemed to shuffle, but it may have been the only way to keep the slippers on his feet.

"What's the deal at this point?"

"Possibly tomorrow. I'm supposed to start cardiac re-hab and he thinks I'm better off doing that on home turf," he said. "Joe Mandel called me this morning with good news. They picked up the guy on that triple homi-cide."

Stacey said, "Good dang deal. Now they can concen-trate on us."

We had the waiting room to ourselves. Up in one cor-ner, a wall-mounted color TV was tuned to an evangelist, the sound turned down low. There was a white-robed choir behind him and I watched the vigor with which they sang. Lieutenant Dolan seemed restless, but I thought it was probably the lack of cigarettes. For him, work and the act of smoking were so closely connected it was hard to do one without the other. We chatted about the case. None of us ever tired of rehashing the facts, though there was nothing new to add.

He said, "Right now, Pudgie's our priority. Time to lean on that guy."

"Waste of time," Stacey said. "He's an old family friend. His prints are easy to explain. Might be bullshit, but nothing we can prove either way."

We moved on to idle chitchat until Dolan's energy be-gan to flag. We parted company soon afterward.

Stacey and I spent the remainder of Sunday afternoon in our separate rooms. I don't know how he occupied his time. I read my book, napped, and trimmed my hair with my trusty pair of nail scissors. At 6:00, we went out for another round of junk food, this time Taco Bell. I was beginning to crave alfalfa sprouts and carrot juice; any-thing without additives, preservatives, or grease. On the other hand, the color had returned to Stacey's cheeks and I'd have been willing to swear he'd gained a pound or two since he arrived.

Dolan was released from the hospital late Monday afternoon just as the dinner trays were coming out. Stacey and I arrived on the floor at 5:00 and waited with patience while Dolan's doctor reviewed his chart and lectured him at length about the importance of staying off cigarettes, eating properly, and initiating a program of moderate exercise. By the time we saw him, he was dressed in street clothes and eager to be gone.

We tucked him in the front seat of Stacey's rental car while I climbed in the back. He carried a manila envelope with copies of the ER report, his EKGs, and his record of treatment. As Stacey turned the key in the ignition, Dolan said, "Bunch of bunk. They exaggerate this stuff, trying to keep you in line. I don't see what's so bad about an occasional smoke."

"Don't start on that. You do what they say."

"How about I'll be as compliant as you were? As I remember it, you did what suited you and to hell with them."

Stacey turned off the key and threw his hands up. "That's it. We're going right back upstairs and talk to the doctor."

"What's the matter with you? I said I'd do as I'm told . . . in the main. Now start the car and let's go. I'm not supposed to be upset. It says so right here," he said, rattling his envelope.

"Does not. I read that myself."

"You read my *medical* records?"

"Sure. The chart was in the slot on your door. I knew you'd lie about things."

I leaned forward, resting my arms on the front seat between them. "Guys, if you two are going to bicker, I'll get out and walk."

All three of us were silent while they thought about that.

Finally, Dolan said, "Oh, all right. This is making my blood pressure go up."

At the Quorum Inn over dinner, Dolan's mood improved and the tension between them eased. Dolan made a pious display of ordering broiled fish with lemon, steamed vegetables, a plain green salad, and a glass of red wine, which he swore he was allowed. After our day of junk food, Stacey and I both ate broiled chicken, salad, and the same steamed vegetables. We all pretended to enjoy the dinner more than we did. By the time our decaf coffee arrived, it was clear we'd run out of conversation. In the morning, Stacey would drive Dolan back to Santa Teresa in the rental car, leaving Dolan's for me. The case had sailed into one of those inevitable calms. We were waiting for paperwork, waiting for test results, waiting for comparison prints; in short, waiting for a break that might never come. I probably should have headed home at the same time they did. I'd certainly join them in a day or two, if nothing further developed.

I said, "In the meantime, what's left? I don't want to sit here idle."

Dolan said, "Just don't get in trouble."

"How could I do that? There's nothing going on."

Tuesday morning, I saw them off at 8:00, giving a final wave as Stacey turned out of the parking lot. I went back to my room, feeling a mild depression mixed with relief at being on my own again. I usually experienced a similar reaction after Robert Dietz had been with me and finally hit the road. It's hard to be the one left behind. If I were home, I'd clean house, but in the confines of the motel, I couldn't even do that. I gathered my wee pile of laundry, rooted in the bottom of my bag for loose change, and walked to the Laundromat half a block away. There's no activity more profoundly boring than sitting in a Laundromat, waiting for the washer and dryer to click through their cycles from beginning to end. If you dared leave your clothes, thinking to return later when the load was done, someone would steal them or pull them out of the machines and leave them in a heap. I sat and did surveillance on my own underwear. It beat doing a records search, but not by much.

24

I hadn't been back from the Laundromat for more than ten minutes when I heard a knock on my door. I peered through the fisheye and saw Felicia Clifton standing outside, staring off across the parking lot. I opened the door. The face she turned to me was pale and undefined, free of makeup. Her eyes, without the black liner and false lashes, were actually prettier, though not nearly as large or as vivid. She wore jeans, a sweatshirt, and running shoes without socks, as though she'd dressed in haste. Her red hair was pulled back in a jumbled ponytail.

"This is a pleasant surprise. Come in."

She stepped in, reaching out a hand to steady herself. At first I thought she was drunk, but I realized within seconds, she was shaken and upset. "Felicia, what's wrong? Is it Pudgie?"

She nodded mutely. I moved her to one side and closed the door after her, saying, "Hey, you're safe. You're fine. Take your time."

She sank onto the desk chair, putting her head between her knees as though on the verge of passing out.

So far, I didn't like the way the conversation was shaping up. I went into the bathroom and grabbed a washcloth. I rung it out with cold water and carried back to her. She took it and pressed it to her face. She made a sound that was half-sigh and half-moan.

I sat down at the foot of the king-size bed, almost knee to knee with her. "Is he all right?" From the way she was behaving, I suspected he was dead, but I was unwilling to voice that possibility until she did.

"They called at seven. They think it's him. They need someone to look, but I can't."

"What happened?"

"I don't know. They told me to come in."

"Where, the Sheriff's Department downtown?"

She nodded. "This is bad. He's been gone for days. If he was hurt, they wouldn't ask me to come in, would they? They'd tell me where he was."

"You don't know that for sure. Did they call you at work?"

"I was still at home. I don't start until eight. I was having a cup of coffee in my robe when the phone rang. I don't even know how I got here. I remember getting in the car, but I don't remember the drive."

"We'll go. Leave your car where it is and we'll take mine. Just let me grab my things. In the meantime, breathe."

I breathed in and out for her, demonstrating the process. I knew her anxiety was such that she'd end up holding her breath. Jacket and bag in hand, I ushered her out and pulled the door shut behind us. She didn't have a purse and her hands were shaking so badly the car keys she carried jingled like a length of chain. I put a hand out to still them. She looked at me in surprise and then stared down at the keys as though she'd never seen them before. She tucked them in her jeans. I opened the passenger door for her, then circled the car and slipped in under the wheel. Once I started the car, I turned the heat on full blast. The day wasn't cold, but she was so tense I knew she'd be feeling chilled. She sat, shoulders hunched, pressing her hands between her knees, while she shook like a dog on the way to the vet's.

The Police Department and Sheriff's Department were housed together in a two-story brick building, which, like everything else in Quorum, was hardly more than seven blocks away. I found parking on the street and went around to the passenger door to help her out. Once she was on her feet, she regained some of her composure. I knew she was still rattled, but something about being in motion helped her assume control. So far, she really hadn't heard any bad news. It was the anticipation that was crushing her.

We went into the station. I had Felicia take a seat on a wooden bench in the corridor while I went into the office. This was strictly no-fuss decor: a counter, plain beige floor tile, gray metal desks, rolling swivel chairs, and government-issue gray filing cabinets. Cables and connecting wires ran in a tangle from the backs of the computers and down behind the desks. A cork bulletin board was littered with memos, notices, and official communications I couldn't read from where I stood. There were also framed color photographs of the Riverside County sheriff, the governor of California, and the president of the United States.

I told the uniformed deputy at the desk who Felicia was and why we were there. He referred me in turn to a Detective Lassiter, who emerged from the inner office to have a chat with me. He was in his forties, clean-shaven, trim, and prematurely gray. He was dressed in civilian clothes, gun and holster visible under his dark gray sport coat. He kept his voice low while he detailed the information he'd received. "We got a call from a woman who lives out on Highway 78, four miles this side of Hazelwood Springs. Are you familiar with the area?"

"I know the section of the road you mean."

"There are coyotes in the hills near her property, so she leaves her dog inside unless she can be in the yard to keep an eye on him. Yesterday, the trash haulers left the gate open and the dog escaped. He was gone all night and when he came back this morning he was dragging a bone. Actually, an arm. The deputy remembered Felicia's call about Cedric. Most of us know him, but we want someone else to take a look."

"I really only met him once and I'm not sure I'd recognize his *arm*. Unless it's the one with all the tattoos," I added. I had a quick vision of his left arm from the one and only time I'd seen him at the Santa Teresa county jail. On it, he'd had a tattoo of a big-breasted woman with long, flowing black hair. In addition, he had a spiderweb, the sombrero-clad skull, and a pornographic sex act he would have been well advised to have tattooed on his butt.

"We had a warrant out on him for a traffic-related felony—this was 1981. Along with his mug shot we have a description of his tattoos that seems to match."

"Can't you use the hand to roll a set of prints?"

"Most of the fingers have been chewed, but we'll try that as soon as the coroner's done whatever he needs to do."

"Where's the rest of him?"

"That's just it. We don't know."

I stared at him, blinking, startled by the notion that had just popped into my head. "I might."

Intuition is odd. After one of those gut-level leaps, you can sometimes go back and trace the trajectory— how this thought or observation and yet another idea have somehow fused at the bottom of your brain to form the insight that suddenly rockets into view. On other occasions, intuition is just that—a flash of information that reaches us without any conscious reasoning. What I remembered was the sound of plastic being flapped by the wind, and a coyote leisurely stripping flesh from what I'd assumed at the time was a recent kill. "I think he's at the Tuley-Belle. The scavengers have been dining on him for days."

Felicia and I sat in the car for an hour on the upwind side of the abandoned complex. By now, the odor of putrefying flesh was unmistakable, as easily identified as the smell of skunk. We waited while the coroner examined the remains. The coyotes must have picked up on the scent of blood within hours, and many of Pudgie's facial features had apparently been ravaged. It was that aspect of his death that seemed to offend even the most cynical of the officers present. Pudgie's troubles with the law had occurred with a frequency that had created something of a bond with many of the deputies. Granted, he was a screwup, but he was never vicious or depraved. He was simply one of those guys for whom crime came more easily than righteous effort.

Eventually, Detective Lassiter came over to the car and asked Felicia if she wanted to see the body. "He's not in good shape, but you're entitled to see him. I don't want you left with any doubts about this."

She glanced at me. "You go. I won't look if it's that bad."

It was.

Pudgie's body had been covered with a length of opaque plastic sheeting, weighted with rocks, and left in a shallow depression out behind the very building I'd toured. Even as I approached the area with Detective Lassiter, I could hear the wind pick up a corner of the plastic and flap it like a rag.

I said, "Where'd the plastic come from?"

"It was tacked across a doorway at the rear of this wing. You can still see the remnants where it was torn from the door frame."

The glimpse I had of the body was sufficient to confirm that it was Pudgie. No surprise on that score. The cause of death was blunt-force trauma: repeated blows to the head that had fractured his skull and left a lot of brain matter exposed.

"What about the murder weapon?"

"We're looking for that now."

There was no immediate estimate as to time of death. That would wait until the coroner did the postmortem. Felicia had last seen him Friday night between 9:30 and 10:00 when she'd turned off the TV and had gone to bed. He might well have been killed that night, though it was unclear how he got to the Tuley-Belle. Odds were someone had picked him up in Creosote and had driven him out here—probably someone he trusted, or he wouldn't have agreed to go. I wondered how long it had taken the coyotes to arrive, their knives and forks at the ready, bibs tucked under their little hairy chins. The hawks and crows, foxes and bobcats would have waited their turns. Nature is generous. Pudgie, in death, was a veritable feast.

The area had been secured. Anyone not directly involved was kept at a distance to preclude contamination of the scene. The coroner's van was parked close by. Detective Lassiter had organized the deputies and they'd started a grid search, looking for additional bones and body parts as well as the murder weapon and any evidence the killer might have left behind. Deputy Chilton, whom I'd met at the McPhees', was one of the men combing the surrounding area. Felicia and I sat in Dolan's car. Technically, she wasn't required to be there at all, and I suspect the detective would have preferred that I ferry her home. At the station, while we'd waited, they'd sent a unit out to the Tuley-Belle to check my guess. The deputy had spotted Pudgie's body and called in the report. Felicia had been given a vague accounting, enough to know it was her brother and the condition of his body poor. She'd insisted on coming. He was far beyond rescue, but she kept her vigil nonetheless.

I watched the crime scene activity as if it were a movie I'd already seen. The details sometimes varied, but the plot was always the same. I felt sick at heart. I avoided thinking about the coyotes and the sounds I'd heard on the two occasions I'd been at the Tuley-Belle. There was no doubt in my mind that he was dead by then. I couldn't have saved him, but I might have prevented some of the mauling that came later. The fact that Pudgie was killed here lent support to my suspicion that Charisse had been killed at this location as well.

At 2:00, Detective Lassiter crossed the wide unpaved parking area and again headed in our direction. I got out of the car and went to meet him midway. "They're getting ready to transport the body. You might have Felicia call the mortuary in Quorum. Once the autopsy's done, we'll release the body to them unless she's made other arrangements. You might ask if she has a pastor she wants us to notify."

"Sure. I'll see what she says."

"You're down here with Stacey Oliphant?"

"Right. He and Lieutenant Dolan are on their way back to Santa Teresa. I was scheduled to follow, but under the circumstances, I'll stay."

"We'll operate on the assumption the two murders are related unless we find out otherwise. I imagine Santa Teresa will want to send down a couple of their guys."

"Most certainly," I said. I gave him my summary of what had brought us to Quorum and what we'd learned. Since Stacey had relayed much of the same information, I skimmed across events, only filling in details when I came to something he hadn't heard, Frankie Miracle being prime. I said, "Lieutenant Dolan and I dropped in on his ex-wife in Peaches as we were heading down to the desert. Her name's Iona Mathis."

"We're familiar with her," he said. "She and my niece belong to the same church, or at least they did."

"Yeah, well her mom says she drove to Santa Teresa to see Frankie as soon as we left. I thought he drove back with her, but I'm not sure. She claims he was at work Friday night in Santa Teresa."

"Easy enough to check. You know the company?"

"I don't, but I'm sure Stacey or Dolan will know. You might want to talk to Iona as well. She called Pudgie Thursday night and was really pissed off, from what Felicia said." I made a verbal detour, telling him about Iona's belief that Pudgie'd made a deal for himself at Frankie's expense. "Felicia doesn't know if Pudgie went out late Friday night or first thing Saturday morning. She told me a call came in before Iona's, but she has no idea who it was. He answered that one himself."

"I'll talk to Iona soon . . . maybe later today. Where will you be?"

I told him where I was staying. "I'll call the guys as soon as I get back to the motel. This business with Pudgie will be a blow. I'm sure Stacey told you they found his prints on the Mustang. We all assumed he either killed her himself or else knew who did. Now it looks like someone killed him to shut him up."

"The downside of being an accessory," Lassiter said. "Meanwhile, if anything comes up, let us know."

I drove Felicia back to the motel. She was quiet, leaning her head against the seat with her eyes half-closed. She had a tissue in one hand, and I could see her dab at her eyes occasionally. Her lids were swollen and her face was splotchy, her red hair lusterless as though dulled by grief. Whatever weeping she did was silent. Now that she knew the worst, there was something passive in her response, a resignation she must have harbored for years, waiting for the blow.

Finally, I said, "If it's any consolation, people did care about him."

She turned and smiled wanly. "You think? I hope you're right about that. He had a sorry life; in jail more times than he was out. Makes you wonder what it means."

"I've given up trying to figure that out. Just don't blame yourself."

"I do in some ways. I'll always think I could have done a better job with him. Trouble is, I don't know if I was too tough on him or not tough enough."

"Pudgie made his choices. It's not your responsibility."

"You know something? I don't care what he did. He was decent to me. He might have sponged, but he never ripped me off, you know? He's my baby brother and I loved him."

"I know. You belong to a church? I'd be happy to make some calls."

"In a town this size, the word's already out. The minister will probably already be there by the time I get home. I just hope I don't fall apart. This is hard enough."

At the motel, I parked near her car and the two of us got out. I gave her a hug. She clung to me briefly. Then she pulled back, eyes brimming, and wiped her nose on a tissue. "Don't be too nice. It only makes it worse," she said.

"You're okay to drive?"

"I'll be fine."

"I'll call you tomorrow."

"Thanks. I'd appreciate that."

I let myself into my room. The maid had come and gone, so my towels were fresh and my bed had been neatly made. I stretched out, reaching for the phone next to my book on the bed table. Stacey's number was a disconnect. I had to smile at that. Since he'd been convinced he was dying, he probably hadn't worried much about utility bills. I called Dolan's number and left a message, asking one or the other of them to give me a call as soon as they rolled in. It was 3:00 by then and even if they'd stopped for lunch, they should arrive in Santa Teresa within the hour. I didn't dare leave the room, for fear I'd miss their call. I tried reading, but I found myself, not surprisingly, brooding about Pudgie's death. I thought about my conversation with Iona Mathis, wondering how she'd come up with that cockamamie notion that I'd made a deal with Pudgie to get him out of jail. I hoped her misconceptions hadn't contributed to his death. If so, then I bore a certain responsibility for what had happened to him. The thought made me ill.

I took my shoes off and slid under the covers, pulling the spread over me. I picked up my book and read for a while, hoping to distract myself. I was warm. The room was quiet. I found myself dipping into sleep so that when the phone finally rang, I jumped, snatching up the handset while my heart thumped. The surge of adrenaline peaked and receded. It was Dolan.

I sat up and trailed my feet over the side of the bed, rubbing my face while I suppressed a yawn. "How was the trip? You sound tired."

"I've felt perkier," he said. "Stacey dropped me off half an hour ago. He's taking a run to the Sheriff's Department to talk to Mandel. On his way back, he plans to stop by his apartment and pick up his things. I guess we'll think about dinner after that."

"Is he staying with you?"

"Temporarily. You know the lease is up on his place and he has to be out by the end of the month. He assumed he'd be six feet underground by then, but I guess the gods fooled him. I asked if he wanted to stay here until he finds some place else. I can use the company."

"Nice. That should benefit both of you if you can keep from quarreling."

Dolan had the good grace to laugh. "We don't quarrel. We disagree," he said. "What about things on your end? We felt bad you got stuck holding the proverbial bag. Did you manage to amuse yourself?"

"Funny you should ask." And then I told him about Pudgie's death, which we discussed in detail. In the midst of dissecting events, Dolan said, "Hang on a second. Stacey just came in. I want to tell him about this."

He put his hand across the mouthpiece to spare me the replay while he brought Stacey up to speed. Even in its muffled form, I could hear Stacey's expletives.

He took the handset from Dolan. "That's the last time I'm leaving you. What the hell's going on?"

"You know as much as I do."

He had his own set of questions about Pudgie, and then we chatted about Frankie. He said they'd do what they could to track him down and see if he could account for his whereabouts from Friday morning on. "Good news on this end. Charisse's dental chart is a match for Jane Doe's, so at least we nailed that down. Forensics is just about willing to swear the hairs we recovered belong to her as well. Now all we need is a match on that second set of prints and we may be in business. Have the McPhees gone in?"

"I assume so. I'll check tomorrow morning to make sure," I said. "When are you planning to drive back?"

"Soon as I can. I'll hit the road the minute things here are under control."

I heard Dolan rumbling in the background.

Stacey said, "Oh, right. Dolan left his gun in the trunk of his car. He wants to know if it's still there."

"I haven't had occasion to open the trunk, but I'll look when I can. What's he want me to do with it?"

Dolan said something to Stacey.

"He says just make sure you get it back to him as soon as you get home."

"Of course."

Dolan said something else to him that I couldn't make out.

Stacey said, "Hang on a minute." And to Dolan, "Damn it! Would you quit talking to me when I'm on the phone with her?"

More mumbling from Dolan.

"Horsepucky. You will not." Stacey returned. "Guy's driving me nuts. He says he'll do fine on his own, but he's full of shit. Minute my back is turned, he'll run out and buy himself a pack of cigarettes. They oughta lock him up."

I heard a door slam in the background.

"Same to you, bub!" Stacey yelled. "Anyway, I'll call and let you know when I'm hitting the road. You can talk to the desk clerk and reserve a room."

After we hung up, I put a call through to Henry. His machine picked up. I left a message, telling him I missed him and that I'd call back. I read for another hour or so and then ordered a pizza. I didn't have the heart to go out and eat a proper meal by myself. Ordinarily, I like eating in a restaurant alone. But with Stacey and Dolan gone, the idea seemed alien. Pudgie's murder had left me spooked. It was one thing dealing with a murder that had happened eighteen years before. Whatever the motivation, time had provided a lengthy cooling-off period. Life had gone on. The killer had managed to strike once and get away with it. I'd assumed there wouldn't be a reason to kill again, but Pudgie's death made it obvious how wrong I was. The stakes were still high. In the intervening years, someone had enjoyed a life that was built on a lie. Now we'd come along threatening the status quo.

I ate my supper and tossed the box in the trash. I watched a couple of television shows with annoying laugh tracks. At 9:00, I decided I might as well work. Keeping a systematic set of notes has its soothing side effects. I sat down at the desk and opened the drawer.

Things had been moved.

I stared and I then looked around the room, wondering if someone had come in. Not *if*. I wondered *who*'d come in and handled the contents of the drawer. The last time I'd taken notes must have been Saturday afternoon.

Stacey and I had been to Creosote, stopping off at the Tuley-Belle on the way home. Once at the motel, we'd decided to take a break. I'd had a phone chat with Betty Puckett from Lockaby and then I'd showered, dressed, and started jotting down the tidbits—events, questions, and conversations. At the end of that session, I'd put a rubber band around my index cards and tossed them in the drawer on top of the murder book. Now they were underneath. It seemed a small matter, but my memory was distinct.

I picked up a pen and used it to lift one corner of the murder book so I could slide the cards out. I held the stack along the edges while I peeled off the rubber band. I'd left the top card upside down as a reminder to myself to have a second chat with Medora Sanders. Now the card was reversed, lined up in the same direction as all the other note cards.

Someone had been in here. Someone had handled the murder book and read my notes.

I got up abruptly, almost as though a shock had been administered through the seat of the chair. I circled the room, carefully scrutinizing every square foot of it. My duffel and the family photo album were in the closet untouched. Except for what was in the drawer, everything else was as I remembered it. Had the maid tidied up? If so, why would she stop and read the index cards? The maid I'd chatted with had barely spoken English. It could have been another employee. There were probably different women who worked weekday and weekend shifts. Maybe the last maid who'd cleaned my room had been curious and had helped herself, thinking I'd never know. I had trouble believing it, but I couldn't prove otherwise.

I rebanded the cards and returned them, using the tip

of my pen to push the drawer shut. I didn't think it would occur to anyone that I'd have such a clear recollection of how the contents of the drawer had been left. If it wasn't the maid, then how had entry been effected? The room door was kept locked. I went into the bathroom and pulled a tissue from the box, then moved to the door and used the tissue to turn the knob. I examined the exterior of the door, the escutcheon and the face plate, but there were no gouges or scratches, and no evidence of forced entry. The windows were latched on the inside and showed no indications of tampering.

On the other hand, the means of access could have been simple. While the maid had been cleaning the room on Saturday, she'd left my door propped open with the pile of dirty sheets. She'd had her radio on in the bathroom, music blaring while she cleaned the toilet and the sink. Anyone could have slipped in and searched the desk, which was just inside the door. There wouldn't have been time to read the murder book itself, but the cards were more important. My notes reflected everything I knew about the case and everything I considered relevant. By perusing my notes, someone could figure out where I'd been, who I'd talked to, and what I intended to do. There was an obvious advantage to anticipating my next move. Someone could step in before I'd had the chance to get the information I needed.

I closed the door and went back to the desk. I studied the stack of cards with Medora's name on top. I didn't think she knew anything she hadn't told me before, but it might be smart to check with her. Briefly, I considered calling Detective Lassiter or someone else at the local Sheriff's Department, but what was I supposed to say? My stack of index cards has been moved an inch? Gasp! I didn't think they'd rush right out and dust for prints. At best, they'd come up with the same suggestion I had, that the maid had opened and closed the drawer in the process of cleaning my room. Big deal. Aside from the rearrangement of my belongings (which they'd have to take my word for), there wasn't any evidence of a break-in. The room hadn't been vandalized and nothing had been stolen, so from their perspective, no crime had been committed.

I grabbed my bag and my bomber jacket, preparing to leave. I was almost out the door when something occurred to me. I retrieved my family album from the closet and then crossed to the desk drawer and removed the murder book and the index cards. I went out, making sure the door was secured behind me. I locked my armload of valuables in the trunk of Dolan's car and then headed for Medora's house. I was heartened by the lingering image of Dolan's Smith & Wesson in the trunk.

25

The night was cold and windy, but the drive was so brief, there wasn't time enough for Dolan's heater to kick in. There was scarcely a building in Quorum more than two stories tall, so there wasn't much protection from the blasts of chill air sweeping in off the desert. The sky was a brittle black and the presence of stars wasn't as comforting as one might hope. Nature has her little ways of reminding us how small and frail we are. Our existence is temporary while hers will go on long after our poor flesh has failed.

I parked in Medora's driveway. The house was dark except for one lamp in the living room. As I crossed the patchy stretch of grass I realized the front door was standing open. I could see the vertical strip of dull light expand and contract as the wind ebbed and flowed. I hesitated and then knocked on the screen door frame. "Medora?"

There was no sound from inside. I opened the screen door and called through the opening. "Medora?"

I didn't like the idea of intruding, but this was odd,

especially given my suspicions about an intruder of my own. If someone had read my notes and spotted her name, her house might well be the next stop. I pushed the door open and eased in, closing it behind me. The room was dark except for a small table lamp. I could see Medora on the couch, lying on her back, her hands folded across her chest. I drew closer. She was snoring, her every exhalation infused with the fumes of metabolizing alcohol. If she woke to find me hovering she'd be startled, but I didn't want to leave until I knew she was okay. A half-smoked cigarette, resting on the lip of the ashtray, had burned down to an inch of ash before it had gone out. The ice in her highball glass had long since melted away. Her prescription pill bottles appeared to be full and the caps were in place. At least she hadn't overdosed in any obvious way, though I knew her practice of mixing whiskey with painkillers was dangerous.

The house was cold and I could feel a breeze stirring. I crossed to the kitchen and flipped on the light. The back door stood open, creating a cross-ventilation that had drained all the heat from the rooms. I lifted my head and scanned the silence for any hint of sound. I remained where I was and did a visual survey. The back door was intact—no splintered wood, no shattered framing, and no broken glass. The windows were shut and the latches turned to the locked position. The kitchen counters were crowded with canned goods, boxes of cereal and crackers, packages of paper napkins, toilet tissue, paper towels, and cleaning products. It looked as if the dishes hadn't been done in a week, though all she seemed to eat was cereal and soup. The trash can was overflowing, but aside from the mess, it didn't appear that anything had been disturbed.

I glanced over at Medora, chilled by the notion of

how vulnerable she was. Anybody could have walked in,
robbed her, assaulted her, killed her where she lay. If a
fire had broken out, I doubt she'd have been aware. I
closed the back door and locked it. I toured the rest of
the house, which comprised no more than one small,
dingy bathroom and two small bedrooms. Her house-
keeping habits, such as they were, made it impossible to
tell if anyone else had been in the rooms doing a quick
search.

I returned to the living room and leaned toward her.
"Medora, it's Kinsey. Are you all right?"

She didn't stir.

I placed a hand lightly on her arm, saying, "Hey."

Nothing. I shook her gently, but the gesture didn't
seem to register. She was submerged in the murky depths
of alcohol, where sound couldn't penetrate and no light
reached. I shook her again. She made a grunting noise,
but otherwise remained unresponsive. I didn't think I
should leave her in her present state. I looked for a telephone and finally spotted one in the kitchen, mounted
on the wall near the hall door. I searched one drawer after another until I found the phone book. I looked up
Justine's number and called her. She answered after four
rings.

"Justine? This is Kinsey. I'm really sorry to bother
you, but I stopped by your mother's house just now and
found both doors standing open. She seems to have
passed out. I think she's okay, but I'm having trouble
rousing her. Could you come over here? I don't think I
should leave her until you've seen for yourself."

"Damnation. Oh, hell. I'll be there as soon as possible."

She hung up abruptly. I was sorry I'd annoyed her,
but such is life. I returned to the couch and perched on

the edge of the coffee table. I took Medora's hand and slapped it lightly. "Medora, wake up. Can you wake up?"

Groggily, she opened her eyes. At first, she couldn't seem to focus, but she finally coordinated her eyes and looked around the room, disoriented.

"It's me, Kinsey. Can you hear me?"

She mumbled something I couldn't understand.

"Medora, did you take something for the pain? Let's get you up, okay?" I slid an arm under her head, trying to lift her into a sitting position. "I'm going to pull you up here, but I need your help."

She seemed to gather herself, pushing up on one elbow, which enabled me to haul her upright. Her gaze settled on mine with an expression of confusion. "What's happening?"

"I don't know, Medora. You tell me. Let's get you on your feet and take a walk. Can you do that?"

"What for? I'm fine. I don't want to walk."

"Well, sit then and let's talk. I don't want you falling asleep again. Did you take something?"

"A nap."

"I know you took a nap, but your doors were wide open and I was worried about you. Did you take any pills?"

"Earlier."

"How many? Show me what you took, was it this?"

"And the other ones."

I checked the labels on the bottles: Valium, Tylenol with Codeine, Percocet, Xanax. "This is not a good idea. You're not supposed to take all of these at the same time, especially if you've had a drink. It's not safe. Are you feeling okay?"

"Dr. Belker gave me those."

"But you shouldn't take them when you drink. Didn't he explain that?"

"That case I couldn't take 'em at all. I drink every day."
She smiled at my goofiness, having settled that point.

We went on in this fashion, with Medora offering
short declarative sentences in response to my continued
questions. While it was hardly scintillating conversation,
it did serve its intended purpose, which was to keep her
in contact with reality. By the time Justine arrived, fifteen
minutes later, Medora was more alert and in control of
herself.

Justine shed her coat and tossed it on the back of a
chair. "Sorry it took so long, but I was waiting for Cornell. I finally called my next-door neighbor and she came
over to watch the girls."

Medora had focused on Justine with an air of humility
and embarrassment. "I didn't tell her to call you. I
wouldn't do that."

Justine sat down beside her mother and took her
hand. "How many times have we been through this,
Mother? You can't keep doing this. I have a life of my
own."

"All I had was one drink and a pain pill."

"I'm sure you did. How many?"

"The usual."

"Never mind. Just skip it. I shouldn't waste my breath.
Are you all right?"

"I'm fine. You didn't have to leave the girls and come
over."

"She says the doors were wide open. What was that
about?"

"I closed them. I did. I remembered what you said."

"Let's just get you into bed. We can talk about this
later when you're more yourself."

"I'm myself," she said blearily, as Justine assisted her
to her feet. Medora was a bit tottery.

"You need help?"

Justine shook her head, intent on maneuvering her mother around the sharp-cornered coffee table, across the room, and into the short hallway that led to her bedroom. I could hear the two of them murmuring, Medora apologizing while Justine went about the business of getting her to bed.

Five minutes later, Justine returned, rubbing her arms reflexively. "I swear she's getting worse. I don't know what to do with her. Geez, the place is *freezing*."

"It's warmer than it was."

She went over to the thermostat. "It's turned off. What's she doing, trying to save money on the heating bill? No wonder she gets sick. She had pneumonia two months ago." She adjusted the lever and within seconds, I could hear the furnace click on.

She sat down on the couch with a sigh that was laden with irritation. "I can't tell you how many times I've talked to her about this. She takes out the garbage or goes to pick up the newspaper from the drive and then she either locks herself out or forgets to latch the door again. On a windy night like this, the doors bang and blow open. She never even knows."

"I'm not sure that's what happened here, but it's giving me the creeps. Could you take a look around and make sure nothing's missing? Suppose someone's been here."

"Why would anybody bother? There's nothing worth stealing."

"I understand, but I don't like the feel of it. Can you make a quick circuit for my sake?"

"All right. You might as well follow me. This won't take long, but you can see for yourself." She leaned over and picked up the whiskey bottle from the coffee table. "Here."

I took the bottle and waited while she snagged the highball glass and the pill bottles lined up nearby. "Her doctor's out of his mind. I've had this discussion with him a hundred times. They're old friends, so she comes along right after me and talks him into it."

She gave the kitchen a cursory look while she poured her mother's whiskey down the drain. She emptied all the pills into the trash, where I heard them rattling toward the bottom like a cupful of BB's. She tossed in the empty whiskey bottle. "I'll take care of this later," she said, referring to the overflowing trash can and the pile of dishes in the sink. "Things look fine in here. The place is a pigsty, but no more than usual."

I trailed after her while she looked into the bathroom and the second bedroom. The latter must have been her room as a kid, the one she'd been forced to share with Charisse. The twin beds were still in place, but most of the remaining space was taken up with piles of clothing, boxes, and miscellaneous junk. I nearly confided my suspicion about someone having entered my room, but I thought better of it. I didn't have proof and I didn't want to sound completely paranoid. Besides, it would only encourage her to ask questions I didn't want to answer.

As we were returning to the living room, she said, "I heard about Pudgie. It's horrible."

"News travels fast."

"Trust me, everybody knows by now."

"Who told you?"

"Todd Chilton called. He's a deputy—"

"I met him. Why did he call you?"

"Oh, right. He remembered I dated Pudgie and he thought I should know. From what he said, it was gross. At least I got that impression reading between the lines. He says you're the one who figured it out."

"Someone would have noticed before long," I said, thinking about the smell. I filled in a few brush strokes, avoiding anything of substance. I was certain Detective Lassiter would limit the information that reached the public.

"Why'd you stop by?"

"I had a question for your mom. I know this seems minor, but I was curious. The first time I talked to her, she said she'd gone to the police the day Charisse disappeared. But according to the police report, she waited a week. I was hoping she'd explain the discrepancy."

"She didn't tell you about the note?"

"From Charisse? Not that I remember."

"She probably forgot to mention it. Her mind's completely shot from all the crap she takes. The note said she'd decided to go see her mother and she'd be back in three days. We thought she'd show up, but a week passed and Mom started getting worried. That's when she talked to the police."

"You saw the note yourself?"

"Sure. She'd left it on the bed."

"And the handwriting was hers?"

"As far as I could tell."

"Did your mother save it?"

"I doubt it. Why would she do that?"

"Could you ask her please?"

"Right now?"

"I'd appreciate it."

She left the living room and returned to her mother's bedroom, where I could hear her insistent questioning and Medora's foggy response. I heard drawers being opened and shut. Moments later, Justine returned. "I don't believe this. She says she saved the note because she didn't want Social Services blaming her when Charisse took off. She thought if they ever asked, she could show the note as proof that Charisse left of her own accord."

"Amazing. That's great. I'd love to see it."

"Well, that's just it. She can't remember where she put it. She thought it was in the chest of drawers, but it's not there now. Knowing her, it could be anywhere. She's such a slob."

"Maybe we can look again when she's on her feet."

Justine gave me a look. "Yeah, right. Listen, I need to get back to the girls. Cornell must be home by now, but just in case. Let me turn off some lights and I'll walk you to your car. It's dark as pitch out there."

I waited while she double-checked, making sure the back door was locked. She turned off the lights, except for one in the hall. She tested the thumb lock on the front door, flipped it to the locked position, and pulled it shut behind her. She took her keys from her coat pocket and crossed the yard to her Ford sedan, which was parked in the driveway behind Dolan's car.

"Did you guys go down and have your fingerprints taken?"

"Edna went Monday, but I haven't had a chance. I'll pop in tomorrow while I'm out running errands."

"What about the others?"

"Adrianne said she'd try later in the week."

"What about Ruel and Cornell?"

"Don't look at me. I don't want to be the one to nag them. It's not my job."

"You're right. Thanks anyway. I'll bug them myself."

I drove to the motel with an eye on my rearview mirror. The wide streets were deserted. Businesses were shut

down and most of the houses were dark. Once in my
room, I spent a few minutes assuring myself everything
was exactly as I'd left it. My book was facedown on the
bed where I'd placed it, the bedspread still rumpled
where I'd pushed it aside. The table lamp was on and the
warm light made the room seem cozy. The windows
were latched and I made sure the drapes were properly
closed. Didn't want any boogeymen to peek in at me.
After that, I stripped out of my clothes and into the over-
size T-shirt I use as a nightie. I washed my face, brushed
my teeth, and slid into bed. I thought my paranoia might
keep me awake, but since I'm a person of no depth whatever, I fell asleep right away.

At 2:06, the phone rang. I reached for the handset
automatically, noting the time as I placed it against my
ear. "What."

"Kinsey?"

"What."

"This is Iona."

"Okay."

"Frankie wants to talk to you."

"About what?"

"Pudgie."

"Put him on."

"In person."

I leaned over and flipped on the table lamp, which
made me squint painfully and probably put permanent
wrinkles on my face. "Why are you calling me in the
dead of night? I'm asleep."

"I would've called earlier, but he just got here."

"Got here where?"

"Quorum. He wants you to meet us at the all-night
diner. Know the one I mean? On Main Street. It's called
the Chow Hound."

I closed my eyes. "No offense here, but there's no way I'm going out at this hour to talk to Frankie Miracle, so scratch that idea."

"What if he comes there? We're calling from a pay phone. We're not far."

"Like how far?"

"A block."

"Why isn't he on the phone instead of you?"

"He's afraid you'll say no."

I laughed. "He's worried about me? Iona, the guy's a *killer*. He stabbed a woman fourteen times."

"But he's paid for his crime. He went to prison and now he's out."

"Oh, crap. Why am I arguing with you? If you want to come over, I'll open the window and talk to him through the screen. That's as much as I can offer."

"Okay."

I hung up and went into the bathroom to brush my teeth. This was not the kind of hotel that offered complimentary robes (hell, I felt lucky they offered complimentary toilet paper!), so I pulled on a sweatshirt. I thought about it briefly and pulled on my jeans. By then, I could see headlights arc across the drapes. I turned off the lamp and crossed to the window, peering out as Frankie's white pickup pulled into a slot two doors down. Iona was at the wheel. She waited in the truck with the engine running, probably trying to keep warm, while Frankie got out on the passenger side and slammed the door. I said, "Great. Wake everybody up. I'll feel safer that way."

I watched him check room numbers until he got to mine. As soon as he was close, I slid the window open a crack. "Hello, Frankie."

"Hi. Can I come in?"

"No."

"Come on. I can't stand around out here. It's fuckin' cold."

"I don't need a weather report. I know it's cold. You want to talk, I'm listening, but get on with it."

"All right," he said, irritably. He paused to light a cigarette. Despite the low-watt outside lighting, I could see him clearly—the brown wavy hair, the smooth baby face. He peered over his shoulder, his manner embarrassed. "I heard about Pudgie. I just wanted you to know I had nothing to do with it."

"Good for you."

"Don't you want to know the rest?"

"Sure."

"The cops have already been around—Lieutenant Dolan and some pal of his. I thought my landlord was talking about you, but he said it was an old guy."

"Stacey Oliphant."

"That's him."

"They're good guys. They're fair. You should be talking to them."

"I hate cops. What pigs. I'd rather talk to you."

"What for? I'm just going to turn around and ask you the same questions Lieutenant Dolan would have asked."

"You want to know where I was Friday night, right? I was in Santa Teresa, working my regular shift. Eleven to seven. And that's the truth."

"I thought you were down here with Iona."

"Who told you that?"

"Weren't you with her when she called and talked to Pudgie Thursday night?"

"Sure, but I left Friday morning and drove back to Santa Teresa."

"Anybody see you at work?"

"Two-thirty in the morning, I'm moppin' floors, not entertaining the troops. Reason I like the job is it's quiet and nobody's there to hassle me."

"You were completely alone."

"At that hour? Of course. Who's going to be there? The place's all locked up."

"I don't know. Someone else on the cleaning crew? A lawyer working late? A building that size can't be empty."

"For starters, there's nobody else on the crew. I'm it. And second, even if there was someone in the building, how would I know? Six floors is tough. I got a lot of ground to cover. Some lawyer's workin' late, he's not going to stop and make small talk with the likes of me. So. Nobody saw me. You'll have to take my word that I was there all night."

"You drove all the way down here to tell me this?"

"Hey, I could've had her alibi me, which she'd've done in a heartbeat, but I wanted to play straight."

"Good boy. Now what?"

"Iona thought you might put in a good word for me."

"Frankie, come on. You know better than that. No one gives a shit what I think. My opinion carries no weight at all. It's like Iona thinking I had the clout to offer Pudgie a deal. It's ridiculous."

"Those cops like you."

"Sure they do, but so what? Look, I'm perfectly willing to pass the story along, but trust me, without an alibi, my big, hot endorsement won't help."

"But you believe me?"

"Let's put it this way; nothing would make me happier than your telling the truth. I'm sure the cops will be crazy about the idea, too."

He dropped his cigarette and stepped on the ember with the toe of his boot. "You try, okay?"

"I'll call Lieutenant Dolan tomorrow. Meantime, if I were you I'd get back to town before your PO gets wind of what's going on."

"I'll do that. And thanks."

"You're welcome."

I closed the window and had it latched again before Frankie reached the truck. I heard the door slam and she backed out, the headlights doing a reverse angle on the draperies as she pulled away. I shook my head. What a baby. Gone was the tough guy I'd met the first time around. As for his story, I wasn't sure whether to believe him or not. Sincerity aside, he was capable of manipulation if it suited his purposes.

In the morning, I changed rooms. There were far too many people who knew where I was and I didn't feel safe. I chose an innocuous location on the second floor in the middle of a stretch of rooms. No ice machines. No vending machines. No reason to be up there unless you were a paid motel guest. At ground level, I figured I was a sitting duck for Peeping Toms or guys with a penchant for picking locks. Up here, even if the housekeeper propped my door open for hours on end, it would take nerve for someone to climb the stairs and pretend to be wandering around lost. From the second floor I had a nice view of the parking lot. I'd left Dolan's car in a row of cars to one side so there was no way to associate the vehicle with my whereabouts.

At 9:15, I called Dolan's house. Stacey picked up. I told him my concern that someone had entered my room and had taken a long hard look at my notes. He told me to change rooms, which I told him I'd done. He told me Dolan had left for an appointment with the cardiologist. I told him about Medora's house, the note, and Frankie's late-night visit. He told me I better watch my step and I said I would. Then he said, "What have we picked up in the way of elimination prints?"

"We're not doing so well. Last I heard Edna had gone in, but none of the other four."

"What's up with that? I don't like them thinking they can bypass us. Go back and threaten. Tell them it looks bad, like maybe one of them has something to hide."

"So how's Dolan doing?"

"He's good. I'd say good. Doing better than I thought."

"You think the living arrangements are going to work?"

"Jury's still out on that. I could probably do worse—though, frankly, the guy's a colossal pain in the ass. Of course, he says the same thing about me."

"Makes you the perfect pair," I said. "Better than some of the marriages I've seen."

"Amen to that. What's the latest down there?"

"I haven't heard anything since I was at the Tuley-Belle last night, but I can stop by the sheriff's office and talk to Lassiter."

"Do that and call me back. I've been trying to get in touch with him, but so far no luck. Meantime, we'll see what we can find out about Frankie's whereabouts on Friday night."

"Great. Tell Dolan I said hi. I really miss you guys."

Stacey said, "Ditto. And you take care of yourself."

I retrieved Dolan's car and drove the few short blocks to the Sheriff's Department. Todd Chilton and a civilian clerk seemed to be the only ones in. He was chatting with one of the church ladies I'd seen at Edna's. She was in her seventies, wearing a pale green leisure suit. Her hair had just been done and it puffed out as nicely as a dandelion. She'd placed a parking ticket on the counter, and I waited politely while she wrote out a check and tore it from her register. I flicked a quick look at the name printed on the face of the check: Adele Opdyke.

"How are you, Adele? We met at Edna's on Saturday. Nice seeing you again."

"Nice seeing you, too." She seemed flustered to realize I was standing close enough to see what she was doing. "Don't go thinking this ticket's mine. It's my husband's. He parked in a fire lane Friday night, late going to a movie. He's always doing that. Doesn't matter how many times I tell him not to."

Deputy Chilton said, "Why are you the one paying? He'll never learn this way."

"You're right, you're right. I'm entirely too good to him. I should make him take care of it. It would serve him right." She glanced at me. "You're that private detective, but I forget your name. Edna told us all about the fabric in her quilt."

"Kinsey Millhone," I said. "Did you get that mailing out?"

"It's done and it's been delivered by now." She turned back to Chilton. "How's the investigation? That poor Cedric had a sorry life and what a terrible end."

"We're all working overtime, doing everything we can. Quorum PD's pitching in so we're on it."

"That's good." She tucked her checkbook in her handbag. "Well, I'm off to run my errands. I wanted to get this done first before I forgot. Nice talking to you."

As soon as she left, I said, "I was looking for Detective Lassiter, but I gather he's not here."

"He's at the Tuley-Belle. The coroner thinks Pudgie was killed with a tire iron, which hasn't turned up yet. Detective Lassiter thinks it's possible it's still out there—dumped or buried. Detective Oliphant left a couple of messages for him, but they'll have to wait. I know he's concerned about this business with the McPhees' fingerprints, but we've got all our personnel at the crime scene, so even if they came in there's nothing we could do."

"Well. First things first. I'll tell Stacey someone will get back to him later in the day. I'm sure he'd like an update."

26

I sat in the car in front of the Sheriff's Department, thinking about tire irons. As murder weapons go, the lowly tire iron has the virtue of being genderless and easily obtainable. Lots of people have tire irons. They're probably not as common as a set of kitchen knives, but they're cheap, readily available, have no moving parts, and no one would think to question your possessing one. You don't need a license to buy one and you don't have to worry about a three-day waiting period while your local hardware salesman runs a background check.

I'd seen a tire iron in the past week. I knew it was only one of millions in the world, and the chances were remote that I'd seen the very tire iron used on Pudgie's head. Still, it seemed like a good mental exercise. Where had I seen tools? McPhee's automobile upholstery shop, both in the two-car garage where he sat to smoke and in the second garage where Dolan and I had found the Mustang. Also Cornell's garage where I'd seen him at work constructing a dog house for his daughters' pup. The question was, did any of these locations warrant another look? It seemed like a waste of time except for the fact that I had nothing else to do. While Detective Lassiter and the deputies were out combing the area surrounding the Tuley-Belle, the killer might have scrubbed the blood and brains off the murder weapon and put it back where it'd been. So finding it wouldn't mean anything and not finding it wouldn't mean anything, either. Well, that was dumb. I decided to try something more productive.

I started the car and went back to the Ocean View. I wanted to call Felicia and see how she was doing. I was also interested in the arrangements she'd made for Pudgie's funeral. My message light was blinking. I dialed 6 and picked up a message indicating that Lieutenant Dolan had called at 10:00. It was only 10:20 now, so I was hoping I'd catch him before he left the house again. He picked up on the first ring.

"Hey, Lieutenant, this is Kinsey. How are you?"

"I'm fine. Sorry I missed your call earlier."

"That's okay, though with all these phone calls flying back and forth, Stacey really doesn't need to come back. I think I'm talking to you guys more now than I did when you were here."

"Don't tell him. He can't wait to get down there and back to work."

"So what's up?"

"Nothing much. We're restless and bored. Hang on. Here's Stacey. He has something he wants to say."

He handed the phone to Stacey, and we went through an exchange of pleasantries as though we hadn't spoken in days. Then, he said, "I've been thinking about this Baum guy and he bothers me. I got sidetracked and left without asking him for leads. Stands to reason she was killed by someone she knew, so let's broaden the search. Can you check it out for me?"

"Sure. Give me the address of the car lot and I'll pay him a visit."

Before I left for Blythe, I put in a call to Pudgie's sister. She sounded better; subdued, but not weepy. She probably found it therapeutic to be caught up in the clerical work that follows in the wake of a death. I could hear the murmur of voices in the background. "You have people there?"

"Friends. Everybody's been great. A cousin stayed with me last night and another one's driving in from Phoenix."

"Are you having services?"

"On Friday. I'm having his body cremated as soon as the coroner releases him, but people are stopping by this evening if you'd like to join us. The memorial on Friday probably won't amount to much, but I thought I should do something. The pastor keeps calling it 'a celebration of his life,' but that doesn't seem right to me with him in jail so much."

"Up to you," I said. "What time tonight?"

"Between five and eight. I've borrowed a big coffee urn and there's tons of food."

"I'll aim for seven. Can I bring anything?"

"Please don't. I'm serious. I've already got far more than I can use," she said. "If you run into anyone who knew him, tell them they're invited, too. I think he'd be happy if people turned out for him."

"Sure thing."

The Franks Used Cars lot looked like just about every other car lot I'd ever seen. The business was housed in what must have been a service station once upon a time,

and the showroom now occupied one of the former service bays. An assortment of gleaming cars were lined up
street-side with slogans painted in white on the wind-
shields. Most were spotless and polished to a high shine,
making me glad I'd parked Dolan's half a block away.

George Baum was the only salesman on the premises.
I caught him sitting at his desk, eating a tuna sandwich,
the open packet of waxed paper serving as a handsome
lunch plate. I hated to interrupt his feeding process—I
tend to get cranky when someone interrupts mine—but
he seemed determined to do business. I sat down in the
visitor's chair while he rewrapped half his sandwich and
tucked it in the brown paper bag he'd brought from
home. I detected the bulge of an apple and imagined it
held cookies or a cupcake as well.

On his desk, he had a formal family portrait in a silver
frame: George, Swoozie (who still looked perky as could
be), and three stair-stepped adolescent boys wearing
jackets and ties. The color photograph was recent, judging by hair and clothing styles. While only in his mid-
thirties, George was already portly, wearing a brown suit
of a size that made his head look too small. Stacey was
right about his teeth—even, perfectly straight, and
bleached to a pearly white. He wore his hair short and
the scent of his aftershave was fresh and strong.

I introduced myself, watching his enthusiasm fade
when he realized I was there to pump him for information. "This is your father-in-law's place? I didn't realize
you worked for him."

"You know Chester?"

"No, but I heard you were married to Swoozie
Franks. I put two and two together."

"What brings you here? I already talked to someone
about Charisse Quinn."

"That was my partner, Detective Oliphant. He's the one who thought we should have another chat."

"What now?"

"We need the names of the guys who were involved with her. 'Involved' meaning screwing, just so you know what I'm talking about."

He smiled uncomfortably. "I can't do that."

"Why?"

"What's the point in asking me? Why don't you go over to the high school and get names from the year-book? It'd be the same list."

"I could do that," I said, "but I'd rather hear it from you. And skip what's-his-name—Toby Hecht. Cornell says nobody's heard from him in years."

"That's because he's dead. He was killed in Vietnam."

"Sorry to hear that. Who else would you suggest?"

George shook his head. "I don't see the relevance. So maybe a few classmates had sexual relations with her. What bearing does that have on where they are now in life?"

"I'm not worried about where *they* are. I'm worried about Charisse. Somebody killed her. That's what I'm here to discuss."

"I understand that. Of course. And if I thought any one of them was capable of murder, I'd speak up."

"Let me tell you something, George. The person who killed her turned around and killed Pudgie Clifton. And you want to know why? Pudgie knew something he shouldn't have. I'm not sure what, but it cost him his life. You keep quiet and you could end up putting yourself at risk. That's not a smart move, especially if your only motive is to protect a bunch of horny high school dudes."

"I do business with a lot of those *dudes*. Honest, I don't mean to be uncooperative, but I don't like being put on the spot."

I was watching him, fascinated, because he'd started to perspire. I'd never really seen that, a man breaking out in a sweat while he talked. I said, "All right. Try this. Let's just talk about you. Were you intimate with her?"

"Swoozie would have killed me."

"You never made it with Charisse?"

"I'd rather not answer that."

"Which means yes."

He paused, taking out a handkerchief to mop at a trickle of sweat running down the side of his face.

"George?"

"Okay, yes, but that's just between us. If it ever got out, my marriage would be over. Swoozie thinks I was a virgin. I told her she was the first. She hated Charisse. All the girls did."

"I'm listening."

"I was kind of nerdy. You know the type—smart and earnest and inexperienced. I'd pretend I'd made out. The guys'd be talking about sex and I'd act like I knew what they meant when I didn't have a clue. Then Charisse came along and she was really nice to me. I liked her—I mean that sincerely—so when she offered to, you know, I just figured what the hell, no harm was ever going to come of it. I felt better about myself after that, a lot more confident."

"How many times?"

"Three. Swoozie and I had been dating since we were kids. I knew we'd get married and then I'd never have a chance to be with anyone else. I didn't want to live my whole life only knowing one girl."

"And afterwards?"

"I wasn't sorry I'd done it, but I was scared Swoozie would find out. I already had a job lined up with her dad."

"You must have been relieved when Charisse disappeared."

"Well, hey, sure. I'll admit that, but so were a lot of guys, including Mr. Clean."

I smiled. "Mr. Clean?"

"Sure. Cornell. We called him that because he worked for his dad and his hands were always dirty. He used to scrub 'em with lye soap, but it never did any good."

My smile had faded because I'd blocked out his explanation and tuned into what he'd actually said. "Cornell was screwing Charisse?"

"Sure. Justine was holding out for marriage. She came up from nothing. And I mean her family was for shit—"

"I know about that," I said, cutting him off.

"She saw Cornell as the answer to her prayers. She wasn't about to put out unless he married her."

I thought about that. "I did hear Charisse had the hots for him."

"Oh, sure. She was also jealous of Justine. Compared to her life, Justine's already looked better, so she got competitive."

"And Justine knew about this?"

"Oh, no. No, no. Charisse knew better. After all, she was living at Justine's. She wasn't about to get herself thrown out on the street."

"You're telling me Cornell was in the same jeopardy you were."

"Big time. Even more so. He was everybody's hero— scholastics, sports, student government, you name it. We all looked up to him."

"Who else knew about this, aside from you?"

"Adrianne, I guess. She walked in on 'em once over at the Tuley-Belle. That's how she found out."

"How do you know that?"

"Because she told me."

"Why? Were you a close friend of hers?"

"No, not really. We were in the same church youth group. We went on a weekend retreat and I could see she was upset. I asked and she told me what was going on. She thought she should talk to our pastor, but I disagreed. I said it wasn't her job to save Cornell's soul. He was a big boy and he could work it out for himself."

I arrived at Felicia's house in Creosote at precisely 7:00 that Wednesday night. Cars were lined up at intervals along the darkened street. I didn't think I could manage to parallel park in Dolan's tank so I was forced to leave his car around the corner and walk back. Cornell's white pickup truck was parked in front of the house, behind Justine's dark Ford sedan. The moon had been reduced to the size of a fingernail paring. The air was dry and cold. The usual wind whiffled through the trees, making the shaggy palms sway, fronds rustling like rats running through an ivy patch. Lights shone from every room of Felicia's small house. Despite her admonition, I'd brought a dense chocolate cake in a pink bakery box.

A neighbor answered the door, introducing herself while relieving me of the box, which she carried to the kitchen. I stood for a moment and surveyed the room. I counted eight flower arrangements, about half of them containing leftover Easter lilies. Felicia had dimmed the lights, using votives and candles to illuminate the rooms. The effect was nice, but the air had been warmed to a feverish temperature. I suppose the gathering could have been called a wake, though there was certainly no corpse present. Perhaps "visitation" was the better term. That's how Felicia had referred to it.

On a purely self-centered note, I hadn't thought I'd need to pack my illustrious all-purpose dress. That long-sleeve black garment is tailor-made for such occasions, but how could I have known? Cheap shit that I am, earlier in the day I'd ducked into a Goodwill thrift store, where I'd found a pair of serviceable black wool slacks and a short black jacket of another fabric altogether. I'd also bought preowned black flats and a pair of (new) black panty hose. My shoulder bag was brown, probably a fashion faux pas given the rest of my ensemble, but it couldn't be helped. I'd looked better in my day, but I'd also looked a lot worse.

I had no way of guessing how many people had come and gone in the hours before my arrival, but the number of mourners I saw was embarrassingly small. I wouldn't have referred to them as "mourners," either. They came closer to being talkers, Nosy Parkers, and consumers of free food. Clearly some of those assembled were Pudgie's relatives. I could tell because they all looked faintly surprised he hadn't been shot to death in the process of an armed robbery. I caught sight of Cornell talking to his sister, but both avoided eye contact, and I got the impression neither was eager to talk to me. I didn't see Justine, and the rest of those gathered were total strangers, except for Felicia, who was standing in the kitchen talking to a fellow I'd never seen before. I'd hoped to see George Baum, to whom I'd given the address before I'd left the car lot. Maybe he didn't want to risk running into Cornell, having tattled on him.

Since I didn't recognize anyone except people who didn't seem to want to talk to me, I crossed to the buffet table on the far side of the room. Felicia hadn't fibbed about the copious amounts of food folks had brought. There was every kind of casserole known to man, platters of cold cuts, crackers and cheeses, chips and dips, plus an assortment of cakes, pies, and cookies. A big pressed-glass punch bowl had been filled with coral liquid that looked suspiciously like Hawaiian Punch. There was one lone bottle of white zinfandel. I unscrewed the top and filled a clear plastic cup to the brim, then drank it down an inch so it wouldn't look like I was hogging more than my share.

I moved through the smattering of people, hoping to corner Adrianne so the two of us could have a chat. I saw Cornell go out to the front yard to grab a cigarette, so at least I didn't have to worry about him. I drifted through the living room and into the kitchen. Felicia passed me with a plate of cookies in hand. I touched her arm and said, "How're you doing?"

Her red hair was pulled away from her face. "I'm all right for now. I think the hard part comes later when everyone goes home. I'll try to catch you in a bit. I have to get back with this."

"Have you seen Adrianne?"

"I think I saw her go out there," she said. "Cedric would have been glad you came."

"I wouldn't have missed it," I said, and she was gone.

I set my wine cup on the counter and pushed the kitchen screen open. Adrianne was on the back porch, sitting on the top step. I took a seat beside her, my shoulder bag between us. "Are you okay?"

"I'm fine. This depresses me, that's all."

"I have a question for you."

"Geez, would you give it up already? This is hardly the time."

"You can talk to me or you can talk to the cops. Take your pick."

"Oh hell. What do you want? I'm sick of this business."

"So am I. Unfortunately, it isn't over."

"It is as far as I'm concerned. So ask me and get it over with. I'm about to go home."

"Did you know Cornell was fooling around with Charisse?"

She looked at me sharply and then she looked away. She was quiet for a long time, but I decided to wait her out. Finally, she said, "Not at first."

"And then what?"

"Do we really have to talk about this? That was eighteen years ago."

"I hear you were at the Tuley-Belle and walked in on them."

"Thank you, George Baum. If you knew the answer, why'd you ask?"

"Because I wanted to hear it from you. Come on. Just tell me what happened. Like you said, it was years ago so what difference does it make?"

"Oh, for heaven's sake," she said, with disgust. "A bunch of us had gone out there. We used to do these big scavenger hunts and play stupid games. That Friday night, it was Hide-and-Seek. Cornell and Charisse were in a room on the second floor. I stumbled in, looking for a place to hide, and there they were. I was horrified and so was he."

She stopped. I thought that was the end of it, but she picked up again. "I guess I was naive, but I genuinely liked Charisse. I didn't know she was using me to get to him."

"What'd she say to you?"

"What could she say? I'd caught them in the act. Not that she was ever one to apologize for what she did. I told her she was a shit, but she shrugged it off. She didn't care for my opinion or anyone else's. Afterward, I begged her to stay away from him, but she was obsessed. I hated her for that. She nearly ruined his life."

"How?"

Silence again. "Ask him. It's really his business, not mine."

"Let me guess," I said. "She told him she was pregnant."

Again, she was quiet.

"Am I right?"

"Yes. She was determined to marry him. She told me about it before she told him."

"Why?"

"Because she thought I'd help. I told her to blow it out her butt, but she threatened to tell Mom and Dad unless I talked him into it."

"Did anyone else know?"

"No. She was sure he'd marry her to avoid the embarrassment. Once he did that, it'd be too late for anyone else to interfere—meaning Justine, of course."

"And he was willing to go along with this?"

"He didn't have any choice. You know how straightlaced my parents are, especially Mom. If they found out, they'd have forced him to marry her anyway."

"So what was the plan?"

"There wasn't a *plan*. She had it all figured out. They were going to run off together. She knew a place where they could get a marriage license even if they were underage."

"He must have been in a sweat."

"He was really scared. I told him he was being dumb. How could he even be sure the kid was his? All he had to do was get five or six of his buddies to swear they'd screwed her too and he'd be off the hook."

"Nice move, Adrianne. Did you come up with that yourself?"

"Well, what was I supposed to do? I couldn't let her wreck my brother's life! Besides, it was true. Why should he pay? He only did what every other guy was doing. Why's that so wrong?"

"Oh sure. I can see your point. There's only one tiny problem."

"What."

"She wasn't pregnant."

"Yes, she was."

I shook my head. "I read the autopsy report."

She stared at me, a hand lifting to her mouth as though pulled by strings. "Oh, shit. She made it up?"

"Apparently. So when she disappeared, what'd you think? That she'd gone off on her own to spare him the disgrace?"

"I didn't know she was lying. I thought she might have decided to have an abortion."

"If she'd been pregnant in the first place."

There was another long silence and I stepped in again. "When you heard Medora'd filed a missing-persons report, weren't you worried they'd find her?"

"I hoped they wouldn't, but it did worry me."

"But there might have been a way to head them off."

"Head who off?"

"The cops who were looking for her."

"I don't know what you're getting at."

"The phone call."

She looked at me blankly, but I didn't know her well enough to know if she was faking.

I said, "Someone called the Sheriff's Department, claiming to be Charisse's mother, saying she was home again, alive and well. The Lompoc Sheriff's Department and the one down here were on the verge of linking the two—the missing girl and Jane Doe. Then the call came in and that was the end of that."

"Well, it wasn't me. I swear. I didn't call anyone."

"I'm not the one you have to persuade." I got up and brushed off the back of my pants. "I'll talk to you later."

"I sincerely hope not."

I went into the kitchen, feeling hyped up and tense. I was treading dangerous ground, but I couldn't help myself. These people had been sitting on their secrets far too long. It was time to kick in a few doors and see who'd been hiding what. I wondered where Cornell was the night that Pudgie was killed. That was a subject worth pursuing.

In my absence, someone had drained off my entire cup of wine. I tossed the empty plastic in a trash can. As I went into the hall, I glanced into the bedroom Pudgie must have occupied. There was a single bed, covered with a plain spread, the blanket and pillow stacked together at the foot. The room had all the cozy charm of a jail cell. There were no curtains at the window, and the plain white shade had been pulled down halfway. No pictures, no personal possessions. The closet door stood open, revealing an empty hanging rod. Felicia must have swept through, boxing up everything he owned, and then called the Goodwill. I felt a pang of disappointment. Given my curious nature, I'd hoped for the opportunity to search his things. I wasn't even sure what I thought I'd find—some sense of who he was, some feeling for why he'd died. I didn't imagine he'd left a note about his final rendezvous, but there might have been a hint of what he'd meant to do in life.

"Bleak," someone said.

I turned. Justine was standing to my left, making the same sad assessment of the room that I had. I saw her gaze linger on my jacket. "What."

"Nothing. I used to have a jacket just like that."

"Really? I've had this old thing for years." I felt a spark

of fear and a second lie sprung to my lips. "Hey, what was Cornell up to Friday night? I thought I saw him downtown about ten."

She gave me a little smile of negation and bafflement. "He was home with the kids. I was out doing stuff for church."

"He was home alone?"

"Not at all. The kids were there. I told you that."

"Well, that's odd. You sure he didn't pop out to get a video? I could have sworn it was him."

"It couldn't have been. I went out at nine after the girls were in bed. He was folding laundry when I left and sacked out on the couch when I got home at midnight."

"The church is open that late?"

"I wasn't at the church. I was over at Adele's, working on a mailing. That's why he ended up baby-sitting."

"I thought they did the mailing Saturday at Edna's."

"They finished it then. We started Friday night."

I didn't point out that Cornell could have driven to Creosote and back in an hour, with plenty of time left for a stop at the Tuley-Belle to deliver forty whacks to Pudgie's head. She could have done it, too. Three hours would have been more than adequate. I tried to remember what Adele had said when she paid her husband's parking citation. He'd been ticketed Friday night because he was late for a movie, but I couldn't remember if she said she'd been with him or not. Changing the subject, I said, "You want some wine? I'm out. I'll be happy to bring you some."

"No, thanks. I don't drink. I've seen enough of that."

"I'll be right back."

I bumped into someone as I entered the living room. I said, "Pardon me," and looked up to find Todd Chilton. He wasn't in uniform and it took me an instant to realize who he was. I said, "Hey, how are you? I didn't realize you'd be here. Can I talk to you a minute?"

"Sure."

We stepped to one side. Music had started up. Someone had apparently put together a tape of Pudgie's old favorites, starting with Chubby Checker. *"Come on, baby, let's do the twist . . ."* Nobody seemed to think it was inappropriate. I was just happy to have the noise to cover my conversation with the deputy. He bent his head, a hand cupped to his ear.

I said, "Have they found the murder weapon yet?"

He shook his head. "We searched until six and then we had to give it up. No point fumbling around in the dark. Detective Lassiter did say he'd return Detective Oliphant's call first thing tomorrow morning. Lot of paperwork's piled up since we've been out in the field."

"I'm assuming Pudgie's murder hit the news."

"Oh yeah. Big spread this morning, asking for volunteers. I was just talking to Cornell. We got a lot of desert out there and a weapon like that's easy to hide. We've searched that whole area behind the Tuley-Belle and now we'll head toward the highway. You're welcome to join us. We could use the help."

"Thanks. I may do that."

Chilton moved away. I scanned the room, looking for Cornell. Adrianne had reappeared and she gave me a look of dark distaste before she walked away. I'd probably overplayed my hand with her. I didn't want to think she'd tell her brother what I knew, but she was capable of that.

Felicia passed me again. "They're about to cut that chocolate cake if you're interested. It looks great."

"I'll have some in a bit. Have you seen Cornell?"

She glanced around. "He was here a while ago. He

might be in the kitchen. I saw him talking to Adrianne. He might have left to pick up the kids at the baby-sitter's. I hear he's a doll about things like that."

"I'm sure. Thanks."

I crossed to the front window and peered out to the darkened street. Justine's sedan was still there but Cornell's truck was gone. I didn't like that. His departure seemed abrupt. Maybe it was true he'd gone to pick up his kids, but it was also true he knew the search for the murder weapon was heating up. I let myself out the front door, struck by the chill night air after the suffocating level of artificial heat inside. My thrift store jacket, which had probably belonged to Justine once upon a time, was too light to offer much protection from the cold. I read-justed my shoulder bag and broke into a trot, heading for Dolan's car.

I unlocked the door and slid in under the wheel. I jammed the key in the ignition and turned it. The car coughed and died. I tried again. No deal. I pumped the gas pedal twice and then realized I was only flooding the engine. I sat and waited and then tried again. The starter ground and turned over. I gave it way too much gas and the engine roared to life. I pulled out, tires chirping as I took off. I turned on the heat, hoping to warm up. My sense of urgency coupled with the dry cold was making me shiver.

Half a minute later, I was on Highway 78, driving north toward Quorum. At this hour of the evening, traffic was light. I thought I caught a glimpse of Cornell's truck up ahead. There were four cars on the road between us and I was having to peer around and through them to keep an eye on him. Approaching the Tuley-Belle, the car in front of me slowed and I realized that, at the head of the line, Cornell had slowed to a stop. His turn signal winked merrily and he turned left as soon as oncoming traffic allowed.

I slowed as I passed the entrance, watching his tail-lights disappear into the dark. I drove on a hundred yards and pulled over to the side of the road. I doused the headlights, set the handbrake, and let the car idle while I debated with myself. I'd be foolish to follow him. The Tuley-Belle was a mile and a half from the main road, not only isolated, but riddled with hiding places better known to him than they were to me. I peered over my shoulder and stared into the darkness, picking up the parallel rounds of his headlights, now facing me. He hadn't driven to the complex. For some reason, he'd turned the truck around and was now parked by the road, facing the highway. I saw the headlights go out. Soon after that, I picked up a faint smudge of light off to the right of the four-lane blacktop. What was he doing out there? Burying the murder weapon? Digging it up to move it? But why take that risk? Simple. He knew the sheriff's investigators had been and gone. He also knew they'd return the next morning to start the search again. Todd Chilton had described the terrain the deputies had covered. If the weapon was out there, he could either move it into an area they'd already searched or remove the weapon from a section yet to be combed. Why would the tire iron be out there in the first place? Because he didn't want the damn thing hidden anywhere close to home? Because he hadn't had time to dispose of it any-where else? Whatever he was up to, he must have de-cided this was his only opportunity to act.

I reached up and snapped the cover from the dome light and unscrewed the bulb. I got out, pushing the door closed without snapping it shut. I walked to the rear of the car and opened the trunk. I wasn't worried about the trunk light. Nothing on the back end of Dolan's vehicle worked, including the taillights. I felt my way across the darkened space until my hand came down on Dolan's Smith & Wesson, snug in its holster. I picked up the gun and the holster, eased down the lid of the trunk, and returned to the driver's seat. I slipped under the wheel again, leaving the car door ajar. I fumbled in my bag until I found my pen light. I snapped it on and placed it on the passenger seat, keeping my inspection process well below the level of the dashboard. This was the gun Dolan carried on duty; a 9mm Parabellum, with a clip that held fifteen rounds. I hit the clip release button and checked the magazine—fully loaded—and then smacked it back into place. I pulled the slide back and released it, then checked to see that the safety was on. I hefted the weight of the gun, close to twenty-eight ounces, feeling its clumsiness in a hand as small as mine. At least it was an equalizer, wasn't it?

I stripped off my jacket. Dolan's shoulder holster had a Velcro and leather strip shoulder strap that I adjusted and secured under my left arm, the gun tucked snugly in place. I pulled on the jacket again, tugging at the front until it lay flat. I kept an eye on the rearview mirror, waiting for a break in the flow of cars. As soon as I was clear in both directions, I made a wide U-turn, swinging across the two-lane highway and onto the berm on the far side of the road. I eased the car along on the berm until I found a spot that seemed to provide at least a modicum of cover. I was now facing in the direction of Creosote instead of Quorum on the same side of the road as the entrance to the Tuley-Belle. Cornell was laboring away somewhere to my right, though I couldn't really see him from where I sat.

I killed the engine, tucked the keys in my jacket

pocket, and got out of the car. It wasn't my intention to do anything dumb. I wasn't going to tackle the guy or try to make a citizen's arrest. I just wanted to see what he was up to and then I'd slip back to the car and be on my way. Even so, if there'd been a public phone in a five-mile radius, I would have bagged my scheme, called the Sheriff's Department, and let them handle him.

The entrance to the abandoned property had been blocked by bright orange plastic cones and a sign mounted on a sawhorse designating the entire area as a crime scene. Someone had moved the No Trespass warnings aside and the sawhorse now lay toppled on its side.

The thin crescent moon worked to my advantage. The road itself was dark, but the sky was a muted gray. The landscape—largely sand and gravel basins—gradually came into focus as my eyes adjusted to the dark. I could make out a number of features: clusters of tumbleweeds, like giant beach balls, creosote bushes, bayonet cactuses, yuccas, and the leggy branches of the palo verde trees. Ahead of me, I caught glimpses of a stationary light, possibly a lantern or a good-sized flashlight. I was getting closer, but as I'd noticed before, distances were difficult to calculate.

I could hear the peeping of ground frogs, probably poisonous, and the intermittent hooting of an owl. Unbidden, my brain suddenly played back in excruciating detail Dolan's earlier recital about Mojave insect life, specifically the tarantula hawk, a species of desert wasp, the female of which sniffs out a tarantula, stings it into a state of paralysis, drags it back to her burrow, and lays an egg in its abdomen. Once hatched, the tiny grub feeds daintily until its final moult, then rips open the spider's abdomen, thrusts its head and part of its thorax inside and devours everything in sight. Sometimes the tarantula is even dead by then. I was grossing myself out. This is the very same Nature that some people find spiritually uplifting. I picked up my pace, trying to block the interminable list of other insects he'd mentioned, scorpions and fire ants among them. Whatever else happened out here, I wasn't going to sit down.

The road made a slight bend, and I found myself not ten yards away from Cornell's white pickup truck, its engine still ticking as the metal cooled. Tucked in behind Cornell's truck was Justine's dark Ford sedan. I stared in disbelief. The last time I'd seen it, it was parked in front of Felicia's house. Apparently, while I was struggling to get Dolan's car started, Justine left the house in her car and followed him. By the time I was finally under way, it hadn't occurred to me to glance back and see if her car was still there. She must have caught up with him, passed him, and turned off the highway before he did. She was the one who'd moved the barrier from the entrance to the place. She'd been back in her car and heading up the road before I'd caught sight of him making his turn.

I reached out and laid a hand on the hood of the truck, steadying myself, then eased to my left, using the cab as cover. I could hear the persistent chunking of a spade. He was digging. Were they burying the weapon or digging it up? I lifted on tiptoe. He'd set the flashlight on the ground. I saw the occasional distorted shadow as one or the other crossed the path of the light as the work progressed. I could hear them arguing, but the subject wasn't clear. I wasn't sure if they'd collaborated from the first or if Cornell had done the killing and she'd finally figured it out. My heart began to bang and a cloud of fear, like indigestion, burned in my chest. I tried to get my bearings, noting two nearby Joshua trees and a clump of sagebrush on my left that formed a mound the size of a pup tent. Directly across the road, there was a massive flowering shrub where white moths the size of hummingbirds had gathered to feed. Their wings beat audibly in the still night air, like the far-off thrumming of helicopter blades.

I turned back, suddenly aware that the chunking sound had stopped. I looked again. Cornell was on his knees, reaching into the hole. He hauled out the tire iron and wrapped it in a fold of cloth. The two of them started kicking soil back in the hole, intent on eradicating any evidence of their work. Justine picked up the spade and used the flat of the blade like a spatula, smoothing the sand like frosting. He bent and picked up the flashlight and gave a cursory sweep to make sure they hadn't left anything behind. They headed toward me.

I pivoted and ducked, silently retracing my steps, hoping to gain the bend in the road before the two reached Cornell's truck. If they climbed into their respective vehicles and returned to the highway, their two sets of headlights were going to pick me out of the dark like a startled bunny rabbit. I heard the slamming of two doors. I left the pavement and scurried out into the dark. I spotted a furrow in the earth, a channel where flash flooding had cut a shallow trench. I dropped flat and propelled myself on my elbows, belly-crawling, until I reached the shallow ditch and rolled into it. I put my head down, my arms folded under me, and waited. Only one engine sparked to life. I expected the flash of passing headlights, but none appeared. Cautiously, I lifted my head and peered in time to see the taillights of the pickup truck. One or both of them were on their way to the Tuley-Belle. I scrambled to my feet and ran. If I was mistaken and she'd been left behind, posted by the sedan, I was in bigger trouble than I thought. I slowed my pace as I rounded the bend. The Ford was still parked by the side of the road and there was no sign of her.

I reached her Ford and snatched at the door on the driver's side. She'd left her keys behind, dangling in the ignition. I got in and started the car. I released the hand brake, left the lights off, and made a wide sweeping turn, bumping off the road and back, this time driving, as they had, toward the sprawling complex ahead. If they intended to hide the tire iron at the Tuley-Belle, it might never turn up.

When I was as close as I dared drive, I took my foot off the gas pedal and let the sedan coast to a stop. I turned the engine off and put her car keys in my pocket, again reaching up to disable the dome light before I opened the car door. I took out Dolan's Smith & Wesson. I moved off the road, circling out and to my left so that I was approaching the complex at an angle across raw land. Cover was better out here. The huddled shadows tended to form and reform, shifting, as the wind pushed the tumbleweeds across the uneven ground. I spotted the truck, which Cornell had parked between the two half-finished buildings, looming silent and dark. In the second building, upstairs, I saw a glimmer of light. I moved forward with caution, hoping Cornell had left his keys behind as she had. If I could steal their only means of transportation, it would force them to walk the mile and a half to the main highway. By the time they reached the road, I could be speeding back to Creosote and return with help. Let them explain to Todd Chilton what they'd been doing out there. There was no motion in the patch of darkness immediately surrounding the truck.

I circled the vehicle, noting that the window was rolled down on the driver's side. I peered in, catching the glint of his keys right where I'd hoped they'd be. In my mind's eye, I was already opening the truck door, sliding under the wheel. I'd turned the key in the ignition, slammed the gear lever into drive, and sped off, leaving the two of them behind. As it turned out, I celebrated my achievement prematurely. I heard a scuffling behind me and a little voice inside piped up, saying "Uh-oh," but by then it was too late. I turned, expecting to see Cornell, but it was Justine sailing toward me. With her pale flyaway hair and her icy pale green eyes, she looked like a banshee sweeping out of the dark. Cornell must have left her to stand watch, acting as a sentinel in case a horny pack of teenyboppers showed up at the Tuley-Belle for a midweek screwfest. Maybe I hadn't been as quiet as I'd thought. Perhaps, given the peculiarities of desert acoustics, she'd heard my every step and simply waited for me.

She had the shovel in her hands. I saw her lifting her arms, raising the shovel overhead like an axe. I had to admire her strength. What she was doing wasn't easy. The shovel looked heavy and I hadn't thought she'd developed that much upper-body strength. Still, from her perspective, this was an emergency, so she might have been calling on reserves she didn't know she had.

As with many moments of crisis in life, the swiftness with which the ensuing events unfolded created the reverse effect, emerging with the soft, dreamy qualities of slow-motion footage. Like a sequence of time-lapse photographs, Justine's arms continued to rise until the shovel reached its apex. I saw the first shimmering instant of its descent. I curled to my left and lifted my right arm, trying to aim and fire Dolan's S&W before the shovel hit its mark. If she'd brandished the shovel with the blade perpendicular, striking me side-on, she probably would have chopped my arm to the bone. As it was, the flat of the shovel collided with my forearm and the gun spun off into the dark. I never even heard it land. The shovel came down again. A ringing pain radiated outward from my left shoulder and disappeared. It was odd. I knew she'd landed a blow, but I was so flooded with adrenaline the pain vanished. I staggered, my knees buckling, nearly felled by the impact.

I spotted the Smith & Wesson lying six feet away. The shovel came down again, this time clanging against the top of the truck cab with a force that wrenched the tool from her grip. I ran at her and shoved her as hard as I could. She stumbled backward but managed to catch herself before she hit the ground. She was making guttural sounds, probably trying to marshall her forces to yell for Cornell. I grabbed the shovel and used it like a scythe to crack her across the shins. She screamed. I looked back and saw she was down. Cornell came running from the building. Just as he spotted me, I saw Justine scramble to her feet and reach the truck door. She yanked it open and got in on the driver's side, screaming at him, "Get in the truck! Get in the truck!"

I scrambled forward, snatched up the gun, and pushed off the safety.

He flung himself at the tailgate as she started the truck. She backed up and shifted gears, gunned the engine, and turned the wheel, peeling out. I watched him haul himself over the side and into the truck bed, disappearing from view. I turned and extended my arms, both hands on the gun as I aimed. It helped that I was pissed off. I was talking aloud, admonishing myself to take my time. There was no reason to panic. The ground was flat and I'd be able to see them for a long time. I located one of the rear taillights between the niche in the gun's rear sight and the niche in the foresight as I squinted down the barrel. I hadn't paid attention to Dolan's choice in ammunition, but if I remembered correctly, the baseline 9mm 100-grain slug moves out at muzzle velocities of between 1,080 and 1,839 feet per second, depending on slug rate. My figures might have been off, but not by much. I fired. The recoil was like a quick sneeze, kicking the barrel up and back. I missed, corrected, fired again, and heard a tire blow. Cornell had flattened himself in the bed of the truck. I altered my sights slightly and fired again, missing. I took aim again and fired four more rounds, trying to make each one count. By the time I paused, both back tires were flat. After that, the truck veered off course and came to a stop almost of its own accord. I approached on foot, taking my time, knowing I had sufficient rounds left to take care of business if Justine and Cornell still felt like arguing.

Epilogue

Justine was arrested and charged with two counts of first-degree murder, with a string of related offenses thrown in to sweeten the pot. Edna and Ruel prevailed on Cornell to hire a lawyer of his own, and his lawyer, in turn, persuaded him to make a deal with the DA. After all, he'd had nothing to do with the murder of Charisse Quinn and he'd had no part in Pudgie Clifton's death. That Saturday after I'd gone to the house to talk to Justine, she'd panicked and begged for his help in moving Pudgie's body and subsequently burying the tire iron with which she'd killed him. Cornell pled guilty to being an accessory after the fact, for which he's serving one year in the county jail. Edna and Ruel have taken on the responsibility for Amelia, Mary Francis, and Cissy McPhee until their father's release.

Justine's motivation wasn't difficult to fathom. She'd killed Charisse for seducing Cornell and trying to steal the life she'd envisioned for herself. It was indeed Pudgie who'd stolen the Mustang and loaded Charisse's body in the trunk. While Justine packed the dead girl's clothes and forged the note explaining her fictional departure,

Pudgie drove the body to Lompoc and dumped it at the quarry Iona'd told him about. Justine waited a week and then called the Riverside County Sheriff's Department, pretending to be Charisse's mother and claiming her daughter was safely home again.

Once Pudgie reappeared in Quorum with news that the investigation had been reactivated, Justine had been forced to eliminate him. She'd enlisted Cornell's aid in disposing of Pudgie's body as she'd once enlisted Pudgie's aid in disposing of Charisse. His was certainly too unwieldy a corpse for her to manage on her own. The day I'd startled her in the laundry, it was his blood and brains she was washing from her clothes. It dawned on me later that the business with Medora's doors standing open was Justine's doing as well, affording her the opportunity to pump me for information about the progress I'd made.

For once in his life, Frankie Miracle was innocent of any complicity in these crimes, a fact that went some way toward brightening his outlook.

With the trial date approaching, Justine's attorney is insisting on a change of venue, maintaining she'll never get a fair trial in Riverside County after the media circus generated by her arrest. I love it when killers want to argue about what's fair.

On a more homely note, Stacey's still living with Dolan, an arrangement that suits them surprisingly well. Both are currently in good health, limiting their consumption of tobacco and junk food, and continually grousing about each other, as good friends are sometimes inclined to do. As for me, I'm back in my office in Santa Teresa, unpacking my moving boxes while I wait to see what else life has to bring.

Respectfully submitted,
Kinsey Millhone

Author's Note

About this novel . . .

There is one additional, quite lengthy note about the writing of this novel. *Q is for Quarry* is based on an unsolved homicide that occurred in Santa Barbara County in August 1969. The catalyst for the book was a conversation I had with Dr. Robert Failing during a dinner party at the home of our friends Susan and Gary Gulbransen in early September of 2000. Dr. Failing is a forensic pathologist who worked, under contract, for the Santa Barbara County Sheriff's Department from 1961 until 1996. I had just completed and submitted the manuscript of *P is for Peril*, and the dinner conversation turned, not surprisingly, to what I might do next. Bob mentioned the Jane Doe victim, whose body had been dumped near a quarry in Lompoc, California, about an hour north of Santa Barbara. He had performed the autopsy, and, in passing, he remarked that the Coroner's Office had retained her maxilla and mandible. It was his feeling that Jane Doe's distinctive dental features should have sparked public recognition. Unfortunately, at the time, she was either never reported missing or the missing-persons report somehow failed to reach the detectives working this case. Despite months of tireless effort, they were never able to identify Jane Doe, and her killer was never caught. To this day, no one knows who she is, where she came from, or who murdered her.

As a novelist, I've been offered countless plot ideas, stories, personal anecdotes, "real life" events, and "true" murders—experiences that were important to those who suggested them, but which, for one reason or another, didn't stimulate or excite me. This idea took root. I expressed an immediate interest, knowing full well that the survival of an idea is unpredictable. I'd met the coroner's investigator, Larry Gillespie, retired now, on previous occasions while researching earlier books in the series. Bob offered to speak to Larry about rounding up the jaw bones. He also offered to introduce me to some of the Sheriff's Department detectives he'd worked with during his association with this law-enforcement agency.

I keep a journal during the writing of these books, a ritual I began in rudimentary form with *A is for Alibi* and have continued, with ever increasing breadth and depth, through the seventeen novels in the series to this point. The early portions of the journal for any given novel are usually a record of my fumbling attempts to find a workable story line. I ruminate, I chat with myself, I fret, I experiment. Oddly enough, from my perspective, the first journal note on the subject of Jane Doe didn't appear until November 8, 2000, some two months after my initial conversation with Bob Failing. I had, at that point, already accepted the subject matter as the basis for this book, though it took me many more months to work out the details. I loved the word "quarry" because its meaning, particularly in this instance, could do double-duty, referring to the place where the body was found and to the search for the killer.

On January 11, 2001, Bob Failing and I met with Sergeant Detective Bill Turner and then Commander Bruce Correll of the Criminal Investigations Division, Santa Barbara Sheriff's Department, and the four of us drove to Lompoc to see the quarry. I met with Bruce Correll and Bill Turner again on January 19, 2001. At that time, in a gesture of incredible generosity, they gave me a copy of the murder book for the Jane Doe case. It contained case notes, investigative reports, and both color and black-and-white photographs of the body and the area where she was found. I was also given photographs of her effects, including her leather sandals and the home-sewn pants with the daisy-print, dark blue with a dot of red on a white background.

Over the ensuing year, with the blessings of then-sheriff Jim Thomas, I met with these two detectives on numerous occasions. Bill Turner, in particular, became an invaluable resource, providing information about procedural issues, technicalities, and the myriad nuts and bolts of his work. He answered my many (sometimes stupid) questions with unfailing patience and enthusiasm, responding with the sort of detailed replies that make a writer's job a joy. Any errors, herein, by the way, are either the result of my faulty understanding or license I took in the interest of the story.

My fascination with the case rekindled the interest of the department, and the possibility arose of an exhumation of the body so that a facial reconstruction might be done, in hopes that Jane Doe might be identified. I wasn't privy to the discussions that must have gone on behind the scenes. In Santa Barbara County exhumations are uncommon, and budget considerations became an issue, not only because of the cost of the exhumation itself but for the expense of hiring a forensic sculptor, who would use Jane Doe's skull and jaw bones to re-create her likeness. There was also the matter of the rein-terment, to accord Jane Doe the ultimate dignity of a proper burial, which we all considered essential. I offered to underwrite the plan because I, too, had become hope-ful that something might come of it.

The exhumation was scheduled for July 17, 2001. On that day, we traveled again to Lompoc, this time to the cemetery where Jane Doe was buried thirty-three years earlier. Dr. Failing flew in from his vacation home in Col-orado. My husband, Steve Humphrey, made the journey with us, as did Sergeant Detective Bill Turner. Also pres-ent were Detective Hugo Galante, his wife, Detective Kathryn Galante, and Detective Terry Flaa, of the North County Detective Unit of the Criminal Investigations Division; Detective David Danielson; Coroner's Investi-gator Sergeant Darin Fotheringham; Sheriff's dispatcher Joe Ayala; his wife, Erin Ayala; the coroner's office secre-tary; Sheriff's trainee Danielle Goldman; Lieutenant Ken Reinstadler of the Santa Maria station, Patrol Division; Commander Deborah Linden, of the Santa Barbara Sheriff's Department, South Coast Patrol Division; and Mr. Mark Powers, the graveyard superintendent. The procedure took the better part of the day. Once Jane Doe's body was recovered, she was removed to the Santa Barbara County Coroner's Office.

In anticipation of the exhumation, Bill Turner had contacted Betty Gatliff in Oklahoma, whose work as a forensic artist is internationally recognized. Betty Gatliff is a retired medical illustrator who not only practices fo-rensic sculpture but teaches workshops and seminars across the country. She is a fellow of the American Academy of Forensics Sciences, an emeritus member of the Association of Medical Illustrators, and an associate member of the International Association for Identification. Jane Doe's skull, maxilla, and mandible were sent to Ms. Gatliff, whose services had been engaged.

In the meantime, I had begun a re-creation of my own, constructing a wholly fictional account of a young girl whose fate was similar to Jane Doe's. Where possible, I used details from the Jane Doe murder book, including fragments from the autopsy report, case notes, and the investigative reports submitted by the detectives originally assigned to this case. There are two exceptions of note: (1) There was no tarp. I manufactured that detail to give my fictional detectives yet another means of pursuing their inquiries; and (2) there was, in fact, found at the scene a blood-soaked man's Western-style blue denim shirt with white-covered snaps, size 14H neck. I omitted this detail in the interest of simplicity. That aside, I must assure the reader that every character in this novel is fictional. Every event is purely the product of my invention. Whatever the personality and nature of the "real" Jane Doe, my assertions are the figment of my imagination and are in no way purported to be real, true, or representative of her. I emphasize this point out of respect for her and out of consideration for those who must have loved her and wondered about her silence as the years have passed.

By mid-September of 2001, Betty Gatliff had reconstructed a likeness of Jane Doe and returned her skull with its mandible and maxilla. She also sent numerous color photographs of Jane Doe, four of which are reproduced here in black and white. Jane Doe was reinterred on Tuesday, February 26, 2002, with a uniformed Sheriff's Department Honor Guard accompanying her from the coroner's office to the cemetery, a sheriff's chaplain conducting the service, flowers, and the heartfelt prayers of those of us who have been a small part of her life. It is our hope that someone reading this novel and seeing the photographs will recognize this young woman and step forward with information about her. Though both Bruce Correll and Bill Turner retired in the summer of 2002, Bill Turner will be available to respond to queries by mail at: Sheriff's Department, County of Santa Barbara, 4434 Calle Real, P.O. Box 6427, Santa Barbara, CA 93160-6427, or through the Sheriff's Department's website, www.sbsheriff.org.

Respectfully submitted,
Sue Grafton

TURN THE PAGE FOR AN EXCERPT

R IS FOR RICOCHET.

And R is for romance: love gone right, love gone wrong,
and matters somewhere in between.

"Sue Grafton is brilliant. We'd follow
Kinsey Millhone anywhere." —*Newsday*

 Penguin Random House

1

_____

The basic question is this: given human nature, are any of us really capable of change? The mistakes other people make are usually patently obvious. Our own are tougher to recognize. In most cases, our path through life reflects a fundamental truth about who we are now and who we've been since birth. We're optimists or pessimists, joyful or depressed, gullible or cynical, inclined to seek adventure or to avoid all risks. Therapy might strengthen our assets or offset our liabilities, but in the main we do what we do because we've always done it that way, even when the outcome is bad . . . perhaps *especially* when the outcome is bad.

This is a story about romance—love gone right, love gone wrong, and matters somewhere in between.

I left downtown Santa Teresa that day at 1:15 and headed for Montebello, a short ten miles south. The weather report had promised highs in the seventies. Morning cloudiness had given way to sunshine, a welcomed respite from the overcast that typically mars our June and July. I'd eaten lunch at my desk, feasting on an olive-and-pimiento-cheese sandwich on wheat bread, cut in quarters, my third-favorite sandwich in the whole wide world. So what was the problem? I had none. Life was great.

In committing the matter to paper, I can see now what should have been apparent from the first, but events seemed to unfold at such a routine pace that I was caught, metaphorically speaking, asleep at the wheel. I'm a private detective, female, age thirty-seven, working in the small Southern California town of Santa Teresa. My jobs are varied, not always lucrative, but sufficient to keep me housed and fed and ahead of my bills. I do employee background checks. I track down missing persons or locate heirs entitled to monies in the settlement of an estate. On occasion, I investigate claims involving arson, fraud, or wrongful death.

In my personal life, I've been married and divorced twice, and subsequent relationships have usually come to grief. The older I get, the less I seem to understand men, and because of that I tend to shy away from them. Granted, I have no sex life to speak of, but at least I'm not plagued by unwanted pregnancies or sexually transmitted diseases. I've learned the hard way that love and work are a questionable mix.

I was driving on a stretch of highway once known as the Montebello Parkway, built in 1927 as the result of a fund-raising campaign that made possible the creation of frontage roads and landscaped center dividers still in evidence today. Because billboards and commercial structures along the roadway were banned at the same time, that section of the 101 is still attractive, except when it's jammed with rush-hour traffic.

Montebello itself underwent a similar transformation in 1948, when the Montebello Protective and Improvement Association successfully petitioned to eliminate sidewalks, concrete curbs, advertising signs, and anything else that might disrupt the rural atmosphere. Montebello is known for its two-hundred-some-odd luxury estates, many of them built by men who'd amassed their fortunes selling common household goods, salt and flour being two.

I was on my way to meet Nord Lafferty, an elderly gentleman, whose photograph appeared at intervals in the society column of the *Santa Teresa Dispatch*. This was usually occasioned by his making yet another sizable contribution to some charitable foundation. Two buildings at UCST had been named for him, as had a wing of Santa Teresa Hospital and a special collection of rare books he'd donated to the public library. He'd called me two days before and indicated he had "a modest undertaking" he wanted to discuss. I was curious how he'd come by my name and even more curious about the job itself. I've been a private investigator in Santa Teresa for the past ten years, but my office is small and, as a rule, I'm ignored by the wealthy, who seem to prefer doing business through their attorneys in New York, Chicago, or L.A.

I took the St. Isadore off-ramp and turned north toward the foothills that ran between Montebello and the Los Padres National Forest. At one time, this area boasted grand old resort hotels, citrus and avocado ranches, olive groves, a country store, and the Montebello train depot, which serviced the Southern Pacific Railroad. I'm forever reading up on local history, trying to imagine the region as it was 125 years ago. Land was selling then for seventy-five cents an acre. Montebello is still bucolic, but much of the charm has been bulldozed away. What's been erected instead—the condominiums, housing developments, and the big flashy starter castles of the nouveau riche—is poor compensation for what was lost or destroyed.

I turned right on West Glen and drove along the winding two-lane road as far as Bella Sera Place. Bella Sera is lined with olive and pepper trees, the narrow blacktop climbing gradually to a mesa that affords a sweeping view of the coast. The pungent scent of the ocean faded with my ascent, replaced by the smell of sage and the bay laurel trees. The hillsides were thick with yarrow, wild mustard, and California poppies. The afternoon sun had baked the boulders to a golden turn, and a warm chuffing wind was beginning to stir the dry grasses. The road wound upward through an alley of live oaks that terminated at the entrance to the Lafferty estate. The property was surrounded by a stone wall that was eight feet high and posted with No Trespassing signs.

I slowed to an idle when I reached the wide iron gates. I leaned out and pushed the call button on a mounted keypad. Belatedly I spotted a camera mounted atop one of two stone pillars, its hollow eye fixed on me. I must have passed inspection because the gates swung open at a measured pace. I shifted gears and sailed through, following the brick-paved drive for another quarter of a mile.

Through a picket fence of pines, I caught glimpses of a gray stone house. When the whole of the residence finally swept into view, I let out a breath. Something of the past remained after all. Four towering eucalyptus trees laid a dappled shade on the grass, and a breeze pushed a series of cloud-shaped shadows across the red tile roof. The two-story house, with matching one-story wings topped with stone balustrades at each end, dominated my visual field. A series of four arches shielded the entrance and provided a covered porch on which wicker furniture had been arranged. I counted twelve windows on the second floor, separated by paired eave brackets, largely decorative, that appeared to support the roof.

I pulled onto a parking pad sufficient to accommodate ten cars and left my pale blue VW hunched, cartoonlike, between a sleek Lincoln Continental on one side and a full-size Mercedes on the other. I didn't bother to lock up, operating on the assumption that the electronic surveillance system was watching over both me and my vehicle as I crossed to the front walk.

The lawns were wide and well tended, and the quiet was underlined by the twittering of finches. I pressed the front bell, listening to the hollow-sounding chimes inside clanging out two notes as though by a hammer on iron. The ancient woman who came to the door wore an old-fashioned black uniform with a white pinafore over it. Her opaque stockings were the color of doll flesh, her crepe-soled shoes emitting the faintest squeak as I followed her down the marble-tiled hall. She hadn't asked my name, but perhaps I was the only visitor expected that day. The corridor was paneled in oak, the white plaster ceiling embossed with chevrons and fleurs-de-lis.

She showed me into the library, which was also paneled in oak. Drab leather-bound books lined shelves that ran floor to ceiling, with a brass rail and a rolling ladder allowing access to the upper reaches. The room smelled of dry wood and paper mold. The inner hearth in the stone fireplace was tall enough to stand in, and a recent blaze had left a partially blackened oak log and the faint stench of wood smoke. Mr. Lafferty was seated in one of a pair of matching wing chairs.

I placed him in his eighties, an age I'd considered elderly once upon a time. I've since come to realize how widely the aging process varies. My landlord is eighty-seven, the baby of his family, with siblings whose ages range as high as ninety-six. All five of them are lively, intelligent, adventurous, competitive, and given to good-natured squabbling among themselves. Mr. Lafferty, on the other hand, looked as though he'd been old for a good twenty years. He was inordinately thin, with knees as bony as a pair of misplaced elbows. His once sharp features had at least been softened by the passing years. Two small clear plastic tubes had been placed discreetly in his nostrils, tethering him to a stout green oxygen tank on a cart to his left. One side of his jaw was sunken, and a savage red line running across his throat suggested extensive surgery of some vicious sort.

He studied me with eyes as dark and shiny as dots of brown sealing wax. "I appreciate your coming, Ms. Millhone. I'm Nord Lafferty," he said, holding out a hand that was knotted with veins. His voice was hoarse, barely a whisper.

"Nice to meet you," I murmured, moving forward to shake hands with him. His were pale, a tremor visible in his fingers, which were icy to the touch.

He motioned to me. "You might want to pull that chair close. I've had thyroid surgery a month ago and more recently some polyps removed from my vocal cords. I've been left with this rasping noise that passes as speech. Isn't painful, but it's irksome. I apologize if I'm difficult to understand."

"So far, I'm not having any problem."

"Good. Would you like a cup of tea? I can have my housekeeper make a pot, but I'm afraid you'll have to pour for yourself. These days, her hands aren't any steadier than mine."

"Thanks, but I'm fine." I pulled the second wing chair

closer and took a seat. "When was this house built? It's really beautiful."

"1893. A man named Mueller bought a six-hundred-forty-acre section from the county of Santa Teresa. Of that, seventy acres remain. House took six years to build and the story has it Mueller died the day the workers finally set down their tools. Since then, the occupants have fared poorly . . . except for me, knock on wood. I bought the property in 1929, just after the crash. Fellow who owned the place lost everything. Drove into town, climbed up to the clock tower, and dived over the rail. Widow needed the cash and I stepped in. I was criticized, of course. Folks claimed I took advantage, but I'd loved the house from the minute I laid eyes on it. Someone would have bought it. Better me than them. I had money for the upkeep, which wasn't true of many folks back then."

"You were lucky."

"Indeed. Made my fortune in paper goods in case you're curious and too polite to inquire."

I smiled. "Polite, I don't know about. I'm always curious."

"That's fortunate, I'd say, given the business you're in. I'm assuming you're a busy woman so I'll get right to the point. Your name was given to me by a friend of yours—fellow I met during this recent hospital stay."

"Stacey Oliphant," I said, the name flashing immediately to mind. I'd worked a case with Stacey, a retired Sheriff's Department homicide detective, and my old pal Lieutenant Dolan, now retired from the Santa Teresa Police Department. Stacey was battling cancer, but the last I'd heard, he'd been given a reprieve.

Mr. Lafferty nodded. "He asked me to tell you he's doing well, by the way. He checked in for a battery of tests, but all of them turned out negative. As it happened, the two of us walked the halls together in the afternoons, and I got chatting about my daughter, Reba."

I was already thinking skip trace, missing heir, possibly a background check on a guy if Reba were romantically involved.

He went on. "I only have the one child and I suppose I've spoiled her unmercifully, though that wasn't my intent. Her mother ran off when she was just a little thing, this high. I was caught up in business and left the day-to-day raising of her to a series of nannies. She'd been a boy I could have sent her off to boarding school the way my parents did me, but I wanted her at home. In retrospect, I see that might've been poor judgment on my part, but it didn't seem so at the time." He paused and then gestured impatiently toward the floor, as though chiding a dog for leaping up on him. "No matter. It's too late for regrets. Pointless, anyway. What's done is done." He looked at me sharply from under his bony brow. "You probably wonder what I'm driving at."

I proffered a slight shrug, waiting to hear what he had to say.

"Reba's being paroled on July twentieth. That's next Monday morning. I need someone to pick her up and bring her home. She'll be staying with me until she's on her feet again."

"What facility?" I asked, hoping I didn't sound as startled as I felt.

"California Institution for Women. Are you familiar with the place?"

"It's down in Corona, couple of hundred miles south. I've never actually been there, but I know where it is."

"Good. I'm hoping you can take time out of your schedule for the trip."

"That sounds easy enough, but why me? I charge five

hundred dollars a day. You don't need a private detective to make a run like that. Doesn't she have friends?"

"Not anyone I'd ask. Don't worry about the money. That's the least of it. My daughter's difficult. Willful and rebellious. I want you to see to it she keeps the appointment with her parole officer and whatever else is required once she's been released. I'll pay you your full rate even if you only work for a part of each day."

"What if she doesn't like the supervision?"

"It's not up to her. I've told her I'm hiring someone to assist her and she's agreed. If she likes you, she'll be cooperative, at least to a point."

"May I ask what she did?"

"Given the time you'll be spending in her company, you're entitled to know. She was convicted of embezzling money from the company she worked for. Alan Beckwith and Associates. He does property management, real estate investment and development, things of that type. Do you know the man?"

"I've seen his name in the paper."

Nord Lafferty shook his head. "I don't care for him myself. I've known his wife's family for years. Tracy's a lovely girl. I can't understand how she ended up with the likes of him. Alan Beckwith is an upstart. He calls himself an entrepreneur, but I've never been entirely clear what he does. Our paths have crossed in public on numerous occasions and I can't say I'm impressed. Reba seems to think the world of him. I will credit him for this—he spoke up in her behalf before her sentencing. It was a generous gesture on his part and one he didn't have to make."

"How long has she been at CIW?"

"She's served twenty-two months of a four-year sentence. She never went to trial. At her arraignment—which

I'm sorry to say I missed—she claimed she was indigent, so the court appointed a public defender to handle her case. After consultation with him, she waived her right to a preliminary hearing and entered a plea of guilty."

"Just like that?"

"I'm afraid so."

"And her attorney agreed to it?"

"He argued strenuously against it, but Reba wouldn't listen."

"How much money are we talking?"

"Three hundred fifty thousand dollars over a two-year period."

"How'd they discover the theft?"

"During a routine audit. Reba was one of a handful of employees with access to the accounts. Naturally, suspicion fell on her. She's been in trouble before, but nothing of this magnitude."

I could feel a protest welling but I bit back my response.

He leaned forward. "You have something to say, feel free to say it. Stacey tells me you're outspoken so please don't hesitate on my account. It may save us a misunderstanding."

"I was just wondering why you didn't step in. A high-powered attorney might have made all the difference."

He dropped his gaze to his hands. "I should have helped her . . . I know that . . . but I'd been coming to her rescue for many, many years . . . all her life, if you want to know the truth. At least that's what I was being told by friends. They said she had to face the consequences of her behavior or she was never going to learn. They said I'd be enabling, that saving her was the worst possible action under the circumstances."

"Who's this 'they' you're referring to?"

For the first time, he faltered. "I had a lady friend. Lucinda. We'd been keeping company for years. She'd seen me intercede in Reba's behalf on countless occasions. She persuaded me to put my foot down and that's what I did."

"And now?"

"Frankly, I was shocked when Reba was sentenced to four years in state prison. I had no idea the penalty would be so stiff. I thought the judge would suspend sentence or agree to probation, as the public defender suggested. At any rate, Lucinda and I quarreled, bitterly I might add. I broke off the relationship and severed my ties with her. She was much younger than I. In hindsight, I realized she was angling for herself, hoping for marriage. Reba disliked her intensely. Lucinda knew that, of course."

"What happened to the money?"

"Reba gambled it away. She's always been attracted to card play. Roulette, the slots. She loves to bet the ponies, but she has no head for it."

"She's a problem gambler?"

"Her problem isn't the gambling, it's the losing," he remarked, with only the weakest of smiles.

"What about drugs and alcohol?"

"I'd have to answer yes on both counts. She tends to be reckless. She has a wild streak like her mother. I'm hoping this experience in prison has taught her self-restraint. As for the job itself, we'll play that by ear. We're talking two to three days, a week at the most, until she's reestablished herself. Since your responsibilities are limited, I won't be requiring a written report. Submit an invoice and I'll pay your daily rate and all the necessary expenses."

"That seems simple enough."

"One other item. If there's any suggestion that she's backsliding, I want to be informed. Perhaps with sufficient warning, I can head off disaster this time around."

"A tall order."

"I'm aware of that."

Briefly, I considered the proposition. Ordinarily I don't like serving as a babysitter and potential tattletale, but in this case, his concern didn't seem out of line. "What time will she be released?"

2

On my way back into town, I picked up my dry-cleaning and then cruised through a nearby supermarket, picking up odds and ends, which I intended to drop off at my place before I returned to work. I was hoping to touch base with my landlord before the arrival of his lady visitor later in the day. I was running the errands to provide myself with props to explain my unexpected midafternoon appearance. Henry and I confide in each other on many issues, but his love life isn't one. If I wanted information, I knew I'd do well to proceed with finesse.

My studio apartment was originally the single-car garage attached to Henry's house by way of a now glass-enclosed breezeway. In 1980 he converted the space to the snug studio I've been renting ever since. What began as a basic square fifteen feet on a side is now a fully furnished "great room," which includes a living room, a bump-out galley-style kitchen, a laundry nook and bathroom, with a sleeping loft and a second bathroom up a set of spiral stairs. The space is compact and cleverly designed to exploit every usable inch. Given the pegs and cubbyholes, walls of polished teak and oak, and the occasional porthole window, the studio has the scale and feel of a ship's interior.

I found a parking spot two doors away and hauled out my cleaning and the two grocery bags. My timing couldn't have been more perfect. As I pushed through my squeaky metal gate and followed the walkway around to the rear, Henry was just pulling into his two-car garage. He'd taken his bright yellow five-window Chevy coupe for its annual checkup and it was back now, the exterior polished to a fare-thee-well. The interior was probably not only spotless, but scented with faux pine. He bought the vehicle new in 1932 and he's taken such good care of it you'd swear it was still under warranty, assuming cars had warranties back then. He has a second vehicle, a station wagon he uses for routine errands and the occasional trip to the Los Angeles airport, ninety-five miles south. The coupe he reserves for special occasions, today being one.

I have trouble remembering that he's eighty-seven years old. I also have trouble describing him in terms that aren't embarrassingly laudatory given our fifty-year age difference. He's smart, sweet, sexy, trim, handsome, vigorous, and kind. In his working days, he made a living as a commercial baker, and though he's been retired now for twenty-five years, he still makes the best cinnamon rolls I've ever eaten. If I were forced to accord him a fault, I'd probably cite his caution when it comes to affairs of the heart. The only time I'd seen him smitten, he was not only deceived, but nearly taken for every cent he had. Since then, he's played his cards very close to his chest. Either he hadn't run into anyone of interest or he'd looked the other way. That is, until Mattie Halstead appeared.

Mattie was the artist-in-residence on a Caribbean cruise he and his siblings had taken in April. Soon after the cruise ended, she'd stopped in to see him on her way to Los Angeles to deliver paintings to a gallery down there. A month later, he'd made an unprecedented trip to San Francisco, where he spent an evening with her. He'd kept mum on the subject of their relationship, but I noticed he'd spiffed up his wardrobe and started lifting weights. The Pitts family (at least on Henry's mother's side) is long-lived, and he and his siblings enjoy remarkably good health. William's a bit of a hypochondriac and Charlie's almost entirely deaf, but that aside, they give the appearance of going on forever. Lewis, Charlie, and Nell live in Michigan, but there are visits back and forth, some planned and some not. William and my friend Rosie, who owns the tavern half a block away, would be celebrating their second wedding anniversary on November 28. Now it looked like Henry might be entertaining similar thoughts . . . or such was my hope. Other people's romances are so much less hazardous than one's own. I was looking forward to all the pleasures of true love without suffering the peril.

Henry paused when he caught sight of me, allowing me to fall into step with him as he proceeded to the house. I noticed his hair had been freshly trimmed, and he wore a blue denim work shirt with his crisply pressed chinos. He'd even traded in his usual flip-flops for a pair of deck shoes with dark socks.

I said, "Hang on a second while I drop this stuff off."

He waited while I unlocked my door and dumped my armload on the floor just inside. Nothing I'd bought would go funky in the next thirty minutes. Rejoining him, I said, "You had your hair trimmed. It looks great."

He ran a self-conscious hand across his head. "I was

passing the barbershop and realized I was long overdue. You think it's too short?"

"Not at all. It shaves years off your age," I said, thinking Mattie would have to be an idiot if she didn't understand what a treasure he was. I held open the screen door while he pulled out his keys and unlocked his back door. I followed him inside, watching as he set his groceries on the kitchen counter.

"Nice that Mattie's coming down. I'll bet you're looking forward to seeing her."

"It's only the one night."

"What's the occasion?"

"She did a painting on commission for a woman in La Jolla. She's delivering that one plus a couple more in case the woman doesn't care for the first."

"Well, it's nice she can manage a visit. When's she getting in?"

"She hoped to be here by four, depending on traffic. She said she'd check into the hotel and call once she's had a chance to freshen up. She agreed to supper here as long as I didn't go to any trouble. I said I'd keep it simple, but you know me."

He began to unload his sack: a packet wrapped in white butcher's paper, potatoes, cabbage, green onions, and a big jar of mayonnaise. While I watched, he opened the oven door and checked his crock of soldier beans bubbling away with molasses, mustard, and a chunk of salt pork. I could see two loaves of freshly baked bread resting on a rack on the counter. A chocolate layer cake sat in the middle of the kitchen table with a glass dome over it. There was also a bouquet of flowers from his garden— roses and lavender he'd arranged artfully in a china teapot.

"Cake looks fabulous."

"It's a twelve-layer torte. I used Nell's recipe, which

was originally our mother's. We tried it for years, but none of us could duplicate her results. Nell finally managed, but she says it's a pain. I ended up tossing half a dozen layers before I mastered the thing."

"What else are you having?"

Henry took out a cast-iron skillet and set it on the stove. "Fried chicken, potato salad, coleslaw, and baked beans. I thought we'd have a little picnic on the patio, unless the temperature drops." He opened his spice cabinet and sorted through the contents, taking down a bottle of dried dill. "Why don't you join us? She'd love to see you."

"Oh please. Socializing is the last thing she needs. After six hours on the road? Give the woman a drink and let her put her feet up."

"No need to worry about her. She has energy to spare. She'd be delighted, I'm sure."

"Let's just see how it goes. I'm on my way back to the office, but I'll check in with you again as soon as I get home."

I'd already decided to decline, but I didn't want to seem rude. In my opinion, they needed time to themselves. I'd pop my head in and say hi, primarily to satisfy my curiosity about her. She was either widowed or divorced, I wasn't sure which, but during her last visit, I'd noticed she'd made a number of references to her husband. At one point, when Henry was nursing a bum knee, she'd gone hiking alone, taking her watercolors with her so she could paint a spot in the mountains she and her husband had enjoyed for years. Was she still emotionally entrenched? Whether hubby was dead or alive, I didn't like the idea. Henry, meanwhile, was busy being nonchalant, perhaps in denial of his feelings or in response to covert signals from her. Of course, there was always the possibility that I was imagining all this, but I didn't think so. At any rate, I intended to have my supper at Rosie's, resigned to my usual weekly allotment of her bullying and abuse.

I left Henry to his preparations and went back to the office, where I put a call through to Priscilla Holloway, Reba Lafferty's parole agent. Nord Lafferty had given me her name and phone number at the end of our appointment. I was already back at my car, opening the driver's side, when the elderly housekeeper had called from the front door and then hurried down the walk, a photograph in hand.

Winded, she'd said, "Mr. Lafferty forgot to give you this. It's a photograph of Reba."

"Thanks. I appreciate that. I'll return it as soon as we get back."

"Oh, no need. He said to keep it if you like."

I thanked her again and tucked the photo into my bag. Now, while I waited for Parole Agent Holloway to answer her phone, I plucked out the photo and studied it again. I'd have preferred something recent. This had been taken when the woman was in her mid- to late twenties and almost puckish in appearance. Her large dark eyes were intent on the camera, her full lips half-parted as though she were on the verge of speaking. Her hair was shoulder-length and dyed blond, but clearly at considerable expense. Her complexion was clear with a hint of blush in her cheeks. After two years of prison fare, she might have packed on a few extra pounds, but I thought I'd recognize her.

On the other end of the line, a woman said, "Holloway."

"Hi, Ms. Holloway. My name is Kinsey Millhone. I'm a local private investigator—"

"I know who you are. I had a call from Nord Lafferty, telling me he'd hired you to pick up his daughter."

"That's why I'm calling, to clear it with you."

"Fine. Have at it. It'll save me the trip. If you're back in town before three, bring her over to the office. Do you know where I am?"

I didn't, but she gave me the address.

"See you Monday," I said.

I spent the rest of the afternoon taking care of paper-work, mostly sorting and filing in a vain attempt to tidy up my desk. I also did some boning up on parole regulations from a pamphlet printed by the California Department of Corrections.

Returning to my apartment for the second time that day, I saw no sign of picnic items on the patio table. Perhaps he'd decided the meal was better served indoors. I crossed to his back door and peeked in. As it turned out, my hopes for their romantic interlude were squelched by William's presence in the kitchen. Looking aggrieved, Henry sat in his rocking chair with his usual glass of Jack Daniel's while Mattie nursed a goblet of white wine.

William, two years Henry's senior, has always looked enough like him to be his twin. His shock of white hair was thinning where Henry's was still full, but his eyes were the same hot blue and he carried himself with the same erect military bearing. He wore a dapper three-piece suit, his watch chain visible across the front of his vest. I tapped on the glass and Henry motioned me in. William rose to his feet at the sight of me, and I knew he'd remain standing unless I urged him to sit. Mattie rose to greet me, and though we didn't actually hug, we did clasp hands and exchange an air kiss.

She was in her early seventies, tall and slender, with soft silver hair she wore pulled into a knot on the top of her head. Her earrings glinted in the light—silver, over-size, and artisan-made.

I said, "Hey, Mattie. How are you? You must have arrived right on time."

"Good to see you. I did." She wore a coral silk blouse and a long gypsy skirt over flat-heel suede boots. "Will you join us in a glass of wine?"

"I don't think so, but thanks. I've got business to take care of so I have to run."

Henry's tone was morose. "Have a glass of wine. Why not? Stay for supper as well. William's invited himself so what's the difference? Rosie couldn't tolerate having him underfoot so she sent him over here."

William said, "She had a small conniption fit for no reason at all. I'd just returned from the doctor's office and I knew she'd want to hear the results of my blood work, especially my HDLs. You might want to take a look yourself." He held the paper out, pointing with significance at the long column of numbers down the right side of the page. My gaze slid past his glucose, sodium, potassium, and chloride levels before I caught the expression on Henry's face. His eyes were crossed so close to the bridge of his nose I thought they'd trade sides. William was saying, "You can see my LDL-HDL risk ratio is 1.3."

"Oh, sorry. Is that bad?"

"No, no. The doctor said it was excellent . . . in light of my medical condition." William's voice carried a hint of feebleness suggestive of a weakened state.

"Well, good for you. That's great."

"Thank you. I called our brother Lewis and told him as well. His cholesterol is 214, which I think is cause for alarm. He says he's doing what he can, but he hasn't had much success. You can pass the paper on to Mattie once you've studied it yourself."

Henry said, "William, would you sit down? You're giving me a crick in my neck." He left his rocker and took another wineglass from the kitchen cabinet. He poured wine to the brim and passed the glass to me, slopping some liquid on my hand.

William declined to sit until he'd pulled out my chair. I settled myself with a murmured "Thank you" and then I made a show of running a finger down the column of reference and unit numbers from his doctor's report. "You're in good shape," I remarked as I passed the paper to Mattie.

"Well, I still have palpitations, but the doctor's adjusting my medication. He says I'm amazing for a man my age."

"If you're in such terrific health, how come you're off to the urgent care center every other day?" Henry snapped.

William blinked placidly at Mattie. "My brother's careless with his health and won't acknowledge that some of us are proactive."

Henry made a snorting sound.

William cleared his throat. "Well now. On to a new subject since Henry's apparently unable to handle that one. I hope this is not too personal, but Henry mentioned your husband is deceased. Do you mind my asking how he was taken?"

Henry was clearly exasperated. "You call that a different subject? It's the same one—death and disease. Can't you think of anything else?"

"I wasn't addressing you," William replied before returning his attention to Mattie. "I hope the topic isn't too painful."

"Not at this point. Barry died six years ago of heart failure. I believe cardiac ischemia is the term they used.

He taught jewelry making at the San Francisco Art Institute. He was a very talented man, though a bit of an eccentric."

William was nodding. "Cardiac ischemia. I know the term well. From the Greek, *ischein,* meaning 'quench' or 'seize,' combined with *haima,* or 'blood.' A German pathology professor first introduced that term in the mid-1800s. Rudolf Virchow. A remarkable man. What age was your husband?"

"William," Henry sang.

Mattie smiled. "Really, Henry. I'm not sensitive about this. He died two days shy of his seventieth birthday."

William winced. "Pity when a man's struck down in his prime. I myself have suffered several episodes of angina, which I've miraculously survived. I was discussing my heart condition with Lewis, just two days ago by phone. You remember our brother, I'm sure."

"Of course. I hope he and Nell and Charles are all in good health."

"Excellent," William said. He shifted in his chair, lowering his voice. "What about your husband? Did he have any warning prior to his fatal attack?"

"He'd been having chest pains, but he refused to see the doctor. Barry was a fatalist. He believed you check out when your time is up regardless what precautions you take. He compared longevity to an alarm clock that God sets the moment you're born. None of us knows when the little bell will ring, but he didn't see the point in trying to second-guess the process. He enjoyed life immensely, I'll say that about him. Most folks in my family don't make it to the age of sixty, and they're miserable every minute, dreading the inevitable."

"Sixty! Is that right? That's astonishing. Is there a genetic factor in play?"

"I don't think so. It's a little bit of everything. Cancer, diabetes, kidney failure, chronic pulmonary disease . . ."

William put his hands on his chest. I hadn't seen him so happy since he'd had the flu. "COPD. Chronic obstructive pulmonary disease. The very term brings back memories. I was stricken with a lung condition in my youth—"

Henry clapped his hands. "Okay, fine. Enough said on that subject. Why don't we eat?"

He moved to the refrigerator and took out a clear glass bowl piled with coleslaw, which he plunked on the table with rather more force than was absolutely necessary. The chicken he'd fried was piled on a platter on the counter, probably still warm. He placed that in the center of the table with a pair of serving tongs. The squat little crockery pot now sat on the back of the stove, emitting the fragrance of tender beans and bay leaf. He removed serving utensils from a ceramic jug and then took down four dinner plates, which he handed to William, perhaps in hopes of distracting his attention while he brought the rest of the dinner to the table. William set a plate at each place while he quizzed Mattie at length about her mother's death from acute bacterial meningitis.

Over supper Henry steered the conversation into neutral territory. We went through ritual questions about Mattie's drive down from San Francisco, traffic, road conditions, and matters of that sort, which gave me ample opportunity to observe her. Her eyes were a clear gray and she wore very little makeup. She had strong features, with nose, cheekbones, and jaw as pronounced and well proportioned as a model's. Her skin showed signs of sun damage, and it lent her complexion a ruddy glow. I pictured her out in the fields for hours with her paint box and easel.

I could tell William was reflecting on the subject of terminal disease while I was calculating how soon I could make my excuses and depart. I intended to drag William with me so Henry and Mattie could have some time alone. I kept an eye on the clock while I worked my way through the fried chicken, potato salad, coleslaw, baked beans, and cake. The food, of course, was wonderful, and I ate with my usual speed and enthusiasm. At 8:35, just as I was formulating a plausible lie, Mattie folded her napkin and laid it on the table beside her plate.

"Well, I should be on my way. I have some phone calls to make as soon as I get back to the hotel."

"You're leaving?" I said, trying to cover my disappointment.

"She's had a long day," Henry said, getting up to remove her plate. He took it to the sink, where he rinsed it and set it in the dishwasher, talking to her all the while. "I can wrap up some chicken in case you want some later."

"Don't tempt me. I'm full but not stuffed, which is just the way I like it. This was wonderful, Henry. I can't tell you how much I appreciate the effort that went into this meal."

"Happy you enjoyed it. I'll get your wrap from the other room." He dried his hands on a kitchen towel and moved off toward the bedroom.

William folded his napkin and scraped back his chair. "I should probably run along as well. Doctor urged me to adhere to my regimen—eight full hours of sleep. I may engage in some light calisthenics before bed to aid the digestive process. Nothing strenuous, of course."

I turned to Mattie. "You have plans for tomorrow?"

"Unfortunately, I'm taking off first thing in the morning, but I'll be back in a few days."

Henry returned with a soft paisley shawl that he laid across her shoulders. She patted his hand with affection and picked up a large leather bag that she'd set beside her chair. "I hope to see you again soon," she said to me.

"I hope so, too."

Henry touched her elbow. "I'll walk you out."

William straightened his vest. "No need. I'll be happy to see her off." He offered Mattie his arm, and she tucked her hand through the crook with a brief backward look at Henry as the two went out the door.